THE BODY LOOKS FAMILIAR

This was no crime of passion. The killer sat patiently on the girl's satin-covered bed, drinking Scotch and soda, awaiting her return. He didn't smoke—some Sherlock might trace his brand. He had already taken care to plant the leads, to weave together the web of evidence that would direct the police unerringly to the wrong man.

He didn't know the girl. When she entered, he thought it a pity to kill such a good-looker; then he held the cushion over the gun, and fired. The silk and feathers made an excellent muffler. It was too bad about the girl, but she was just a means to an end—and the end was to send another man to the chair...

THE LATE MRS. FIVE

When factory representative Paul Porter arrived at the small rural town of Lowndesburg, he little suspected that he would soon be under arrest for murder.

Soon after his arrival he had been shocked to see his beautiful ex-wife Edith, getting into an expensive limousine. He had never seen her for years. Nor had he any idea that she was now married to the rich landowner John Hilliard the Fifth, to whose mansion he had later made a visit hoping to sell agricultural machinery—only to find nobody was at home. But the local police knew of his visit, and when they discovered Edith's dead body there, he became the prime suspect as the slayer of the late Mrs. Five!

The Body
Looks Familiar

■ ■ ■ ■ ■

The Late Mrs. Five

■ ■ ■ ■ ■

Richard Wormser
Introduction by Bill Crider

STARK HOUSE

Stark House Press • Eureka California

THE BODY LOOKS FAMILIAR / THE LATE MRS. FIVE

Published by Stark House Press
1315 H Street
Eureka, CA 95501
griffinskye3@sbcglobal.net
www.starkhousepress.com

ISBN-13: 978-1-944520-42-7

Layout by Mark Shepard, SHEPGRAPHICS.COM

First Stark House Press Edition: January 2018

FIRST EDITION

Contents

Contents

Not the Usual Suspects
■ ■ ■ ■
Bill Crider

Once upon a time in a place called San Antonio, Texas, there existed a place known as Brock's Bookstore. It was owned and operated, or presided over, by Norman Brock, a well-known local character who usually dressed in overalls and listened to country music. He was a booklover, and he must have had a bit of the hoarder in him because the store was certainly a place where books were hoarded. There was no order, no system, just books everywhere, thousands upon thousands of them: in short stacks, in towers, on shelves (sometimes double-shelved), tossed higgeldy-piggeldy here and there at random. I believe there were three stories in the building where the store was located, including the basement, and eventually no one could go to the second floor, which was in danger of collapse.

The books weren't priced. If you could find something you wanted, you took it to the counter where Brock would look at the each book, look at you, and decide on a price. The buyer's strategy was to take at least three books, slip anything valuable into the middle of the stack, look poverty-stricken, and hope for the best. Using this method, a graduate student I knew got a first edition of *The Catcher in the Rye* for a dollar.

I never got a bargain like that, and in fact I seldom looked around for long. The place intimidated me, and I found I couldn't really search for anything. The task was too daunting. But that's not the end of the story. Around the corner from the main store was a place I called Brock's Annex. I have no idea of that was its name or if it even had a name. It was seldom open, and it was even more disorganized than the main store. What caught my eye through the front window one day in 1969 or 1970 was a rack of paperback that had fallen over onto its back. Every book in it looked brand new, although all of them were a bit over ten years old at that time. Once I was able to persuade someone open the place for me—or maybe it was open already—I bought one copy (fool that I was) of just about every book on that rack. And that's how I got my copy of Richard Wormser's *The Body Looks Familiar*.

I was already a fan of Richard Wormser's work at that time. He began his writing career with Street & Smith in the 1930s, and by the middle of the decade was writing the lead novel for that publisher's revival of the Nick Carter character. He wrote for the pulps but also published hardcover novels, wrote for the movies, and did many paperback novels both under his own name and as "Ed Friend." The latter name was used mainly for movie and TV novelizations, of which Wormser wrote a good many under his own name, including those for *McClintock, The Thief of Baghdad,* and *Torn Curtain.* Under his own name he wrote both crime fiction and westerns and excelled in both genres. For those who like westerns, I recommend *On the Prod,* one of the most unusual westerns you'll ever encounter, but all his work in that genre is rewarding. An accomplished and versatile professional, Wormser is one of a handful of writers to have won both the Spur Award from the Western Writers of America (twice) and the Edgar Award from the Mystery Writers of America in 1973 for a Gold Medal novel entitled *The Invader.*

Wormser also worked in Hollywood, and *The Big Steal* (1949, directed by Don Seigel and starring Robert Mitchum, was based on his original story "The Road to Carmichael's." The screenplay was done by two writers, one of whom was Geoffrey Homes (Daniel Mainwaring), who adapted his own novel *Build My Gallows High* for the film *Out of the Past,* also starring Mitchum. While *The Big Steal* doesn't reach the heights of *Out of the Past,* it's very good, and it has a fine pedigree.

The Body Looks Familiar was first published in abridged form in *Cosmopolitan* as *The Frame,* and it's worth a mention that in the 1950s work by writers like Wormser, John D. MacDonald, and Charles Williams regularly appeared in that magazine. Times and tastes have changed, and you're not likely see hard-boiled or noir tales there anymore. At any rate, whereas *The Body Looks Familiar* is a generic title that doesn't fit the novel, *The Frame* is an appropriate title for a book about, well, a frame-up.

And what a frame-up it is. Dave Corday, an assistant district attorney in a large, unnamed city, frames the city's police chief, James Latson for the murder of his mistress. This happens in the first chapter, so I don't think this is much of a spoiler, although it's certainly a surprising and shocking opening for a crime novel. Corday waits in the mistresses' apartment (paid for by Latson), and when Latson and the woman return from a night on the town, Corday surprises them, takes Latson's gun, and kills the woman with it, leaving Latson to deal with the consequences. Why? Because Latson had an affair with Corday's wife, who then left him. When Latson tossed her aside, she became a prostitute and later died.

So Corday gets his revenge with the perfect frame. Or does he? As it happens, Latson's not the kind of guy to quit that easily, and he believes that he's a real man while Corday is a weakling. The result is a dandy cat-and-mouse game that reveals Wormser's knowledge of police procedure, big-city politics, and human nature. It's full of twists and turns right up until the end.

There's no way to classify *The Body Looks Familiar*. It's nothing like any other crime novel you'll run across. Is it noir? I like and agree with Otto Penzler's definition of *noir*. Here's part of it: "Pretty much everyone in a noir story (or film) is driven by greed, lust, jealousy or alienation, a path that inevitably sucks them into a downward spiral from which they cannot escape." Some noir stories, however, include characters who are basically good, and so does this one. There are a good cop and a good reporter who get involved and help bring the story to its conclusion. My own conclusion is that the novel is hard-boiled, it's noir, and it's a great story, well told.

And now for something completely different. Wormser was nothing if not versatile. *The Late Mrs. Five*, instead of being set in a large city, is set in a small, rural midwestern town named Lowndesburg. It's told in in first person, and the narrator isn't any bigwig. Here's how he describes himself "My name is Paul Porter, I am vice-president in charge of marketing for Hydrol Machines, Inc., a Chicago firm. I am at present engaged on a field trip visiting users and sellers of our machines."

Here's the thing about that field trip and the visit to Lowndesburg. They result in a couple of really big coincidences. It just happens that Porter's ex-wife, a greedy and grasping woman, has found herself another sucker and now lives in Lowndesburg. She's married to Mr. Five, or to give his real name, John Hilliard the Fifth, the richest man in town. Everybody just calls him Mr. Five. Porter doesn't know that his ex lives in town, much less that she's remarried, so when he finds out, he decides to pay her a visit. No one appears to be at home when he arrives at her door, however, so he leaves. The next thing he know, she's dead and he's become the primary suspect in her murder.

Porter eventually goes on the run and tries to prove his innocence, but there aren't a lot of places to run to in a small town. Luckily for Porter, he has a few allies. One is the daughter of the local police chief (part-time; he also sells farm implements, and he's the one Porter has come to town to visit). The daughter's name is Andy, short for Andrea, and she falls for Porter immediately, which is the kind of thing that often happens in '50s paperbacks. Her grandfather is also on Porter's side, as is the local hotshot lawyer. Her father isn't, however, and neither is the state cop who's investigating the murder. Wormser shines at presenting small-town politics just as he did in showing how things work in the city of *The Body Looks Familiar*. The conflict between the local and state lawmen is particularly well done.

It's also worth a mention that Wormser also knows a lot about farm machinery. That's because in addition to being a writer, he was a rancher, and for a while he was a mounted patrolman with the U.S. Forest Service, another facet of his career that he makes use of in *The Late Mrs. Five.*

The characters in this novel are as skillfully delineated as those in *The Body Looks Familiar*, with the difference being that *The Late Mrs. Five* has a number of genuinely likeable folks, including Paul Porter (in spite of the number of dumb things he does) and Andy, who's a quite competent and intelligent young woman.

Richard Wormser was never less than a competent and professional writer, but more often than not he rose to greater heights than those labels would imply. The pairing of *The Body Looks Familiar* and *The Late Mrs. Five* in one volume gives readers an excellent opportunity to see him at the top of his game in works that are strikingly different but equally entertaining.

—September 2017
Alvin, TX

The Body
Looks Familiar

■ ■ ■ ■ ■

Richard Wormser

CHAPTER 1

Neither a disgrace to the city nor its great pride, the neighborhood lay, solid and well lighted, between the really expensive Hill to the east and the badly lighted, poorly swept Bottoms to the west and south. You could find people living in the area who were on civil service; you could also find an occasional small manufacturer or store owner who might conceivably float a million-dollar loan at the banks.

They called it the Park section, and, indeed, there was one big park and three little ones there. It had the best supermarkets in the city and the least crime; housebreakers and similar professionals naturally headed for the lusher pickings of the Hill, and the people of the Park didn't have the passionate pressures on them that made Bottoms folk beat and stab and purse-snatch and rape each other.

Nevertheless, the Park was about to have a crime, and it was going to be a lulu, a whopper, a front-page item. Maybe not right away, but within a day or so at the most.

David Corday was sure of that, for two reasons: In the first place, he was chief assistant district attorney, and he knew crime. In the second place, he was about to commit the crime, a murder, himself.

He waited, at his ease. He had on gloves—who leaves fingerprints these days?—and he did not smoke as he waited—because some Sherlock might trace his brand. It was a real fancy precaution, he thought, since he smoked the second most popular cigarette in the country.

But he lounged on a satin-covered bed, and he listened to a softly playing radio, and he had a highball, good Scotch and soda, in his hand. No prospective murderer was ever more comfortable, David Corday reflected; but he didn't chuckle or smile as he thought it; he was in deadly earnest.

The sound of a rising elevator caused him to turn the radio off, finish his highball. He dropped the glass into the pocket of the light overcoat he wore, stood up, turned off the one light that showed him the very expensive furnishings of the bedroom.

Then he crossed, using a little flashlight, to the living room of this three-room apartment. The elevator had stopped; its door was opening. He got just behind the entrance door of the apartment.

A key grated; the door began to open. It seemed to him that it had hardly cracked an inch before he could smell perfume, perfume as expensive as the satin covering in the bedroom, the plate glass mirror in the living room, the—

A girl entered. She was every man's dream of physical perfection, in complexion, length of leg, depth of breast and fineness of hair; and she was dressed in a cocktail gown and short silk coat that showed she'd cashed in on what nature had given her. David Corday had also heard that she was not stupid; but he'd never talked to her.

She entered, walked to the middle of the room, turned on a standing lamp and—what else?—looked at herself in the plate glass mirror. She must have seen David Corday then, because she gasped, and the long, thin man who followed her caught the gasp and turned.

But by that time the heavy door had closed, and it was too late. David Corday had a .38 automatic pointed square at the tall man's midriff. Corday said, "Evening, Latson."

Latson made a noise that might have been, "Dave." His hands instinctively rose a little, away from his sides. He was bone-thin, except for curiously thick lips set in a skin-covered skull.

"Yes," Corday said. "Dave. Old pal Dave. Good old dog, Dave. Turn around, Chief, face the young lady. She's not hard to look at. Now get your hands up, reasonably high... You carry your gun in your left armpit, don't you?" As he talked, he crossed quickly to the little love seat next to the mirror. He snatched up a silk pillow, held it under his right armpit, in no way inhibiting the right hand that held his gun.

Then his left hand darted out, around the thin Latson, and got the gun from Latson's shoulder holster.

He took time for a quick look at the girl. She was about to scream. He was deft switching his gun for Latson's, pushing the pillow over it, and firing; the silk and feathers made a good muffler, and there wasn't much noise.

The girl's dress was at once ruined, her face immediately drained of blood; it had been a direct hit to her breast. But he held the pillow steady and sent the other five bullets into her before she hit the floor.

The room was filled with feathers now, with the smell of singed feathers. Latson stared, immobilized either by surprise or by the automatic in David Corday's left hand.

Corday said, calmly, "That does that, Chief." He slid the empty revolver back into Latson's holster and smiled.

Latson spoke for the first time, except for his gasp of Corday's first name. "I got to get out of here."

David Corday said, "Trite, but true. Take your hands down." He opened the front door with his gloved hand and bowed a little. "With me, Chief?"

Latson had never had a chance to take his hat or coat off. He walked stiffly to the opened door, and out, to where David Corday was pressing the button of the automatic elevator. The door opened at once; no one had called for the car since Latson had ridden up with the girl.

Corday switched the automatic to his right hand again, and gestured. "Though I don't have to use this," he said. "You couldn't reload before I killed you." He put the gun in his pocket.

Still in his nightmare trance, Latson joined him in the car. His voice seemed to be coming back. He said, "When did you know her?"

David Corday had pressed the G button for the ground floor. He said carefully, "I didn't. Never spoke to her. Saw you once with her, in a crowded joint... When Elsa left me, I thought it was her business... I still thought so when I found out she left me for you. Besides, a stink would have upset all our apple carts."

"Still would," Latson said gruffly.

"I've lost my taste for apples," David Corday said. There was an overeducated precision to his speech. "But when I heard you'd ditched my wife for"—he pointed upstairs—"I was still thinking of my job. Last week Kansas City notified me. Elsa's dead. My name was still on her driver's license, Mrs. David Corday... She'd been working cheap joints along the river there."

Latson shook his head, beginning to smile a little. He reached out and pushed the emergency button, stopping the car. Then, amazingly, he chuckled.

David Corday's eyes got wide. He retreated as far as the little car would let him. His lips twitched, and the blood drained out of his face. "Listen. We got to—"

Latson said calmly, "We don't have to do anything. And watch your grammar; that word 'got' is pretty crude for a high-grade lawyer. A minute or so won't hurt us. If anybody presses a button, we hit the emergency again and run away from them... I've got a little speech to make. It goes like this: I hate to see anyone kid himself, especially a distinguished political ally like you."

It was certainly not hot there in the elevator car. But Dave Corday's whole appearance was that of a man pinned against a furnace.

"What did you think I'd do?" Latson asked, "Run away, like some candy-pinching kid? You don't know Jim Latson. I don't panic. And somehow, some way, I'll be out of this, and leave you holding the bag. No pun."

Dave Corday said, "Jim—"

Jim Latson was chuckling happily now. "Little man, don't kid yourself. You didn't do this because I took Elsa away from you. If I hadn't, the next real man that came along would have snitched her, because that was the way she was. And she didn't amount to anything, because how could she, or she wouldn't have married you."

Dave Corday half brought the pistol out of his pocket.

Latson said, "I ought to yawn, or do something dramatic like that. You aren't going to shoot me. You don't have the guts. Which is why you've hung this frame on me. Because you hate me. You've always hated me and you always will because I'm too much for you. Too much man and too much brain and too much guts. You worked your way into law school—"

Jim Latson reached out, pushed the ground-floor button. The car started to move again.

"And out of law school," he went on, "and into the D.A.'s office and almost to the top of it. And nobody pays any attention to you, because there are real men around, real men like me, with power and brains and nerves we never had to work for. So you hate me, and you dreamed up this cockeyed frame to fix me."

The car stopped and the door opened automatically. At this hour, well after one in the morning, there was no one in the lobby. Dave Corday said, "I took a risk someone would see me coming in. The only risk I took."

They were walking to the street door now, and out into the well-lighted, quiet street of the Park district.

"The risk you took," Jim Latson said, "was in going up against a better man." He turned and started walking away.

"Your girl," Corday said after him. "Your gun. The apartment you rented for her." He sent the words after the tall, thin figure of Jim Latson in a sharp whisper.

Latson turned, and his voice came back, composed, casual. "If your wife ended up in a Kansas City hook-shop," he said, "maybe it was because that was better than you."

Then he turned the corner and was gone.

CHAPTER 2

James Latson stopped when he had gotten around the corner. It was pretty hard to realize—Hogan was dead. Hogan DeLisle. He'd never known her real name. As deputy chief of police for the city, he could have found out; but it hadn't been her name that interested him.

He shook his head, began to walk again. Corday was crazy. Stark, raving nuts. It didn't hurt Jim Latson to get de-womaned—though the dame who called herself Hogan DeLisle had been a good one; pleasant, good-looking as they come, easy to get along with. There would be other ladies, other apartments, other pleasures.

And if Corday's idea had been to involve Jim Latson in a scandal, he could not do so without involving himself. Latson had never given the girl anything but cash, she'd paid the apartment rent in person, paid her own way at the department stores.

About all Corday could do was offer himself as an eyewitness, and that was one thing no murderer had done yet; Jim Latson had been a police officer quite a while.

Which was a good thing, he thought wryly, beginning to get a little grip on himself. A thing like what happened in the apartment would have shaken the ordinary person. But he'd seen killings before. Plenty of them.

He stepped into a doorway, and carefully reloaded the revolver from a little ammunition box in his overcoat pocket.

The thought came to him that David Corday must have meant the girl's killing as a warning: *You are next, Latson.* Well, Jim Latson took precautions, but he didn't scare. One of the precautions had been to leave his car a few blocks from the girl's house, to use cabs when he took her out. Not that there'd been anything hidden about his affair with her; he'd hardly get a girl like Hogan to keep hidden. They'd been seen in every nightclub in town, in the Zebra House tonight. But he'd never driven her a block in his city-owned sedan, never parked it in front of her door all night; never parked it there at all after dark, in fact, because he had never been sure when he would want to spend the night. A damned alluring female.

He clucked regretfully as he crossed the last street. There was his heap, the big sedan that the department provided, in keeping with his position as number two man on the police. Jim Latson fished his keys out of his overcoat pocket, got in behind the wheel. He lit a cigarette with a gold lighter marked with the number of a precinct; the boys there had given it to him when he was promoted from being their captain.

I'm a sentimental cuss, he thought. I wouldn't sell that lighter for a new Cadillac.

Then he reached out to put the key in the ignition switch, and at once knew something was wrong. The switch was one of those from which the key can be taken while the ignition is still on; and that, for the first time in his life, seemed to be what he had done.

He frowned, tried the starter. The motor turned over lazily once, and was still, frozen.

Jim Latson began to whistle, noiselessly. It could be a coincidence. He had seen some damned funny ones in his time. He'd once sent a man to the chair on coincidence, only to get a deathbed confession from the real criminal two years later...

Sweat popped out along his narrow brow. That had been an extremely uncomfortable thought. He tried another one; coincidence had broken a lot of cases for him, given him a lot of credit he hadn't really earned.

That thought hadn't been any better. This was a case he didn't want broken.

Futilely, knowing it was futile, he tried the starter again. It got him just where he expected it to get him—no place.

But he didn't panic. You don't get on top of the police list—the chief was just a politician—by panicking.

He grinned, suddenly remembering a wisecrack that had been going around town a few months ago: If you can keep your head when others are losing theirs, maybe you don't really understand the situation.

He understood this one clearly enough. This was the tight spot, the squeeze, the hot one.

Characteristically, he wasted no time regretting that he hadn't parked on a hill. If he had, Corday would have done something else to the car or waited for another night. Dave—it was hard not to think of him still as a co-operative intimate—had said Elsa died last week.

This particular night had been chosen for some reason. But he'd gotten where he'd gotten by never underestimating himself. He was as smart as David Corday. Anything Corday could spin, he could unravel. Period.

Now—the radio was on a separate battery, under the turtle deck. He could radio in, and a police car would push him to a start. But that would mean that the patrol car would log the time and place, and he was not far enough from Hogan's apartment in the Belmont to have that happen.

He could just walk away, and have the car picked up in the morning, but that was hardly better. It kept him from being placed here in time, but not in location...

He could get a taxicab to push him.

That, of course, was the solution. Even if the cabby recognized him, the channels for connecting him up to the Belmont, to the girl's death, were impossibly complicated. And hackmen were not the kind to go out of their way to make enemies of the Deputy Chief.

He got out of the car again, looked around. One of the phone company's aluminum booths was scarcely a block away in front of a market. A routine call. Cabs pushed people all the time, especially in the middle of the night when the stalled motorist couldn't beg a friendly shove from some other citizen.

Jim Latson took two steps toward the phone booth, and as he did so, a car came around the corner. A white spotlight played up the back of his sedan, crossed over to hit him, and a cheerful young voice said, "We came as soon as we got the call, Chief."

The light, politely, went off him. He crossed to the police car, peering. He was a good commander; he knew half the men on the force by first and last names. Sunk, he played his hand out; he said, "Evening, Jimmy; how are you, Page?" to the radioman and the driver.

Page was already maneuvering behind the sedan. It wouldn't do to say too much; obviously someone—and who but Corday?—had used his name and call letter in radioing in. Corday, as Chief Assistant D.A., had a police radio in his car though he seldom used it.

He put the car in second, turned the switch on, and slowly was pushed ahead. They went through a stationary stop sign before they got up enough speed, and then he let in the clutch, and the motor caught at once.

He pulled to the curb and put the car back in neutral, keeping his foot down on the accelerator.

The cruiser came alongside. Page leaned out and said, "Want us to follow you, Chief?"

Jim Latson said, "I'll be all right. Resume patrol. I just had a low battery."

"That city garage," Page said. "They can't even keep up a chief's car." He gave an awkward salute, pulled ahead, made a U-turn and went back the way he had come.

In the dim glow of the radio, Jim Latson had seen Jimmy Rein making a note on the cruiser's log. Which was to be expected.

Jim Latson drove slowly home, raced the motor for a couple of minutes to make sure he had a good charge for his next start, and took the elevator—a self-service one like the one in the Belmont—to his own apartment.

He slowly and carefully mixed himself the single highball he always had before sleeping, smoked the single cigarette that always went with it, and then methodically undressed, put his gun and wallet and badge on the stand next to his bed, and got between the pleasantly cool sheets.

Winter was setting in, he thought. He'd have to tell the maid to put an extra blanket on his bed. Though, in all probability, she'd do it without being told. This was a good apartment hotel, better than the Belmont, for instance, though not as expensive.

And then Jim Latson was asleep. Tomorrow would bring what it would bring; no day in his life had yet brought more than he could handle.

CHAPTER 3

At eleven o'clock the next morning a very well dressed man named Ronald Palmer gave his card to David Corday's secretary and murmured that Corday had sent for him.

He was at once admitted.

David Corday came from behind his desk to hold out a hand to Palmer. "Hope I didn't get you up," he said. "In your business, I imagine you sleep till two."

Palmer chuckled, shaking his head. "You'd be surprised," he said. "No, I'm usually up at eight." He made a mockery of looking for eavesdroppers, and said, "The truth is, I sleep at my desk. I'm usually at the club from four in the afternoon till three in the morning; but there's nothing to do most of the time. So—I sleep."

Corday gave a politician's chuckle and waved the nightclub man to a seat. "I won't tell your partners," he promised. "Cigar?"

"Have one of mine," Palmer said. "They're a gift from a wholesale liquor dealer. Quite unusual."

They lit each other's cigars. Everything up to now had been manners, as formal as the preliminaries of a bullfight. Now, a silent bugle had blown, and it was the third part of the fight: the sword had come from its sheath, the playing cape had been exchanged for the red flag of death. When a D.A. sends for a nightclub owner, he is not inviting him to a game of tiddlywinks.

Corday blew out smoke and said, "It's the Arnaux matter. It's been on my desk for three weeks, and I should have called you sooner; but it goes to trial next week, and you'll have time."

Ronald Palmer frowned. "Arnaux? Let me see, that's the young couple that got robbed and beaten up by a prowler?" The question mark said, strongly: "What's this got to do with me, with the Zebra House?"

"They are going to testify," Corday said, "that they were a little drunk. It is an essential part of the case, my case. The burglar, a mug named Harris, is a three-time loser. I'm sending him up for life this time, and I don't want any slip-ups. The bizarre behavior of the Arnauxs—for one thing, she had mixed a drink for Harris, offered it to him—is likely to prejudice a jury if they don't know that the young couple had been drinking."

Palmer began to nod. He said, "Let me finish. They had been drinking at the Zebra House. And Mrs. Arnaux—she was Paget Stinnell, wasn't she?—is under age."

Corday said, "Nineteen."

Palmer said, "Thanks for letting me know. If it becomes court record, the Alcoholic Control Board will have to act, I suppose."

"Well, I haven't spoken to them," Corday said. "None of my business. But if I were on the ACB, I know I'd act."

Surreptitiously, Corday glanced at his wrist watch. It was eight minutes past eleven. Eleven o'clock was the regular hour for Miss Hogan DeLisle's maid to clean her apartment.

He stalled, "I can't give you legal advice, Palmer. It wouldn't be ethical."

Palmer said, "I can see that. And I've got lawyers. Will it be necessary for you to ask the Arnaux kids where they got their liquor?"

"Not I—" The phone rang, and Corday made his eyebrows say "excuse me" as he picked up the red phone that was direct with police headquarters. He said, "Corday," and listened. Then he hung up the phone, carefully frowning, and said, "I've got to roll, Ronald. Homicide. And I don't know when I'll have time—" Impulsiveness was in every fold of his face as he said, "Want to come along, and we can talk in the car?" He was already moving to the door.

"If I won't be in the way," Ronald Palmer-said. He followed the D.A. quickly. "I've never seen anything like this."

Corday said over his shoulder, "I guess all citizens are interested in police work. It's remarkably like the movies."

They were in the corridor now. Corday's secretary listened in on and recorded all calls over the red phone; he didn't have to tell her where he was going. She had already buzzed for his car to be brought around.

Once in the car, Corday switched on the radio, the red light, and the siren. Traffic melted around them, and Palmer said, "This is fun."

"Glad to oblige," Corday said. He laughed. "In more ways than one. The Zebra House pays big taxes to the county. Now, as I said, I have no intention of asking Paget Arnaux where she got her liquor. It isn't pertinent to the case."

"Irrelevant and immaterial," Ronald Palmer said. He dug his fingers into the upholstery as Corday took the car around a bus and into the wrong side of the street. The siren wailed and they cut back again around a traffic island.

"That's the legal expression," David Corday said. "However, counsel for Harris might think there was something pertinent—relevant and material—in my not asking. He's certainly going to cross-examine; he might cross-examine on that point." He added wryly, "I understand until Harris threw his empty glass at Don Arnaux and knocked the wife down with a backhanded swipe, the kids had thought the whole incident too priceless for words."

"A fun thing," Ronald Palmer said. "That's the current expression. You don't grow to love humanity, running a nightclub. Or being a district attorney either, I imagine. Who's Harris's lawyer?"

"Mort Tucker," Corday said. Ahead a group of city cars—some marked, some plain—clustered around the entrance to the Belmont Apartment Hotel. Corday cut his siren and left the red light on for a moment; then, to the dying wail of the horn, cut the red light and coasted into the slot a uniformed officer indicated.

"Mort Tucker," Palmer said. "I think I can get him to keep the club out of the case. And maybe I could throw a little legal business his way. Who's the judge?"

"Judge Minelli's going to preside," Corday said, beginning to get out of the car. "But I wouldn't go near him. And be careful that nothing you do with Tucker looks like bribery."

Palmer joined him on the sidewalk, watched Corday nod in return to salutes from the patrolmen who were moving curiosity seekers along. Hurrying into the building, Palmer said, "I'm grateful for this, Corday."

"Standard procedure," Corday said, pushing him ahead into the self-service elevator, now run by a patrolman. "My interest is in convicting Harris, not in making trouble for businessmen." He turned, faced Palmer. "You know that about concludes our business," he said. The patrolman's ears were wide on his head; no cop could help but be interested in a conversation between two of the high and the mighty. "If you want to go on your way, I'll get an officer to drive you back to the Civic Center to your car."

"I'm really interested in this," Palmer said. "I've never seen a homicide squad work."

Corday said, "It's likely to be gruesome," and led the way out of the elevator.

Hogan DeLisle's little apartment was full and overflowing. Corday's voice was irascible as he said, "Will someone pass the word to Captain Martin that I am here?" and a uniformed sergeant at the door said, "You, Levy, Abner, Jones, out of this and wait in the hall," and three cops, two of them in the white coats of the ambulance division, crowded out and made room for the D.A. and his guest.

Captain Martin of the Homicide Squad, Doctor Shaefer of the Medical Examiner's office, Captain. Fink of the precinct stood around the body. Chalk marks on the carpet indicated that the squad had started work; that and half a dozen exploded flash bulbs. The light powder of the fingerprint men was on everything.

Corday joined the three head men and stood staring down at the girl.

"You got anything?" he asked Fink and Martin.

Martin shook his head. An overly burly man, he had a surprisingly light voice an Irish tenor He said, "Maid found her. Registered as Hogan DeLisle, occupation actress, she said." He had everyone's eye on him, expectantly; but his mouth closed and stayed closed.

Dave Corday looked around at the other men furtively, with suspense. This Captain Martin, head of Homicide, was a sort of legend; the police told stories about his incredibly clear head, lawyers proudly exhibited their scars after trying to twist him up on the witness stand, as though it were a badge of honor to be defeated by Captain Martin.

The legend was strong enough for Dave Corday to feel a pang of terror; he almost expected Captain Martin to say in his famous laconic style, "Brought home by Jim Latson. Shot by Dave Corday," and, perhaps, to add, "Handcuffs."

Like most lawyers, like most human beings, Dave Corday enjoyed talking. There was something frightening about Captain Martin—Captain B. L. Martin, he never used a first name—who seemed to loathe the sound of his own pleasant voice.

But Captain Martin, having talked and stopped, remained silent, and the heavy-faced Fink took it up: "Real name—we found letters—Beverly Hauer, father's on the assembly line of a car factory in Detroit. Murder committed by party or parties unknown, dead on arrival—hell, he put six slugs in her bra-seer—Doc here says she croaked about two this morning."

"Within the hour either way," the M.E. said.

Corday shrugged. "A party girl. We find out who was paying her rent, we'll probably find out she was blackmailing him."

Fink said, "The manager says she paid her own rent." He nodded across to the corner by the window where a group of witnesses—one of them the maid in a striped uniform embroidered with the name of the hotel—huddled unhappily.

Corday said, "Well, I'll want the slugs. Photographs. Wire Detroit, pick up any mail to her folks that was en route at the time of her death, any recent letters from her. I'll want—" He stopped. "Wait a minute. Palmer, want a look? You said you'd never seen anything like this." He made a gesture around the group. "You all know Ronald Palmer, don't you? Manages the Zebra House. We were talking business in my office when this call came in."

Having focused all their attention on the nightclub man, he stepped back, giving Palmer a clear view of the dead girl's face.

Palmer looked, and Corday heard him catch his breath; but when Palmer finally spoke, he said, "I've seen dead bodies before. Car accidents.

I guess this is the first murder though."

"That's one thing," Captain Martin said. "This is one we don't have to call an alleged murder or a possible murder or homicide. Six slugs in her... Take another look, Mr. Palmer. She ran in your circles."

Palmer said, "Yes." Corday, listening for it, heard caution in the words; but the others wouldn't be able to. He bent over. "Yes," he said. "I think I've seen her... But, really, my maître d', my captains, could do a better job. I'm in the office most of the time. Unless she was involved in a row or wanted to cash a check, I wouldn't know her."

Fink said, "That one cashed no checks. She was strictly a girl for the deposit window. Twenty-three years old, and eighteen thousand dollars in the banks."

Corday said, "Well, it's one commodity men have always paid for. Let's see. I'll want a careful file of all the fingerprints in the apartment; even the maid's. Until you make an arrest, I have no idea whom I'll have to prosecute. You know my slogan, gents: You catch 'em, I send 'em up."

"This one won't be hard for us," Captain Martin said. "She fancied her looks. Seven different poses of herself in the bedroom. I'm having them all copied, toted around the city to places she could have been. Places like yours, Mr. Palmer, like expensive clothing stores. We'll turn up her boy-friend, and he'll be the man. After that you'll have it tough, Dave."

Corday said, "Oh?"

"Money," Martin said. "He'll have heavy sugar. That kind is hard to send up."

"We'll do it," Corday said. "I think that's all. Coming, Palmer?"

Palmer nodded, and they turned away. But they were stopped by Latson; in fact, Corday had already seen him come into the room before he made his good-by speech. The lower ranking officers near the door gave way for the deputy chief as they had not for the district attorney.

Latson walked right up to the girl's head, said, "Sorry. Traffic Two had a four-car crash, I got away as soon as I could. What we got, Martin?"

Captain Martin was older than his superior, longer on the force. But his voice was quietly respectful as he said, "Murder, Chief. Murder one or murder two"—meaning premeditated, or unpremeditated—"that's all we don't know. Party girl. Probably blackmailing someone."

Latson nodded, shoved his gray felt hat back on his head, put both hands on his hips as he bent over. "Good looker," he said. And then, "Well, hell. That's Hogan DeLisle. I've dated her myself. Hey! That's too bad. She was fun."

He straightened up, looked around. "I—" he said, and then he saw Palmer and choked a little. "What are you doing here, Palmer?"

"We were talking business in my office," Corday said. "The Arnaux

case, you know, Latson. We finished it up in the car coming here when
I got the call, and I invited Palmer up."

Jim Latson laughed. "You've got damn funny ideas of how to entertain a friend, Dave." He straightened up, looked around the circle.
"Well, Marty, you don't need me, except to say what you need on this
case the department'll give you. Off-duty men and all. We'll want a quick
windup, a clean case for Dave here." He looked at Palmer, the only out-
sider there. "Not that we don't always want that, but it's more a matter
of what we can get... There are just so many men in any given police department."

"I know how it is," Ronald Palmer said. "And in my business, I'd just
as soon not see taxes go up. So don't apologize to me, Chief."

"I wasn't," Latson said flatly. He stepped away, looked at the medical
examiner. "Don't bother with special copies to me, Doc. I'll look over
Marty's shoulder. And I imagine the sooner your boys get the body out,
the better the management here will appreciate it. We're cluttering up
their lobby downstairs."

Captain Fink said, "I'll get my men back on patrol right away, Chief."

Latson nodded, and started for the door after Fink. From the corner
the plaintive voice of the manager said, "How long will you want this
apartment bottled up, Chief?" He was speaking to Latson, was obviously
glad that authority had finally boiled down to one man who could be
spoken to.

Latson said, "How long's her rent paid up?"

"First of the month."

"That's twelve days. Ought to be enough. You can clean up, redeco-
rate, whatever you do, on your own time; you would for a live tenant
moving out." He was at the door now. He straightened his hat, said,
"Give Dave Corday a nice clean case now, boys," and left.

Corday said, "Palmer and I were just leaving," but he moved slowly
enough so that they did not have to share the elevator with Latson. The
man's assurance, his ease, had shocked Corday. He had at least expected
Latson to take charge of the case himself, to stay in a position where he
could suppress the wrong kind of evidence.

He was shocked but, riding down with Ronald Palmer, he took a little cold comfort. Palmer obviously had known the girl, had probably
known that she had been at the Zebra House with Latson the night before. It was why he had maneuvered Palmer so skillfully into the scene.

It hadn't been hard; there was always some reason the chief trial
deputy could find for wanting to see a night club manager, a bar owner.
But it had apparently come to nothing, and that was what amused Corday.

Because if Palmer planned on blackmailing Jim Latson, he was in for some very uncomfortable moments. So was Jim Latson, which mattered more to Corday; but Latson's discomfort would be as nothing compared to Palmer's; his would go quickly from mere discomfort to the dire plight of a man reaching out to pet a Pekingese, and finding his hand on the back of a wolverine.

As Corday and Palmer went through the downstairs lobby, the reporters and photographers had broken through the thinning cordon of Captain Fink's men. Corday had to stop four or five times to say, "No comment. See Captain Martin," before he got to the car.

He drove Palmer rapidly back to the Civic Center.

CHAPTER 4

Now Homicide was in charge of the case. That meant Captain Martin and his small squad of regulars, plus a few of the utility men always on duty at headquarters and available for any division that needed them.

Two of these utility men were named Lyons and Koch, and Captain Martin had given them their orders: "The basement."

Koch, who was thin and worried about his hairline, looked at Lyons, who was stocky and athletic, and sighed. They had been lent to Homicide before; they knew Captain Martin and his terse orders. What he meant was, "I want you to give the service department of this hotel a thorough search. Go through all the lockers of all the help, question everybody, get me lists, inventories, floor plans, backgrounds, criminal records if any, and do it now."

What they found down below was a small but efficient unit. Although the apartment hotel had no dining room, room service could be had at any hour, and to order. It was nothing for the Belmont to furnish Chinese pheasant with truffles at four-fifteen in the morning.

With drinks. Also fresh linen, as many times a day as you wanted it.

This was daytime, and no personnel were on shift who had been on when Hogan DeLisle was murdered. But the executive housekeeper gave Lyons and Koch a list of night personnel, a master key to the lockers, and her blessing.

It was unpleasant work. Koch found one busboy's locker that apparently hadn't been emptied in a year; when he unlocked the door, filthy clothes came cascading out, and he swore as he pawed through the sweat-caked linen, searching for nothing.

Koch said, "Waste of time. If this was robbery, it'd make sense, working down here. Only it wasn't."

His partner looked up, grunted. "Here's a screwball. Night floor waiter. He's got a book for translating Lithuanian into French, and one for going the other way." He slammed the locker door shut again.

"This guy never takes anything home," Koch said. He shoved the busboy's dirty clothes back into the locker, kicked the door shut and went over and washed his hands. "Two more lockers and we can move over to the women's locker room."

"That'll be fun," Lyons said. "Stop bitching. If this had been short of homicide, we'd be working for Cap Fink. Martin's easy to get along with."

Koch opened a locker for himself, one for Lyons. "Sure," he said. "Martin's easy to get along with. All you gotta be is perfect." '

Lyons reached in the locker and took out a box. "Maybe the lady's diamonds'll be in here," he said, "and we can all go home. Well, when Martin gives you an order, it sticks; later on he don't pretend he told you to do something else." He had opened the box, pulled something out. He gave it a casual glance, and then, perhaps because he had been talking about Captain Martin's high standards, he held the object close to his eye and squinted.

Then in an oddly strangled voice, he said, "Hey. I got something."

Koch looked up from his own search. Dangling from Lyons's hand was a string of beads. They were irregularly shaped, greenish blue, hooked together with silver links.

"Turquoise," Koch said. "So what? They come all prices. My wife bought a string of them out west one summer vacation."

Lyons said, "But look," and handed over the stones, clasp first.

Koch had to move over under the unshaded center light to peer. The silver clasp was somewhat larger than the turquoise merited, and it was initialed. Not with very large letters, but with plain ones. *H. DeL.*, for Hogan DeLisle.

Neither detective wasted time speculating; the initials were too unusual. Lyons went at once to the house phone fastened on a center pot near the washbasin and said, "Gimme the housekeeper." He identified himself, looked at the name on the locker, and said, "How's about an employee named Ralph Guild." He took his notebook out and started writing. "Night waiter...been here over a year... All right, gimme his home address." He cleared his throat. "Naw, we'll go out there. We need the air."

When he hung up, he turned to his partner and said, "West side, Jacobi Avenue."

Koch said, "Should we phone upstairs, tell Cap Martin?"

Lyons spat on the cement floor. "He'd just say where is he? You know

Cap."

So they went out, two unexcited men, and got in their squad car, illegally parked in the alley. They both lit cigarettes, and Lyons drove.

The car rolled west, away from the Civic Center, through the wholesale produce section, through a block—covered entirely with used machinery shops, past the freight terminal, and then into an area forgotten by progress where small frame houses sat huddled as close together as possible, each with a fourteen-by-twenty foot back yard, a fourteen-by-ten foot front lawn.

After a minute or so of this, Lyons said, "Here we are." Koch slid the car to the curb and then got out. Koch moved his gun from his hip holster to his coat pocket, ready to shoot through the cloth, and they went up the rickety wooden steps.

But the very pregnant young woman who answered the door did not look formidable. Her two-piece smock-type dress only accentuated her condition as she hitched the top part down and looked at them. Lyons said, "Mr. Ralph Guild live here?"

She said, "But he's asleep. He doesn't get home till after seven every morning, he has to, get his sleep."

Koch said meaninglessly, "That's all right," and shoved forward till she gave way.

Lyons pulled his gun, and the woman—Mrs. Guild, beyond much doubt—screamed a little. Koch said, "It's all right, lady," and when her eyes went to one of the two doors opening off the living room, he promptly palmed the knob and threw the door open.

The man in bed muttered, "Coming right up," as they slammed into the room, and then he sat up: a skinny guy, about thirty, in polka-dot undershorts. The bed looked as though no expert had made it. Koch said, "Ralph Guild?" in a hard, businesslike voice.

"Yeah, sure. My papers are on the bureau."

Lyons slid a hand under the pillow, down among the sheets and then put his gun away. Koch crossed and picked the papers off the bureau. "Immigration," he said, "naturalization. Court order changing his name from something—thank God, I don't have to phone it in—to Ralph Guild. He's a Czech."

"He's a bad check now," Lyons said. His normally cheerful face was grim. "Out of it, Guild, and on your feet. Get some pants on." He backed up, started throwing clothes at Guild, first feeling each garment for weapons.

Guild said, "Yes, sir," standing up. He was going a little bald, one tooth was missing among his, uppers. "May I ask what you want me for, sir?"

Koch's voice was kindly. "Take it easy, boy. Don't mind Mr. Lyons here,

it's just his way. Do you know a girl named DeLisle, Hogan DeLisle?"
Guild nodded eagerly, fastening his pants. Almost at once he had to un-
zip them again to tuck his shirt in. "Yes, sir, of course I do. Miss DeLisle,
I am her regular waiter. She always asks for me.... I must explain, I am
night waiter, ten till seven, at the Belmont Apartment Hotel." He was
fumbling with a hideously bright necktie—the only thing in the room that
had any kind of color.

The knot wouldn't tie to Guild's satisfaction. He stopped fumbling and
suddenly got a thought. "Nothing has happened to Miss DeLisle, sir?"

"She's dead," Lyons said. "Take him to the car, John, while I search the
house for the murder weapon."

Koch marched Ralph Guild to the car. When Lyons rejoined them, he
said absently, "That dame can sure cry," and started the car.

CHAPTER 5

As deputy chief, one of Jim Latson's duties was to wander, without
schedule or map, through headquarters building. It kept the men on their
toes. And so, when he returned from the murder suite (as the papers were
already calling Hogan DeLisle's apartment), he signed a few letters on his
desk and took off.

Missing Persons, Arson, Radio Room, Personnel. He paused there and
lit a cigarette, perched on the edge of the bureau chief's desk, swinging
one leg, idly watching the clerks. When he left, a half dozen civil-service
fingerprint cards were in his pocket.

He went on to Loft Squad, Taxi License Bureau, Juvenile, and into Identification. Two clerks were busily putting together a bundle of prints from
the DeLisle apartment; flustered by the personal attention of Chief Latson, they never noticed that the envelope for the FBI was six cards heavier when he left than before he visited them.

Jim Latson wandered back to his office. The second mail of the day had
not been sorted. Two little piles were on his desk: one personal, the other
duty. Seeing his wife's handwriting on the top of the personal file, he went
through the other one first.

But there was no putting it off. He examined the Italian stamp and the
flimsy *Avion* paper until it was more boring not to open the letter than
to open it, and used a knife on his desk, a souvenir of a national meeting of peace officers.

Yeah, she was in Rome. She had an audience with the Holy Father, not
a private one to be sure, but the Pope had spent more time blessing her
than any of the other pilgrims. She had lit a candle for Latson's return

to the church, and she needed another five hundred dollars.

Yeah. Except for the amount, which sometimes—but not often—went as low as two hundred, he hadn't needed to open the envelope at all; habit was an X-ray that could read her letters folded. Yeah.

He hadn't been to confession in ten years. But officially he was a Catholic and in politics that meant that his behavior was subject to Cathedral inspection. The archbishop had let it be known, clearly, that divorce or overt infidelity meant the withdrawal of Cathedral support for any party that kept Jim Latson in high office.

He wrote a short glad-you-are-enjoying-yourself note, and got his private checkbook—one of his private checkbooks—out of the locked drawer. But when he thumbed through the stubs, he saw that this, the New York book, was not the one he had been using to send Marie her money. He put it away and got the San Francisco book, and that was right.

There was no use letting her know any more than she had to know. He wrote the check, and was just about to sign it when his red phone buzzed. Orders—his own—were that any man with a red phone dropped everything when it rang, but he took time to lock the checkbooks away before scooping the phone up.

"Got an arrest in the DeLisle case," Captain Martin said. "A room waiter. Motive, robbery."

Some day Martin was going to drop from the exhaustion of wasting a word.

"Where are you?" Jim Latson asked.

"Girl's flat. Lyons and Koch brought him in. Necklace of hers in his locker."

"Keep him there. The body still around?"

Captain Martin said, "M.E. took it."

"Too bad. Looking at bodies is good exercise. I'll be over. Keep it from the papers if you can."

"Can't. News-Journal was here."

"No great harm. Be there in five minutes."

"Okay, Chief."

Phone on the hook. Note and check in an envelope. Airmail to Italy was—yeah, he remembered, stamped the envelope, addressed it by hand and shoved it in his pocket. The buzzer from downstairs said his car had been brought to the Street level.

But still he took time to check his gun. The suspect might try to escape, and so get killed.

He wondered as he put his hat on, started out, what the name of the room waiter was.

Also, he wondered if the guy's fingerprints would show up at Hogan DeLisle's. Funny if they didn't. Not that it mattered. Fingerprints would not be used in this case when it was found that those lifted in the girl's apartment had gotten mixed up in some way with a bunch of police officers' prints from Personnel.

Some clerk would get fired over that. And Captain Martin would have to work the DeLisle case without fingerprints... Too bad, but Martin was a good man, he could do it. You never got fingerprints in a case these days anyway.

Not to do you much good.

CHAPTER 6

"She gave it to me," Ralph Guild said. "Every night, nearly, she phone down for warm milk and crackers, for Ralph to bring it up. When I got there, she would make a little joke; has the new Guild started yet? You see, my name it is the same as a union or something... And I would say no, not yet. So she gave me this string of beads, and she says, when the baby comes and they let you see your wife, give her these; it will make her feel beautiful again. They were not valuable, she said."

"Fifty bucks." This was a detective lieutenant named Sands. "I was on pawnshop detail before I got on Homicide."

"Sure," Jim Latson said. "Fifty bucks is no tip at all for a room waiter. Fifty-buck tips happen every night, sometimes two or three a night."

"Please," Ralph Guild said, "I know fifty dollars is much money. But from a regular patron, one I—"

"How was she dressed?" Jim Latson asked. "I don't mean on the night you killed her, last night, but usually. When you brought her"— he dropped one eyelid, drawled his words—"her bedtime crackers and milk."

Ralph Guild licked his lips nervously. "Dressed? She would be in bed. She would phone down and unlock her front door; I would bring her her—snack, you call it—and I would lock up when I left."

"Snack's a good word for it," Sands said. A heavy-fleshed, small-eyed man, he had been a certainty to pick up Chief Latson's insinuation.

"Have sex with her?" Captain Martin asked.

"Me? A waiter? No. She was very rich, she knew fine gentlemen."

Sands was snorting through his broad nose. "Money don't do a guy much good in bed," he said. "And after the rich gents went home, there was a nice young waiter, looking for a good tip. A fifty-buck tip."

Jim Latson was thinking that Sands would make a good captain. Put him on the Vice Squad, and he'd work for nothing.

The half dozen reporters present were breaking for the door. They could now tell their desks that it was safe to say that a sex angle had been turned up in the DeLisle case.

Harry Weber of the *News-Journal* remained behind. "You got a robbery motive," he said, "why search around for rape, too? The papers haven't been that good to you." The *News-Journal* was the biggest paper in town; it always had two men on a big story, one to ask fool questions.

But the police are public servants. They should be polite to the press. "Get him into court," Captain Martin said, "and we can't prove the beads weren't a tip. Tip for doing what?"

Dave Corday strolled in, followed by the reporters returning from their phone. "Nice work, boys," he said. "That was a quick catch. This the defendant?"

Jim Latson laughed. "That's up to you, Dave. If you don't like him for it, we will be happy to catch you another one. A happy district attorney's office, that's the slogan of my department."

Corday said, "Jim, that's the way to talk. After all, arrests without convictions don't do either of us any good."

You smug bastard, Jim Latson was thinking. You size six feet in number twelve shoes. You sure stepped out of your league when you tried to frame me.

But a sneaking, lonely thought remained: the graceful figure, the laughing face of a girl who called herself Hogan DeLisle. He missed her, and he had never thought another woman would get under his skin.

For that, some day, Dave Corday would end up in the gutter.

Corday was asking Martin what the situation added up to; Captain Martin was telling him in his curt way.

Corday nodded. "Okay. I like the sex angle better than the robbery. It makes more sense. He was her lover, and she either broke off with him or refused to give him any more money…we'll find out which. I'll put the D.A.'s officers on Guild: his background, his financial position. From your men, I'd like to get a tie-in on the gun, on his relations with his wife, and, of course, anything else you get."

"Can do," Captain Martin said.

"Particularly the gun," Dave Corday said. He was talking directly to Jim Latson now; but his eyes were not on the chief's eyes but on his left armpit, where the gun bulged the carefully tailored suit not at all. "By now ballistics will have a good deal on the slugs that came out of the corpse; and I want the gun that fired them. I want that gun, Chief. If you have to drag every river, open every manhole in the state, we'll need that gun. Without it, there's no case."

Jim Latson grinned and bowed deeply. "Mr. Prosecutor, you have but to command and us lowly cops'll break our tired bones for you. You want a gun, we'll get you a gun." He reached in his armpit, came out with his own weapon, butt first. "Take mine, counselor. Anything to keep you happy, as I said before."

"I never owned a gun in my life," Ralph Guild said. But none of the policemen were listening to him.

CHAPTER 7

Evening papers under his arm, Dave Corday went past the bowing doorman and into the Zebra House Bar. This was not the regular night-club but a big anteroom off it; at night it was mostly used by people waiting for tables, but from five to seven it was a prosperous cocktail lounge.

The cocktail maître d' bowed low. "A table, Mr. Corday? We don't often get honored this way."

"Yes, I'd like a table, Ernest. Small one will do. I'm not expecting anyone."

Palmer was not in sight, neither was Jim Latson. Dave Corday, a man not given to public drinking, had not changed his tastes; he was there to watch Latson squirm. It was an absolute certainty that the chief would show here, wanting to find out as soon as possible what Ronald Palmer was asking for his silence.

Hating Latson as he did, Corday still had a twinge of sympathy for him. They were both public figures, politicians in a sense, and blackmailers were, of all criminals, the only ones they feared.

Ernest himself brought the Bloody Mary Corday had ordered. He sipped it, looked at the paper. It would be something if the case against Ralph Guild stood up. One for the books.

He skimmed the stories in the big *News-Journal*, the tabloid *Tribune*, the conservative *World* and the reformer *Record*. It was a rare thing for the city's papers to be in agreement on anything. But this time they were: Ralph Guild was guilty.

The *Record*, trying for an angle, had a front-page editorial suggesting that room service men be licensed by the police, as hack drivers were. The *Trib* practically said that Hogan DeLisle—nobody used her real name— had been raped before she was shot.

His lawyer's mind automatically went over that story a second time. They were smart at the *Tribune*; when you first read their stories, you thought you saw grounds for a libel suit; but they were masters of the alleged-possible-no-statement kind of writing.

Dave Corday wondered if there were courses in that kind of work in journalism school.

And this took him back to his own school days, the bitter days of his undergraduate life, when he had washed dishes and worked a laundry route to get through; the almost as hard times when, a G.I., he and Elsa had lived in part of a Quonset hut while the Veterans' Administration helped him get his law degree.

Stop crying, Corday, he told himself. Those times weren't so horrible. Elsa was wonderful, for one thing; she'd gotten jobs to augment the hundred and a quarter a month the government had allowed them; she'd cooked spaghetti and hamburger forty-one different ways—they had counted once—to keep them fed tastily and cheaply—she'd never complained.

What had gone wrong? At what step in their lives had he written a brief when he should have admired a new dress, said no when he should have said yes, done something when he should have done nothing?

There had been no big fight between him and Elsa. Just all at once, they were miles apart, drifted, and she was leaving him for Jim Latson. He remembered at the time thinking that Latson was a fool; no woman was worth what a divorce would cost the chief...

But there'd been no divorce. Instead, there had been a new girl for Jim Latson, a girl called Hogan De Lisle—ridiculous!—and Elsa had gone out of town, to die on Kansas City's Skid Row.

She called me, Dave Corday thought. I couldn't take her back—I'd have been laughed out of politics for that—but I should have helped her. With money, maybe...

And there was Jim Latson. His long legs carried him into the bar as they carried him every place; a man going where he was going on purpose. There was an accident in Jim Latson's life. He controlled it, himself, and the people around him.

Dave Corday suppressed a grin. Life had caught up with Jim Latson. Oh, how it had caught up with him.

Sooner or later all those little bits of evidence were going to come to light; the ballistics report on the gun should start it. You couldn't tamper with those records; city regulations—put in by Latson himself—required all sworn personnel in the department to register their guns with the FBI.

Latson had seen him, was hard-heeling toward him, smiling. But, as he approached, Corday ticked off the case against him.

One, the bullets. Two, Latson's fingerprints all over the DeLisle apartment (Latson had tried to cover that by frankly admitting that he had "dated" DeLisle).

Three, the cruiser log placing Latson within six blocks of the Belmont at the time of the murder. Four—"Hi, Dave! Ernest, a martini and a dividend for me, and another one of those things for Mr. Corday."

"Yes, Chief Latson. If you're through with those papers, Mr. Corday, I could remove them."

"I'm through, Ernest: And switch me to a Tom Collins; I've had my vitamins."

Ernest's teeth were the whitest any man ever owned; his hair the smoothest. He gathered up the four papers, and was gone like a genie.

"I hate waiters," Jim Latson said. "Always make me feel I should have changed my shirt."

"You're about to get your revenge on the Waiters' and 'Stewards' Union," Corday said.

Latson laughed, his easy, thumb-on-the-world laugh. "Guild? That case is shaping up nicely. We got one set back: negative on the paraffin test. But I got a statement from the food checker at the Belmont; one of her duties was to see that no waiter left the kitchen without having his white gloves on. So we dug around, and there, by golly, were a pair of white gloves behind a garbage can; whataya know?"

"Paraffin positive," Corday said. "And done without my crystal ball. I'll bet I can tell you where you were this afternoon. Answer: the pistol range."

"Yep," Latson said. "Sure. Departmental regulation one-one-seven thirty-two: all officers will carry gun and badge at all times, on and off duty; one-one-seven thirty-three: each officer of the department will fire eighteen rounds of ammunition per month on the Police Club range, said ammunition to be paid for by the officer firing; and in the event that the score for said rounds shall average less than seventy, PPC standards, an immediate report shall be made to the Personnel Bureau, which will take steps to see that the officer firing this—"

Corday interrupted rudely: "That's enough, Latson, that's enough. You're God's great cop, aren't you? You can recite the manual backwards, fire a hundred target, PPC, repair a police radio, take lab tests and—" he paused, swallowing, "and frame waiters."

"What are you sore about?" Latson asked mildly. "You swung and you missed. Result—I'm building you up a case that'll probably get you elected D.A. next term. Smith tells me he's stepping up, the party likes him for governor... Ernest, if you'd let your hair grow, I'd marry you."

The maître d' was setting up for a ceremony as intricate as a voodoo rite. In front of Jim Latson he placed a glass holding an ice cube; off to one side was a martini mixer, with the long glass stirrer cocked at its most

alluring angle; on a little plate covered with a glass dome were two pi-
mento-stuffed olives, two anchovy-stuffed olives, and two pickled onions.

Now Ernest dumped the ice cube into a little bucket, placed the bucket
on the floor. He wiped the chilled glass with a spotless napkin, placed it
back in front of Latson, gave the cocktail two slow stirs, and lifted the
glass dome.

This was the time for a breathless pause; Ernest was duly breathless as
his eyebrows raised at Jim Latson. The chief gravely pointed a little finger at one of the onions, and Ernest breathed again, the crisis past.

The onion went in the glass, was drowned in the almost colorless cocktail, and again the maître d' lost his breath. Jim Latson gravely lifted the
glass, sipped, and smiled.

Ernest breathed, placed Corday's Tom Collins in front of him briskly,
removed the tomato-stained glass, and was gone.

Dave Corday gave a disgusted grunt.

"I still hate waiters," Jim Latson said. "But I'm a guy believes in
spreading sunshine as I go. You came here to watch Palmer blackmail
me, didn't you?"

Corday's stomach knotted. Jim Latson was, at one time, all the things
he hated most in the world. The ease with which the cop had gotten to
the top of the department, the careless grace Latson showed with
women, the social expertness with waiters, college professors, businessmen—they were all the things Dave Corday did not have and knew now
he would never have. He said, "Yes. I wanted to see you suffer."

Jim Latson laughed. "By the way, Dave, I have a little bad news for you.
You know McCray, that con-man who's out on bail? The case on him
has fallen apart. Lack of clear identification. I'm sorry."

Corday had been about to take a swallow of his Tom Collins. He set
the glass down with a click. "McCray? That was Donald Munroe's
nephew he conned. I promised Mr. Munroe we'd send him away for ten
years, make him pay the nephew back and—" He stopped, sick.

Jim Latson said, "Now, if I'd known that... Why, Dave, as I understand
it, Mr. Munroe got you into the D.A.'s office in the first place... He's about
all the sponsor you have in politics, isn't he? Why, that's too bad."

Dave Corday felt the blood pushing at his eyes. "Too bad? Too bad?
He's kicked in to the party funds every time I've asked him. You—"

Jim Latson laughed. "Take it easy, Dave. Drink your drink."

Dave Corday gulped at the glass unhappily, then flushed as he realized
he'd taken an order from Jim Latson.

Jim Latson said easily, "Don't let it worry you. If you get a conviction
on Guild, you'll be made, a famous man; you won't need a sponsor.
There'll be dozens of men waiting to back you for any office you want

to run."

Dave Corday was reminding himself of his training, his practice in thinking on his feet. He said calmly—though he didn't feel calm— "You didn't just do this to get me in trouble with Donald Munroe."

"I didn't do it at all," Jim Latson said. "I'm a cop; I like to get convictions. But McCray's lawyer, Steve Sigel, was too smart for me."

Corday set down his glass so hard that some of the drink splashed over the top, though he'd drunk more than half of it. "Steve Sigel! That's it. He's lawyer for the syndicate, isn't he? I wouldn't doubt he was more than counsel, a big owner—"

"Easy, boy, you're in a syndicate bar. They don't like to be talked about."

"They wouldn't like one of their nightclub operators, Ronald Palmer, testifying against a man who'd done Steve Sigel a big favor, would they?"

"It must be wonderful to go to law school," Jim Latson said. "How they train you! Everything comes out easy for a boy with a good education. Me, a little high school, and I was on my own. Yep. A little favor for the syndicate, and they'd make hamburger of one of their men who annoyed me—such as Mr. Palmer. After all, all he's doing is saving me newspaper embarrassment. Since Guild is guilty, it doesn't occur to Palmer that he's withholding pertinent information in a murder case, thereby laying himself open to a charge of accessory after the fact, a serious felony. He's just—"

Dave Corday slapped the table, but neither glass was now full enough to slop over; all he did was make a sharp sound that caused heads to turn at a couple of tables. "And at the same time, you louse me up with my sponsor."

"Two birds with one stone," Jim Latson said cheerfully. "My, that's a pretty girl there."

Despite himself, Corday looked. The girl was auburn-haired, and it looked natural. Dark blue eyes and a milkmaid complexion gave an overall Irish look. He said, "This isn't the time or place to discuss girls. You killed Hogan DeLisle and, brother, you are not going to get away with it."

Jim Latson suddenly dropped his light manner. "You really believe that, don't you? But you killed her, pal. And she was my girl. And cops don't take to having their girls killed. It wounds their *amour propre*—French phrase, meaning love of self—I may not have gone to college, but I read. It would hurt the party to hurt you, and I know enough to keep my friends in office. It saves you— You know something? The couple with that gal are Tommy Beale and his wife. He runs a small cab line. Whatya bet he'd be flattered if the deputy chief of police stopped by?"

Dave Corday said. "Your girl's hardly cold, and you're looking for another."

"Ah, she's cold enough now," Jim Latson said. "You son-of-a-bitch." He picked up his martini pitcher and his empty glass, and strolled toward the red-headed girl's table.

CHAPTER 8

Ballistics came in first. Dave Corday hardly had his mail in front of him when police headquarters called: Ballistics had the murder gun, had fired slugs out of it, and it matched.

Corday had trouble keeping his voice steady. This was it. This was the payoff. There was no way Jim Latson could get out of this one; the slugs would lead right to his registered gun. He said, "Where'd you find the gun?"

The lab officer over at headquarters said, "Routine. We asked all city workers to keep an eye open. A sewer inspector found it under a manhole on Fifth Street. No fingerprints, of course."

"Serial number?"

"For what it's worth. It's a Skoda, they're reasonably rare, but a lot of G.I.'s smuggled them home as souvenirs. It's never been registered in this country that we can find out. Of course, some states don't have registration, and some are slow reporting to Washington."

Corday leaned forward till the edge of his desk cut into his belly. "But it's never been registered in this state?"

The ballistics man was probably thinking that the D.A. was a little slow this morning. He said, "That's right, sir."

Dave Corday said, "How about fingerprints from the apartment? I know, don't tell me; they've gone to the FBI for a quick check. How about a long distance call to them? This office will pay for it."

An unmistakable political tone came into the ballistics man's voice. "I'm pretty sure Chief Latson phoned them this morning."

It was barely nine o'clock. Jim Latson must be sweating to be on deck that early. Corday grinned, but not with too much gusto, and said, "Switch me to him."

The phone clicked noisily, and Dave Corday held it away from his ear. When Jim Latson's voice came on, saying, "Deputy Chief Latson," he was oily. "Jim, it's fine about the gun, isn't it?"

"Fine?" Latson asked.

"Yep," Dave Corday said. "It's a Skoda. That's a Czecho-Slovakian make, and our man is a Czech; it's all closing in. Your man said you'd called the FBI lab about the fingerprints. Do they make them?"

"I'm sorry as hell," Jim Latson said. "Dave, old boy, I don't know how to tell you—we botched that. Not that we can't straighten it out, but it makes the report a little long; they're sending it on by collect day-letter. What happened was a whole batch of our personnel prints got in with the ones from the DeLisle flat; but I can tell you this..."

He went on. But Corday wasn't listening. A cinch. A lead pipe cinch. Latson had fired the gun—probably one he'd palmed from an arrest, or maybe even one he'd had since the war—at the range, so it would look used.

Then all he had to do was get it down a manhole.

Dave Corday felt his legally trained mind take hold of the facts, start aligning them. It was a process he always enjoyed; as a boy, he had not been a very clear thinker; he had been inclined to daydream, and to leave out—as gaps in his daydream—all the difficult process of thought and reality.

So he knew that logical thinking was a thing he had bought, and bought hard, at law school.

The gun was not registered and the fingerprints were so confused that they would do no good; not only Latson's were on the FBI report, but those of a half dozen other police officers who could not possibly be tied into the case.

Those were the facts; the lawyer's mind deduced from them that the first fact, the gun fact or set of facts, was luck: Latson luck. Many a police officer keeps several guns: souvenirs of dangerous arrests, gifts from other peace officers, souvenirs of shooting matches. Latson had been wearing one of these, a light pistol, a Skoda, and he had probably been wearing it for no other reason than that its size would not bulk out his evening clothes. And Latson would be the last police officer in the world to take seriously the rule that all guns must be registered; Latson considered the law his servant and not his employer.

So much for that. The fingerprints were not luck. It had been Jim Latson, and no one else, who had messed up the mailing of the prints from DeLisle's apartment.

Of course, if Dave Corday insisted, he could take over the return from the FBI and distinguish between Personnel Department photostats and those from the Homicide Squad camera.... But he would have to warn Latson he was going to do that, and give the policeman plenty of time to botch up things better.

Latson was talking, had been talking. "You'll have to ride this case out without fingerprints, Dave. One thing the Washington report does show:

Guild was not among the prints. Some weirdies were, though, including a couple of telephone operators and the reports clerk out at the Park Precinct."

Dave Corday reminded himself that he was a trained lawyer. The Guild case was a case. He said, "What a botch. Well, as you say, fingerprints hardly apply; he wore gloves." He strengthened it: "He always wore gloves. We've got the checker's word for that; room waiters had to put on white gloves before leaving the kitchen. Always."

"Yeah," Latson said slowly, "but we'd better soft pedal the sex angle. With gloves on, Dave? Bizarre, but unlikely." His chuckle was genial.

Dave Corday managed a chuckle in return. "I see what you mean," he said "The *Trib* would call her 'The Immaculate Call Girl.'"

"It's better with your shoes off," Jim said, going on with the gag.

"Well, nothing's happened to weaken our case, and that's the big thing. Want to meet me at county jail, and we'll talk to Guild together?"

"Sure, Dave, sure."

Corday hung up and leaned back. It looked very much as though Ralph Guild was in for it... Well, a thief was a thief. He shouldn't have taken the necklace. And that he'd done; people don't give waiters a fifty-dollar piece of jewelry, and if they do, the waiter sells it for cash.

He glanced at the desk clock. Almost ten. A hell of a lot of paper work to catch up on before he met Jim Latson...

He found himself wondering how Latson had made out with the auburn-haired girl last night. What a guy...

Then, as his mind faded into his work, he forgot all about Latson. Once he was suddenly stabbed with a chilling, paralyzing feeling of loss that made his mind refuse to absorb the words he was reading.

He pushed back in his swivel chair, and realized that he was sad because Elsa was dead; he would never see her familiar walk come striding around a corner, never have her come back and tell him she was wrong, she should never have left him.

It was a good thing she was dead, he told himself. He would have made a fool of himself and taken her back. His position, his rise in life had cost him too much for him to throw it away doing a thing like that. He couldn't afford to be laughed at, not ever. He had thought of that when she called him, and then it had been too late; he had no number to call back once he had hung up.

He shook his head and dived back into the papers carefully—conscientiously reading the reports from his subordinates, carefully and conscientiously passing up short summaries to the district attorney himself, his only superior.

At exactly five minutes of eleven, he pressed the button for his car, stood

up, took a quick look in the little mirror in his breast pocket, and
walked briskly but not hurriedly out to the car.

He did not carry any papers because he thought that officials who did
paper work in the streets gave the appearance of being eager beavers. Bad.
But he did let his chauffeur—a patrolman assigned to the D.A.'s office—
drive. There was no use in wasting his energy.

The driver put the car through the gate that said *Police Cars Only*, and
parked in one of the four stalls reserved for the district attorney's office.
This put him right next to the press parking, and so he ran into Harry
Weber of the *News-Journal* just coming out of the back entrance of the
jail, lighting a cigarette and looking pleased.

The press was important; Dave Corday said, "Hi, Harry! How's it going?"

"Dandy, Mr. Corday. Just fine."

"You were with Cap Martin when they brought in Ralph Guild,
weren't you?" He watched, and he thought Harry Weber's face changed;
but the reporter didn't ask him for a statement. Corday gave it anyway:
"We're going to hang that man, Harry."

This brought a reaction. Harry Weber reached for the folded copy paper and the pencil: "Any developments, D.A.?"

"We have found the murder weapon."

The reporter scribbled something without taking his eyes off Corday's
face. "Where?"

"In a manhole on Fifth Street."

Weber said, "And it ties in with Ralph Guild?"

Corday cleared his throat and hated himself for doing it. It sounded like
an old-time, Phogbound type of politician. "It is a Skoda, which is a
Czecho-Slovakian make. Guild has confessed to being a Czech."

"Want to give me a statement on that? If the gun had been a Luger, the
murderer would have been German; Webley, English; Colt, a horse?"

Dave Corday felt his face reddening. "Of course I won't give you any
statement like that!"

Another car was pulling into the courtyard. Out of the corner of his
eye, Dave Corday saw with relief that it was Jim Latson's car. He needed
reinforcements badly.

Harry Weber said, "Well, then, how about a statement that the gun
doesn't tie into Ralph Guild at all."

"He's a Czech!" Corday said.

"Which is of what significance in this case?"

"The gun is Czech, too. Surely—"

"Czech, Spanish, and Belgian pistols are the rule down on Skid Row,"
Harry said. "Because they're cheap."

Corday's temper slipped. He had been told in law school that that was the one thing no lawyer should ever indulge himself in: uncontrolled and uncalculated anger. "Young man, you can't badger me!"

Jim Latson, followed by his patrolman-secretary, had ambled up. "Sounds like he's doing it, Dave, old boy. Hi, Harry. Getting plenty?" Harry Weber's face lost that taunting grin. "Hello, Chief."

And there it was again. Dave Corday was entitled to be called Chief, but no one ever gave him the courtesy; after all, he was Chief Deputy of the District Attorney's office. It was a job calling for education, experience, tact, brains. Really, he rated higher than anybody in the police department; but no one ever thought so. The minute Latson appeared any place, any time, everyone turned to him. But a district attorney rated much higher.

"I'm just trying to get a howgozit on the Guild case," Harry said.

Jim Latson said at once, "The District Attorney's office is well satisfied that the department was justified in arresting Ralph Guild; but, mindful of his oath to protect the innocent as well as prosecute the guilty, Chief Deputy David Corday is not yet prepared to say that the evidence against Ralph Guild is complete."

"You know I can't turn that in, Chief," Harry Weber said. "If I phoned that to the desk, they'd take the dime for the phone call out of my pay."

"Okay," Jim Latson said. "That's what you get for heckling the D.A.'s office. If you'd been a good boy, you might have picked up a story. Come on, Dave." And somehow he managed to leave Harry Weber unsatisfied but not angry. It was a pretty good trick.

CHAPTER 9

The interview room at the jail was sunny; but that was about all that could be said for it. The furniture consisted of four straight chairs and a swivel chair, all bolted to the floor; the single table had no drawers because a man could whip out a desk drawer and bean a district attorney.

Jim Latson had had to leave his gun out at the front gate; Dave Corday was not carrying one. They entered the interview room, and Latson waved at the swivel chair. "Your honor, D.A."

Dave Corday said, "Someday I'm going to shove that deferential grin down your throat."

"Any time, Dave, any time. Want me to quote some more police manual to you? Want me to quote the part about physical fitness of all personnel? About periodic physical examinations? Or shall I quote you my last rating in judo?"

"I don't want you to quote anything to me!" Dave Corday said.

Jim Latson was calm. "Shush." He gestured at the door into the jail proper. It was opening. Ralph Guild came in, followed by a turnkey. The officer looked at Jim Latson who made a gesture with his thumb; the turnkey went out again. Ralph Guild stood in front of the closed door uncertainly.

"Sit down, Ralph," Jim Latson said. "You know who we are?" He told him their names and titles, and added, "This is just a talk. We're not nearly as hot as my boys who have been handling you. We've arrived; they're ambitious."

Ralph Guild didn't smile. But after a moment, he moved toward the straight chair Jim Latson had indicated. He wore the standard jail clothes, old Marine dungarees—war surplus—on which the name of the jail had been block-printed below each knee, on the left breast, and between the shoulder blades. The dungarees didn't fit too well.

Jim Latson looked at Corday, which he didn't have to do; it was up to the district attorney to question. Corday said, "Before we start this talk, Ralph, I want you to notice there are no reporters in this room, neither electronic or personal. In other words, you can talk freely. So, is there anything you want to tell us?"

Guild's accent had gotten worse since he had been arrested. His English was good, but his g's and th's were badly slurred. He said, "Gentlemen," first and then stopped uncertainly. Suddenly his words came in a spurt. "Please, they tell me the baby has come, my wife— Could I see my wife, gentlemen?"

Corday gave Latson a theatrical look, got one back. Then both men shrugged.

"I don't see why not," Latson said. "If you're cooperative, I'm sure Mr. Corday would give me permission to have one of my boys take you over to the hospital. Mr. Corday recently lost his wife himself; he's sympathetic."

Dave Corday heard the prisoner say, "Oh, I'm sorry," through the roaring that his blood was making in his ears. He swallowed hard, and said, "Yes, yes, of course, no objection. Anything more you want to say?"

"Only that I didn't kill Miss DeLisle. She was a very nice lady, very good to me." The voice was sad as November sweeping the last dead leaves out of a street; it was obvious that Ralph Guild already saw himself convicted and executed. Dave Corday had a picture, wholly sympathetic for the moment, of Guild's background; a Czech of thirty would have no mature or adolescent memory of a fair government, of any kind of government except that of a foreign secret service organization.

Corday said, "This is the United States. If you are innocent, you will have plenty of chance to prove it. Who is your lawyer?"

"Mr. Justin."

Jim Latson coughed. Jule Justin was low-ranking man on the public defender's totem pole; only the fact that he was the mayor's nephew kept him there. The gamin *Trib* had once said that Jule Justin was to the executioner as a plunger was to a plumber: a friend.

"Well, exactly," Dave Corday was saying. "Mr. Justin is a native-born citizen, graduated from one of our best universities. Why, he is connected with the mayor."

Jim Latson said, "First you tell him everything's on the up and up in this country, Dave. Then you imply that being related to the mayor is what a guy needs. Stick to one story or the other." He leaned forward, tapped on the table that separated them from Guild. "Ralph, here's the real scoop—the truth, if you don't understand. If you get into court and pull something that clears you, it will hurt Mr. Corday's record, it will hurt the record of my whole department."

Ralph Guild made a European gesture—hands spread, shoulders hunched almost to his ears. The law officers both had the same thought— get an all-American jury, a few gestures like that'll finish him. Guild said, "What can I say? She gave me the necklace, because she said having a baby was the most important thing in the world for a woman, and—" He paused. "It was a funny expression she used, about the necklace. Very much slang. I try to remember it— Yes. And having a new piece of jewelry would put icing on it for my wife. Icing, yes. I had to ask the checker—a nice lady, my friend—to explain it."

Jim Latson said, "But you didn't give her a receipt or anything. If you did, it wasn't among her papers."

Dave Corday said, "I think we've got enough. Guild, you might as well know; I do not believe you. Let's go, Jim." He reached in front of Latson and pressed the buzzer for the turnkey; his lips were a thin set line as he sat—per regulations—until Ralph Guild had been taken back into the jail. Then he turned to face the astonished look of Jim Latson. "We'll have to let him go, Latson."

Latson said, "For goodness' sake, why?"

"That one thing: the slang expression. He asked the checker about it! He probably asked some of the other waiters or cooks first. Two, three days before she was killed! They'll remember. Waiters and cooks are great ones for chattering; I used to wash dishes up in the capital when I was going to the university."

Jim Latson whistled. "Yeah. You would get that. A lawyer. And there's also the business about her not having called room service that night."

Dave Corday said, "Oh, that's covered. Anybody who ever took a course in cross-examination knows it is impossible for a witness to swear that anyone was present during a whole evening; he could have slipped around to DeLisle's when he was out on another call or supposed to be in the men's room or—it doesn't matter. But this business of the checker and the slang phrase, the cake on the icing—that's a real big stinker."

Jim Latson said softly, "You're sure this room isn't bugged?"

"Sure."

Jim Latson fished a thin, pale cigar out of his pocket. He had his cigars sent from New York, and he was sparse with them; most of the time he contented himself with cigarettes. But now he bit the end off with care, spat that end on the floor, and lit up with precision. There was, of course, a sign in the room that said that Peter Poldear, Sheriff of the County, forbade smoking.

Jim Latson said, "Dave, drop it. Drop the act, poodle-boy. Frame the checker if you have to; she's a woman, isn't she? Send her up for streetwalking. I'll loan you a guy off the vice squad if you need him. Because I love you."

Dave Corday stared.

"It won't wash, Dave," Jim Latson said. "You started out to frame me. So okay, I maybe thought more of you for it. I'd have done the same for you, if you were worth it, which you're not. Then you got cold feet and decided to let Guild take the rap, to drop your efforts—your feeble, floor-wetting efforts—to fix me. Now something's put some red into your pus-colored blood, and you're going back to framing me, dropping Guild. Don't do it, boy."

The words poured out in a smooth, effortless purr; Jim Latson had never raised his voice.

"I'm on the level," Dave Corday said. His voice sounded too eager, and he hated himself for it. "On the level. A witness testifies that he talked about those turquoise beads days before the murder, and we're done for."

"I told you. Get rid of the witness. Get rid of all the witnesses. I'm not going to tell you again."

Dave Corday was on his feet; his fist pounded the interview table. "I'm not dropping it! I'm going to nail you, Latson. I was ready to make friends again, call it even, but no stinking cop talks to me that way. I'm going to get you!"

"One question," Jim Latson said. "One word. How?"

If he had hated his own meeching voice before, Dave Corday hated worse the ranting sound now. "I don't know," he shouted. "But there are always two stages in a case. Where you know who's guilty, and where you can prove it! And I know who shot Hogan DeLisle. You did, and all the losing of prints and finagling of—"

Jim Latson's arm shot out and grabbed Dave Corday's wrist, hard. The pressure and the pain were enough to shut Corday's mouth in surprise. He followed Jim Latson's glance and saw the door opening; he kept quiet.

Peter Poldear, sheriff of the county—in effect, jailer—came in, genial, stupid looking, self-satisfied. "Saw your prisoner had gone back down, boys," he said. "Thought we might chew the rag awhile. Who do you like for governor, Jim? I hear the gov's swinging for the U. S. Senate, ain't gonna run again."

"Well, I don't like you, Pete, or Dave here. Congressman Patrice might do; or the mayor."

"Yeah," Pete Poldear said, "but—"

The two voices droned on. It was noticeable, Dave Corday thought bitterly, that Poldear had asked the question of Jim Latson, though Latson was civil service and Dave Corday was, theoretically at least, in politics.

The gossip was drowned out by the blood in his ears. He hated Jim Latson! Just that. And he knew now why he had made his move, why he had planned so well, and hidden so artfully in Hogan DeLisle's apartment; because he could never be a whole man, a top dog, so long as Latson was around. Jim Latson had been riding him since he first came to the city, went on the D.A.'s staff.

Latson had been a detective-sergeant then. He had nicknamed Corday "Country Boy," and it had taken years to get rid of it. He had—

His own name called him back to the conversation. Pete Poldear was saying, "Dave, what's with this Guild case? I just got notice that Frederick Van Lear's filed as associate counsel with that punk Justin."

Dave Corday said, "Van Lear?"

Jim Latson whistled. "Hey. Frederick Van Lear hasn't taken a criminal case in years, and there's no dough in this one—not that he needs money.... Hey. It must be the old boy's got his eye on the state capital. This is a case with plenty of newspaper angles."

Dave Corday said, "Yes. Yes. Guild has no friends, no money."

"A good guy to send up," Peter Poldear said jovially.

"I'd better have a talk with Van Lear," Dave Corday said. He was thinking: If Frederick Van Lear finds out about that checker—

"Let me do it," Jim Latson said. "Let me talk to the old fox. We don't want any slip-ups, Dave."

Dave Corday went deaf with rage again.

CHAPTER 10

Captain Martin had long since come to the realization that he would probably never be an inspector; most certainly never anything higher than that. Examination marks, good conduct and seniority had carried him where he was; here the line separated routine police work and politics; and Martin was not fool enough to think he could out-politic the Jim Latsons of the city.

Therefore he didn't try.

His work was superb. As head of Homicide, he had once looked up the figures and found that he had a higher percentage of cases solved than had any city of comparable size and population in the United States. Having found this out, he destroyed his notes and his neat chart; he told his wife and no one else.

If a thing like that got out, he reasoned, he'd be called on to make speeches at police conventions. The Chamber of Commerce, or the Kiwanis, or someone might get to bragging on him. And this sort of thing started intra-departmental jealousy, and the next thing you knew, a fifty-year-old captain was buttoned up in blue serge, running a precinct house. Martin, a man with brains and reasoning power, wanted a job where he could use them; and such jobs are not found in a precinct commander's routine.

The DeLisle case had not particularly interested him at first. A quick glance at the dead girl's apartment had told him this was not a robbery case; jewelry well worth a heist-man's time was left in plain view.

Not robbery and not, the clothing told him, rape; therefore blackmail or any one of the motives lumped together as passion; one of those killings that happen when one partner in an affair moves out or wants to move out to more stimulating activities.

Routine.

The arrest of Ralph Guild had surprised him; in the sense that a man picking up a sugar jar in a cafeteria is surprised when he finds it empty. Captain Martin's quick, unruffled mind said at once, "Sure. He stole the cheap beads, she found out, he was going to lose his job. So, bang."

The "bang" had now become "*bang (?)*." The good mind was now beginning to reject the obvious.

That the *News-Journal* would try and get Guild off was nothing. The *News-Journal* was backing Frederick Van Lear—who was their attorney and one of their directors—for a political office, that was what that meant. But that Van Lear would pick this particular case, with a dozen easier bolting ones on the docket—that had significance.

Yeah.

Cap Martin leaned back, put his feet on the desk. A buzzer was at his hand; it would take him only a moment to get the file on Guild.... But he knew enough. It was just a matter of putting things together a little differently.

So: The hour of the killing would indicate that she had been at a night-club or at a private home. Which, and with whom...?

He let that go for a moment. She had come home, opened her door, walked in and been shot, at once... Yeah. Lights were not on in the bed-room or bathroom, and that kind of dame would head at once for a good place to repair her face or—

He picked up the phone, asked for the medical examiner. "Two questions, Doc, both easy. Did DeLisle's shoes fit her, and what was the state of her lipstick?"

The M.E, chuckled. "Marty, you're something. We just got the bullets out and checked her stomach for food. She'd eaten about two hours before. Want to know what?"

"Chicken sandwich?"

Another chuckle. "Close enough. Club sandwich—bacon, tomato, and either chicken or turkey."

"Can you tell which?"

Captain Martin permitted himself a slow smile. He was about to un-veil one of those little bits of knowledge that so astounded his colleagues and even, after all these years, his wife. The sputtering on the other end of the telephone was his reward. Doc was asking what possible business of the Homicide Squad it could be if the dead girl ate chicken or turkey in her sandwich.

"Easy," Cap Martin said. "Restaurants always make a club sandwich out of turkey. Private homes almost always use chicken. Could tell you why, but you don't deserve it. Want to know where she was."

"Call you back," the M.E. said.

Cap Martin said, "And if her feet were tight in her shoes, and had she fixed her lipstick after she came home."

"I get you," the M.E. said. "Put 'em together, you'll know whether she was alone."

"Right." He hung up the phone, and gave the ceiling of his office a hard stare. He had been a fool. Never judge a case an easy one. There's a rule that ought to be hung in every squad room in the country.

He'd take a run out to Guild's house, take a *News-Journal* man with him since they were obviously in with this Van Lear who now thought he could clear Guild.

Cap Martin called headquarters press room, asked for the *News-Journal*, and got Harry Weber. He said, "Come on up here. Something for you."

Then he used is memory. Koch and Lyons had made the pinch. He told Jake, his patrolman-secretary, to get them out to Guild's house, to wait for him.

By which time, the M.E. had called back. He said, "In your own language, Marty: tight shoes, fresh lipstick, turkey."

Cap Martin said, "Thanks," hung up, got his hat and coat. Young Weber was in the outer office. Cap said, "Can you keep something off the record?"

Harry Weber said promptly, "Not if it's something I can find out some place else."

"I'll take a chance. Here it is: I'm pretty sure now a man took DeLisle home." Then he stood, waiting; Weber's answer would tell him a lot about the kid.

Finally Harry Weber said, "If you're right, this man was the murderer or a witness who fled the scene."

They were moving downstairs now. Cap Martin nodded. Smart boy. A dumb one would jump to the conclusion that the unidentified man was the murderer.

He said, "Your paper paying Frederick Van Lear?"

"Who knows?" Harry Weber asked. "Maybe he's paying us. He owns a lot of stock in the paper."

"Yeah." Cap Martin flipped open the heavy glass door to the parking lot. His unmarked car, those of two precinct commanders, and a marked H.Q. car were all in the section reserved for the brass, their drivers out of them smoking together. Chief Jim Latson was leaning against a wall in the sun, his hands in his pockets, his feet crossed, chatting with the flattered drivers.

Jim Latson took a hand out of his pocket, waved it at them. "Hi, Marty. Who do you like in the fights tonight?"

Cap Martin said, "Who's fighting?" in his driest voice.

The drivers were scattering back to their cars, giving the two brass a chance to talk alone if they wanted to.

Jim Latson chuckled, raked a glance across Harry Weber's face, and said idly, "Old Strictly-Business Marty. Where you off to?"

"Guild house. First chance I've had."

Latson nodded. He winked in the direction of Harry Weber. "Aren't you scared of taking the opposition along?"

Captain Martin said, "No."

Jim Latson chuckled his easy laugh. "Brave old Marty." He raised a hand, and his driver was there, fast. "I'm going for a ride with Captain Martin. Tell my office and give them the number of the car."

"H-four," Cap Martin's driver said. He opened the door of the big sedan, and all three of his passengers got in the back seat.

Jim Latson sat down, fished out a cigar, offered the other two smokes, and settled back, sighing. Unlike Martin and Harry, he was bareheaded and without a coat, but he didn't look cold. He said, "This is damned bad practice. I should have taken my own car, in case you and I get separate calls, Marty. But it gets plenty lonesome, being a chief."

Martin said, "Yeah." He leaned forward and tapped the driver's shoulder, waved his flattened palms downward twice for "slower," and then decided to shoot a whole lot of words, despite Latson's presence. "Koch and Lyons are meeting us. Use their car." He paused again, and added, "If you need it."

Latson said, "Sure." He seemed interested in a construction job they were passing, and suddenly said, "Mind if I stop?"

Cap Martin said, "No," and the car came to a smooth halt. At each corner of the block, traffic patrolmen stiffened a little, but they didn't stare directly at the car; they were under orders not to when a car was unmarked and its passengers un-uniformed.

But Jim Latson raised a hand, and one of the patrolmen trotted over. Down in a hole that had been the Lakemen's National Bank, a steam shovel and some bulldozers were digging away, in preparation for a new Lakemen's National Bank building that would be twenty stories taller.

The Chief, grinning, called the patrolman "Benny" and jerked a thumb at the crowd of sidewalk spectators.

"Tell the super here to put a railing on the curb," he said. "Those briefcase superintendents are crowding out in the street and cutting down traffic by a full lane."

The uniformed man said, "Yes, sir," and Latson dropped a friendly hand on his shoulder, then climbed back into the sedan. As the door closed and the car moved ahead, Jim Latson said, "Traffic. I never had a day of it till I got to be deputy chief. You ever bothered with it, Marty?"

"Only cooperation, when I was precinct lieutenant."

"Yeah," Latson said. They slowed up for a streetcar stop and he frowned again. "Those tracks ought to go... Marty, you got something more on Guild, or is this a fishing expedition?"

Cap Martin said, "Fishing."

Latson chuckled politely, and turned to Harry Weber: "Mind telling me why your paper's out on a limb over a dumb cluck?"

"We're not on a limb," Harry said, promptly. "We feel that even

dumb clucks shouldn't be railroaded for what they didn't do."
Latson stopped smiling. "That's kind of rough language, young man."
Harry said he was sorry.

The broad street turned here to follow the river. What had been a slight breeze in town became a wind here, and Latson looked with appreciation at the fluttering skirts of the office girls. There were enough of them on the street to indicate that it was lunch hour; but none of the men suggested eating.

When they had crossed the poor district that was Guild's, and stopped at the Guild house, the detective car with Lyons and Koch in it was already there, and Lyons was standing on the porch. Koch appeared from a neighboring house, dangling a key. He and Lyons said polite hellos to their superiors; Latson returned them, Cap Martin grunted, and Harry Weber said, "Hi, John," to Koch.

Koch unlocked the door. "What do you want us to do, Chief?"

"It's Captain Martin's detail. I just came along to get some fresh air."

Cap Martin said, "Lyons and Koch. Go over the place first. I want any changes since you made the arrest."

Jim Latson leaned just inside the front door, watching them, his hands in his pockets, his face relaxed. They had not shut the front door, and the police radio could be heard faintly, as Cap Martin's driver kept in touch with headquarters. Harry Weber moved around, looking at things.

John Koch came out, and said, "There's baby stuff in the bedroom that's new. A bassinet, a rubber bathing table, a little chest to keep diapers and stuff in."

Cap Martin said, "New to here, or new from a store?"

Koch seemed to blush slightly. He said. "I'm sorry, Captain. Secondhand, but new to this house." He went back into the bedroom.

Jim Latson said, "What's this all about, Marty?"

Cap Martin looked at him. There was a long silence; the noise of the car radio seemed to get louder. Finally, Cap cleared his throat. "Routine."

Lyons and Koch stopped their bustling, and came to a sort of semi-attention in front of the homicide captain. Lyons said, "Those are about the only changes, Captain. Of course, there were dirty dishes, an unmade bed before; they've been cleaned up."

Cap Martin nodded. He said, "Good. Now. Guild makes a waiter's pay and tips. Check. See if he made any more."

They went off, and Latson said, "I see. If you can hang one more theft on him, we'll have a pretty good case. But what if you can't?"

Cap Martin shrugged.

Harry Weber said, "What does the district attorney's office think of their case, Chief Latson?"

Jim Latson smiled without charm this time. "I ought to tell you to find out for yourself. You did a good job this morning, rubbing Dave Corday the wrong way. You know a newspaper man without entree doesn't last long. Dave Corday is an important man, and a good one."

Harry Weber said, "I'm sorry. I was trying to needle a story out of him. I didn't think he'd hold it against me; just doing my job."

"I didn't say he did, kid," Jim Latson said. "Why, you'd have to go to him to get the district attorney's point of view. From the angle of the police department, let's say we feel we're justified that we arrested Guild; and that we're still investigating. Say that Captain B. L. Martin has taken over the investigation personally. Okay, Marty?"

Cap Martin shrugged.

Lyons and Koch were back again. They were carrying a towel, each by an end. They laid the thing down on a lumpy looking couch, and spread the ends, started pushing jewelry around with their fingertips to make a display. Stones and metal glittered in the weak sunlight that came through a white curtain.

"All the jewelry in the house," Lyons said. "No furs. No silk underwear, anything like that."

Cap Martin put his hands on his hips, bent over. He grunted once or twice. "He coulda bought better," he said.

Harry Weber said, "He was saving to have a baby."

Cap Martin grunted. "Put it back, boys. Be neat." He looked up at the ceiling as though expecting something to be written there.

He was not a very highly paid man. And what he did get paid, he was likely to misspend—a poker game, a symphony record, books he didn't really need. But still his wife had earrings, perfume, silk lingerie. There was something feebly pathetic about this little pile of junk. No jewelry at all would have been better than these half dozen specimens of dime store art, filled out with two or three old-world brooches that hadn't been worth anything a hundred years ago and had, somehow, failed to turn themselves into antiques.

Cap Martin said, "Put 'em back where you found them. Lyons, you used to be on hockshop detail. How much do you think everything in this house it worth?"

Lyons shrugged. "Nothing here would hock," he said. "Maybe seventy-five bucks, selling it outright. Clothes and all."

Jim Latson said, "That's about an all-time low," and turned toward the front door. Feet were clumping on the porch. It was Cap Martin's driver. He was saying, "Call your office, Captain. Something they didn't want to put on the air."

Cap Martin nodded. He stood there a moment, looking at the floor, a blocky man, strong and bright and at home in his job. Then he stared at Harry Weber, but Weber made no move to give him privacy.

Finally Cap Martin shrugged, and walked to the phone that the hotel had probably required Guild to have. Or maybe the waiter had put it in when his wife got near the end of her term of pregnancy. Considering the sparseness of everything else in the Guild house, the telephone was sheer wanton luxury.

Cap Martin took a last look at Jim Latson who, as senior officer present, should have asked Harry to step outside. But Latson was cheerfully lighting a cigarette, a mere spectator of another man's work. Martin dialed the number.

Then he said, "Homicide," and then, "Martin." No reporter would grow healthy, wealthy and wise from Cap Martin's end of a phone conversation. What Barry heard was, "Yeah," and "I see," and "I'm starting right in." There was not even a goodbye.

Cap Martin put the phone down and smiled a little. He said, "Put this stuff back like it was, boys, and resume your standby." Then he went out the front door, leaving his chief and Harry to follow him.

The driver was already back behind the wheel. When Martin said, "Office," he picked up the handphone, said, "H-four to H-one. Coming in, over and out," and started the car. Martin said, "Code two," which meant the driver could use his red light and siren.

So they went back the way Lyons and Koch had come down here the other time, instead of by the more traffic-free riverfront boulevard. Occasionally, the siren moaned a short cry as they pushed through the machinery center, the produce belt.

Jim Latson smoked his cigarette. Cap Martin kept his face stolid. Harry Weber made no effort to keep his face from looking curious.

Finally Martin spoke; they were only a couple of blocks from the Civic Center now. He said, "The federals want Guild if we don't. Illegal entry."

Latson whistled, cranked the window down a little, and dropped the cigarette out. "I'd say we want him. This about ties up the case."

Harry Weber said, "That's right. Never hit a man when he's down; wait till someone else comes along to hit him first."

"The guy's already a criminal," Jim Latson said. "You can't expect us to exactly make love to him. It's not what the people pay policemen for."

"Oh, lay off," Harry Weber said. "What you're saying is, the guy's likely to confess to save himself getting deported."

Jim Latson laughed. "Think again," he said. "He's going to get deported any way you look at it. It's a question of whether he does time first or not."

"Or gets electrocuted first."

Jim Latson's careless voice said, "Oh, Dave Corday won't ask first degree. You never get it without a witness."

Harry Weber stared. Cap Martin had told him, just before they started down to Guild's house, that a man had brought Hogan DeLisle home, had been there when she was shot. It seemed funny he hadn't told the chief.

Latson's voice was sharp. "Or was there a witness?"

Cap Martin said, "Yeah. Man brought her home."

The car stopped at headquarters then. The homicide captain and the newsman waited politely for the deputy chief of all the city's policemen to get out. He did, fast.

"I won't have time to see your federal man, Marty," he said. But he said it over his shoulder and was gone.

CHAPTER 11

Dave Corday sat in his nice office, and wrote careful words on a sheet of fine bond. The district attorney's suite was high in the County Building, and, as chief deputy, he had the corner that faced north and west. The district attorney himself had chosen the south and east exposures, one for the sun and the other for its magnificent view of approaching storms.

Next year, Dave Corday could have that office. The district attorney had announced this morning that he was running for governor. He hadn't put a hand on Dave Corday's shoulder to tap him as successor, but the party would do that; there hadn't been a chief deputy yet who hadn't been offered the top job when it became vacant.

Dave Corday was writing his platform, his declaration of how he would run the office when he got it.

Once in office, he'd be the equal, the superior of the Jim Latsons. He'd get the good tables at the restaurants, the salutes of the doormen, the invitations to speak at luncheon clubs. He—

His phone rang. He frowned at it. A good secretary ought to know better than to interrupt her chief when he was thinking.

But he picked up the phone and the girl's voice said, "Chief Latson, Mr. Corday."

"Put Mr. Latson on."

"He's not on the phone. He's out here."

"Send him in." Well, she'd been right not to use the box; he didn't want Jim Latson hearing everything he had to say.

He didn't get up as the policeman ambled in. He waved a hand at the straight chair next to his desk that he used to interview witnesses, defendants.

But Latson picked up one of the heavy side chairs that sat by the couch and carried it across the room with one hand, no easy feat. He slouched down in it and shoved his hands deep in his pants pockets, his suit coat and topcoat open over an immaculate white shirt.

"We're in the soup, Dave."

Dave Corday split his lips in a polite smile. "You are, Jim."

"We, boy, we. Your frame never got off the ground. If I'm in, you're in."

"Don't growl at me, Latson. What's your trouble?"

Jim Latson got up, his coat bunched over the clenched fists in his pockets. He walked to the west window, stood looking down at the river and the traffic that ran alongside it. "That Martin," he said. "He's got it established that a man brought Hogan home."

Dave Corday laughed. "Of course. A man did." The laugh faded. "But he hasn't said anything to me. After all, I'm the one supposed to be working up a case on this." He took the folded handkerchief out of his breast pocket and dried his hands.

Jim Latson's grin was ghoulish. "Hot, boy? You might be... That Martin doesn't miss much. Cap Martin. I should have put him out in the sticks years ago. He's the best cop in the city. Maybe one of the best in the country."

Dave Corday's voice was a full octave higher, to his own ears. "Why did you let him take the case?"

Jim Latson shrugged. "Routine. It seemed to me that the more natural I let this thing be, the better it would look. Matter of fact, it still seems that way." He put a foot on the window sill, continued to stare down. "What this city needs is half as many people and twice as many streets."

Corday said, "I'll send for Martin, talk to him."

Jim Latson turned and faced the attorney squarely.

"Do that. And right away."

Corday shoved the swivel chair back with his thighs, jumped to his feet. He leveled a finger at the police chief in his best courtroom manner. "Don't bark orders at me! I'm practically acting district attorney from now on; the boss is going to campaign for governor. You'll mind your manners in this office."

Latson walked over to the desk. At the last minute he swerved and went around it, came behind Corday's symbol of office, until he was facing the district attorney. Only then did he take his hands out of his pockets. The right hand shot up with ferocious speed and caught Corday's nose; Latson twisted it with all his force.

Then he let go, and put his hands back in his pockets. He strolled with his back to the desk to the door. Then he turned, smiling. Corday was dabbing at his nose with the white handkerchief that had formerly cut such a nice line across his left breast. "Try putting a cold key on the back of your neck," Jim Latson said. "I'm giving a cocktail party at the Zebra House this afternoon," he added. "Six o'clock on. If you're swinging for the D.A.'s place on the ballot, you could pick tip a little help there."

After Latson had gone, Corday crossed the room quickly and locked the door. By lying down on the floor and stuffing paper under his lip, he managed to stop the nosebleed without any of his staff knowing he had it.

There was a little mirror in the center drawer of his big desk. He examined himself in it, and decided he looked like a man with a touch of hay fever, nothing more. After he had thrown the bloody handkerchief out the window and replaced it with another from his desk, he felt himself able to go on with the day's business.

But he didn't continue writing his speech. Instead, he had his secretary get Captain Martin on the line. Corday's joviality—he was aware of it himself—was a pale imitation of Jim Latson's habitual manner, but it would have to do. "Marty, how's my big case coming?"

"Which one?"

"Guild, of course."

"Was going to call you," Cap Martin said. "Complications. Guy from the U.S. Immigration Service was just here. Guild's an illegal entrant."

"But he's naturalized."

"Illegally. He bought another Czech's quota number and entered under the other man's name. Makes his naturalization illegal, too."

Dave Corday said, "Now, wait a minute. I wasn't aware that you had a lawyer's degree, that you were admitted to the bar, Captain."

Apparently Cap Martin didn't think that was worthwhile answering. The phone remained completely silent, and Corday had to carry on the conversation himself. "Immigration would have to prove all this," he said. "At any rate, I have no intention of releasing Guild to a federal court. He's ours, and we are going to try him—that is, if you work up a good case for me." Again he waited. This time he said, "Are you still there, Martin?"

Cap Martin said, "Sure."

"Has anything developed in the case itself?"

Cap Martin's calm voice said, "No."

Dave Corday took a deep breath. If Latson had been lying, why? If Cap

Martin was lying now, why? He asked, "You mean, nothing you can prove, but some good leads for you to investigate?"

Cap Martin said, "Sure."

Dave Corday's voice had its solid, judicial boom back in it. "Well, report to me the moment you have anything."

"Sure," Cap Martin said, and then there was a click as the captain hung up.

Dave Corday laid his hands flat on the desk blotter, rested his weight on them. The box said, "The district attorney would like to see you, Mr. Corday. I told him you were on the phone."

Dave Corday said, "Sure." He raised his hands, and saw that they had left damp marks on the blotter.

But the district attorney only wanted him on a matter of magistrates; one was resigning, and the mayor wanted advice as to the appointment of a successor. It was just a routine matter.

CHAPTER 12

After he finished talking to Dave Corday on the phone, Cap Martin allowed himself to smile, something he rarely did in office hours. As he saw his duty, his primary function at the moment was to be the conscience of the city's law-enforcement agencies; and in goading Dave Corday, he had insured his intangible boss, Justice, that the D.A.'s office would not drop the Guild case for another twenty-four hours.

He sighed.

Though the head of no homicide squad can ever be absolutely certain when his day's work will end, Cap Martin indulged himself in a daydream of leaving the office at five-thirty, getting home at six. The barb he had sunk in Dave Corday's rather thin hide would keep on working, festering. Frightened—but not so frightened that they struck back and wiped out one Captain B. Martin—the politicians would turn up his witness for him... He could go home pretty soon now.

His wife would have martini makings laid out, and he would stir two good ones for himself and one for her; with the cocktail he would have—if there were any in the house—some of those little cocktail sausages that Lora broiled under the electric skillet...

Unless the missing witness was a very, very big man indeed, no Dave Corday, no mayor, no politician at all would cover up for him at the risk of his own career. Politicians are not that unselfish.

Renewed by the cocktails, he would suggest that Lora have her brother and his wife over for the evening. Matt was as silent as Cap Martin pretended to be around headquarters; unlike traditional brothers-in-law, Matt's idea of a big evening was sitting in a deep chair and listening to Cap Martin sound off. On any subject—art, politics, the movies.

Let the wiseacres over at City Hall and the County Building sleep in fear tonight. Tomorrow they'd make a, move that would go to Chief Latson and draw utility men to help him and—

At the silent mention of Jim Latson, Cap Martin stopped rubbing his hands together and looking at his wristwatch.

Instead of running for cover—and leaving a trail to that cover—Jim Latson was perfectly capable of doing something so wild and unpredictable that the whole case would disintegrate.

To hell with it. He had earned his pay today.

He got up, put on his hat and coat, moved to the door. Then he stopped, and stood there. From somewhere around his toenails he gathered a sigh, shot it out into the empty room.

Then he went over to the closet, put his hat and coat away again, went back to his desk, sat down, and flipped the intercom. "Jake? Bring me the logs of every cruiser that was working within three miles of Hogan DeLisle's apartment on the watch when she was killed, and the watch before it."

He flipped the box shut and picked up the phone, dialed his home and got ready to tell his wife he'd be late for dinner. He didn't think he'd surprise her.

She had been with him most of the years he had walked his tightrope in the department. She was used to his hours.

He told himself fiercely that it was not civic conscience, the desire to earn all his pay that made him stay. It was simple self-defense.

Somebody big enough to get personal protection from Jim Latson, who was the big shots' hatchetman in the department.

Captain Martin did not permit himself to curse Jim Latson. There had been hatchetmen before; there would be others if Latson quit, died, or moved on to higher glories.

But Jim Latson was a smart hatchetman as well as a ruthless one. So long as Latson held the hatchet, it was necessary for. Captain Martin to do what he had to do now, not leave it overnight.

If the protected witness was big enough, rich enough and scared enough, it would not be unbelievable for him, Latson, to burn all the departmental files overnight.

Or the department itself.

Captain Martin did not want to do his work in the open air. He was used to his office; he would hate to see it burn down.

CHAPTER 13

Dave Corday was enjoying a sensation he had never felt before. It was as though his nerves had been cleaned with something refreshing and cooling—perhaps cologne or pure alcohol. Everything that came to him—sight, sound, smell—made more of an impact on him than it ever had before.

This is success, he told himself. This is what it feels like to be a successful man. The world, the air, the very pavement is made to comfort a successful man.

The difference between being a district attorney, he thought, and being one of the deputies—even the chief deputy—is the difference between being a prison guard and being one of the trusties, even the chief trusty, if there is such a thing.

After I take office, I will look back at my jealousy of Latson and wonder at it. Because he will be a thing compared to me; he'll be a cop among cops and I will be the only one of my kind in the whole city.

He regretted for just a moment the killing of Hogan DeLisle, and then put the thought firmly away from him. He had not killed Hogan DeLisle. He had not! Nor had Jim Latson. A man named Ralph Guild, alias a couple of unpronounceable strings of Czech syllables, had shot the girl. The only thing unusual about it was Frederick Van Lear's offer to defend Guild. And that could be explained by Van Lear's need for publicity, the rumor strong around town that the corporation lawyer wanted to be governor. Losing a popular case was as good as winning one for that purpose; the point was to get known by the public.

He had arrived at the Zebra House. The doorman opened the door snappily; the maître d hurried forward to greet him. "Your party's waiting for you in the Turf Club Room, Mr. Corday. Just this way, sir."

The man was helping him off with his coat, handing his hat to the check girl. "You won't need a check, Mr. Corday. Freda could hardly forget you, could you, Freda?"

The girl was pert in velvet toreador pants and a white blouse, open far enough down. She shook dark hair at him, blinked dark eyes. "Certainly not, Mr. District Attorney." Hugging his coat to her expensive looking bosom, she danced to hang it up, deposit his hat on a high shelf.

He straightened his cuffs and followed the maître d'. Long before the padded, brass-studded door was opened for him he could hear the happy hum of the party; his party, the one gotten up to welcome him to the big leagues.

Then the door was opened; a cloud of expensive cigar smoke and alcohol fumes and lemon juice came pouring out. He went in, and the maître d followed him and murmured, "Your drink, Mr. Corday? I'll get it myself."

"Bourbon and branch water."

"*Tout de suite.*"

A hand was grabbing his elbow. Dan Dryce, the State Commissioner of Motor Vehicles, "Dave, ol' boy."

"Didn't know you were in the city, Dan."

"Drove down with the governor. We made it in an hour and twelve minutes, from the Mansion to the State Office Building here."

Dave whistled politely. It was ninety-two miles, exactly; he'd turned it in on mileage reports often enough, before he had a-county-owned car check issued to him. "Who was driving?"

"The governor. You know how he is on martinis."

There was a surge, and the two men were separated. Chuckling, Dave moved into a group of brass from the Highway Department. One of the men told a story about three capons and a hen, and the resultant laughter increased the crowd; suddenly Dave found himself standing shoulder to shoulder with Jim Latson.

Another highway man started a story. Latson said, "I've heard that one," and turned away. Dave Corday went after him, and found him holding out his glass to the bartender with one hand, using the other to point to things on the buffet; a waiter was piling a plate for him.

Dave Corday said, "Give me one of everything Mr. Latson takes. And a bourbon and branch water."

Jim Latson's sardonic face creased into a grin. He peered down at Dave Corday; a haze of blue cigar smoke curled around his face. "Thought you were a vitamin drinker, Dave. Bloody Marys and long, cool Collinses."

Dave Corday said, "Tastes change."

Jim Latson chuckled. "Men don't," he said. "Thanks, Lawrence." He took his plate and shoved his chin at the waiter's burden. "Take your food, Dave."

Dave Corday did. With a drink in one hand and the plate in the other, he found himself hopelessly tied up. He looked over at Jim Latson. The chief's long fingers were functioning perfectly: thumb and forefinger of his right hand held the plate, the other three fingers hooked around the glass.

But Dave Corday's fingers were short and stubby. In desperation he gulped his drink and set it down on the edge of the buffet.

Jim Latson popped a caviar-covered cracker into his mouth, picked up Dave's glass and put it on the bar; the barman promptly refilled it and held it out to Dave Corday. He took it, while Jim Latson ate a deviled egg and washed it down with scotch and soda.

"I hear the D.A.'s gonna be our next governor," he said.

"I also hear that Frederick Van Lear's going to oppose him," Dave said. Larson peered at him. The big banquet room was getting smoky. "You can hear anything," he said. "Fred Van Lear's not affiliated with any party. He could belong to ours as well as the opposition... A man of great stature, serving the public weal," he intoned, and grinned his devil's grin.

Dave Corday said, "You mean he might run against the D.A. in the primaries?" He frowned. The district attorney was not likely to resign unless he was sure of the nomination.

"Between you and me," Latson said, "I talked to Van Lear this afternoon. Your boss is a shoo-in for the party nomination; stop worrying about that."

Dave Corday's embarrassment fell away. He set the full glass down, ate a stuffed celery stalk, picked up his glass and took a swallow, then put the glass down again. He was the next district attorney. It didn't matter if he used part of the public buffet for a private table; what might have looked like hick manners in an assistant prosecutor was eccentricity in an important man.

"So they tell me," he said. "Now, if the police chief would just resign, Jim, you and I would have the running of this town to ourselves."

Jim Latson shook his head. "Not me, buddy. The chief's a fine front for my nefarious practices. I run the department, he takes the credit. What I take is cash."

Dave Corday felt himself goggling. It was a bad habit; he thought he'd broken himself of it when he was a clodhopping freshman at State U. "You're mighty frank."

"Sure," Jim Latson said. "Tell the truth and nobody believes you. Anyway, there's no one here but friends, damn it."

"Damn it?"

"I like to see the enemy. In other words, women, dames, girls. Man's natural enemies, aren't they? God bless them." He laughed and half turned. "Hi, son."

Ronald Palmer, Dave Corday realized with sudden perception, was a man who had studied as hard to get where he was as Dave Corday had. There was no telling now where Ronald Palmer had started; but at one point in his career he must have had the slick servility of a waiter, and then the insinuating friendliness of a maître d'. (A phrase Dave Corday had only learned a couple of years ago.)

But now, look at him, in a tweed suit, a blue shirt and a very narrow tie. You would be a very clever man to know that he managed this place; just an occasional sideways look at the waiters and the bartenders gave him away.

He said, "Gents, are you festive?"

"Hilarious," Jim Latson said. "Bubbling over."

"Any complaints, don't bring 'em to me," Ronald Palmer said. "This is my day to howl. I'm just another guest, eh, Oliver?"

The passing waiter heard his name, and pulled up gently, did a right face, took Palmer's glass and Jim Latson's and headed for the bar with them. Before he left, however, he murmured, "Certainly, Mr. Palmer."

Ron Palmer said, "You don't come in here nearly often enough, Dave. And, by the way, I like the way you handled that Arnaux case. If a case of champagne shows up at your apartment some time, don't have me indicted for bribery."

This was big league stuff. Dave Corday laughed, and said, "I'll keep it down to a misdemeanor."

Jim Latson said, "Dave's a bright man, Ronald. The governor was saying all kinds of nice things about him before. Wheel horse of the party was the mildest one."

Dave Corday felt himself getting red in the cheeks. He didn't know when he'd enjoyed a party more. He said, "Ron, you interrupted Jim just when he was giving a speech on Topic A. He's the professional lady-killer of the administration, you know."

Ronald Palmer said, "I know, Dave. I know. Lord, he's in here so often with so many little beauties, I can't keep track. I'd hate to be put on one of your witness stands and told to identify any of your escorts, Jim."

"Just as well," Jim Latson said. "Especially the one I had in here last Tuesday. The little schnitzel told me she'd never been married, and two days later I see where her husband's bringing suit against her. And speaking of the devil—"

"What? What?" It was the governor. His appearance was just as famous as his name; he had the sort of face that would appear well on a silver coin, he had the walk and stature of success. "What's all this about the devil?"

"You, Governor," Jim Latson said. "I was just talking about you, and here you are. I was telling Dave Corday how highly you thought of him."

The governor nodded. A couple of state capital men were bustling around him, one getting his glass refilled, the other ordering a plate for him. Those well-packed cheeks of his demanded constant stoking; the Governor's appetite was notable. "That is a fact, Dave. Jim was telling me what a good man you are, and I was outdoing him in your praise... Thanks, boys." He crammed his mouth and chewed carefully, getting every bit of nourishment out of the food. When his mouth was empty, he absentmindedly drained his martini glass.

"Teamwork," Dave Corday said. "Without it we'd none of us be anything. Jim's department gives us good cases. My staff works up clean, hard cases. When I go to court, that battle's almost over."

"Your staff?" The governor looked puzzled for a moment. "That's right, you're chief trial deputy, aren't you...?" He didn't look at his glass as it was taken away and a new one put in his hand. He drained that one, too, said, "Gives a man an appetite," and his short, blunt fingers went working around the plate, carrying samples of the different kinds of tidbits to his happy mouth. Around a large stuffed olive, he said, "Let's see. You're pretty close to Donald Munroe, aren't you?" He posed a toothpick load of sour-cream herring in front of his mouth, told it, "A fine man, Mr. Munroe," and ate his audience.

The liquor, the high company, the luxurious air of the place, all this was having its effect on Dave Corday. He said, "Mr. Munroe's been a good friend to me. He's from my home town, you know, downstate. I had a letter to him when I first came here, a green punk out of law school. Well, Governor, he said he could get me placed with the law firm that does his corporate work; but when I said I was interested in politics, he offered to use his influence with the administration, and I became an assistant district attorney; about the least experienced one the office has ever seen."

The governor accepted another martini, and held out his plate to be refilled. "Made it down here in seventy minutes, door to door," he said. "Man, we were really balling the jack. What I wanted to see you about, Dave, was—how much do you think Munroe'll go for in the next election? We're going to need a sizable war chest, if we want to make a sweep of it—and we do." He grinned. "I'm up for senator, you know."

Dave groped in his mind. "Last general election he contributed five thousand."

"Not enough," the governor said, put his martini glass down, waved his hand over it to forestall a refill. The blue eyes under the noble brow were suddenly cold, and the firmly chiseled lips narrowed meanly. "Not nearly enough."

Jim Latson said idly, "He gave the opposition that much last time, too."

Dave Corday cleared his throat. "Mr. Munroe has very wide interests."

"What the hell does that mean?" the governor asked. "He's with us, or, hell, we clobber him next time he wants something. And those rich bastards always want something."

Jim Latson said lightly, "We can get ten out of him easy, Governor, maybe fifteen. He owns some lots over in Traffic Three, and he wants an exception made to the zoning. You know, over there you have to have parking facilities for one and a half cars per apartment. He wants to build a two-hundred-apartment building. He'll deal. Just think how much land it takes to park three hundred cars."

His Excellency said, "Handle it, Jim," and the blue eyes gleamed again, the lips expanded from cracker-barrel waspish to toga-wearing classic. "Hey, I'm out of drinking liquor."

"That we can fix," Ronald Palmer said, and snapped fingers at the bar.

The governor said, "Old Dave Corday. Dave, it's men like you on whom the structure of our party rests. I was telling the attorney-general the other day, an assistant like you is worth ten of these shadow-boxers he sends into court."

Dave Corday nodded. He wondered if the governor would take offense if he went to the bar for a drink. He needed one, but he hardly dared move away.

"You heard there's going to be a change in the D.A.'s office?"

Dave Corday said, "Yes," but he hesitated first. Was he supposed to know?

"Yep," the governor said, "a big change. Old Fred Van Lear's decided he's made his pile in private practice; he'd like to hold office for a while. He'll make a wonderful D.A. for you. If I were your age, Dave, I'd give anything for a chance to work under Fred for a few years. He'll round you off, boy, put a polish on you."

Dave Corday swallowed, and turned, and walked to the bar. He set his hands on the edge of the bar, and said, "Double rye on the rocks." When the drink came, he swallowed so fast he got a chunk of ice in his mouth; it rolled against one of his back teeth, and a shock went up his temple; he'd have to have his dentist look back there.

After he left the bar, the governor was telling a new group of admirers how he came down from the capital building in sixty-eight minutes. "The sirens were howling like wolves in a burlesque show. The head of my escort told me later it was the first time he'd ever had his motorcycle wide open."

Jim Latson came away from the group and gave Dave Corday his sardonic smile. "Four more martinis, and he'll be here before he left the capital. How's it going, Dave?"

"Okay."

"Don't get drunk, kid. The governor hates a man who can't hold his liquor. Him, he's got a stainless steel gut. I don't think the stuff touches him at all."

"He can certainly hold it."

"That's right, Dave, he certainly can. It's amazing how a man can stay that high and still be such a bore."

Jim Latson had not bothered to lower his voice at all. "But he likes you, Dave. I was with him when he called on Fred Van Lear. Van Lear wanted to bring one of his boys in as chief dep and the governor was firm as an old secondhand iceberg. Nobody was going to shove his boy Dave down."

"Decent of him."

Jim Latson squinted his eyes, bent down to peer into Dave Corday's face. "Man, you don't look good. You didn't expect to be D.A., did you? You just don't have what it takes, Dave. Some boys have it, and some don't. Van Lear does; it was his price for not running for governor. My idea. Look, cheer up. How's it if I get a couple of dollies later and show you the town? You're too serious, Dave."

Dave Corday was thinking. He was thinking, or maybe it was feeling, because it went much farther than his head; it filled his whole body. I was a fool, was the feeling. I should have killed Jim Latson in the first place. No substitute should have ever been thought of.

"Go to hell," Dave Corday said, and swung on the grinning face.

Jim Latson caught Corday's fist in his palm, squeezed it. "Take it easy, boy. You spoil the gov's party and you'll be a retired D.A."

He held the fist a moment, and then threw it away.

Dave Corday turned and looked wildly for the exit.

CHAPTER 14

Cap Martin had taken his shoes off. He leaned far back in the high-backed swivel chair; he had blocks nailed to the floor to stop the front legs of the pedestal from sliding too far and dumping him on his back.

He had a board laid across his lap; a board about fourteen inches wide and a good three feet long. It was covered with papers, each of them marked with the seal of the City Police Department.

But he wasn't reading anything just now; the papers were in case he forgot a fact and needed to locate it. That sometimes happened, but not often.

He had read an article once about mechanical brains; the ones that the young geniuses were building and giving such weird names to: "The Maniac," "The Idiot" and so on. The principle was what fascinated him. You fed a given fact in, and it was held in a series of vacuum tubes. Thereafter, any other facts fed in were automatically affected by the first fact. Like the average man is five-feet eight inches. So if you told the machine to start figuring how many yards of goods it would take to uniform a regiment, it would be on its way....

But if you told the machine that it took ten thousand yards of cloth to uniform a squad, it would light up something that probably said, "Tilt," considering the youth and cuteness of most of the geniuses who built the machines...

I am the same, Cap Martin thought. I know a few things, and I don't have to repeat them over and over. I automatically say, "Tilt" when I run up against something that doesn't fit facts I've always known. Like—

Well, like Patrolman Ray Page. Page had been in the department five years, including his rookie time. He had tried twice for the Motor Squad, but had failed to pass the written tests, though he had done well enough on the physical. He had been in Traffic Control during a flu epidemic, but they had made no effort to keep him when their regular men returned to their desks.

A patrolman, half of a cruiser crew, best put on duty with another man.

But here, yesterday, Patrolman Ray Page had been put into plain clothes and made a hack inspector; an easy job and a nice one and a coveted one.

Tilt.

It was not the only "Tilt" among the records of the men who had been on watch in Hogan DeLisle's neighborhood at the time of her death. But it was the biggest Tilt, really the only one worth noticing.

Now we go back. Lay aside all the other watch reports, the typed logs from the cruisers out and around that night, and concentrate on that one car: James Rein, radio operator, Ray Page, driver.

Rein, too, had gotten a little promotion—to the detective bureau. Third Grade Detective, no raise in salary, but a chance at the ladder of promotion. But this made sense. Rein was a damned good man. Second best, stolen car recovery on the cruiser list. Rein had already passed his sergeant's examination, was fourth in line for promotion as vacancies occurred.

But Page? Ray Page?

There was nothing in the typewritten log to show any irregularity. Their patrol did not run along either the side or the front of the Belmont....

Cap Martin found a pipe in his desk, filled it, lit it. It occurred to him that he was as absolutely certain of his own sense of correctness as a machine would be. It was conceit, and he rather liked himself for it. He picked up the phone, dialed his home. "Babe, I'll be there in about half an hour. Get the chow warm again... No, I haven't eaten yet. This stuff you get around town, it doesn't deserve the name of food... Put some records on, too. Hell, a man deserves a little home life."

He hung up, grinning, and puffed his pipe as he walked down to the Records Department. The clerk on night watch there was a civilian employee; Cap Martin was careful with him. "I want the rough logs of all the two-hundred series cruisers for the last week."

The clerk walked down a row of files and presently came back with the sheaf of long sheets from the cruisers' clipboards.

These were turned in at the end of each watch and copied by girl typists. The rough logs weren't kept very long...

Rein and Page's sheet for the crucial night was missing.

Cap Martin had shielded the logs with his body as he looked through them. Now, satisfied that the clerk did not know which car he'd been interested in, he shuffled the papers a little, handed them back. "Afraid I got them out of order."

"I'll straighten them, Captain. Glad to have something to do."

"Good."

The Communications Room, and then he could go home. Communications was sorry. Deputy Chief Latson had taken their log for that night. Wasn't that the night there was the murder, the Guild case?

Cap Martin shrugged, and went to get his hat and coat. Jim Latson, and it didn't surprise him. Latson was cover-up man for the politicians. Latson was the politician in the department.

Yeah. Transferring Rein and Page was a good trick. Anxious and nervous over learning new jobs, they would not gossip around about something that had probably not been very big in the first place—in their eyes. Yeah. Jim Latson. The chief was smart. A campaign was coming up, and somebody was going to kick in big for this cover-up...

Cap Martin considered. It was highly probable that whoever was being covered up had not committed the murder.

Latson and his politicians were much more likely to entertain bribes from a witness than from an out-and-out murderer; such a man would be very likely to freeze up, to tell no one, both from fear and from the knowledge that an admission of murder to the politicos would cause them to bleed him white.

But that was deduction on a purely mental basis. Let's pin it down a little.

Let's picture two people, Hogan DeLisle and a gent, coming to her apartment. Gent would be full of courtesy and attention, expecting both to pay off.

So he would take her key from her, and open her door for her, and stand aside to let her enter first—

Or maybe not, if this were an affair of long standing. Maybe she'd open her own door, go on in and—

Suddenly Captain Martin was grinning. Key. Of course.

The key was the key.

There had been no key in the girl's handbag, none in the door, none on the floor.

So the sandwich-buyer had carried it away with him.

Which meant panic, not premeditation. Also, Captain Martin thought it unlikely that a man planning on murdering a girl would take her out on the town first.

So the gent was a witness, not a killer, for there had been no signs of a fight, and no time for an argument; they hadn't gotten far enough into the apartment.

The missing man was missing because of fear of scandal, not because of guilt.

Just to be sure, Cap Martin checked. No key on the girl, none found any place except in the back of a dressing table drawer, and that would be a spare.

Problem: Was it worthwhile fighting City Hall for a mere witness? For a killer there would be no doubt, but get Jim Latson and the machine mad just for a witness who, at best, could clear Guild only so he could be deported?

Cap Martin, sadly deciding to call it a day, already knew the answer. It was worthwhile. It might mean going out to a precinct, it might mean even being framed out of his pension, but he knew he was going to do it.

For a final act of the day, he put in a note: Rein and Page were to report to him when they came on for the day watch tomorrow. And a memo to Jake: Call Latson's secretary and ask for an appointment as early as was convenient for the chief.

The egg, as the kids said, had hit the electric fan. From time to time, other things hit that fan, too. But Cap Martin, a family man, believed in clean talk.

CHAPTER 15

Fog covered the city, had even managed to find its way into the interview room at the County Jail. It mixed with the sweat on Dave Corday's face, but it didn't cool him.

He slapped the picture with the palm of his hand. "This is your man," he said. "You shot Miss DeLisle, and this man was present."

Guild shook his head. He seemed to have shrunk since he had been in jail; probably all that had happened was that the damp air made his dungarees droop even more than when they had been issued to him.

"I did not shoot Miss DeLisle," he said. "I am a family man, I cannot dishonor my name."

Dave Corday let his voice out a couple of notches. "Your name? You fool, it isn't your name! You came into this country under a name that wasn't your own, and then you even changed that! What was the idea, were you going to send the papers you came in under back to the old country, sell them over again?"

"Please, I am sorry I came in that way, outside the law. But I have worked hard since I have been here; I am good American."

Dave Corday used the dramatic fall in volume now. He put a hissing quality into his voice, he chose plenty of words with S's in them. A good legal education pays off. "The United States stinks for your presence. I'm sending you back out of the States. Back behind the Iron Curtain!"

That hurt. That was the line to take. Little Guild's face collapsed. He said, "Well, I know. I did not kill Miss DeLisle, but yes, I bought another's papers to come here. His quota number."

"And you'll go back without ever seeing your baby," Dave Corday said. He did not have to bother with voice tricks now; what he was saying carried its own weight. "Why should anyone give you a favor?"

Ralph Guild began to cry.

Dave Corday leaned over, and spoke harshly: "There's only one man can save you: me! Sign this thing, and identify this man, and I'll drop the charge against you down to murder two—second-degree murder. It means you'll go out on bail; and I'll see you get that bail."

Ralph Guild said, "And—and then?"

Corday said, "Time, man, time." He leaned back, used his kindly tone. "Think it over, Guild. Time to spend with your family. Mr. Van Lear will ask for postponement after postponement. He's a smart man. Think, Guild, think."

He thought to himself: This is the way. This will get Jim Latson into court, stripped of his power. By the time the trial starts, he won't have a friend left; they'll scare off quick when they find he was involved in a murder. And then—hell, then we can trace the gun to him. He got it some way; took it off a criminal, got it as a gift, bought it.

And whatever he did about the fingerprints will come out, too. And I'll look like an honest prosecutor who mistook a witness for a murderer and a murderer for a witness.

Publicity? Fred Van Lear's perfectly right; this case is going to be page one-all the way. All my way. I won't settle for D.A. I'll be governor myself. And I certainly will sign no reprieve for Jim Latson.

Ralph Guild was talking. "I am afraid."

"Afraid? You, a Czech, afraid? Think what they'll do to you if you go back home. Just think of that."

"I'm afraid of this man here." Guild gingerly touched the photograph of Jim Latson. "He was here with you when you came before. Such men!"

"For every one we have here, there are six in Czecho Slovakia. And you'll be free, man. Tomorrow morning! Free to go to the hospital, to see your wife, to look at your son!"

Ralph Guild stared at him. "How do I know you are not another? You were with him!"

Dave Corday knew he had won: He only had to say one word more and he was through. "If I am, Guild, you can't be worse off than you are: in jail, booked for murder, with me about to try you. Can you?"

Ralph Guild reached for the pen, and slowly signed.

Dave Corday pressed the buzzer.

Peter Poldear himself came up. "Through, Dave?"

"He's confessed, Pete. Send for the press."

CHAPTER 16

The county jail was a mess. It had never been meant to accommodate a full-scale news break; but now more than forty newsmen—daily papers, wire-services, radio and TV reporters, plus a few people from the weekly magazines—were all storming in to see Ralph Guild.

Peter Poldear, the sheriff, wasn't having any. Jim Latson, jumping out of the patrolman-driven car, counted at least two dozen of his men thrown around the jail; and that many more turnkeys were on duty in their clumsy blue uniforms and old-fashioned looking badges.

They saw Jim Latson, and stormed him; the yells of "Chief" were reminiscent of newsreel sound tracks from the old Mussolini days. He saw two of his big motor cops heading for him and shook his head at them.

Policy was at stake. That ass, Poldear, had damn near alienated the entire local, state, and national press. He raised a hand for silence, and said, "Boys, give me five minutes. I just got the flash. In fact, I got it after you did; Wade Cohen and I were both in the Oak Bar, and his call came in first. But I was soberer."

It got a laugh, it got a couple of minutes before the Fourth Estate pulled the jail down. He kept a grin on his face; but when he got inside, he was going to skin Peter Poldear and throw the hide out to the reporters. It would make a story—the idiot Poldear had acted stupider than Dave Corday.

He said, "I'm going in and get some order. As soon as I get inside, I'll see Sheriff Poldear and arrange to have the big visitors' room set open for you" He raised a hand and pointing at the bigger of the motor cops, yelled, "Come here, break center for me." He smiled back at the reporters. "Let me in, and you'll have your story in five minutes. We'll bring Guild up there, and you can talk to him."

The big officer—Sid Harrison, his name was, six years on the force, two and a half on a motorcycle—started over.

Carl Glidden of the *Trib* said, "Is it true Guild confessed?"

Jim Latson raised his voice so he wouldn't be giving Glidden an exclusive. "All I know is that I got a phone call to that effect. More to come, as it says on the tele-type."

Patrolman Harrison came through the crowd, Jim got out his wallet, thumbed some bills out. "Sid, get coffee and a load of sandwiches for the press, and have them set up in the visitors' room upstairs."

Not a reporter there—all men at this hour—really wanted coffee and sandwiches. Not a man there but could afford to buy his own easily. But Latson knew his working press—suckers for a free load, any time, any hour. They let him go into the jail, and waited, quietly for newspapermen.

Peter Poldear took one look at Jim Latson's face, and said, "I only—"

"You only raised hell," Jim Latson said. "Is there an assistant dog catcher in this city? If there is, I'll see you're it, come next election. Now, here's what you're to do: Get your screws back in here, have them make a cordon, so the newsmen can get to the visitors' room and no place else. A motor cop named Harrison's bringing free grub for them; be a gracious host. Set up an interview room for me, and get some hot coffee. I'm drunk."

Pete Poldear grinned.

"Get Guild up there," Jim Latson concluded. "And fast."

Poldear said, "My prisoners—"

"Your prisoners aren't going to escape with cops all over the sidewalk... An idea; as each newsman comes in, check his card, make him put it in his hatband. It's an excuse to stall awhile."

Poldear nodded. His jowls wobbled when he did. He said, "Interview Room Three."

Jim Latson went toward the stairs.

Pete Poldear's blatting voice followed him: "Guild's already there." Then, as Latson paused, the sheriff cried, "Dave Corday's with him."

Jim Latson turned; he was up a couple of stairs, and he let all the fury he felt shoot down at Poldear.

"What!"

But Poldear had turned away.

A turnkey stood in the square hall, guarding Interview Three. Jim Latson started around him and the guard put out a hand, saying: "The sheriff—"

Jim Latson struck the hand down. "You know who I am," he said. "And your name is Larner, and you've been taking a cut from the restaurant across the street to bring in special meals for the prisoners."

Larner got out of the way. The interview rooms locked from the outside; the key was in its hole. Jim Latson twisted it and went in.

Behind him he could hear Larner locking them in.

Dave Corday, rumpled and tired looking, was sitting at the interviewer's desk. Little Guild, across from him, had been crying.

Jim Latson said, "Let's see that confession," and reached for it. When he picked it up, he uncovered a picture of himself lying on the table. Ralph Guild groaned and Dave Corday moved away a little, but Jim Latson just grunted.

He read the confession through once, and then again.

Then he said, "Your handwriting, Dave?"

Corday nodded. His eyes were very wide.

Jim Latson grinned. "I'm not going to hit you." He took his pen and blacked out a few lines. "Better copy that over," he said. "Without all that crap about witnesses."

Corday said, "There are two copies."

Jim Latson said, "Then copy 'em both. And hurry, man! You got the press outside, howling like cats with their tails stepped on! Poldear can't stall 'em much longer."

He reached out casually arid picked up his photograph, tore it in two. "Write, you son-of-a-bitch," he said to Corday. "And you, Guild. Sign it!"

Dave Corday shook his head.

Jim Latson said, "At a party tonight, given for the governor by Deputy Police Chief James Latson, David Corday, Assistant Trial Deputy in the D.A.'s office, was to be informed of his party's nomination of him for district attorney. However, Corday became so drunk before the announcement was made that the governor decided he was unsafe to hold public office.

"Chagrined and disappointed, Corday then went to the County Jail where, together with a known illegal entrant and accused murderer, he conspired—"

Corday said, "God!"

Jim Latson said, "Pete Poldear was never without a bottle in his desk. Not since I've known him, maybe not since that desk was in the third-grade room at a fourth-rate public school. Sid Harrison, one of the biggest patrolmen on the motor squad, is on his way here with coffee for me. If you think he won't hold you while I pour Pete's bottle of whisky into and on you, you don't know what I've got on Sid Harrison."

And what have I? he thought. Nothing that I can remember, and my memory is pretty good.

"You'd look hot, Corday, holding a press conference reeking drunk. I don't know if there is a job in this town called assistant pet shop inspector, but if there is, you wouldn't be able to get it when the newspapermen got through with you."

It was nice timing. Somebody knocked on the door, Larner twisted the key, and big Sid Harrison came in with the chief's coffee.

Jim Latson took it from him, and said, "Wait a minute, Sid."

Dave Corday let his breath out in a long, almost moaning sigh, and began to write. "That's all, Sid," Jim Latson said, and the motor cop went away.

Jim Latson looked down at Ralph Guild, and his voice got soft. "When caterpillar-guts here gets through writing," he said, "you'd better sign it. Maybe you can see why: we are now in no position to convict you, because a man going to the chair would spill all he'd heard tonight. No, Guild, you're sitting better. We'll postpone and postpone, and you'll be out on bail." He walked to the door, rapped for Larner to let him out. "Won't we, pal Dave?"

Corday, writing fast, had nearly replaced the mutilated page. "Yes," he said, without looking up. "Yes. We'll postpone. And you can't be deported till the case is over."

Guild said, suddenly, "I will sign." He pointed at Latson. "I believe him. I will sign."

Larner had the door open now. Jim Latson let out a guffaw, said, "Have a good press conference, Dave," and went out.

Poldear had cleared the stairs and corridors of newsmen. Jim Latson went out into the damp, foggy night. He was thinking: If Cap Martin ever hears of that one, we're sunk. I'd better pull him off the case tomorrow.

But the thought came bouncing back like a cheap ball on an elastic. Marty doesn't pull easy.

CHAPTER 17

Cap Martin liked a neat desk. He sat down in front of an absolutely bare slab of wood the next morning, took a pad from the center drawer, and laid it in front of him. He stared at it awhile, and then pressed the buzzer for Jake.

His secretary came in promptly, his badge shiny on his alpaca coat, his face closely shaven, his shoes polished; all correct. He had a stenographer's notebook and a handful of pencils all ready.

"No letters," Cap Martin said.

Jake said, "Page is outside. Rein's on his way here. I haven't been able to get you in to Chief Latson yet."

"I'll see Page right away. And bring me a copy of the *News-Journal*."

"Yes, sir."

Door open, door shut; door open again, and Jake very properly ushering Ray Page in. As soon as Page was seated, Jake came across the office and put a folded copy of the paper on the desk. Then he went out again.

From Jake's competent back, Cap Martin's gaze went to Ray Page's inadequate face. Cap kept his own face smooth; there was no use telling the patrolman—now a hack inspector—that he was unlikable. But it did seem that a man of thirty could have pulled his features together, just a little bit.

"Routine, Page," Cap said. He unfolded the paper. The four center columns of the front page had been run together into one bank; the confession of Ralph Guild, reported by Harry Weber. Just glancing down, Cap Martin could see the words: "skirt," "negligee," "bed," "nightgown," and that was enough for the moment. He sighed, and turned to Page, who was looking as intelligent as possible. Possible wasn't enough.

"The night the DeLisle girl was killed," Cap Martin said, "you and Jim Rein were on patrol, not too far away. Anything happen out of the ordinary?"

"Aw, we woulda reported, Cap," Page said.

Cap Martin said, "Captain."

"Yes, sir, Captain. Like I say, we kept a good log, kept our noses clean."

Cap Martin opened a side drawer, took out the typed log sheet. "Here, study this, Page. Refresh your memory."

He found he was physically reluctant to read the confession. It was such obvious junk. "Protect my wife and unborn child..." Bunk. No self-defense there. "I was driven frantic by her obvious and naked appeals to my sex..." sounded about as much like a Czecho Slovakian waiter as he did.

His eye kept drifting to other stories. But war and the rumors of war had been relegated to the inner pages of the *News-Journal*. This was hot, this was the essence of life: an immigrant waiter had confessed to killing a high-class hooker. Don't call her a whore, Captain Martin, because she got paid too much to be a whore.

A red light on his box went on, and he flipped the switch for Jake to say, "Rein's here, Captain."

"Send him in." With Rein, he was more cordial, asked him how he liked the detective bureau, told him to sit down next to Page. "I'm filling in the picture on the Hogan DeLisle thing, Jimmy. Just smoothing off the top. You and Page look over your typed log there, and see if you can recall anything out of the ordinary."

It was noticeable that Rein didn't offer to shake hands with Page. Cap Martin had done his uniform patrol back when there was still a lot of walking done, and a patrolman walked alone; but when he had become a detective, he had frequently been teamed with insufferable partners. He imagined that being penned up in a patrol car with a man like Page was as rough duty as could be found.

Rein was leaning on the back of Page's chair, reading over the other man's shoulder. He said, almost immediately, "That was the night we started Chief Latson's car for him, Ray."

Ray Page shook his head. Plain clothes didn't help him; he wore a nubbly tweed with an under-shade of purple to it. "It ain't here, Jim."

"The girl left it out," Rein said. Across the top of Page's head, he looked at Captain Martin. What he saw there must have led him to say, "Or maybe I'm wrong."

"Sure you're wrong," Ray Page said. "It ain't here. And we kept a good log."

"My mistake," Rein said. "It was some other night."

"Well, if that was just a routine patrol," Cap Martin said, "I won't need you any more, Page. Thanks for your cooperation."

"Any time, Cap, I mean, Captain. Any time at all."

Cap Martin said, "There was something else I wanted to see you about, Rein. Your commander phoned while you were on the way here."

"Yes, sir...?"

They waited till Ray Page had left. Then Cap Martin tilted his chin at the chair closest to the desk. "Sit down, Jim. Cigarette?"

"Thank you, sir." It was Rein who got the match lit. They blew out smoke silently.

Finally Cap Martin said, "Tell me about it."

"Not much to tell," Jim Rein said. "We got a call that a department car was stalled and where. Went there, and pushed Chief Latson's sedan with our cruiser. It started at once. I saw Page log it."

"Good report," Cap Martin said. "You'll make an excellent detective. If I asked for you for Homicide, what would you think?"

"I would think," Jimmy Rein said, "that the captain thought me competent."

Cap Martin nodded and stood up, something he seldom did for his inferiors. "Exactly what you're supposed to think. It may take a few days.

I wouldn't want to ask Chief Latson for the transfer."

"No," Jimmy Rein said. "If you did, I wouldn't want to take it."

The red light lit up; Cap slipped the switch to hear that Harry Weber was outside.

He sighed, shook hands with Rein and escorted him to the door. Then he stuck his head out and called Harry Weber.

Weber came in silently, and silently took the hard chair Captain Martin pointed to Harry Weber said, "Any statement on Guild's confession, Captain?"

Captain Martin shook his head, smiling a little. "Nope. You covered the story?"

"They dragged me away from a game of Russian bank. My wife was taking a beating for the first time in a month."

"Tough," Cap Martin said.

"And rough," Harry Weber added.

"Typed confession?"

Harry Weber said, "No. Corday's handwriting. I happen to know it."

Cap Martin nodded, staring at the ceiling. He was going to have to spend a few words; and Weber was not stupid. What did the military call it: a calculated risk? Cap Martin didn't usually believe in them. But maybe the time had come. He asked, "Was Chief Latson there?"

Harry Weber's eyes narrowed. He said, "Why, no. Should he have been? We got to see Guild, talk to him. He hadn't been beaten up."

It would hardly do to smile now. Cap Martin said, "What's the political gossip these days, Harry?"

Weber's reaction proved to the captain that it paid to be taciturn. In a Civic Center lousy with first names, having yours used by Captain Martin was a rare honor. Harry Weber beamed, and said, "The governor's swinging for the United States Senate. The scoop is, Frederick Van Lear will take the nomination for D.A. in exchange for not running for governor. He's a shoo-in here in the city, where he's known; he'd have tough running in the state, where he's not."

Captain Martin smiled a good, broad smile, almost a home-use smile.

Harry Weber said, "Of course, the D.A. resigns to start campaigning, Van Lear is appointed pro tem, and he can't act on either side of the Guild case. Lawyers' ethics."

Captain Martin said, "I never said a word."

"Not a mumbling word," Harry said. "It'll never come to trial. Or if it does, it'll be a strange, bumbling kind of mess. Say Corday decides to prosecute. He can't use anybody on his staff who is working with his new boss, Van Lear, on anything, or the opposing counsel will jump all over him."

Captain Martin smiled.

Harry Weber said, "They'd almost have to get an outside prosecutor, someone not in the D.A.'s office at all. Means a special appropriation, and this case wouldn't justify it. Much easier to drop the whole thing."

Captain Martin shook his head gently.

Harry Weber snorted. "You can't be naïve enough to think this case will be tried."

Captain Martin said, "You know—and off the record, though I hate the phrase—it will. Maybe not with Guild as defendant, but it will. And I can't tell you why."

Harry Weber started laughing. He said, "I'll end up with the reporters' cliché: If you do decide to let the public in on what its servant is doing, don't forget the *News-Journal*."

The phone rang twice. It was Jake's signal to his boss: *Urgent*. Cap Martin scooped it up, said, "Martin," and Jim Latson said, "Understand you want to see me, Marty. Let's make it right away, before I'm snowed."

"I'll be right down." He hung up the phone, stood up, held out his hand to Harry. "I've got to see the brass."

Harry said, "You're probably the only man in the city government who doesn't look in the mirror before that exercise."

"They don't hire me for pretty," Captain Martin said.

The reporter walked along with him as he went downstairs to where the offices were larger, the pickings lusher. But the reporter didn't talk, and Captain Martin was glad; he had an awful decision to make. If he told Jim Latson he knew about the stalled car, he immediately entered a field of intra-department politics he'd always avoided.

He might possibly enter a field in which the murder of a police captain was not too big a price to pay for silence.

He was still thinking of this when, having passed Jim Latson's three secretaries without speaking, he found himself in the chief's office, the door closing pneumatically behind him. He grinned at the thin man behind the desk, and said, "Chief," falling again into his silent role.

Jim Latson was telling him to sit down, and start talking. "It's your nickel, Marty. I didn't send for you. I'm never likely to; you're the only man in the department completely on top of his job."

Captain Martin did not return a cynical thanks for the cynical compliment. Instead, he said, "The Guild case."

Jim Latson yawned and pushed around so his feet could come up on his desk. "Yeah. The DeLisle killing. Tell you about that, Marty. We're out of it, the department that is, and damn glad to be. Corday's satisfied that the confession's all the case he needs; so I'm pulling you and your men off it. I told Dave Corday he could borrow a couple of men if he needed them and direct them himself."

Captain Martin kept his own feet firmly on the floor, side by side. "I see."

"Sure," Jim Latson said, and he yawned again. "Maybe you think I don't appreciate you? I do. The department does. You've put in a lot of overtime on this Guild thing. Well, I won't have the D.A.'s office overworking my best man. If Corday can't get a conviction on a signed confession, that's his hard luck."

Captain Martin felt a great weight come off his lungs. He knew now where he had to go and what he had to say when he got there. But he took his time about it. He had walked a tightrope for twenty-nine years, and that is a very long tightrope; he had put one foot ahead of the other, and he had never fallen off on either side: the side of outright dishonest or the side of such righteous indignation that the machine had to break him.

He was getting off the tightrope now. It had gotten too greasy for his feet.

He said, "The Guild confession is no good, Chief."

Jim Latson's eyes were a bright green. They let themselves be covered with the lids for a moment, and then they dulled a little, and looked bored. "What do you mean, no good, Marty? Forged? Gotten under bodily duress? Misunderstood by the signer? Guild's English is good enough for him to read what he signed."

"It's a phony," Captain Martin said quietly. "It's a deal, and the dealers can't deliver. There's no bail in a murder case."

"Murder two? Homicide?"

Captain Martin said, "Murder one to me, until proved otherwise."

Jim Latson shook his head. He clucked a little, his tongue clicking against the back of his front teeth. "Marty, Marty, you're due for some time off. An old cop like you! You know better. What the D.A.'s office wants to prosecute for, that is what they charge; not us, not the public, not the victim's family. That is the law, Marty, and you've known it— how many years?"

"I'm one short of my pension."

"Twenty-nine years... But we wouldn't graduate a rookie from police school who couldn't tell you the division of responsibility between police, district attorney, magistrate, and grand jury... You've slipped, Marty." Suddenly Latson's voice got brisker; his feet came off the desk and he leaned forward, openly smiling. "You've slipped, and I like you better for it. You've been a cold one, Marty, to me. The perfect cop! Well, I never believed in the perfect anything; nobody does, and nobody'd like it if he met it. You're human now, Marty, and human beings get tired when they've been overworking. I'm authorizing two weeks' leave for you, starting right now, and it's not to come off your annual leave; it's in lieu of all the overtime you've put in."

Captain Martin said, "No."

But Chief Latson went on as though he hadn't heard. "And when you come back, it won't be to Homicide. It'll be to an inspector's desk and an inspector's shield; in charge of the Criminal Investigation Division. Chief of all detectives; how do you like those apples, Marty?"

And as he said it, Jim Latson remembered Dave Corday saying he'd lost his taste for apples; but Dave had regained that taste, had hesitated at tipping over the machine's applecart. Martin wasn't Dave Corday; but Martin was a man with only a year to go for his pension.

Captain Martin said, "I appreciate the offer, Chief; but I won't be able to take leave just now. The Guild case needs reopening."

Latson's dull eyes brightened again. There was the bite of anger behind his mild words: "Marty, even from you I expect listening when I'm talking."

"It may not take me long," Captain Martin said. "But there was a witness to the killing. I want to question him. After that, it will be up to the district attorney and his staff; they can drop it if they want to. But not till I give them this one piece of evidence, this story from the witness."

Jim Latson leaned forward. "That's a long speech—for you. This witness got a name?"

"It's one you know," Captain Martin said.

"Better than I do my own?" But the mockery didn't have much depth to it.

"Not better. As well."

Latson's right hand slowly curled into a fist; Captain Martin, watching him, wondered if the chief knew. Latson slowly rose to his skinny height, and Captain Martin wasn't sure that Jim Latson knew he was doing that, either. Latson said slowly, "Why, Marty? With a year more to run, why?"

Captain Martin shrugged.

Jim Latson said, "You think I killed her?"

"I wasn't there," Captain Martin said, "so all I know is when she was shot, where she was shot, and with what she was shot—an unregistered Czech pistol."

"And that I was there."

Captain Martin looked at the floor. He held his hands out, turned them over, and inspected them as though they were strange to him. He said, "You said that, Chief Latson, I didn't. Here is what I know: that you dated her, from time to time. That a man came home with her. That she had eaten nightclub food shortly before. And that you were in the neighborhood and went to a good deal of trouble to conceal the fact."

"Illegal trouble. Doctoring of department records. Yeah, Marty, I took her home."

Captain Martin said nothing.

Jim Latson slowly sat down again. He studied Captain Martin, Captain Benjamin L. Martin, though no one in the department called him Ben, never had. Marty, Captain Martin, commander Homicide Squad. "You're married, aren't you, Marty?"

Captain Martin said, "Yes."

Jim Latson said, "It's a funny question right now, I know. The reason I asked it, it just occurred to me I know less about you than almost any man in the department. We've served together twenty-five years—you were an acting sergeant when I was a rookie—and I don't know the first damn thing about you. You've never brought your wife to a department party, you've never had another officer in your home, have you?"

"No."

Jim Latson said furiously, "You were chatty enough a minute ago—when you were hanging it on me. Why dam up now?"

Captain Martin smiled. It was a slow smile, calculated to enrage a suspect; he had used it often. So, he was sure, had Jim Latson. Shakespeare's expression, worn to a cliché by its years of aptness, came to mind: "hoist by his own petard." With the slow, sarcastic smile still on his face, he thought: Latson would know the phrase, or a reasonable approximation of it, but he wouldn't know where it came from.

"I guess I'm heisted by my own derrick," Jim Latson said. "If I'd put a poorer man in Homicide and shoved you in Traffic, I'd have been better off."

Captain Martin waited.

Traffic was distant, headquarters was not on a main street. Some place in the building, the direct wire from fire headquarters rang its bell; a one-alarm fire in the Park district. Rubber-heeled feet tramped in the corridors, and Captain Martin waited.

"Damn it," Jim Latson said finally, "I didn't shoot her."

Captain Martin spared him two words: "I see."

"But I can't prove it," Chief Latson said. He was out of his chair again, ranging the room, flinging his long arms around. "And don't give me that crap about a man being innocent until he's proven guilty! You know that isn't so, and I know it isn't so. A man's innocent till the cops decide he's guilty, and that's that!"

Captain Martin said, "Is it?"

Jim Latson came to rest. He leaned on the back of one of the easy chairs, his arms folded. He said, "It isn't with you, is it? An honest cop!" He made it sound like the worst sort of insult. But when it didn't erase Martin's smile, he raged again: "Who sold me out? Rein, Page, one of the girls in the log-typing room? Go on, tell me. I can find out. I can find out anything in this department. It's my work. I built the department up from a lousy, small-time police force, and I run it! Me, Jim Latson."

Captain Martin was thinking: I've got all the time in the world. If I have to pinch the chief, the newspapers'll explode all around me. I'll be over my head in reporters for a week, and I'm in no hurry for that. All the time in the world.

Latson was off on another tack, now. "I didn't kill her! Do you think I did?"

Captain Martin said, "You're still wearing your gun."

"And you'd have taken it off me if you thought I was guilty? Not you! Not the longest, sunniest day of your damn smug life! The cop doesn't live who could take Jim Latson's gun away. Not here, not in the FBI, not in Scotland Yard."

Captain Martin thought vaguely that a pipe would be a nice thing to smoke just now.

Jim Latson came as close to pleading as he would ever come in his life. "What's the percentage, Marty? You haul me in on this and you ruin my career, you maybe get the whole administration thrown out at next election, and who gains? Say you don't get broken, say you only get transferred to the sticks, and where does that leave any of us? It means the department has a worse deputy chief than it had before, and it means it has a worse head of Homicide. The city's the loser, the department's the loser, and who gains?"

"I don't know," Captain Martin said. "Who shot Hogan DeLisle?"

"You wouldn't believe me," Jim Latson said.

"Try me."

Jim Latson came around the chair. He started to sit in it, and then thought better of that, went behind his desk, placed himself in his swivel chair of command; the high-backed, expensive chair of the deputy chief.

"Dave Corday," he said.

Captain Martin reached in his pocket and took out a notebook and pencil. And then the whole story came out; came out in such a rush that the captain had trouble getting it all down, though he had taught himself shorthand.

When it was all through, he closed the notebook and put it away, put his pencil back in his inside coat pocket.

He stood up, and went to the door. "Thank you, Chief Latson," he said.

Jim Latson was red-eyed, his hair wild about his head. "My God," he said, "believe it or not, I feel better for getting that off my chest."

"Sure," Captain Martin said. "By the way, I want James Rein transferred to Homicide. Detective second grade, till he makes sergeant."

"Okay," Jim Latson said. "He's almost at the top of the promotion list now. Wouldn't detective first grade be better?"

"This isn't a bribe," Captain Martin said. "It's a promotion for the good of the department." He walked to the door.

But the chief called him back, as Captain Martin had known he would. "What's going to happen? I haven't signed anything, and I'm not going to. You know the truth now, but you can't use it in court."

Captain Martin shrugged, an almost imperceptible motion. "Who knows?" he asked. "I'm going to see Corday." And he went out.

Jim Latson reached down in the double drawer of his desk and got out the bottle with which he entertained visiting brass. He took a shot, all by himself. Then he gathered the half dozen bank books from his locked drawer.

He put them in an envelope, addressed the envelope to Norman Wright, Hotel Plaza, New York. In the upper left-hand corner he put his own name and his apartment address.

If he had to take off, it was simple to go to New York and register as Norman Wright. If he didn't have to take off, it was equally simple to write to the Plaza and tell them his friend, Mr. Wright, had decided not to go to New York after all, and would they return the envelope to the addresser.

Life remained something that came in doses no bigger than a man could swallow, one at a time. For him. But for Dave Corday, who was about to be interviewed by that iceberg, Captain Martin, the pills were about to grow to horse-doctor size. And no man has a throat as big as a horse's.

Jim Latson grinned. The door opened, one of his secretaries brought in the mail, he saw there was another letter from his wife and he stopped grinning.

CHAPTER 18

Dave Corday's girl, Alice, held the door for Captain Martin and then closed it behind him.

Martin crossed the office at his steady pace, looked down at Dave Corday, and held the pose for a full minute. It was a lovely day over the city, a beautiful morning, and the clear light came into the high office and made Martin's features clearer than usual. Still, Dave Corday could read nothing there.

Finally, Captain Martin said, "Tell your secretary to hold all calls."
Dave Corday started to bluster. He said all the usual things: this was
his office, he would run it; a chief deputy district attorney amounted to
something, and so on. He used phrases like common courtesy, chain of
command, and perhaps the word protocol got in there.

When he finished, Cap Martin was still standing in front of the desk,
still impassive. Dave Corday flipped the intercom and said, "Hold all
calls, Alice." This, of course, did not cut off the red phone hooked to the
high emergency desk at police headquarters.

Cap Martin looked Dave Corday over. He was sure that there was no
gun on the man's body, but there was undoubtedly one in his top desk
drawer; experience knew the type. Well, Captain Martin could stop Corday getting at that gun; he did not want a suicide on his record. He went
and sat down.

"I'll give it to you straight, Mr. Corday," he said. "Short and simple. I
have an accusation against you. The DeLisle case."

Then he leaned back. His eyes kept steady on Dave Corday's; his ears
let a wave of indignation go by them. Preposterous, unheard-of and in-
solence left him untouched, as did incompetent and irresponsible; but he
felt a slight twinge of respect for vaporous extravagations. He hoped he
would remember to work that into a conversation with his brother-in-
law.

When the noise subsided—with, of course, a threat to get his badge—
he said, "Yes." Then he opened his notebook, keeping his feet squarely
on the floor; he wished he also had a bowler hat, like a Scotland Yard
man in a movie. If he had, he would have kept it on.

"Statement by James Latson, police officer," he read. "Dated yesterday.
I read: 'I escorted Hogan DeLisle, or Beverly Hauer, to her apartment
from the Zebra House. I opened the front door with a key she gave me,
and followed her in. David Corday, known to me personally, was hiding behind the apartment door. When it was closed, he appeared, threatened me with a revolver, and took from my armpit holster a Skoda .38
which I carried there. Using a pillow to muffle the noise of the report,
Mr. Corday then shot Miss DeLisle with the Skoda, emptying the gun
into her and returning it to me. Seeing that she was dead, I then left in
company with—'"

The eyes told Captain Martin what he needed to know; Dave Corday
was involved. Latson might have shot the girl; or Latson might have told
the truth, but Corday was involved.

He shut the notebook, held it ready, and got a pencil from his pocket.
"Want to add anything to that, Mr. Corday?"

Guts Dave Corday didn't have and never had had.

His brain content was a dubious matter; he probably had more brains than he ordinarily used. But his lawyer's training was an asset frequently available to him; he'd bought it hard and it stuck with him when courage and thinking power failed.

So he said, "Is that statement signed?"

Captain Martin shook his head. Dave Corday said, "Then it is worthless." His voice was still clear and firm. But his face was the color of cream left on the coffee table overnight, and his hands were beginning to shake.

"Why, yes," Captain Martin said. "It is. In a court of law. But I have good evidence that Chief Latson was in the neighborhood of the girl's apartment at the time of the killing, and that he committed criminal acts to conceal that fact. Using those for levers, I think he'll sign the accusation against you. Sooner or later."

"Either that," Dave Corday said, "or face a murder rap himself."

"To escape which, he'll formally accuse you."

"Nothing to say," Dave Corday said. "Nothing to say."

"You do not wish to file a counter-accusation against James Latson?"

"Nothing to say," Dave Corday said. "Nothing to say."

Captain Martin nodded, and got to his feet. He stowed his pencil and his notebook away, picked up his hat and bent to the door. He didn't say goodbye.

Before he could get out of the secretary's office, Dave Corday's voice came after him, through the squawk-box.

"Cancel my appointments for the morning; something important has come up."

Captain Martin let himself out quietly. Time was on his side now; time would break Dave Corday down, as it would never do Jim Latson.

CHAPTER 19

Jimmy Rein had reported to Homicide, as ordered, and it was a temptation for Captain Martin to send for him, give him a chair in the captain's office, and invite him to talk over the DeLisle killing. But that was the one thing Captain Martin couldn't do.

The slightest implication that Rein's promotion was a bribe for silence, and discipline would go to hell. And it looked as if silence was what was going to result. The interview with Dave Corday had brought up nothing but ranting and raving. Which was evidence—to Captain Martin—that Latson's accusation of Corday had been true. But was no evidence at all in a court of law.

So—Captain Martin reached in the top drawer of his desk, got out a pack of cards, and started a game of Canfield—what did you have? Evidence that Jim Latson had been near the scene of the crime. Said evidence being the testimony of a police officer, James Rein.

Evidence that Chief Latson had tampered with the department files to conceal the fact testified to by Patrolman Rein... And how did you go about putting that evidence to a court? You subpoenaed the department records, and you dragged a lot of clerks into court, and it all added up to negative stuff.

Captain Martin put a black queen on a red king.

He had been foolish. In the hopes of using surprise to get a little farther, he had confronted Jim Latson. It had never occurred to him that Latson had killed the girl, and he didn't think so yet. The chief was neither half-witted nor impulsive. If he'd wanted to get rid of a party girl like that, he'd have had her floated out of town, firmly and in such a way that any accusation against him on her part would sound like nonsensical revenge.... And the autopsy had shown she was not pregnant, which was about the only accusation she could make that would amount to anything...

Yeah, Dave Corday was guilty... Maybe Hogan DeLisle—Beverly Hauer—had a brother who could be brought here from Detroit, handed a gun, and told to go get Corday. And maybe he'd do it.

Captain Martin turned up the ace of diamonds, and covered it with a whole run, up to the nine. Big deal. He smiled to himself.

Yeah, and supposing all that happened. Then, would Captain Martin, being consistent with the standard he had set for himself, have to go and arrest Mr. Hauer?

It made a nice problem.

The Canfield was about to come out. He gathered up the cards, carefully shuffled them, and put them in their box. He thumbed his squawkbox: "Afternoon papers up yet, Jake?"

Jake said, "Yes, sir," and promptly brought in the eleven o'clock edition of the *News-Journal* and the lesser afternoon sheet; the one that specialized in racing news.

Captain Martin put the cards away and opened the *News-Journal*. Yeah. Guild admitted to bond; trial would probably be postponed until Frederick Van Lear took over the district attorney's post, which might be soon; the D.A. would probably resign in order to campaign, and the governor would appoint Van Lear. The writer—no by-line—pointed out that the new district attorney would be unable to assist in a case where he had once been defense counsel, and that, with a murder case pending, Van Lear's appointment should be postponed. But it is much easier to get a man elected to an office he already holds... The old typewriter exercise was wrong; there is no time that is not the right time to come to the aid of the party.

Having read the late edition of the morning papers, the rest of the front page of this afternoon-paper printed-in-the morning did not interest Captain Martin. He turned to the first page of the second section, to a column called "City Hall" and signed by "The Recorder."

The third item brought him upright in his swivel chair: "Rumors are hot that there will be a change at Police Headquarters that will really crack pavements around town. A high-ranking, high-rated cop, previously apparently happy to serve out his time with railroad bars on his shoulders, is about to make a move to go to the very head of the class. And is also rumored to have the ammunition to do it with."

Captain Martin didn't swear. Swearing without an audience would have been a silly gesture. But he didn't smile, either. Nobody but he and Corday and Latson—well, and Jimmy Rein—knew that he had placed Latson in the Guild case.

Corday could be eliminated as a silly ass, too scared to move for days. Rein could be eliminated because any other conclusion would cause the Tilt light to go on in Captain Martin's head. Captain Martin could eliminate himself because he slept with no witnesses but his wife, and anyway, he didn't talk in his sleep.

Which left Jim Latson. And if Latson had tipped the *News-Journal* to the fact that Captain Martin was about to accuse him of something, Latson had a plan. Latson always had a plan.

Now it was just a matter of figuring out what the plan was. It could be done. Captain Martin told himself how smart he was, how experienced he was, how trained in following criminal reasoning.

Figure out what Latson's plan was, and come up with a counter-plan and—

Captain Martin shook his head. He had never fooled himself. He was not as smart as Jim Latson. More thorough, yes. Perhaps more analytical. But smarter, definitely not.

And before his methodical, analytical mind started asking itself what it meant by smarter, Captain Martin got to his feet. This was no time for armchair pondering. He was about to have his bacon fried for him, with a year more to go for his pension. If he did not kill this story at once, Latson would be well on his way to charge anything Captain Martin said to jealousy.

As he moved past Jake, muttering, "Press Room," at the patrolman-secretary, the Captain saw that his Tilt light had failed him. It had been a major error in strategy and tactics to let time go by between seeing Latson and filing charges against him.

He still believed Latson's story about Corday; but he should have kept Latson with him when he went to see the deputy D.A. Latson could think, and think fast, and act faster and—

There were three reporters in the press room: Cohen of the Tribune, Cahoon of the *World*, and Agatt of the *City News Bureau*. He said, "Hello, gents. Where's everybody?"

Wade Cohen had been typing; the other two playing gin. They all looked a little astounded at seeing him; as astounded as professional police-beat guys allow themselves to look, no matter how they feel. Cohen said, "Mostly everybody is out trying to see you or Chief Latson. How'd you escape them?"

Captain Martin almost grinned to himself. Supposing he told them that he had almost copped Latson and Corday for a murder, and that Latson was trying to write it all off to departmental jealousy.

It would make a sensation, all right. The newsmen might almost believe him for a minute or two. And then he'd be asked for proof—and he didn't have any, except theoretical guff. That, and Jimmy Rein's testimony that Jim Latson had been near the DeLisle apartment when the girl was killed, been there and worried enough about it to steal departmental records to cover it.

And now that Latson had made his move, it was a dead certainty that the chief had figured out a reason why he'd been where he'd been, why he'd doctored the records as he'd done.

All that was left was to deny he was jealous of Jim Latson, and that was as feeble a move as he could think of. But self-respect demanded that he stay on his feet as long as possible.... It was time to answer Wade Cohen's question about the other reporters. "I must have beat it out just a minute before they got to my place. Naturally, they'd see Chief Latson first."

Cohen was the only one of the three with much more standing than an office boy. He slid out from behind the typewriter, and leaned against the battered press desk, his hands in his pockets, his eyes half closed. "What's it all about, Marty?"

"You tell me."

"I know, I know. All you know is what you read in the papers."

Captain Martin laughed. "Don't you guys ever get tired of that act? You can't possibly be as weary as you make out."

Cohen laughed. "Who's interviewing who? It's not my story, really, Marty; we're a morning paper, and by the time we go to press again the *News-Journal* will have covered us firmly and thoroughly. But just for my own information."

"For your own information, I honestly didn't know a thing till I read that squib in the *News-Journal*."

The other two reporters had gone back to their gin game. But Cohen continued to lean against the table. There was a faintly wistful look in his rather heavy features; for once he looked quite young. He said, "If you were to start lying, Cap, it'd hurt me. I dunno why."

"I'm not lying." He had to say it, and thought less of himself because he had to.

Cohen nodded slowly. "That item couldn't have meant anybody else but you. So for once the great *News-Journal* goes flat on its nose. A nice sight."

Captain Martin fished out cigarettes, offered them. "What were you writing up, Cohen?"

Cohen shrugged. "Feature stuff. Eyewitness account of the raid Jim Latson led this morning. Maybe run it Sunday; for tomorrow, we'll use a rewrite of city news or the afternoon papers."

Captain Martin went on fishing: "You've got a nice off-beat style when you want to use it. Some of the best feature stories in the city come under your by-line." He moved over to the typewriter.

Flattered, Cohen moved aside.

Captain Martin read, and having read, felt the pinball hit the jackpot. Deputy Chief Jim Latson had, that morning, culminated weeks of careful waiting by raiding a gambling house. Said gambling house—and Captain Martin did not need to consult a map—was near the Belmont Arms, where Hogan DeLisle had been shot.

It was, in fact, between that spot and the corner where Chief Latson's car had stalled and been pushed by the cruiser. So now Jim Latson had a perfect alibi for being where he had been; and for not wanting anybody, even in the department, to know it.

Hope went. But had hope ever existed? Was his strength, was any man's strength, the strength of ten because his heart was pure? You did not have to serve twenty-nine years in the police department to answer that.

The answer was simply that if a pure heart was ten times stronger than a criminal heart, it was a coincidence.

To learn this, all you had to do was grow old. Maybe old enough to graduate from high school. Or grade school.

We are quite the philosopher today, Captain Martin. Not much of a cop, but a hell of a deep philosopher. What you should have done is frame Latson for something he never did—barratry, maybe, or stealing from blind beggars' hats—and kept him guessing. As soon as he knew what you were up to, he swung, and unfortunately, he fought like a three-armed man.

Back to business.

A big favor had been done the syndicate; and Jim Latson had a clear, logical reason for being where he was, and for concealing that fact at any cost. Later, there would be a department trial, and at least one policeman, maybe more, would be found guilty of taking money from the little gambling joint.

And since department men were concerned, the chief was perfectly right in going to any lengths to keep the department from knowing he was watching the house. Even to altering the logs.

The time had come to quit. A man owes something to his dignity, and that is to beat the world to the kick in the pants. Kick yourself—a neat trick physically—and save what appearance you have left.

Captain Martin said, "I'll tell you, Cohen. I just got to thinking. I'll bet you I know where that rumor came from that I was going upstairs."

Cohen said, "Oh?" Very noncommittal. Very cynical wise guy.

"I've put in for a transfer," Captain Martin said. "I'm getting too old for this job. Too many night calls, too much overtime. I've asked for a precinct house, preferably a suburban one."

"You'll still work night watches."

Captain Martin said, "But on schedule. Night one week, swing the next, day the third. Means I'll eat at least two meals at home every day. Middle-aged stomachs like that."

Cohen swallowed it: He turned to the *City News* man. "How's about we pass the hat for a testimonial dinner for Cap here? It won't be the same headquarters without him."

The *City News* man thought it was a wonderful idea. Captain Martin, touched a little, but not very much, drifted out of there. Precinct captains wore uniforms; he was wondering if he had bought a new one since the cut of the collar was changed about ten years ago. He didn't think so.

Latson's office next. One of the secretaries sent his name in, and he went right through. The chief's room was full of reporters. Jim Latson came from behind his desk, and put an arm around Captain Martin's shoulders. "One of you guys take a picture of this," he said. "Label it, 'How Wrong Can the *News-Journal* Get?'"

Captain Martin said, "I just gave the story to Cohen of the *Trib* and that new boy from *City News*. I've put in for a transfer to a quieter job. I want to sit out my time without ulcers.... I guess it was interpreted as a move for power."

They shot questions at him; they took pictures. Latson intervened to tell them that the department's information and education office would furnish them with a complete biography of Captain Benjamin Martin.

So they left.

Jim Latson went behind his desk and sat down. "Cigar, Marty?"

Captain Martin said, "Just a pipe, sometimes cigarettes."

"Fill up, boy, fill up and light up. Sit down, don't wear your feet out."

Captain Martin sat down, but he didn't lean back and he didn't take his pipe out. "Where am I going, Chief?"

Chief Latson's face creased sardonically. "Shafer, out at the Gardens, retires next month. Mandatory, he's sixty-four."

Captain Martin took it quietly. He neither groaned nor winced. The Gardens, Precinct Eleven, was at the opposite end of town from his home. It was also a dilly; two-thirds of it was taken up with the Zoo and the Municipal Arboretum, both of which were closed at dark, and patrolled from within by gray-coated watchmen....

"Cheer up," Jim Latson said, "maybe somebody'll steal an aardvark, and you can work on the case."

"One year," Captain Martin said. "I can do it on my ear." He cleared his throat. "I'd like to ask you a favor, Jim. After all, it's been twenty-five years."

Jim Latson grinned again. "I didn't think honest cops like you took favors from crooks like me."

"Jimmy Rein," Captain Martin said. "He didn't come to me; I sent for him." It slipped out of him before he knew what he was saying. Suddenly, he became eloquent. "He's a comer. Smart, hard-working, honest. The department needs kids like that. And—hell—he's pretty small game to be shooting at with an elephant gun."

Jim Latson said, "I don't know what you're talking about. Those hoods I rounded up this morning said they'd been paying off to the night patrol car. Ray Page and Jim Rein. You want me to keep a grafter in the department, Marty?"

Marty shook his head, and stood up. "See you in the Zoo," he said and left. He had just decided that his uniform was old-style after all. He would have to buy a new one; he hoped the price hadn't gone up. They used to cost seventy-five dollars.

CHAPTER 20

Dave Corday barked at his squawk-box: "What's the airmail rate to Italy?"

The girl's voice came back and said, "I'll have to find out, Mr. Corday."

"You should know these things."

The girl said, "Yes, Mr. Corday," and shut off the box. Her name was

Alice—Alice Willing, a last name that was unfortunate for a girl who had
to come in daily contact with the ribald humor of the Civic Center—and
she had worked for Dave Corday quite a while without getting very fond
of him.

But it was a job, and she called the mail room downstairs, got the information and told the box: "Airmail is fifteen cents for the half ounce,
regular mail eight cents an ounce."

"I only asked you for the airmail rate," Corday's voice said.

She hit the switch and told the cut-off box: "Now you know something
you didn't know before," and, sighing, went back to the magazine she
had been reading. Usually there was plenty to do; Corday knew his rights
as second biggest man in the office, and raised a fuss over any errors in
his briefs, his letters, even the memos he wrote to himself to guide him
in the court room.

Most of this mass of material she had typed by the stenographic pool,
as was her right. But some was confidential; and all she proofread in person, carefully and a little fearfully. She was not bright enough to know
that the day would go better if Dave Corday had something to yell about
early in the morning, when the typing was laid on his desk. A typo-
graphical error on the first page would have started the day off just fine
for him....

The door from the hall opened, and a messenger girl came in. She laid
three letters down; looked in the out-box, and raised one plucked eyebrow. "Nothin' to go?"

"No," Alice said.

"Ball of fire's slippin'," the mail girl said, and slouched out again.

Alice sighed. Her magazine was not holding her, and the morning had
been long. Lunch had been dull, because it was just before payday, and
it had consisted of a sandwich at the soda fountain. The afternoon looked
even duller than the morning had been; she should have tried to hold the
mail girl around to talk to. Bored, almost unbearably, she decided to write
a letter to an aunt on the West Coast. Not that she cared very much about
her aunt, one way or another; but Alice usually got a Christmas present
from her, and a letter could do no harm.

She took a sheet of engraved stationery and turned to the typewriter.

At once, she noticed that it was not the way she had left it. The paper
release was forward, the margin stops had been changed, and an inex-
pert touch had tangled the "a" and "g" keys. She straightened them out
daintily, and used Kleenex to remove a tiny flick of ink from her fingertips.

Ha! Big shot had typed a letter while she was out to lunch.

Alice couldn't remember him ever doing a thing like that before. If he wanted to write something confidential, he told her it was that before he dictated it, and she was careful not to have it in her machine when anyone was waiting in her office. Super-confidential things, she knew, big shot wrote with his own fountain pen, in longhand.

She shrugged. The letter to Italy, no doubt; that he had asked her about. If he left it in her out-tray, maybe she could get it open and read it. But probably it wouldn't be worth the trouble.

She was telling her aunt the news about their common relatives when Harry Weber walked in.

Harry said, "Hi, Alice. Happy in your work?"

She said, "Hello, Harry. How's your wife?"

That was the way it went. He didn't make jokes about her being willing, and she always reminded him she knew he was married, and then they could gossip a little together. A good secretary, she was pretty sure she'd never given him anything for his newspaper that Mr. Corday might have minded his having; but as a tribute to his being neither a wolf nor a foul-talker, she was more than happy to pass on anything she had picked up from the other girls in the office.

But today nothing had happened. She said, "Keeping busy?" but it was a hopeless gambit, going no place; at any moment he'd go on in and see Corday, and leave her bored again.

"Pretty busy," he said. "You?"

She shrugged. "It's like a rest cure around here. The only letter he's written all day, he wrote himself." She watched. The newspaperman was moving toward the inner door. Desperately she said, "To Italy. I've never been to Italy, have you?"

"I had a brother went there during the war," Harry said. He laughed. "When he came home, he wouldn't even eat spaghetti. Now, he won't pass up a picture that was shot in Italy. He's the world's greatest Italy-lover.... Boss in?"

Alice snapped the squawk-switch, and said, "Harry Weber to see Mr. Corday."

The voice that came out was more of a croak than even the box accounted for. "Send him in."

Harry waited till they were cut off, and asked, "What's eating him?"

"Oh, brother, I don't know. He didn't even eat lunch. I certainly hope it isn't another cold. He had one last year, and I suffered more than he did."

"When you get so you can't stand it, come over to the *News-Journal.* I'm getting so I make friends and so forth over there."

As soon as he opened the door he knew he had been right; something was awfully wrong with Dave Corday. The D.A. was huddled behind his

desk, shoved back from it, looking at a spot on the county's carpet.
Harry looked at the spot, too, and found little interest in it. He said,
"Howzit, Mr. District Attorney?"

Corday shrugged. "What can I do for you, Weber?"

Harry said, "Oh, routine. I got Guild bailed out this morning. I'm just
checking to see if you have any idea when his case'll be on the docket.
Fink said—"

He stopped because he'd gotten too much reaction; or the wrong reaction; or a perfectly bizarre reaction. Corday's head snapped up, he almost twitched his ears, "Fink. Captain Fink?"

Harry said, "Why, yes. Haven't you heard, it's all over the city end of
the Center. Cap Martin's taking over the Eleventh Precinct. Fink's going
to be Homicide."

Color came back into Dave Corday's face. He straightened his coat,
twitched at his tie, and pulled his chair closer to his desk. "I hadn't
heard."

"Sudden," Harry Weber said. "About Guild, now..."

Dave Corday said, "Well, there'll have to be a postponement. Mr. Van
Lear had put himself down, as associate counsel of record, and—this is
confidential, but you've probably heard of it—Mr. Van Lear will not be
available as a defense counsel. So, you see, there will be a postponement,
as is inevitable when—"

He babbled on. There was no other word for it. Harry Weber didn't
have to be a trained newsman; any copy boy on a country weekly
would have known something had happened. He very carefully did not
stare at Dave Corday; he had the idea that somewhere in the course of
the D.A.'s rambling a hint might be dropped.

It didn't come out that way. Corday cut himself off as fast as he had
started; he suddenly reverted to his yellow-cheeked state of collapse.

Harry Weber watched. Corday's eyes went everywhere but one place;
Harry looked at the place.

A good third of an airmail envelope stuck out from under the crisp blotter provided by the county to its good and able servant.

The girl outside, Alice, had said that Corday had written only one letter that day, had written that one himself, and then she had added that
the letter was going to Italy. Now—a sick politician is a scared one.

Jumping the country?

Dave Corday's fingers were creeping toward the envelope under the
blotter. They touched it; they started pushing it out of sight.

Harry Weber quietly leaned forward, grabbed the envelope, and said,
"I'll mail that for you."

Corday's voice was an anguished scream: "Give me that!"

Harry Weber said, "I'm sorry. I didn't know it was important." But he hung onto the letter.

Dave Corday said, "No, no, nothing important, just a personal note."

"Then I'll mail it for you."

Corday tried to get some discipline into his babble. "Well, all right. I'm quite jumpy today. And now, busy, you know."

"Sure," Harry Weber said, and started out, carrying the letter.

The busy D.A. suddenly had plenty of time. He walked with Harry Weber to the door, through Alice's office, to the corridor. He even walked with him part way down the hall, past the wardheelers. Then he stood, watching, until Harry got to the elevator and the mail chute.

So, Harry had to mail the letter right away. But he did by the greatest dexterity manage to see to whom it went. Mrs. James Latson, at a hotel in Rome— When he turned around, Corday had gone back to his office.

There was a coffee shop in the lobby of the County Building, but it would be full of people Harry Weber knew, and he didn't want to talk. So he drove his car till he saw a greasy spoon, parked, bought a cup of coffee and two doughnuts, and took them to a little hard-topped table.

What did he have?

A politico crushed by the world, who revived at once when he heard that a new head of Homicide was coming in.

A big shot in the D.A.'s office writing to the wife of the big shot in the police department, and doing it with great stealth.

Harry Weber paused to savor that word stealth. It was a word you don't often get to use, he thought. In most cases secrecy, privacy, fitted a lot better. But stealth was what Dave Corday had betrayed, and stealth it would be called, if only in Harry Weber's mind.

So you had homicide and you had extramarital relations, and what more do you need for the top story of the year?

Well, according to the old gag, you also needed religion. Rome, Italy, Mrs. James Latson, Hotel something-or-other, Rome, Italy. Seat of the Pope. Yeah. Harry, like all other newsmen in town, had heard that Jim Latson and his wife only stayed married because of their religion, Catholic.

So you had that, too.

Put it together this way: Dave Corday and Mrs. J. Latson were having an affair. She had gone to Rome to get permission for a divorce.

Nice, but it left out one piece: Homicide.

Corday had made an attempt on Jim Latson's life, and Captain Martin knew about it. Charge: attempted homicide. Disposal: removal of investigating officer, i.e., Captain B. Martin, the honest cop.

Harry Weber took a swallow of his cooling coffee, chewed a dough-nut, and told himself it stank: the story, not the food, which was no worse than mediocre.

Dave Corday was merely shaken, not bloody. If he had attempted to injure Jim Latson, he would have had two black eyes and a broken nose, not to mention a few missing teeth.

Harry tried a little more doughnut. It didn't seem to be brain food. Hell, this thing was simple. It just took a little falling into place.... Jim Latson's wife, Captain Martin, Dave Corday. A triangle, but not a very conventional one. Say Cap Martin was chasing Mrs. Latson and—

Harry Weber got up and left. He didn't have enough facts, was his trouble.

The folders he got from the morgue at the paper were thick. Even Mrs. James Latson's. The lady did not spare herself when it came to charities, both her church's and the city's.

But a look at her frequently half-toned picture was enough to tell Harry Weber—or a congenital idiot—that she was not the hypotenuse of any love triangle. No man would throw over a political career for that buxom figure...

Captain Martin's folder was strictly business. The only clipping that referred to his private life at all was yellow and cracking. Benjamin Martin, sergeant in the detective bureau, had gotten married.

His bride had been a trained nurse. Period.

Corday's private life was a little better publicized. After all, the machine might want to run him for office sometime. He had made speeches before veterans' groups, he was a veteran himself. He had spoken to G.I. students' classes. He was married, and a very nice looking dish she was, to be sure.

He was also divorced, and this was the tiniest of clippings. He had been the plaintiff, and the divorce had been granted and that was about all. Mrs. Corday was a resident of Kansas City, and had not come home to contest the divorce.

It was not local newspaper policy to make much capital out of the marital troubles of people like Corday...

Not very long ago, either, about four months.

Harry Weber went to the employees' lunchroom for his coffee this time. Eliminating Mrs. Latson as a love interest, what did he have?

Harry Weber slowly came to the conclusion that he had nothing at all except three unrelated facts: (1) Dave Corday was glad Captain Martin was going to the sticks; (2) Dave Corday had not felt well that morning; (3) Dave Corday had written a letter to the wife of a political associate.

It was all Dave Corday. He needed something more.

There was no use going after Jim Latson. He was too smart; and anyway, he scared Harry Weber. No use sticking the only nose you have into a highly efficient food chopper; the results are predictable.

That left Captain Martin.

Police Headquarters looked much as usual. Chief Latson was lounging on the stairs, cutting up touches with some uniformed sergeants from Traffic; plainclothesmen were coming and going; the usual hangers-on looked their usual genial selves.

Outside the head of Homicide's office, the patrolman, Jake, was cleaning out his desk. Harry said, "Oh? Going with the captain?"

"It's a break for me," Jake said. "I live out in the Gardens. For the skipper, it's a long trip from home."

"I should think he could have any precinct he wanted."

"Y'know, he don't always take me into his confidence," Jake said. "G'wan in."

But Captain Martin wasn't alone. A small man was kneeling at his feet, chalk in one hand, tape measure in the other, pins in his mouth. Captain Martin was wearing blue serge trousers, unfinished at the bottom, and a blue serge coat, pinned together where the brass buttons would go.

Harry said, "Back into harness."

Captain Martin said, "Sure."

The little man stood up, took the pins out of his mouth, and started putting them in his lapel, one at a time. "That will do it," he said. "Like the paper on the wall, Benjy."

Harry Weber was startled. He had never heard anyone call Captain Martin Ben, much less Benjy. He wondered if anybody had ever called ex-President Hoover Herby. It seemed as probable.

The little man turned to Harry. "You are in the police, too?"

"No. Newspaperman. *News-Journal.*"

"My concern dresses your publisher. Of course, that I don't do myself. I have young men for those fittings. But this young man, here; I made his wedding garment."

Harry had a wild vision of Captain Martin in white lace and tulle. But actually the captain was now in shorts and shirt, changing back to his own trousers. "I've known Mr. Coffman here since I was a patrolman."

Mr. Coffman said, "More than twenty-five years ago. I had a little shop. Alterations, and French weaving. My wife did that, God rest her soul. That nobody should have to do French weaving: what it does to the eyes. You want to hear a story, young man? Such a story as you do not read in the newspapers?"

Captain Martin zipped up his pants, reached for his suit coat, "Now, Mr. Coffman."

"It doesn't hurt. Young men should know such things, in these times; it is good for them. We were trying hard to get ahead, my wife and I. Till nine o'clock at the store, ten o'clock, who counts when there is money to be made? Now I have the most expensive tailoring establishment in the city, but the price was my wife's eyes, they were never good after we got rich; and my stomach, I wouldn't wish it on anybody."

Captain Martin said, "Mr. Coffman, Harry Weber here's a busy man. He hasn't time for all this."

"Time," Mr. Coffman said. "Who has time in these times? Your publisher, now, he buys maybe one suit a year from us, three hundred dollars; the rest of the time he is happy in something ready-made. So I was telling you, we worked hard, and we had a son. You know—mama's got an English flannel to mend, papa must cut this suit down two sizes, go home, a glass of milk from the icebox, a peanut butter sandwich. You understand?"

Harry Weber said, "I think so."

"And is it any surprise a boy gets into trouble, both old people at the store till all hours? And this young man, this Benjy Martin was the cop on the beat. So one night we come home from the store, and there is Jules, our Jules."

Jules Coffman, Harry thought. Jules Coffman? He was the president of the municipal chamber of commerce. He was honorary chairman of half the charity funds in town. He was this little man's son.

"He had a black eye," Mr. Coffman said. "Such a black eye you never saw. And such screaming as his mama let out, that you never heard, either." He chuckled. "A mama with one chick, she can yell. So finally he tells us who does this awful thing. The cop of the beat, Patrolman Martin."

Captain Martin was suddenly laughing. He sounded like he wasn't used to it. "She wanted Mr. Coffman to beat me up."

Mr. Coffman laughed, too, an elflike figure against Captain Martin's bulk. He was folding the blue uniform, putting it away in an imported leather valise. "That would have hurt you, Benjy. That would really have caused you pain.... And then Jules tells us. He and another boy, they tried to hold up a cigar store. They were caught; they were in jail. And this Benjy, the big bum, he paid some damages out of his own pocket, he talked to the cigar store man, got him to drop charges, he talked to the district attorney—"

"The tenth assistant," Captain Martin said. "Even so, that was big talking for a uniformed patrolman."

"—and he got our Jules out of that place, took him up an alley, and such a beating he gave him, Jules's nose isn't too straight now." He snapped the valise shut, stood up, carrying it; one of the smallest men Harry had ever talked to. "So I said, Benjy, I said, so long as you are a cop, no one else will make your uniforms."

He shifted the valise to his left hand, held out the right to Harry Weber. "A pleasure, Mr. Weber. Such stories your paper should print, but I should live so long."

He went out and Harry heard Jake offering to carry the valise for him.

Harry Weber said, "Been a long time since you needed a uniform."

"Eight years," Captain Martin said. "Mr. Coffman looked it up. Eight years."

"With a friend like Jules Coffman, you don't have to take a precinct in the sticks. He draws water in this town."

"It's my own idea. No decent home life in this job. No decent meals."

"It's an idea," Harry Weber said, "that you got awful sudden."

"When a tire blows, it doesn't talk about it in advance. All of a sudden, my health was not so good. I've given this department enough; I'm not going to be one of these retired cops who has to walk slowly around the block once a day, and sit in the sun the rest of the time."

Harry Weber nodded as though Captain Martin had said a profound and weighty thing. "You look fine," Harry Weber said. "And I'll tell you who else looks fine, too. Dave Corday. He started looking fine as soon as he heard you were being transferred."

Captain Martin said, "Good."

"What did you have on him?" Harry asked. "Before that, he looked like he was about to take the fatal hemlock."

Captain Martin said, "Come out and see me at the Gardens. I'll get you a pass at the Zoo."

"Admission's free," Harry said.

Captain Martin said, "Not on Tuesdays. Tuesdays it's two bits to get in."

Harry Weber said, "Do we have to talk like this? We sound like two Noel Coward characters from the wrong side of the tracks."

"You came to see me," Captain Martin said. "I didn't send for you."

"What was wrong with Corday that got better when he heard you were out of Homicide?"

"Ask his doctor," Captain Martin said. "Or his dentist. Or his psychiatrist. You might even try asking him."

Harry Weber let his voice out a notch. "You're mighty cute today. I never saw that in you before."

"I'm a lovable old man. Come out to the Eleventh Precinct and watch me be lovable. I'll give you an interview every groundhog day."

"It's a long time since I've been groundhog editor," Harry said. "And your man Jake out there seems to think the move'll be hard on you. Other end of town from your house."

Captain Martin smiled at him.

Harry Weber said, "You can't push the *News-Journal* around this way." The Captain's smile got a little broader.

"Cute," Harry said. "I never thought I'd see the day. Well, let me guess: you had something on Corday, and when you tried to use it, they threw you out of Headquarters, put you out to grass. Right?"

The smile got wider.

"At least you haven't said it was wrong. Let's see. You're Homicide, or were, but Dave Corday hasn't got guts enough to commit a homicide, so it isn't that. Whom did he take a bribe from?"

"Don't end sentences with prepositions," the Captain told him.

Jake looked startled when Harry Weber slammed the office door.

CHAPTER 21

It was quiet weekend. There was a downtown fire just as the big movie houses let out, and Traffic Two had a little trouble keeping a boulevard open for the fire department.

Homicide had a gas call, which Captain Martin let one of his sergeants handle; it turned out to be unmistakable suicide.

Captain Martin and his pleasant brother-in-law, their wives in the back seat, drove around the Garden Precinct. They visited both the Zoo and Botanical Gardens, and Captain Martin began to think that he might enjoy his new life.

Ralph Guild worked as a counterman in a downtown cafeteria. The union had gotten him another job as a waiter, but he was deep in the hole from the loss of time in jail, and planned to work two shifts to get out of it. He had had to borrow to pay a bailsman, too.

Dave Corday tried one of the new tranquilizing pills, and found it more of a help than a cure. But, he assured himself, they weren't habit-forming. If he wanted to go in for barbiturates, he could be as steady-nerved as— He broke the thought and washed down another tranquilizer with a highball.

He fell into a shallow sleep from which terrifying nightmares woke him several times during the night. But he never could remember what the dream had been about...

Jim Latson had a social obligation to perform Saturday night. The capital city chief of police was visiting him; and if there was one thing Jim understood, it was what a visiting chief of police expected in the way of entertainment.

He rented an apartment on the roof of the Belmont, filled it with schnitzels and liquor and food, and he and the visiting chief and a few choice and durable cronies had at it.

Everybody had a wonderful time—except the host. Suddenly, at two in the morning, Jim Latson lost his taste for endless highballs, and for the inevitable flattery of any of the call girls he deigned to notice. He had never before wondered what they really thought of him. It didn't matter; they were paid, weren't they?

But now—I'm over fifty, he told himself. I'm still thin to my friends, but I'm probably just scrawny to these chicks, these schnitzels, these whores.

His mind twisted down into a mood of black, furious despair. Silently he called the girls he had hired all the synonyms for prostitute he had ever heard; called the men every variety of mug he knew.

It didn't do any good.

He had never kidded himself; there was no percentage in starting now. It was himself he hated, not his associates. He was not acting his age, and he despised himself for it.

He could hardly leave a party where he was host, but tomorrow night, he'd stay in his apartment, read a book, and look at television.

Jim Latson remembered that he had to write to the Hotel Plaza in New York for his bank books. He'd do that tomorrow night.

One of the girls settled on his bony knees, and, absentmindedly, he began removing her clothes, hardly hearing her giggles. Too bad he had had to remove Marty. Fink could be handled, but he would need help if anything very complicated came up in Homicide. Unsolved murders did nobody any good.

His hands became aware, then, of what he was doing to the girl, and hot blood flooded his neck, interest rose in him, fast. "What's your name, darling?" he asked.

She said that it was Carolle. She spelled it for him.

CHAPTER 22

The weekend passed. Monday passed, and Tuesday and Wednesday. Ralph Guild continued to work two shifts, coming home almost too tired to admire the new baby.

Jim Latson continued to run the police department.

Dave Corday attended daily conferences with the D.A. and Frederick Van Lear, helping pass the control over.

Planes flew the Atlantic and carried mail.

Captain Martin took over the Gardens Precinct, No. 11, and had lunch with the director of the Zoological Park, the curator of the Botanical Gardens. They seemed delighted at having such an intelligent police officer to work with, and each of them lent him books on zoos and garden parks. He began to wonder if he hadn't been a fool not to get a job like this a long time ago.

On Thursday morning, Jim Latson's secretary put a small stack of mail on his desk. It was so small that he could not long avoid opening the letter with the Italian stamp. He unfolded the flimsy *Par Avion* paper, expecting the usual report on the Pope's health and the usual request for money.

But this was a little different. This was kind of final. This was the request for a divorce.

"I have consulted a Vatican lawyer and—"

He didn't want to read any more. This could be the end, this could be the sort of trouble that couldn't be handled.... The end of political pull, the end of power, but not the end of his life.

Automatically, he unlocked the drawer where he kept his bank books. But they weren't there, of course; he'd mailed them to a cover name in New York.

It didn't worry him that they weren't there, though he would have liked to know how much money he could count on if all his sources of revenue were suddenly cut off.

But it did worry him that he had expected them to be in their usual place; that he had forgotten something as important as that. He flipped his squawk-box and said, "I'm going home for a while..."

During the day the front door of Jim Latson's apartment house was kept open, and a clerk sat at the desk. At night they locked the front door, and there was a night watchman who prowled the lobby, the basement garage, and the halls. If you forgot your key, you had to ring for him.

But this was day, and the desk clerk was on duty. He stood up straight as Chief Latson approached him, and said, "There's a man to see you, Chief!" He was twenty-two and would have liked an appointment to the police department, but could not pass the physical.

Jim Latson turned slowly, and stared at the man rising from the straight-backed Spanish chair and ambling toward him. In the years since he had left the house he had bought for his wife, nobody had ever come to his apartment without an invitation.

So this was a new thing to him, but no more alarming than any of the other new things he'd met in all his years; neither was it stimulating. New things were much like old things to Jim Latson.

The man was a complete stranger; there was not the slightest twinge of memory as his face came into full light. "I'm James Latson. You were waiting for me?"

"Yes, Mr. Latson. I've got a matter to discuss with you."

"Come on to my office tomorrow. I work for the police department." This was sarcasm. But the man neither flinched nor smiled. "It's a private matter, Mr. Latson. I'd better see you in your apartment."

"Mister, anything you've got to say to me—"

The stranger was staring at Eddie, the day clerk. Then he turned his head slowly and looked straight at Jim Latson. Even more slowly the lid of the stranger's right eye came down and rested; then it raised again. He had, Latson realized, extraordinarily large eyes, a small nose, a tight mouth, a weak chin.

Jim Latson said, "Let's get upstairs. I'll give you five minutes."

The man bowed. He didn't just nod his head, which is what most Americans think of when they think of bowing; he bowed from the waist, in the European fashion.

Latson pushed past him and into the elevator. He pressed the button to close the door, and his visitor just managed to push past the sliding gate.

The car went up to Latson's floor, stopped, the doors started opening by themselves. Latson pointed with his chin for the stranger to get out first, but the man gave him a queer, confident smile, and Latson shrugged and went ahead of him, fishing the apartment key out as he did so.

He opened the door, started in; he could almost feel the other man's breath on his neck.

Then Jim Latson stopped abruptly, turned, brought his shoulder up under the stranger's chin, caught the man's wrists and jerked.

The stranger was caught up sharply, his Adam's apple banging into Jim Latson's shoulder, his head snapping back.

Latson shoved the door closed, brought the stranger around in front of him and slapped his face, hard, with each hand.

The man went backward, out of the little hall into the living room. Jim Latson kept after him, jabbing him in the wind with stiff fingers, rapping his belly with hard knuckles, cutting at the bridge of his nose with the edge of a hand.

The man got to a chair, collapsed in it, sobbing for breath. Blood was running from both nostrils.

Jim Latson tore at the heavy cloth of the stranger's blue serge suit till he had the man's wallet. Then he went into the bathroom, got a hotel towel, and threw it hard into the bleeding face. "Keep your dirty blood off my furniture."

There was silence then, as the man mopped at his nose, finally got his breath back. Latson thumbed through the wallet, grunting once or twice, then threw it into the blue serge lap, and went into the kitchenette. He returned with a highball in his hand. He didn't offer one to his visitor, nor a cigarette; just lit up for himself, and sat in the best chair, crossing his legs, sipping at the highball, puffing on his cigarette. Finally he said, "All right. Your name is Neal Harrison, you're from Chicago and you're licensed in a half dozen states to be a private detective. Any part of that give you the idea you can force me into letting you in my apartment? Anything in your past experience give you the idea you can wink at an executive police officer and not get a bloody nose?"

Harrison had pulled himself together a good deal. The bloody towel lay on the floor next to him; his hands were square on his knees, and his face was composed. A shadow under one eye indicated he might well have a black eye by tomorrow. "All right," he said. "You've had your fun, Chief. I came here to do you a favor, and I get a beating. So all right. Now I don't do you the favor. Now I'm getting out of here."

Latson laughed. "Just like that?"

There was a remarkable amount of calm self-confidence in Harrison's voice. "Just like that, Chief. Guys know I came up here; if I don't come back, they'll know who to tell. So now, good-by."

Jim Latson said, "Twenty-five years a cop. I'm the top of the heap in this town."

Harrison told him what it was a heap of. Jim Latson started forward, and then stopped. He said, "I'm fascinated, little man. A two-bit private detective! You've been around. You know what I can do to you, and not a mark on you that you could show anybody. A double hernia, a rib in your lung, a ruptured kidney. You want all those things?"

Harrison said calmly, "Sure, I been around. So have you, Chief. You know I got the cards or I wouldn't be here."

"Play 'em."

"No, sir," Harrison said. "No, sir. I came here to do you a favor. It woulda cost you some money. Sure. You think I want to work all my life? But money, you got plenty of it. You got a bank account in New York, in the Union Bank, you got one in Chicago, in—"

Jim Latson sat quietly, his cigarette smoking in his fingers, his highball warming in his palm, while Harrison recited a list of Jim Latson's bank accounts. When he finished, Harrison added, still in a monotone, "Want to know the amounts? In New York you got—"

"Let it go," Latson said. "How much?"

Harrison shook his head. "I'm being a sucker," he said. "Noses heal, a black eye turns white again. Money, it sticks to your ribs, but I'm being a sucker; I'm going to see you where you sent so many guys. In the

State Pen."

He stood up, moved to the door. His hat had never come off in all the trouble.

Latson said, "You're a good man. The district attorney's office needs one. He doesn't have to come from the police ranks."

Harrison was nearly to the door. "District attorney's office? I don't need you to get in there. It was your pal, the assistant D.A. that tipped Mrs. Latson off." He gave his foreign bow again—it was obvious now that he used it for the mockery that sustained his meager soul—and started for the door.

"Wait a minute," Jim Latson said. "You're working for my wife."

"Right the first time," Harrison said. "Twenty-five years a cop, and he figures things out fast. Sure. I'm to get divorce evidence. She's got a list of your dames; your friend Corday sent it to her in Rome. I hear around town he's about your best friend—and I'm not surprised. By, now."

Latson said sharply, "Drop the cheap patter. We can do business. I just want to get everything straight. Corday sent her a list of the women I've been seeing."

"That's a nice word for it—seeing."

"It smells like Corday," Jim Latson said. "Sneaking to my wife. But how come the checkbooks?"

"You are not very fast," Harrison said. "Not very sharp. A list—what's that? She needs evidence. She sends us—my agency—the list. They give it to me. They say, watch this jerk. What they say do, I do. And I am watching when you write the Hotel Plaza in New York."

"Robbing the mails," Jim Latson said. "A federal squeal."

"You're not likely to turn it in," Neal Harrison said.

"Those books go to the opposition politically, or they go to a newspaper, or even to your own party—and you're through. You are eating in a prison mess hall. And don't say squeal, Chief. Say case. Squeal is language for gutter types like me. Lowdown private detectives without social standing."

Latson went ahead of him, put his thin, high shoulders against the door. "All right. The bank books are no good without my signature. How much do you want, and I'll write a check on any bank you name—and you are the little man who can name them."

Harrison said. "Little, but I got my pride. Isn't it a funny thing, I didn't know it? But I'm sore now, and likely to stay so. The evidence on your dames goes to Mrs. Latson. But the other—I ought to send it to her, too. It would raise her alimony, wouldn't it, and she'd like that, she could give it to the church, and my grandma was a Catholic, I think."

"Stop clowning."

"Little guys always clown. It saves their dignity. Out of my way, Chief." He walked to the door, put his hand on it. "But I'm not going to send the dope on your bank accounts to your wife, 'cause she wouldn't know what to do with it. I'm sending it to the opposition. Your party'll have to ditch you or lose the next election. You're through, Chief."

Jim Latson began to laugh. The deep creases of his face got deeper. "You've overplayed, small fry. I think you're lying."

This was so astounding that it turned Neal Harrison around, the doorknob forgotten. "Lying? Mister, I didn't make up that list of banks. I couldn't."

Jim Latson felt genuine amusement coming up in him. It was going to be all right. He had never had more trouble in one day than he could handle in that day. He said, "Not lying about the list. You intercepted the letter all right. But you are lying about— Let's see what you said—guys knowing you came here. You never told a soul. Cheap chiselers don't."

He stood there, chuckling, and moved forward, his hands swinging at his sides, enjoying the fear that grew in Neal Harrison's eyes. "You don't matter, chiseler. Corday doesn't matter. It's the second time he's tried to get me, and he can have three tries for his dime. You can't touch me, any of you."

He caught the front of Harrison's cheap coat, as he had before, but this time he lifted him off his feet. "You haven't got a gun, and you think that saves your life. But I've got a half dozen pistols in my bedroom, and none of them registered. I plant one on you, and you're a dirty-necked holdup man. Eddie downstairs'll believe what I tell him. I'm his hero."

Neal Harrison gasped. "I told guys. I—if I don't come back I—"

"What guys?"

The thin, slack mouth said nothing.

"You're not even a good liar."

He hit Harrison then, hit him in the belly hard, with a clenched fist. "Give me that list! All my life a cop, and every blackmailer I ever heard of said the papers were some place safe, said people knew where they were going." His fist beat punctuation to the speech. "And they lied! They lied!"

Then he had to let go. Neal Harrison had passed out.

Jim Latson let the little man fall to the carpet, forgetting his worry about bloodstains. He went and mixed himself another highball, and waited. Time was on his side; it always had been. After a while, Mr. Harrison would come to.

And then he would talk. And those bank books would turn up. They would not go to any politician or to any newspaper; Neal Harrison would talk and they would go right back to Jim Latson, where they belonged.

Maybe he would have to resign from office because of the divorce. But he would resign with his money intact and without a trial, and certainly without a prison sentence.

Having sized up the situation, Jim Latson waited. He waited because there was nothing else to do; and he never tried the impossible.

CHAPTER 23

When the edition had rolled, the city editor of the *News-Journal* turned his desk over to the day city editor, and strolled over to Harry Weber's desk. He said, "Let's go see the boss."

Harry had been expanding feature stories for the Sunday paper; he was glad to stop. He followed the city editor down to the rich end of the room, and passed a secretary into the managing editor's plush office.

Ward Candle, the managing editor, was thin, black-haired, very well dressed. He said Harry's name at once, a good boss, and waved them to seats.

"Still hot on that Corday hunch, Harry?" On his desk wat a folder containing the morgue clippings Harry had dug up on Corday and Latson and Captain Martin.

"I'm still convinced Cap Martin got something on Corday and got bounced out to the sticks for it," Harry said. "I am not at all convinced that I am good enough to dig it up. I tried."

"I can add a little something," Ward Candle said. "Corday's wife committed suicide in Kansas City a few weeks ago. Mean anything to you?"

Harry Weber frowned. "Suicide is death and so is homicide. Which could bring Captain Martin in. Where was Corday when it happened?"

Candle laughed. "I thought of that. We put a couple of legmen on it. They place him in a movie—here—that night."

Harry Weber said, "Too bad."

Ward Candle lit a cigarette, smiling. "The good reporter does his work without heat, without personal prejudice... Frankly, the publisher would like to see Corday out of office. But more particularly, he'd like to see Latson out. I want you to get on it, Harry."

Harry Weber said, "Yes, sir."

"It seems obvious that Latson is involved. That letter from Corday to Latson's wife; I happen to know that they don't know each other socially, she doesn't attend political parties, Corday has never been on the guest list, of any of the plush charity affairs she does give."

The city editor said, "It would look like Corday was sending money out of the country. His pal Latson's wife could be banking it for him abroad."

Ward Candle said, "That wouldn't be honest money."

Harry Weber said, "No, sir."

Ward Candle said, "Don't jump at conclusions. All we've really got is your impression that Dave Corday was scared, and got over it when he found out that Martin was out of Homicide."

Harry said, "Which leaves the Italian letter out in left field."

Ward Candle said, "Maybe he thought he was about to go into the soup over the homicide matter—if it was homicide—and sent extra money away quick to take care of him if he had to run."

Harry said, "A man doesn't have to be in Kansas City to kill someone there. Not a man whose work has brought him into contact with paid killers."

Ward Candle's voice got sharp. "This is exactly the sort of conclusion I don't want you jumping to. Get on it, but move carefully. We don't want a libel suit. If we don't get Corday—and Latson, particularly Latson— we want to keep our in with them for stories."

"I'll start with Corday."

Ward Candle laughed. "You're smart. I've always thought Dave Corday was nothing much more than a highly educated dog. But Jim Latson's a hell of a big lion to find in your den."

"My name isn't Daniel, but I feel like him." Harry Weber stood up.

Ward Candle said, "I hope this works. If they hadn't transferred Captain Martin, maybe we wouldn't be bothering. He was the biggest asset Police Headquarters had."

CHAPTER 24

Jim Latson said, "I wish you'd stay with me awhile."

Neal Harrison looked up at the tall cop, and giggled foolishly. His eyes were rolled back in his head and slobber had run down his chin, bloody slobber that stained his shirt. The peculiarly disagreeable odor of the cold sweat of fear pervaded the room.

Jim Latson swore calmly and went and got a jigger glass full of whisky. He wore an expression of extreme distaste as he held Harrison's head up, forced the whisky down his throat. Jim Latson just jumped back in time to keep the liquor from spewing over him.

But some of it had stuck in Harrison. Slowly his eyes rolled down, his lips started moving; he swallowed a couple of times and even coughed.

"All right," Latson said. "You can hear me now. What I've done so far is first-grade stuff, kindergarten. Now, you talk or we go into high school."

Neal Harrison put both hands up, grabbed at Latson's wrist. Latson let him hold it, thinking the man wanted to be helped up to a seat. But after he'd gotten to his feet, lowered himself down into Jim Latson's best chair, Harrison hung onto the wrist.

Latson finally made out that the private detective wanted to look at Latson's wrist watch. He let him. Harrison let out a weird noise, halfway between a moan and a chuckle.

Jim Latson said, "All right. Talk, man, talk up."

"Too late," Harrison said. His breath was ragged. "Too late. Used your own—trick. Western Union boy... If he couldn't deliver the—papers—to me, hotel room, take 'em back to sender."

"Sender?" Jim Latson put a harsh into his voice, sank his fingers into Harrison's shoulder. "You were the sender."

"Didn't tell 'im that," Neal Harrison said. From somewhere he got some strength and for a moment his voice was very clear. "Told him I was Dave Corday, to bring the envelope back to me at my office. I was lying. Stalling for time. Never meant to send 'em any place but to Corday. He hates you the most." He giggled, weirdly.

And then he pitched forward, out of the chair, onto Jim Latson's smooth gray carpet, his wall-to-wall carpeting that the apartment house had been so glad to put in for the deputy chief of police. His blood and his saliva stained Jim Latson's carpet, slightly at first, and then much more freely, because Jim Latson had pulled back his foot and kicked Neal Harrison in the ribs.

Then Jim Latson stood, rubbing his right hand gently through his close-cropped hair. Harrison could still be lying. But the papers weren't on him, and—

Jim Latson said aloud, "When I work 'em over, they don't hold out on me." Then he laughed. Harrison had built up a big scene. He had been going to tell Jim Latson that he, Harrison, was inviolate, because if he wasn't handled at once and with money, Latson's enemy, Corday, would have the evidence to send Jim Latson a long, long way away.

Only trouble was, Jim Latson had hit the little man before he could get the scene built up.

Jim Latson stood there, staring down at his good right fist. It had been his best friend, and in the end it had betrayed him.

He laughed again; laughed at himself, Jim Latson, getting fancy thoughts like that. Still laughing, he looked down at Neal Harrison and said, "Little man, you haven't scratched me. If there's one thing I'm not scared of, it's Dave Corday."

Then he was busy, tying Neal Harrison's hands and ankles with towels, shoving another towel into his mouth, binding it expertly so the man wouldn't choke.

"I'll be back," he said. "Until then, you figure out what I can do with you. If you come up with a real good scheme, I might buy it."

CHAPTER 25

Harry Weber said, "Is the big man in, Alice?"

The girl smiled. "We're certainly seeing a lot of you these days, Harry." She reached out, thumbed the squawk-box, said Harry's name. Corday's voice saying, "All right, all right," was weak and irritated.

Alice winked, and turned off the box. "Temper, temper."

The last time Harry Weber had seen Dave Corday, the district attorney had been jubilant; before that, he had been distraught to the point of collapse; now he seemed to be in a glowering rage that didn't seem to be able to get off the ground; instead of making him terrifying, it only underlined his pettiness.

He greeted Harry with: "What is it now? What?"

Harry said, "A couple of questions, is all."

"More about Guild?" Dave Corday cleared his throat. "Frankly, I haven't done any more on that case. More important things."

"Don't know if it's about Guild or not. Well, a legal question. If a case—say murder—runs into two states, does it become a federal case?"

Dave Corday slapped the top of his desk. "Oh, really, now. Hypothetical questions? Doesn't your paper have a lawyer you can bother with things like that?"

"Oh, I'd just like your opinion. The states involved are this one and Missouri—Kansas City."

It was a shot in the dark; this was a fishing expedition. The shot missed. Dave Corday said brusquely, "Well, if a body is taken over a state line, I suppose the federal attorney might have an interest. If a person is taken over a state line alive and then killed, there is a kidnaping charge under the Lindbergh Law; but since murder is the greater charge, the kidnaping would probably never be filed... In practice, such matters remain with the states."

Nothing had happened that time except the fish had eaten the bait off the hook. But it was apparent that, having gone this far, Harry Weber had to keep on driving. If he didn't, Corday would simply sit still and the interview would be over.

"I was over in Kansas City yesterday," Harry said. "On a story. The funniest thing, I thought I saw Captain Martin over there. What in the world would take him to Kansas City I can't imagine. I must have been mistaken."

Dave Corday looked at him. "You're babbling, Weber," he said. "Whatever is the matter?" He stood up, came around the desk, stared down at Harry Weber. "Did you come here to confess something? Are you involved in some crime you want to tell this office about?"

Anyone else could be bluffing. But not Dave Corday. He didn't have the strength, the guts, to carry on a protracted bluff like this.

Harry Weber said something unintelligible; he wasn't sure what it was himself.

Corday said, "I don't understand you," and then turned sharp...his voice rising to a peevish snarl. "Alice, I have told you—"

But the girl stood her ground in the open door. "Something most peculiar has happened, Mr. Corday. And this boy insists on your signature in person."

She stood aside then, and a kid in a messenger boy's uniform came in, holding out a letter. "I was to try an' deliver this till four o'clock," he said, "and then bring it here. The guy give me ten bucks; I don't want him complaining to the manager he didn't get what he paid for."

Dave Corday said, "Let's see that thing."

He took the envelope from the boy, read the address. "Neal Harrison, Esquire, Mandan Hotel. That's not my name, boy."

"In the corner. For return-like."

Dave Corday looked. He said, "Yes, I see."

"Ya sign here."

Dave Corday signed. As he did so, he said, "I hate mysteries," and took the envelope. The boy waited a minute, perhaps for a tip, and then scooted. Alice went after him, and shut herself out.

Harry Weber said, "Aren't you going to open it?"

Dave Corday held the envelope up to the light, to see which end was safe to tear, and ripped the paper open in his deliberate, prissy way.

"Go on," Harry said. "Maybe your aunt died and left you a millionaire."

"I haven't any aunts," Corday said automatically, and started unfolding the letter.

Because he was Dave Corday, he did not glance at the contents until everything was unfolded, neatly. The bank books he stacked to one side on his desk blotter.

So Harry Weber saw the books first; and saw the name written on them. The whole thing was clear to him before Corday even started read in the letter from Neal Harrison.

Later he would wonder why. He wasn't particularly conceited about his quick-wittedness. And he didn't think, recalling all his conversations with Cap Martin that the captain had ever even hinted at the true story about Corday and Latson.

But when he saw those bank books—all different colors, all different banks—he grabbed one. And when he saw the name James Latson on the cover, he knew what the letter to Mrs. Latson had been—a letter conspiring to pull the props out from under Jim Latson.

A lot of little things fell into place, and he knew Corday was not Jim Latson's friend, but his bitter rival.

So he put his hand down hard on the bank books, to keep Corday from hiding them.

And just then Alice said, on the box, "Chief Latson is here—"

She never finished, because Jim Latson had already charged into the office.

CHAPTER 26

Most of the adjectives in the English language had been applied to Jim Latson at one time or another; the complimentary ones by boards of review and his political allies; the others by men he had sent up, cops he had broken, girls he had used and discarded, and by his political enemies.

But nobody had ever called him slow-witted. Long before Dave Corday had managed to stammer out Latson's name, the police chief had taken in the little tableau; the bank books on the desk, the letter on hotel stationery, and the newspaperman with his hand on the bank books.

"So you sold out, Corday."

But Dave Corday was done for, pulled apart, beaten and ruined. His white face told Jim Latson that, his un-lawyerlike, meaningless gabble, his shaking hands.

"Spilled your guts to the newspapers, didn't you?" Jim Latson could feel the anger growing in him; and after all these years of caution and craft and deep thought, it felt good to him to let go, to let anger take over from his brain.

"Did he tell you he killed the DeLisle girl, Weber?" Jim Latson asked. "Killed her and tried to frame me for it?"

Harry Weber was saying, "Good Lord," or something like that. But Jim Latson was not worrying about Harry Weber. He said, "Cap Martin has the dope, Weber. He'll send Corday up for you. He would have before, but I had to protect that sniveling—" He couldn't think of a noun for Corday, and anyway it didn't matter; the time for talking was over.

Days of practice paid off one at a time, and his draw was a classic for all rookie policemen to study; smooth and fast and on the target a split second after his hand started for his holster.

Harry Weber was jumping back, as though the noise could hurt him, and Dave. Corday was going down on the desk, a mess.

"He isn't dead," Jim Latson said. "I gut-shot him. He'll die in about ten minutes. I'm taking a powder, Harry. Tell your paper, tell the mayor, tell the FBI. I'm betting I'm smart enough to get away with it, too."

Harry Weber said, "The South Seas? Hong Kong? They'll find you, Jim."

"No one ever told you that you could use my first name," Latson said, and turned away, for the door. His mind was already ahead of him; it was getting him past the girl in the outer office, past the people who must have heard the shot, getting him down to the street and—

And then Dave Corday shot him in the back with the pistol from his desk drawer.

Harry Weber grabbed the red phone. He yelled into it, "Get an ambulance crew to Dave Corday's office, on the double."

He heard the police operator answering, and slammed that phone down and grabbed the other one, dialed the *News-Journal*, asked for the desk, gave his name out, and gave them a masterful one-sentence summary: "Jim Latson and Dave Corday just shot each other. They are dying before my eyes."

They got him a rewrite man, fast, and he started dictating an eyewitness account. Over at the office it would be like a movie; they would really be stopping the presses, something he'd never seen done; they, would be re-plating fast, and calling in all the trucks, they would be dispatching reporters to Latson's apartment, his office—

He said, "Hold it. Latson's trying to say something."

Jim Latson had been knocked down by the force of the bullet. But he twisted around, he got a little off the floor. He said, "I didn't think he had it in him. I didn't think so. And you know something? He couldn't have done it if I'd kept my eye on him. He shot Hogan DeLisle; but he never had the guts to put a slug in me, not while I was watching him."

Harry said, "Ambulance on the way, Chief."

"A hell of a chief. Wasn't even man enough to keep watching a louse like Corday. He dead yet?"

"Going fast," Harry said.

"So am I," Chief Latson said, and fell back to the floor.

Harry said, "All right take this: Before he died, Jim Latson said—"

He was still talking when the ambulance men came in, past a screaming Alice; but it was too late for Dave Corday. And for Jim Latson.

CHAPTER 27

Deputy Chief of Police (Acting) B. L. Martin came out of the grand jury room to face a mess of reporters. He stood calmly, one hand raised, waiting for silence. He had chosen to wear his new uniform, with stars instead of tracks, to the hearing, and he was amused at himself for it. Vanity, he thought. At age fifty, I get tracked down by vanity.

He said, "Nothing happened. You can't indict dead men. I've been ordered to clean up Headquarters. See Mr. Van Lear."

Frederick Van Lear had been masterful, he thought, conducting the hearing. Frederick Van Lear would be elected governor in all probability, and what did he want it for?

One of the reporters said, "Has your appointment been made permanent?"

Chief Martin frowned. He had been offered Jim Latson's job on a permanent basis; it meant more money, and he ought to take it.

But the Gardens had been so peaceful. A man could think out there.

And at Headquarters—the temptation was something terrible. The papers were full of denunciations of Latson and Corday. Phrases like "betrayal of great trust," and "perfidy in high places," and "shocking breakdown of leadership," were being used with frequency and unction.

But Chief Martin (acting) didn't see it that way. They shoved temptation at a man like Latson, and they paid him a cop's salary, and they asked him please not to bother the citizens with any troubles. Just run the department.

What did they expect?

And Corday, with his miserable G.I. years behind him, trying hard to make up for poverty and deprivation—and life in a Quonset hut—what did they expect of him?

And B. L. Martin wasn't much better. He'd taken it for years, from the Latsons and the Cordays, the politicos and their sponsors, the rich and the powerful. He had to admit it felt good to have all the strong ones running to him, saying, please, take over our police department, put it back on its feet.

He said, "Boys, I'll tell you. I'm too weak a man and too old a one to stand the gaff in the chief's office. Soon as things are running right again, I'm going back to the Gardens. Come see me when the first crocus blooms through the snow; I'll give you a statement on it."

THE END

The Late Mrs. Five

■ ■ ■ ■

Richard Wormser

CHAPTER 1

I had always thought of this part of the United States as flat, like Kansas, or maybe Indiana, but it wasn't. You came over ridges where the trees had cones, needles and grew in nicely-spaced rows, and then you went downhill and there were the hardwoods, the oaks and the maples and some others—maybe black walnuts—that I didn't know the names of. The leafy trees didn't grow as neatly as the evergreens, and the underbrush was thick amongst them, and little brooks ran to the road and under it in metal and stone culverts.

Then there was a valley, very green now in the spring, and some of the farms had wire fences and raised hogs, and others had whitewashed rail fences and raised horses and cows, but everybody raised corn; it was coming up bravely.

Everything was very fine looking. I felt wonderful. The car was new and it was mine, but the mileage was the company's; and, at the rate I was running it out, the company was going to pay for a year's depreciation in a couple of months.

Cutting across the valley, I came to a split in the road; not a crossroads, but one of those Federal highway splits: LOWNDESBURG BUSINESS, and LOWNDESBURG BYPASS. There was a rig of ours in Lowndesburg that had been unsold for quite a while; I had a card in my pocket from the boss about it.

So I chose business and headed into town.

It seemed like an all right little town, although, in the manner of the Middle West, they had cut down all the trees on the business streets.

Two banks, a small hotel, three movie houses, a big department store and a smaller, classier one; a Chinese restaurant and three non-Chinese ones.

On a street paralleling the main drag, but two blocks nearer the railroad tracks, I found what I was looking for: J. F. Gray's Feed & Seed Co. had one of our terracers in the window.

There was a girl in the front part of J. F. Gray's. Out back, I could see men working on the loading platforms and in the sheds; hay and seed and barbed wire and hog wire were selling that day.

When I asked for the boss, she just looked up from the bills she was posting and said, "Over in the jail, I think." I must have looked surprised.

She grinned. "You're not one of the regular salesmen who call on us, are you? Don't be surprised—Dad's also chief of police."

"Well, if you're part of the firm, maybe you can tell me what I want to know. I'm not a salesman; I'm a factory rep for that terracer you've got on display."

She nodded and stood up. I was surprised at her height—about five feet seven—because it was mostly in her legs. Sitting down she had seemed quite a short girl, and I don't like short girls particularly, maybe because I've had better luck with tall ones.

"I could tell you aren't a salesman," she said. "When I tell them Dad's the police department here, they always say something about having to watch their steps."

"Always?"

"Mostly. What do you want to know about the terracer?"

"Have you ever sold any of them? Do the owners like them? What objections have been made by people you've shown this one to?"

"I guess you'll have to talk to the boss, after all," she said. "I'm mostly the bookkeeper, telephone answerer and taker-of-orders. Offhand, though, I'd say you've got your machine in the wrong place. If a terracer does what I think it does, it's for hilly country. This is all flatland farming around here."

She had moved over to the big, swing-up window as she talked. Naturally, I followed her, and we stood there, looking unintelligently at the leveller. She tapped a natural-polished fingernail on one of her front teeth and said, "Tell me, why did you paint it blue?"

"Well, I'm working up to the paint department, but as I get it, the boss figured land-moving machinery's almost always red or yellow or orange. When people see one of ours, they remember it, and because it's doing a good job, we want them to remember it."

"Who isn't a salesman?" she said, and then turned. "Here's Dad now." The smile she gave me as she went away was polite, no more.

I fished a card out of my pocket and advanced on Dad. About fifty, short and broad, with that facial resemblance to Harry Truman you find so often in small towns. "Mr. Gray, I'm Paul Porter."

He grunted, took the card, read it, and said, "Well, all right, but I'm not Mr. Gray. He's my father-in-law. I'm Otto McLane."

"Sorry. Mr. McLane, your daughter tells me you've had trouble moving our terracer because the land's too flat around here. Now that's just where we have done the most good. Most flatland farmers own the hills behind them, but they don't farm them because—well, because they're flatland farmers. With a terracer, we can reproduce flat conditions on a hillside, and maybe add a third to the arable acreage of the valley-edge farms."

He was moving across the sales floor as we talked. His daughter had gone back to her desk and her books. He patted her sleek hair once in

passing, and said, "Any calls I ought to know about, Andy?"
She gave him her nice smile. "Not if Bill got you."

"Did. Gonna be a month late with his check. Told him it was fine. C'-
mon in my office, Mr. Porter. You interest me." The office was three half-
glass walls set up against the concrete block partition that backed on the
loading clock. We sat down in the proper chairs, fished out our cigarettes,
waggled them politely at each other, and then each lighted his own brand.

"Yep," he said. "You've got the picture wrong, but you interest me.
Here's where you're wrong: our customers don't own the hills behind
them. Here's where you interest me: the man who does own them is
named John Hilliard Five, and he's got all the money in the world. Maybe
you could sell him; I can't."

I asked what Mr. Five did with his land.

"His name isn't Five, it's Hilliard; he's the fifth of the name. And he rides
horses on it. His dad, John Four, used to hunt on it; he doesn't even do
that. Doesn't even bother to raise his own horse feed. Buys hay and grain
from me. About my biggest customer."

I started to say something when a frightful screaming drove the words
out of my mouth. But Mr. McLane calmly pulled a thin gold watch out
of his pocket and set it. "Air raid siren," he said. "Use it at noon for a
test."

Feeling slightly foolish, I played to recover. "May my expense account
take you to lunch?"

"Sure."

As we came out of the office, a boy was coming in from the loading
dock. Andy—what kind of a name was that for a girl with slant eyes and
long legs?—McLane got up, saying something like, "Right on time, Jim,"
and started poking at her hair with her fingertips.

"I'm taking your father to lunch, Miss McLane. Be nice if you could
join us."

There was no coquette in her. She nodded, said, "Give me two minutes," and went through a door behind which a flash of white porcelain
showed.

We made light conversation waiting for her. It was a pretty town. No,
he hadn't lived here all his life. Done thirty years on the police force in
the city.

"I wasn't coming here," he said. "Not my town, and my wife was gone,
two years before. But her father wrote me...he wanted to see Andy, and
he didn't have anybody to leave the business to. It added up."

"So, naturally, they made you police chief."

"Sure. Three hundred a year and some mileage. The force is a traffic
cop and a night marshal."

I said it must be a quiet town.

"It suits me," Mr. McLane said. "I guess."

There was a sort of awkward silence. I broke it by changing the subject. I said, "Funny name for a girl, Andy."

Her voice answered me. "It's Andrea."

"Not a usual name."

"Well, I'm used to it." She was between her father and me, walking to the front door. Fresh lipstick and a hair combing had not been necessary to make her attractive. She rested her fingertips in the crook of my elbow, the other hand was holding her father's arm, a little more tightly. "Dad been telling you how green we are in this business?"

"He's been telling me about Mr. Hilliard. We're going to try and sell him a terracer. Maybe some other stuff."

"John Five? He's got the money for it."

We were moving up the street together. Sometimes you like people right off. That was the way I felt about these two. They weren't stuffy and they liked each other in a father-and-daughter way that wouldn't have interested Freud for a minute.

And, of course, Andy was damned pretty.

"If it's all right with you," Otto McLane said, "we usually eat at the Chinaman's."

"Chinese restaurant, Dad," Andy said.

Otto McLane grunted. "Expect me to change all at once," he grumbled. "A Chink was a Chinaman when I was on the force. Now he's a customer, buys chicken feed from us, so I gotta call him a Chinese gentleman."

The business people of Lowndesburg were coming out of their places, going to lunch. The street was fairly busy. Quite a few people said "Hi, Mac," and about as many greeted Andy. Then Mac said, "Hello, Ralph," to a gaunt fellow, who didn't answer him.

At once Mac tried to swing back. Andy reached out, caught him firmly by the sleeve. "Mr. Polette didn't mean to cut you, Dad. He was just preoccupied."

Mac mumbled something about keeping a good deal of money in that fish-face's bank, but he let Andy lead him on. I had revised my estimate of their relationship. It seemed just as warm as ever, but almost a mother-child deal. Mac hadn't looked old enough to be in his second childhood, but I sensed a worry in Andy: a worry, and a wonderful patience.

As we passed the Lowndesburg National Bank a woman came out and started walking ahead of us.

What is there about a man? I had an extremely nice-looking, nice-talking lady on my arm. I had every chance of getting a date with her tonight, if I stayed over—I'd noticed, no rings—and if I didn't stay over, no Lowndesburg date was going to do me any good.

But here I was, watching the legs of the girl ahead of us with delight, admiring the view of nicely moving hips hugged by a white linen suit. I wanted to see her face... I speculated about her age.... What was it to me? But I looked anyway.

Andy noticed. She said: "*Quelle jambes*, eh, old boy? The shoes cost as much as everything I have on."

Just then the body on top of the costly white shoes turned left to head for a big Buick station wagon.

The bright pleasant day got too hot. The airy, wide street was a choking alley.

It was no wonder I'd admired those legs. I'd married them once.

They were the underpinnings of the only person in the world I really hated, my ex-wife. Edith Stayne Porter. Only that wouldn't be her name now. She'd taken me for a lot, but not for the price of Buicks like that station wagon. Apparently Edith had found herself another sucker.

CHAPTER 2

Somebody had stopped us, was talking to Mac and Andy about something—I don't know what—and I just stood there and watched that big Buick get driven away by its very expensive driver. There'd been no chance to ask who she was, and I probably wouldn't have anyway. If she hadn't been interrupted, Andy probably would have mentioned the name, small-town fashion.

By the time we had given our order in the Chinese restaurant, I was back in shape again. Mac was asking Andy if she knew whether John Five was in town.

Andy said, "Henry Lighton and Mrs. John Five were dancing at the hotel last night. They said John Five had gone up to the city to look at a horse or something. He ought to be back late this afternoon... Henry's the lawyer for the Hilliard estate, Mr. Porter."

I said: "Paul."

"Well, Paul, then. Are you all right? You look a little green."

"Oh, I get tired of being the same color all the time."

I didn't feel like telling an attractive girl that I'd just gotten a shock from seeing my ex-wife. I couldn't talk about Edith without sounding bitter and reproachful, and a girl hearing me could hardly help but wonder what the other side of the story would be. It's a rare marriage that breaks up without there being two sides to the story; I honestly believe ours was the exception.

Mac was saying that he appreciated my staying over, since I couldn't see John Five until late, maybe not till tomorrow. I asked him if there were any other items of our manufacture in the neighborhood, and he said that he hadn't sold any, but maybe the dealer up in the city had, and why didn't I call, and we got into a business discussion.

Andy joined in from time to time—she knew a lot more about the business than she had admitted—and the waitress brought us some very good food. Gradually the nasty feeling I'd gotten from seeing Edith wore off, and I began enjoying myself.

After lunch we went back to the feed-and-seed store, and I phoned the dealer who'd put the terracer in Mac's window. The dealer gave me the names of three farmers around there who'd bought machinery from us, and then he invited me to stay with him and his family if I came through the city. I'd entertained him last time he'd visited the factory, three years ago.

He said, "Your wife with you, Paul?"

"We're divorced," I said. "I'm a bachelor these days."

While he made the usual awkward remarks, I looked up, and Andy was looking at me. Another girl would have jerked her eyes away; she just smiled.

Later, she got out a county map and showed me where the three customer-farms were, and I asked her if she'd have dinner with me that night.

She said at once, "I'd love to. We can get a reasonable meal at the hotel and there's dancing."

"I'll call for you about seven."

"Here." She put a check mark on the map, wrote an address on the margin. "The mailbox is marked J. F. Gray, for Grandpa, but we live there, too."

So I checked into the Lowndesburg House, left my baggage, and started out calling on farms.

One of the customers had a land-leveller that dug in at the turns, so I put on my overalls and adjusted the hydraulics for him. That made him offer me a sample of his hobby, which was apple brandy distilled under a special government farmer's permit. I'd never heard of one before, and that led to a second sample and a genial discussion of the high price of liquor and it was five o'clock when I drove out of his gateway and headed back for Lowndesburg.

It was still light, and I drifted along, well pleased with the evening ahead and the day behind me.

About ten past five I was opposite a big arched gateway that said: "Mr. Hilliard. John Hilliard V, Prop." It said it in stone relief. Pretty fancy.

His lawyer had said he'd be back in late afternoon. I had an hour and three quarters to kill before my date. I turned up the driveway. .

It wound and climbed through hardwood groves that were not always the native woods. One of the John Hilliards—one to five, take your choice—had been a tree collector. I don't know enough about exotic trees to name them all, but I recognized the flaming red of Chinese pistachios, the fleshy green of Korean camphor-laurel. I passed two men in suntan shirts and green riding breeches, and they were unwrapping a eucalyptus after the winter. So Mr. John Five had his own private forestry service. They were efficient, too; there wasn't a piece of underbrush that didn't look as if it had been placed by an expert.

The private road climbed up on a bluff and stopped; this was Mt. Hilliard. I parked near a six-car garage, and looked around.

The land fell off sharply ahead of me and behind me. To my right was the garage and the road I'd come up. To my left was a house, or maybe it was a château or a castle. It was huge, I know.

Perversely, all the plantings around it were natives, mostly laurel and myrtle and blue spruce.

I followed a path around the house, and came out on a half-covered terrace that ran from the front door to the third edge of the bluff. A stone wall kept people from falling down into the common man's valley, but I wasn't there to talk to stone walls.

I pressed a button next to the door, and heard a bell ring deep in the big house and waited. When nothing happened, I rang again. It seemed impossible that a house that big wouldn't have servants, but if they were at the other end, it could take one of them quite a while to get to the front door.

I lighted a cigarette while I waited, and noticed that I'd used the last match in the packet. I made a mental note to get some more packages from the carton in the glove compartment, and put the empty folder back in my pocket. This was not the place to throw litter.

When nobody came, I drifted back to my car. Inside the big garage I could see the vague outlines of four—no, five cars. One stall was empty. I started the motor and drove back to town, to my hotel and a bath and a seven o'clock date with Andy McLane.

CHAPTER 3

She had on what I guess is a cocktail suit, silk or a good imitation, pale blue with a black blouse under it. There were earrings shaped like little baskets of fruit, and a pin on the blouse, and so on. Very pleasing.

She said, "Paul, I'm sorry. Gramps wants us to come have a glass of sherry with him."

I said I had lived through worse things than that.

"You may be talking before you're fully advised. This way."

The house was no Mt. Hilliard but it was bigger than they make them nowadays. There were a lot of plate-glass windows and old-fashioned sliding doors and clear-grained wood paneling, and we walked straight through from the front door to what might have been a back door once; now it led into a conservatory.

It was warmer in there than in the rest of the house, and considering the age of the man seated bolt upright in an armless straight chair, he could use the heat.

He looked as if a couple of greats ought to have preceded his title of Andy's grandfather. The slightest amount of slackness under his jaw indicated that he might once have had a fleshed, human body; but all that had gone, years and years ago. Now, a skeleton sat erect, covered with gray skin to which large, brown freckles failed to give warmth.

Andy said, "Grandpa this is—"

He raised a long hand. "I know. The young man who is taking you out tonight."

"Paul Porter, Mr. Gray." This was Otto McLane. I hadn't seen him, sitting off to one side, under a scrawny palm that was existing in a mat-covered pot. He held a glass, presumably of sherry; not exactly an ex-cop's drink.

"Give him a glass of wine," Mr. Gray said. "Do you drink, young man?"

"Certainly," I said. "But seldom sherry."

Mr. Gray made a noise like *Hmph*, a sound I had previously believed was not a sound at all, but something writers put on paper. "Give him a glass of sherry, Andrea. Pour yourself one... Young man, why are you taking Andrea to dinner?"

"Why do men do anything for women?" I responded. "Because they think the lady in question is charming, attractive." I had decided that servility would get me nowhere with him, and anyway, I didn't care very much.

Andy dipped a little curtsey and said, "Thank you, sir."

Mr. Gray hmphed around awhile. "We have plenty of food in the house," he said. I accepted a glass from Andy and sipped. It wasn't bad; bootless but not repulsive. I waited, and finally the old man said, "Silly waste of money. Eat here."

"No, sir," I said. "How can I get the gal grateful if I don't spend money on her? And, anyway, I'll want a couple of cocktails before my food." '

"Impudent son-of-a-bitch, isn't he, Otto?"

Otto McLane was chuckling. "He wasn't to me, Mr. Gray. I'd say it was you that brought it out in him."

"I'll lay off," J. F. Gray said. He cackled. "Last amusement of an old man. Sticking pins in young ones to see if they'll wriggle. Hell, I've had two heart attacks and a stroke. Three bowls of pap a day, and a glass of sherry for an old-time whiskey drinker. Call that a life?"

"No. But now that you've given up the act, I'd make a guess you've got some pretty gaudy memories to amuse you over your pap, whatever that is."

"Super-boiled oatmeal shoved through a sieve," he said. "With all kinds of protein and vitamin supplements to make it worse. Hell. Remember a salesman coming in somewhere back in the twenties, trying to get me to sell something like it for hens." He laughed, or cackled, again. "I told him it would probably do wonders for the hens, if they could be persuaded to eat it. They couldn't."

The phone rang. Andy looked at her father, who made a flat down-gesture with the palm of his hand for her to keep her seat, and went himself to snatch up an instrument in the hall. We could hear him easily.

Old Man Gray said, "So now I'm eating it myself, and I wouldn't be surprised—"

At the same time, Otto McLane was talking on the phone: "This is Mac... Dead...? What...? All right. I'll go right up there. Give me a couple of minutes start before you tell the state boys. I'd like to be there first...

The old man had stopped talking when he heard the word "dead." He waited, head cocked on one side, and his eyes were as bright as a hen's, and as beady.

Mac stuck his head in, and he no longer looked so much like Harry Truman; his jaw had tightened and pulled all the lines of his face together, so that the benevolence had been replaced with something else, perhaps the cold determination of a cop. He said, "Police business. Don't wait dinner for me, Mr. Gray."

"All right, Otto," J. F. Gray said. "Give 'em hell, boy." And Mac was gone.

Andy said, "Grandpa, if you want us to stay home..."

"Hell no. You and Paul go have yourselves a time. I'll slop down my swill and listen to the radio. My eyes can't stand television, Porter."

"I'll get my hat," said Andy.

There was an inch or less of sherry left in each of our glasses. The old man raised his. "To my granddaughter... You married, Porter?"

I grinned. "What kind of a question is that? No, I'm not."

"Worried about Andrea. Gave Otto the business so she'd live here with me. It's hard to be old, Porter. Supposed to be a dignified thing to be, but I've never noticed it... Sometimes, in summer, she wears a halter and shorts around the house. You ever noticed the small of a young girl's back?"

"Hell, no."

"Talking like an old lecher, eh? Not so. Small of the back, right where the spine ends, that's the youngest thing about a young girl. Like to look at it. If I was an old fool, I'd hire a young nurse or a housekeeper, end up marrying her, making an idiot out of myself. Hope I die before Andrea marries and goes away. Don't want to make a fool out of myself."

"You're quite a guy, Mr. Gray."

He nodded. His bony hand went out and flicked a leaf off a plant. "Ought to die. Nothing in life any more. But nobody ever seems ready to die. Know I'm not. Here's Andrea."

The hat was made out of a piece of the same stuff the cocktail suit was; it was twisted around and pinned up with a chunk of uncut stone, a pebble set in silver wire.

"Grandpa, you're sure you don't mind?" she asked.

"Otto'll be back. He went off on police business, maybe he'll tell me about it," the old man said. "Can't be much, not in Lowndesburg. A big city cop like him ought to get it solved in eighteen minutes, without breathing hard."

Andy looked at him hard, frowning. She said, "Don't be sarcastic," and then she kissed him on the left eyebrow, approximately, and I held out my hand, which he waved away, as though shaking hands would be too much trouble for him, and we went down the long, broad hall towards the front door.

It was dark when we had driven away from the door light, just the headlamps ahead of us, coming down the highway into town. Andy opened a window and the air was crisp and fresh. "I like this car, Paul. Yours or the company's?"

"Woman, you sound mercenary."

"Of course. All girls look at all young men with an eye to marrying them and being comfortably supported the rest of their lives. And what do all young men think of, or don't tell me, I already know."

We were coming into the heart of town, the part where the street lamps were. I said, "You sound like your grandfather."

A red light and siren came at us, fast. I pulled to the sky, and we watched the state car go by. When I started up again, she said something about her grandfather being an old dear, and then we were at the hotel.

We had two cocktails, we had a dance, we had chicken and noodle soup; then we got up to dance again.

I was enjoying myself thoroughly, and I think she was. At least, I know she was dancing closer to me than she had at first, a pretty good sign. I tightened my arm around her, and looked over at our table, hoping the roast beef wasn't there yet.

It wasn't, but my date's father was. Otto McLane, looking grim and tired and unhappy, was sitting in my chair, his hat in his lap. He caught my eye and raised his chin to call me over.

Not surprisingly, I missed a step and stumbled, and Andy looked up abruptly. I let go of her and took her elbow to guide her to the table; then she saw Mac, and made a little noise of distress. "Something's happened to Grandpa—"

We hurried, almost running, to the table. Mac didn't smile at us. He said, "I paid your check, canceled the rest of the order. Let's go."

Andy said, "Grandpa—"

"Naw. You g'wan home, Andy. Take a cab."

"Take my car, Andy," I said. "You can bring it downtown tomorrow."

"Take a cab," Mac said. "C'mon, Porter."

It was hard to recognize him as the small-town hay and grain dealer I'd been seeing, on and off, all day. There was a sour look on his face that might have come from indigestion, the nervous kind—if there is any other.

I said I didn't understand, and I got a look that was almost hatred in return. "If you want to make a scene here," he said, "I got handcuffs, and more than thirty years' experience in putting 'em on. Make something of it, if you want to."

"Let's go, Andrea," I said.

Nobody looked at us in the lobby of the hotel; there was nobody on the street at the moment but a couple of cabdrivers, listening to a radio in one of their cars. Mac said again, "G'wan home, Andy."

She looked wonderful in the lights from the hotel front; her eyes were hot as St. Elmo's fire. "Dad, I didn't want to make trouble in there. But I've got a right to know what you're doing. You're acting as if I were twelve years old."

"It's got nothing to do with you, this is police business. G'wan, scram, now."

"You're arresting Paul for something?"

Mac said, "I'm taking him to City Hall for questioning, yeah. And if you want me to say I'm sorry I busted up your date, so okay, it's said."

"Paul, do you want me to call a lawyer?" she said.

"How do I know? This heavy blanket of mystery's got me covered, too."

"I'll go this far," Mac said. "He needs a lawyer. Henry Lighton's the best in town, Porter, the only good one... You had to be pinched, and I thought it would look better if I came and got you, instead of a uniformed state cop. C'mon." He shut his mouth and it was obvious there was no hope of getting him to open it. I went along smiling apologies—what for?—at Andrea.

She ran across the sidewalk and jumped into one of the cabs. I would have watched her drive away, but Mac's hand on my sleeve was strong.

"Did you have an overcoat?"

"It's in my room at the hotel," I said.

"Suppose you were going to try and get her to go up with you for it, later. You got quite a way with the dames, haven't you?"

"Considering that Andy's your daughter, you'd know better, if you didn't have a cop's filthy mind. And the rest of the crack hasn't cleared anything up. Somebody file bastardy charges against me?"

McLane said, "I haven't got a coat on either. No use us freezing." He jerked my arm and I went along with him.

City Hall was a two-story building, set back from the street with trees and a dying lawn around it. A plaque acknowledged PWA and WPA help, and through the big front doors I could see the murals that the WPA had once spread through the country.

But we didn't go in the front door; we went around to the side. Here a ramp went up into the Fire Department and stairs went down to the Police Department. The ramp was marked with a red light and the stairs with a blue. We went down to the blue light.

The police office was nothing: a desk,, a phone, two chairs and three filing cases., At the back an open pine door showed a barred one—closed—behind it, leading to the lockup.

A triangular sign on the desk said, "Captain Otto McLane." Since he was now a chief, that must have been a leftover from his days on the St. Louis force. A captain of municipal police is pretty good; but then I hadn't rated Mac as a dope.

The office was crowded with men. One of them wore the uniform of a state trooper, wide hat and all; the rest of them were quietly dressed, but there was too much muscle under their conservative suits. More state cops, no doubt.

"This is it," Mac said, and pushed me into the room by the arm he was holding.

I staggered, and bumped into the desk. The uniformed boy steadied me and one of the older men said, "Take it easy, Chief."

"Easy, he says," Mac said. "It's you I ought to be swinging at. This guy was a guest in my house, he represents one of the solidest companies I do business with, he was out with my daughter, and you guys make me pinch him."

I said, "Will somebody tell me what I'm charged with?"

The gray-haired man who'd talked before said, "Mr. Porter, take it easy. This is very likely to come to nothing."

"Sure," Mac said. "A great big coincidence. I don't believe in them."

The older man—but he wasn't as old as Mac—said, "But they happen. Mr. Porter, I'm Lieutenant Detective Gamble, State Police. So we'll know whom we're talking to. You admit you are Paul Porter, of Chicago?"

"If Mac hasn't convinced you of that, I carry a good deal of identification," I said.

Gamble said, "Get it out."

"Very official," Mac said. "Big shot—in my town."

I had my wallet out by then, held it out to Gamble. He said, "Please take the money out first," and I did. He thumbed through all the I.D. and credit cards, the driver's license, the insurance cards. Finally he came to the little separate compartment that held my business cards. He looked at these. "He certainly seems to work for Hydrol Machines, Incorporated, Mac."

"What detective school did you go to? You can read."

Gamble said, politely—he was the smoothest thing I'd seen in weeks— "Yes, but printing's cheap. Still, these look good, and since his identity is the only reason for picking him up, let's all act as though he had proved he's Paul Porter."

"So maybe he bumped off the guy whose I.D. he carries," Mac said.

Lieutenant Gamble said, "Mac, no officer likes arresting another cop's friend. Try and get along with us. Mr. Porter, would you mind telling us what you did after lunch today? In as much detail as you can remember, please."

"Well, after I finished eating," I said, "I paid the check, including Mac's lunch—and now you can charge me with bribery."

The uniformed trooper smiled a little, but Lieutenant Gamble said: "This is far from being a funny matter, Mr. Porter. On second thought, I think we'll have this taken down and signed by you. If you don't mind."

"Don't I get a lawyer or something? I'm supposed to be told what I'm accused of."

Mac jerked a thumb at the cell door behind his office. "Take a coffee break, Gamble. Leave him here till he gets a lawyer."

After Mac's snarl, Gamble's patience and courtesy were monumental. He said: "Mr. Porter, you have been accused of nothing. But if we're going into talk about lawyers and so on, we can book you, and then you can name your attorney, and then we can wait till we find a magistrate— and so on, and so forth. But if you give us a statement, perhaps we can release you at once."

Mac said: "Ha!"

Gamble said, "All right, Chief McLane. But let me point out to you that when you called in the State Police, you ceded authority. I am, at present, in charge of this case and shall remain so until relieved by a superior."

"All right." That was me. "Let's get it over with. I didn't get to finish my dinner... My name is Paul Porter, I am vice-president in charge of marketing for Hydrol Machines, Inc., a Chicago firm. I am at present engaged on a field trip, visiting users and sellers of our machinery. My boss's name is Harvey Planne, and if you want to check with him, his home phone number is on that card in my wallet..."

The uniformed man, surprisingly, was the stenographer. He had sat down in one of the two chairs, and was writing all this down in his notebook. Perversely, I tried to snow him by talking as fast as I could. I told about the three customers we had here in Lowndes Valley and how I had called on each of them, how long it took, what we talked about. I did not forget the third one's hobby of making apple brandy, and how we sampled it. The lieutenant seemed to show interest in this. Mac was jumping around like a terrier on a leash.

I hadn't succeeded in snowing the steno at all; he was well up with me when I got to ten past five and the gate at Mt. Hilliard.

"I noticed the time particularly because I naturally didn't want to call on a prospect at a time that might annoy him. It didn't seem too late; I drove up the hill."

Gamble interrupted me. "Did anybody see you?"

"I passed two men who looked like foresters or tree surgeons. Whether they noticed me or not I don't know... Anyway, I got up to the house at whatever time it takes from five-ten to get there, driving reasonably fast on a strange road. I parked, and walked around to the front of the building, rang the bell. When nobody answered, I had a cigarette, and waited. It's a big house...might have taken some time to get to the front door. I admired the view, and after a while I went back to my car and drove into town here. It was just about six o'clock when I got my key from the room clerk at the hotel."

Lieutenant Gamble nodded. Mac was a little quieter; he was watching the lieutenant. Gamble said, "Now, and this is important, when you got back into your car at Mt. Hilliard, were you still smoking, or did you throw your cigarette away up there?"

So Mt. Hilliard was the important part of the day. I said, "Let me think... I was still smoking. As you come to the gates of Mt. Hilliard, there's a Stop sign. I stopped, being a lawful citizen, and before starting up again, I put the butt out in the ashtray of the car."

"Did you see the two tree surgeons on your way out?"

"Never thought of them. No, I don't think I did."

Gamble nodded, and chewed his lower lip. "You are willing to sign this?" When I nodded, he turned to the trooper, and said: "You'll find a typewriter up in the city clerk's office. Type this up, and while you're there, try and get in touch with those men who take care of Mr. Hilliard's trees."

The trooper said, "Yes, sir. They're dendrologists, by the way. I asked them once."

Gamble said that was fine, and the trooper went out. I could hear him clattering up the outside stairs to the ground level.

Gamble continued to chew his lip. Sometimes he would look at Mac and sometimes at me. Finally he said, "It's an awfully straight story, Mac. You've heard as many as I have in your time. What do you think?"

Mac was more like a well-trained boxer than a terrier now. He said, steadily, "Don't know. If he was lying, he'd have a lot more details. But why ask me? It wasn't my idea to pinch him."

There was some more silence. Then Gamble sighed and turned to me. "I can't see what possible harm there can be in telling you what you're up against. John Hilliard got home a little after six, and found his wife dead in the garage. In her car."

"I thought it must be murder from the way Mac was carrying on. But why me?"

"We didn't even know you'd been up there," Gamble said. "You told us that. It makes the case against you just that much worse, and, for some strange reason, makes me begin to believe in your innocence."

"Why should there be a case against me at all? Just being up there wouldn't be anything—I had a reason; I'd discussed it with McLane here, in fact it was his idea that I go up there. I never heard of John Hilliard or Mrs. John Hilliard before today, before Otto McLane here mentioned him."

Lieutenant Gamble said, "Now you're lying. Now I feel a lot better about this." He looked at one of his men, said, "Take this down. When Trooper Rainier gets back, add this to the statement before Porter signs." He turned.

"If you'll sign that, too."

"Of course I will."

Lieutenant Gamble said, slowly: "Mac, get one of our local J.P.'s down to act as magistrate. It's too bad your district attorney's out of town, but we'll take a chance and arraign Porter without a D.A. I wish you had a real jail here, but I'll take Porter up to the city and hold him there as soon as I can."

"Sure," said Mac and he started out.

He didn't make it. An extraordinarily tall, thin man came walking in. I remember thinking, his clothes must have cost as much as all the rest of ours put together.

He said, "Evening, Lieutenant, Mac, gentlemen. Mr. Porter, I am Henry Lighton. Andrea McLane said you might need an attorney."

"I think I do, sir."

"Think?"

"I seem to have been near a place where a woman died today. These cops are trying to make it murder, with me the murderer."

The trooper was back with a sheaf of papers. There seemed to be several copies. Lieutenant Gamble handed them all to the plainclothes man he'd told to take down my statement that I didn't know the Hilliards; he whipped out a fountain pen and wrote rapidly at the end of each copy. Gamble handed them to me.

"Read and sign each one. And please initial the written addendum."

Henry Lighton smoothed his beautifully graying hair, and said, "Not so fast, I do not think my client is going to sign anything." He reached out and I handed him a copy.

We both read rapidly; Lighton was humming a little under his breath. "All of this true, Mr. Porter?"

I said it was.

He said, "The Hilliard part is obviously the crucial time... Oh, sign it. It doesn't mean anything much until it's sworn to."

When I finished, Henry Lighton said, "Well, you know where my office is, gentlemen. My client and I are going over there to talk." '

Gamble said, "I don't think so."

Lighton asked him if he was in charge of the case.

"I am in charge, Mr. Lighton, yes," Gamble said. "And I think we'll try for an arraignment, without bail. You see, that's a false statement, and a false statement in a murder case—"

Henry Lighton held up his hand. "Please don't tell me the law, Lieutenant. Leave me in my ignorance. Do I tell you how to repair motorcycles?"

"That's a low dig," said Gamble. "All right, I'll ask you. When a man says he does not know, has never heard of, a woman to whom he was married for four years, would you consider him completely on the up and up?"

I never heard what Mr. Lighton answered to that because, then, I couldn't hear at all. There was too much blood in my head; and too many memories, one of them not a day old, of Edith's legs crossing the sidewalk ahead of me and sliding into a big Buick. I tried to say something; the noise that came out didn't make sense, even to me. Lieutenant Gamble said, "Get him a glass of water—"

I heard that, and I felt hands lowering me into a chair, and then the water was at my lips. I swallowed with,' difficulty, but it helped me. I said, "Edith? I saw her in town today—" My head wasn't throbbing so badly. "McLane was with me. On our way to lunch."

Mac said, "Yeah, I was. I remember."

"Ah, yes," said Henry Lighton, "you'd remember, all right. She could make a man's day—"

"Why didn't you tell me she was Mrs. Hilliard?"

Mac turned to me. "Why didn't you tell me she was your wife?" There was a querulous, little-boy note in his voice. "We found it out when we talked to John Five. Asked him about enemies; he said maybe her ex-husband, Paul Porter. Then the two tree surgeon guys said an Illinois car had been up there, didn't stay long."

"I think a mistake has been made," Lieutenant Gamble said. "I think I'm going to turn you loose. When you heard your wife—your ex-wife—was dead, you were not faking that reaction... Let me tell you, most killers and many other felons are psychotics. Where other people react sharply, they react by becoming more calm. I took you for one of them."

McLane was changing back into the small-town businessman. Having been a boxer and a terrier, he now began to resemble a basset—a whole kennel of dogs in one man. I hoped I'd be able to see him again some day without thinking of canines; I doubted it. He said, "See how it looked to me. A guy comes in, says he is with the company that makes a rig I got in my window. I don't ask him for credentials; why should I? He buys me a cheap lunch, and steers the talk around to where I give him—me, the chief of police—a reason to go to a woman's house where he wants to kill, maybe has good reason to kill—the woman. I even tell him that she'll be alone there, 'cause her husband'll be out; and it's Thursday, when even a cop knows rich people's servants get off."

I said, "I didn't know that. I didn't know Mrs. Hilliard was—who she was."

"But see how it looked to me," Mac said. "It looked like a guy'd deliberately set out to use me for a patsy. Me, that was a captain of detectives in one of the ten largest cities in the United States." There was a wail in his voice that was hard to explain. "Gone out of his way to make a sucker of me!" ,

Henry Lighton said, "Now, Mac, take it easy. There's life in the old dog yet."

Considering my kennel-reflections, this startled me, and I grinned at

Lighton. He remained grave. But he had explained what was wrong with the chief: Mac was afraid he was all washed up, too old to be of any use in the world. Considering the age of the father-in-law he lived with, he should have thought of himself as a pup, with many years ahead in which to be a gay dog. Apparently he didn't. He hadn't been trying to clear me because he loved me, but because he' didn't. He was afraid that the cops were regarding him as useless, were laughing at him.

"Believe me, Mr. McLane," I said, "I had never heard of you before today. And I didn't know Edith was remarried." This time I said the name without difficulty.

Lieutenant Gamble said, "Mind telling us the circumstances of your divorce?"

"You're damned well right I do!"

"Take it easy, client," Henry Lighton said. "You don't swear at police officers any more than you call them cops."

"Or motorcycle repairmen," Gamble said.

This got a smile from Henry Lighton. It was as aristocratic as the rest of him. He made the dingy office look dingier when he smiled. He said, "I think that all the lieutenant wants to know is whether you went to court, defaulted...the legal circumstances of the case."

Gamble said, "I wanted a good deal more than that, but if Mr. Lighton says that's all you're going to give me, I'll settle for it."

We were all very polite with each other. Henry Lighton bowed to the lieutenant, and gestured to me, and I said: "We had been separated a year, eleven months to be exact, when I got a letter from a Nevada lawyer. He enclosed a copy of the divorce decree, and advised me to hang onto it if I wanted to remarry. I haven't. I—"

"That's enough," Henry Lighton said. "May we go now, Lieutenant?"

Gamble said, "I'd like your client to see me before he leaves town. I understand he's paid for a room till morning; maybe by then I'll know more about the case." He paused. "Mr. Porter, whether it damages your feelings or not, by morning I'll want to know more about the deceased's background."

I nodded. Henry Lighton took my arm, and we started out. McLane suddenly came to life. "Wait a minute. I noticed something today: you don't carry a cigarette lighter."

He was very proud of himself; you could hear it in his voice. "A thing I've noticed, since I've been in business. Salesmen all carry matches with their company name on them. You say you smoked a cigarette up at John Five's; you put it out down at the Stop sign. How about the match?"

Lieutenant Gamble was getting impatient; but I could see Mac's point. If the tree surgeons saw me come down the mountain, they'd say I'd just had time to smoke one cigarette, and a man wouldn't hold a smoke while killing a woman. I said, "This is going to look so pat it's suspicious. I threw the match away right at the front door of the house, mansion, whatever you call it. It hasn't rained since then, maybe you can find it. And here's the book it came from. It was the last in the book, and Mt. Hilliard looked too neat to litter up."

I fished the book out and threw it on the desk. "I was never a big-city police captain, like our friend McLane, here, but I imagine anybody with a magnifying glass can tell if a match was torn from this pack or another. You're not going to accuse me of murdering with one hand and holding a cigarette with the other, are you?"

"If the match is there—and somehow or other I am sure it will be—it will either fit the tear or not. It is impossible, without machinery, to tear two matches exactly alike."

Mac growled something I couldn't get, but Lieutenant Gamble said: "Yes, Mac. It does look pat, as though he'd planted the match to account for his time up there."

Mac said, "Sure. Who carries empty matchbooks in his pocket?"

"I do," I said. "If you're going to sell expensive machinery to a man you don't start out by dirtying up his front lawn with a piece of advertising."

Henry Lighton said, "Mr. Porter, please stop bickering with these officers. You have me to do that for you."

"This sews it all up," Mac said. "Honest men don't set up alibis for themselves. He expected to get pinched when he threw that match away, and that's why he kept the match folder!"

Lieutenant Gamble said, "Oh, Chief," in a weary voice.

"He wanted to account for his time," Mac barked. "Honest men don't care about that."

This time Lighton took it. "Oh, Mac, take it easy."

A state trooper I hadn't seen before came in, saluted Gamble, and said: "Sir, I made a pickup on those tree men. They were at a movie in town."

Henry Lighton laughed. "Who's being pat now? We talk about tree surgeons giving Mr. Porter an alibi—and tree surgeons show up."

McLane said, "That kind of coincidence can happen, sure. But—"

Lieutenant Gamble waved a tired hand. "Gentlemen, we're talking ourselves to death. Would you ask the dendrologists to step in, Trooper?"

The word startled the trooper so that he forgot to salute. He opened the door, and said, "In here, please."

Two big guys came in, and a woman. Lieutenant Gamble said, "I didn't send for the lady, Trooper."

The state trooper said, "Lieutenant, I don't know what a dend—what you said is."

Henry Lighton made a contribution. "At any moment the chorus will dance in, singing something appropriate from Gilbert and Sullivan."

The big guys looked alike, though they no longer wore John Five's uniforms. One of them said, "Dendrology is the study of trees. A dendrologist is—"

"All right," Lieutenant Gamble said. "I didn't invite you here for a lecture on English. What are your names?"

I know the one on the left," McLane said suddenly. "He goes out with my daughter. He calls himself Daniel Banion."

"Well, it's my name," the one on the left said. "This is my partner Harold Crosley. The lady is his wife. And what's this all about, Mr. McLane?"

Mac said: "The lieutenant is in charge."

"Well, that's right," Lieutenant Gamble said. "You two men saw Mr. Porter here drive up to Mt. Hilliard this afternoon. Right?"

Banion said, "We saw a car with an Illinois license drive up. I didn't see the driver, to recognize."

"How about you, Crosley?"

"We were talking about the red spiders that have gotten in the Pfitzers up there," Crosley said. "We were pretty absorbed."

Gamble said, "If anybody wants to know what Pfitzers are, or what red spiders do in them, please wait till you get outside... Did you see this Illinois car come down off the hill again?"

"No," said Crosley.

Lieutenant Gamble said, "The first short answer all evening, thank the Lord." He turned to Henry Lighton. "The whole thing about the match doesn't signify anything now, does it, counselor?"

Henry Lighton smiled his urbane smile, and said: "Mr. Crosley, did you or your associate *hear* the car come down? And Pfitzers are a variety of low-growing juniper, Lieutenant."

Lieutenant Gamble said: "God."

Banion said, "Why, yeah, we heard a car come down, about fifteen minutes after Mr. Porter went up."

"As John Five's lawyer," said Henry Lighton, "I'm familiar with Mt. Hilliard. No way for a car to come down without seeing this Illinois tagged automobile—which might have been anybody's from Illinois, Lieutenant—parked up there, would there be, Mr. Crosley, Mr. Banion?"

Banion said: "Nope."

Henry Lighton said, "Client, let's go to my office for a chat."

"God help the district attorney when he comes up against you, Mr.

Lighton," Gamble said. "My men are up there searching, and if the match is there they'll find it. I suppose if it doesn't fit the book, or if they don't find it, you'll accuse me of tampering with the evidence."

"I wouldn't think of it," Henry Lighton said. "And don't use the name of the Deity so often, Lieutenant. It becomes banal, after a while." We walked out.

CHAPTER 4

It was colder than when Mac had taken me into City Hall. I shivered. Henry Lighton looked at me, and said, "Is your overcoat back there?"

"In my hotel room. I wasn't going to be out except in a heated car—"

There were quite a number of people around the Hall now; they were watching the front door. Then they saw us and hurried over. One of the men said, "That must be the murderer now."

Lighton had hold of my arm again, was hurrying me across the crisp, frost-killed grass. "Don't say anything, Porter. Act as if they aren't there."

A fat woman said: "They wouldn't be letting him go if he was guilty."

A man said: "If he wasn't guilty what'd he hire Henry Lighton for?"

The hand on my arm tightened, and Henry Lighton chuckled. "Such is fame."

The people tried to stop us but Henry Lighton glared them out of the way. They were much more polite than a city crowd. They didn't actually block us; they were just slow in giving way.

Then a kid, not more than eighteen or nineteen, said, "I'm from the *Loundesburg Journal,* and the A .P. I'd like to know—"

Lighton said, "No comment, Max. I'll call your dad if we have a statement later."

The kid looked crushed, and we went on. Henry opened the plate-glass door of what looked like a remodeled Colonial dwelling. "They're either too young or too old," he said.

I looked surprised. He went on: "My office is upstairs here... Weren't you thinking that, over in the police office? Mac's worried that you picked his town to commit a murder in because he's too old to be a serious menace to a murderer. Makes no sense at all, but, you know, people seldom do make sense."

We were at the top of the curving staircase now. What must have originally been bedrooms were now offices, each with a different name on the door. Mr. Lighton had no partners listed, but maybe the whole building belonged to one firm.

He opened the door and bowed me in. "Here's your boy, Andy." She got up from a deep, leather chair. The place was furnished like an Englishman's club in a movie—heavy desk, high-backed swivel chair in a bay window, and all the rest, deep carpet and leather furniture and hunting prints on the wall—and the result was to make Andy McLane look fragile and thoroughly feminine and very desirable. Well, she'd looked desirable before, but not the other things.

Henry Lighton went behind the desk and sank down in the swivel chair. "I can turn," he said, "and the City Hall, with all its entrances and exits, is spread before me like a panoply of virtue and vice." He turned, and was hidden from us by the high back of his chair.

Andy held out both hands to me. "I'm sorry our date was ruined," she said. "I was having a good time." She smiled, and got her fingers back from me. "By the way, I called Grandpa. He said he'd pay Henry Lighton's fee. He must have taken quite a liking to you."

"Maybe he thinks you like me. He's pretty crazy about you."

She let me make what I wanted out of a smile.

I said, "For what it's worth, I didn't kill her. Or anybody. And you knew I was divorced."

Andy said, "That's hardly my business... And it really isn't my business, either, how Grandpa spends his money. A man his age is entitled to his—his—"

"Eccentricities is the word you want," I said. "Do you consider it eccentric to like me?"

She let me have another smile on that.

Henry Lighton turned. "Since you aren't going to neck," he said, "there's no use my being delicate."

Andy said: "Blush, blush."

"We've got a long night ahead of us," Henry Lighton said. "I have to get to know my client, inside out, right side back again, upside down. Andy, darling, if you are not afraid of going out into the night, how about cruising down to Larry Genauer's emporium of good cheer and getting (a) a bottle of Scotch, (b) two large bottles of soda, and (e) a sack of ice cubes? Put it on my bill and I'll charge it to Mr. Gray."

"Mr. Gray doesn't have to pay your fee. I'll be glad to."

"Take blessings as they fall, Paul, if I may call you Paul. On your way, Andy. Give her a slap on the rear to get her started, Paul."

"I never slap girls' rears on the first date."

Andy said she had a good deal to look forward to, and gathered up her coat from one of the club chairs.

When she was gone, Henry Lighton stopped grinning. He said: "It's going to hurt you, kid, but I have to know. Did you have any reason for killing Edith Hilliard?"

I sat down in the chair nearest the desk. The room was lighted by a brass Federalist lamp on the desk. I stared at it and said: "Yes."

Henry Lighton said, "Want to wait till you've oiled your tongue a little? It's why I sent for the Scotch." Without waiting for me to answer, he went on, "You ought to know a little more about me. Several years ago I was one of the best criminal lawyers in New York. My income ran into six figures, which is no hay, especially when it comes to paying the income tax. But I saw no sense in all that and came out here and bought a farm out in the valley. You passed it today, right next to that of our apple-brandy-loving friend, Jack Lutyel. Farming bored me, so I rented this office. I do a little law work, but I am no hick, friend, and you are damned lucky I'm not. You're in trouble."

"Seemed to me when they let me go, they meant it."

"Mac's like a bulldog... Why do people always think of dogs when they talk about Otto McLane...? I guess it's his sad eyes."

"No one can say a word against McLane. He was the one who brought up the match, and tried to clear me."

"Just to prove he was smarter than Gamble...and, then, for the same reason, he proved the match meant nothing. But Mac doesn't matter. The trouble you're in is a big one. It's an awful coincidence that an ex-husband would drift into town just on the day a woman gets killed. An ex-husband with rancor, if I'm right."

"You're right."

"She didn't send for you? If she was going to take you back, it would give John Hilliard Five a motive that would fix him. If she sent for you, now's the time to tell me."

"She didn't send for me. I didn't know where she was, didn't know she was remarried."

He cleared his throat, made a steeple out of his fingers, leaned back in his regal chair. He stared at the ceiling. "Oh, brother. You must live right, as the kids say. If you'd gotten here tomorrow, or any other day in the long history of Lowndesburg, you'd have been all right..."

"Tell me about McLane and his father-in-law," I said. "It's really weird that the old man would hire me a lawyer on the strength of five minutes and a glass of sherry."

Henry Lighton shrugged. "Maybe Andy told him she'd fallen in love with you on first sight... But I don't think so. I think he doesn't like Mac, and when he thought Mac arrested you, he decided to take a hand, show Mac up for a fool."

"But he gave Mac the business."

Henry Lighton began chuckling. It was a very musical sound. "In more

ways than one. The old man wanted Andrea around. Mac's the price of
that. Call them two superannuated dogs, fighting over a manger..."

"There you go comparing Mac to a dog again. And Andy's the
manger?"

He said, "We're way off the point. Did you kill Edith Hilliard?"

"I didn't know she was here. I didn't see her."

"You're getting shrill. Watch that. Juries send people to the chair, not
because they're guilty, but because they don't like them, and being shrill
is an easy way to be disliked."

I said, "Damn it, Mr. Lighton, I—"

The outer door opened, and Andrea McLane was back. She had
turned the big collar of her tweed coat up, and it framed her head; her
hair was glistening. "It's beginning to rain out."

Henry Lighton turned in his big chair, and looked out at the City Hall
and its lawn and its sycamores. "So it is," he said. "And some more cops
have arrived. Big brass, from the size of their cars... It's a curious thing.
The lowest grade of policeman, the patrolman, has to get to what the
newspapers call the scene of the crime fastest, so they give him the cheap-
est, slowest car. The very top grade of policeman can take his time, so
he gets the fastest car. Well, I guess it makes as much sense as anything
in this..."

He went on. But I had long since given up listening to him. I was staring at Andy as though I'd never seen a girl before. The color the cold had
brought to her cheeks, the shine that the rain had given to her hair, made
her seem finally, and without doubt, the most desirable thing I'd ever seen.

So this is how it comes to you. After a marriage, after a half dozen more
or less comfortable love affairs, this is how it hits. It is not a completely
pleasant sensation, I learned; nor have the better poets ever claimed it was.

She went by me and put her two paper bags down on Henry Lighton's
desk. He was still talking; something about the over-complications of a
totally mechanical civilization. Her packages unloaded, she turned back
to me. Slowly her hands came up and were held out to me, a curious gesture, because the arms must have come up with them, since I knew that
only the hands were for me.

I grabbed them both, and pressed them in my own palms. Her hands
were very cold, but their touch melted the ice in my belly, and I was self-
confident again.

The slight creak of Henry Lighton's swivel chair brought us back to
earth. He said, "Well, it's time for me to make hostly gestures and
noises. You'll have a drink with us before you go, Andy?"

She jumped a little. "Yes. Of course."

Henry Lighton moved around the office, getting glasses from a hard-pine cupboard, opening bottles, fishing ice up with his long fingers. He handed a glass to Andy, one to me. "Here's to litigation, the lawyer's life blood."

Andy said, "You're damned funny, Henry."

"The light touch," Henry Lighton said. "Convinces the jury that you are sure of getting your client off. Or sometimes it does."

Andy said, "I'm dying of laughter. Every time you mention the jury, I choke with glee. Didn't you ever try and stop an injustice before it got to a jury?"

"End of humor," he said. "Appearance of serious-minded attorney. Paul hasn't a chance of not going to trial—unless they catch the murderer— or frame one. The circumstances are too damned weird." He stopped, then added, "None of this is any of your business, Andy. I don't want to talk about it till I figure out a defense."

I had only drunk half my highball. Now I set it down on the edge of the desk so hard that the liquor jumped and spilled on the wood, where it fizzed shallowly. "Damn it, I didn't kill her. And before I got through over at the police station, they didn't think I had; or they wouldn't have let me go. Whose side are you on, anyway?"

"Yours," Henry Lighton said. "And they didn't exactly let you go. There's no district attorney available for this county tonight. With me on your side they were afraid of arraigning you illegally, so I could throw the arraignment out later, and I would have seen it was done that way. But they didn't let you go. Try getting out of Lowndesburg! They know where you are: in my office. They impounded your car a long time ago; try getting another one. Try going any place except to the hotel from here, and then try getting out of the hotel."

I told him I saw his point.

Lighton said, "Well, don't let it crush you. I'm a good lawyer, and I'm not so damned frivolous as I sound. As soon as Andy's out of the way, we'll start on the story of your marriage, and somehow or other I'll start building up a case." He smiled. "There's another room, Andy. Take your drink with you."

She smiled at me and went into what I guess was the secretary's office, and I was alone with my lawyer.

"Andy didn't have to go," I said. "It's a quick story. I had some money; some saved, some inherited. She told me she was pregnant to get me to marry her and then she told me it was a mistake and then she ran through my money and then she ran out. Period."

Henry Lighton said, "She had the most beautiful legs I've ever seen. And a face that made you dream of a woman without guile, malice or greed... It almost surprised you that she had to eat, like other mortals."

I must have looked almost as amazed as I felt.

"All right," Lighton said. "I had a case for her, a yen, a crush on her, whatever the current vulgarism is. Where did John Five meet her, do you know?"

"I already told you I didn't know she'd remarried. The divorce papers came from Reno."

"John Five was west, California, Las Vegas, San Francisco, for a while. I paid his bills for him while he was away."

"She liked money," I said. "She'd go where it was."

"We all like money," Henry Lighton said. He got up and refilled his glass, gestured to me. I shook my head. I had the feeling I'd stepped into a new world where everyone's objective was to trap me. I would be a fool to trust anyone in Lowndesburg. The time to get drunk was not now.

The phone rang. Henry Lighton raised his thin eyebrows at it, and then lowered them and picked up the phone. He said his name. "No, I'm not...not yet... I do not see that that matters... No, I couldn't. But before you ask anyone else, I'd like you to come to my office, now...to meet him. You might change your mind...Well, do that."

He hung up and smiled. "John Five. Wanted to retain me as special prosecutor. I told him to come up here and talk to you. He said he'd think it over."

"I don't see what's to be gained by—"

"Don't be a child," said Lighton. "John Five laid the original finger on you. If he takes it off, it would help."

"Is he likely to because I'm pretty, or wear a nice blue suit?"

"The only picture of you that he's had was from Edith," Henry Lighton said. "She may have made you out as a monster of some kind. Meeting you can't help but be to our advantage... He might come here. He just might. Men are curious about their wives' ex-husbands... That's enough for now." He pressed a button and a buzzer sounded next door.

"You are the most peculiar lawyer I've ever seen," I said. "You don't seem to plan at all. You just let things happen."

Andy came back in. With another smile for me

"They happen whether we let them or not, don't they?" my attorney said. He stood up, and started walking around the room. After a while he started talking local politics to Andy. She answered him, and I lost interest in a conversation that was all about people I didn't know.

I got up and fixed myself another highball. "Perhaps I ought to call my boss, Harvey Planne. Our lawyers would know somebody down here to represent me, or maybe one of them could come down himself." I reached in my hip pocket to get Harvey's home phone number and then I remembered: Lieutenant Gamble had kept the wallet.

He'd be checking everybody in it, to find out about me. And that wasn't good. I had no more to hide than the next man, but it is not very good for a businessman to have police around asking questions about him.

I hadn't been with Harvey Planne and Hydrol very long. Why should he send legal help or any kind of help?

And I didn't have much money. I was barely back on my feet again after the wreck Edith had made of my bank account and my career. A divorce never leaves you exactly as it found you, I suppose...

Perhaps a third highball would help... Before, getting drunk had seemed a very bad idea, the worst in the world; a man in a trap should keep his wits steady. But now that it was reaching me that, outside the trap, I didn't have a friend in the world—not a real friend—drinking seemed the dandiest of ideas, and I'm not a heavy drinker.

Andy and Henry Lighton were talking about some people named Madge and Jimmy, who seemed to be local politicians, or as reasonable a facsimile of same as Lowndesburg could be expected to produce. Madge, it seemed, was for Jimmy, but susceptible to flattery, and might desert him at any moment. "Fond as she is of Jimmy, she'd always go for three men against one," Andy said.

Henry Lighton said, "But if we had one voice there, to put our side forward, it would get on the record." He turned to me. "What are you up to?"

"I'm going over to the hotel."

"No. I'm not through with you yet."

"But, I should think, the client—"

His voice turned very harsh. "My clients do what I tell them. You stay."

"The law isn't a license that gives you the right to play with people like—"

He cut me off. I didn't know what I was going to say anyway.

"Liberty," he said. "Not license. I can play around with people...because I get them off in court. Look up my record some time. Come in tomorrow—if I decide you're still loose then—and my secretary will get it out for you. People are so frightened I won't defend them that they gladly surrender their lives, their fates, their very wives to me—if I want them to."

Andy said, "Really, Henry."

He flung himself around his desk and fell into his high-backed chair. "Just histrionics," he said. "All criminal lawyers are hams. Just showing off. Did I dominate you, Porter?" I didn't answer. I hated him thoroughly just then.

"That was a sample of what I would have been if I'd stayed in big-time practice. So... I got out. Just about in time, too."

A siren wailed down in the square. It sounded like a loon I'd heard once, in a camp in Maine. I had fallen among loons, I felt, but not the bird kind.

Another one appeared then, as though conjured out of the air by my thoughts. It was McLane, Otto McLane. He had on a blue uniform, with an eagle on each shoulder, like an Army colonel's eagle, but in brass.

He put his hands on his blue serge hips, and said, "What the hell are you doing here?" to his daughter.

"Sitting and talking to Mr. Lighton and Mr. Porter."

"I went home to get my uniform," he said, "so Gamble wouldn't have to keep explaining me to the brass, and you weren't there. I didn't raise you to hang out with murderers and shysters. G'wan home."

"Dad, leave me alone," she said.

Henry Lighton said, "You know, Chief, this is my office. You ought to say something like 'permission to come aboard,' or 'thanks for the use of the hall,' before you call me a shyster. You really should, Chief." His use of the word "chief" was a masterpiece of understated insult.

Mac glared at him and walked across to me. "Leave my daughter alone, punk."

I said, "Mac, before we start anything else, thanks for the help you gave me over there."

"I don't frame innocent guys. And I don't let state brass, no matter how big, crowd me out of my own department. But that's nothing to you. I don't want a guy who's suspected of murder chasing after my daughter. Get it, punk?"

I understood him. A washed-up man still trying to be impressive. But I'd been pushed too far. I'd had it.

"Chief McLane," I said, "I'm not a known pickpocket that you can tell to get out of your one-horse town. Float, isn't that the word that cops use? You can't float me."

"Big shot," Mac said. "Chicago big shot."

"Has-been," I said. "Lowndesburg has-been. From now on, if you talk to me, do it through my lawyer here, or Lieutenant Gamble."

Dogs don't turn whitish-green with rage, so Mac longer looked canine. He said, "Gamble! I was a police officer when Gamble needed changing on the hour!"

"And he's a police officer when you're part-time day watchman in a feed store!"

Henry Lighton said, "Your relationship with the police department deteriorates rapidly. Hold it, Chief."

I turned and looked at Mac. He was getting out a gun from under the blue skirt of his tunic, "You and me, punk, are going for a walk. When I bring you back, you'll be willing to talk! You're going to tell me how, when, why and dot your i's and cross your t's, and then we'll see your great pal Gamble, and—"

Lighton said: "I said, Chief, hold on."

We both looked over at the desk. Henry Lighton was pointing a small, efficient looking automatic at Mac. Lighton said, "I'm sorry, Mac. I like your father-in-law, I'm mad about your daughter, and I used to like you. But the dignity of the bar is not to be trod on lightly, like the snake in the old Revolutionary flag."

Mac called him one of the more obvious epithets.

Henry Lighton said, "I must also warn you that a tape recorder has been running since you first insulted my client. Don't add any more to it."

McLane turned on his heel and slammed out. The building was well made, or it would have shook from the banging he gave the door.

"What an unrewarding conference... Oh, for God's sake," said Henry Lighton.

Andrea McLane had burst into tears.

I must have hurried over to her, because I found myself standing in front of her, holding out my arms, trying to take her in them. But she side-stepped, smiled a wan smile that wasn't more than kindly and friendly, and reached up and patted my cheek.

Suddenly I realized that I'd been living in a fantasy, a dream world where Andy McLane loved me. But all that was between us was a couple of dances and a bowl of noodle soup, two cocktails. Well, she'd held my hand a couple of times, which is hardly a passionate affair for a modern girl.

She had cried, and maybe it was for me and maybe it was because her father had just shown himself a jerk and a washout. Reason enough to be sad, especially when I remembered how protective she'd been towards him that morning.

Lighton said, "Now you know why Mr. Gray was willing to pay your bill here. All of Mac's friends are afraid he's blown his stack... Oh, call it...call it the male change of life."

He stopped and considered this, and his eyes brightened with admiration for his own words. When he spoke again, he didn't sound so angry. "I hate crying women. I should hate to hate you, Andy, you're so pretty. Stop crying, and I'll let you take Mr. Porter to his hotel where you can kiss him good night. I'll pick you up at the lobby entrance in ten minutes and drive you home where you can—hope springs eternal—kiss me good night. Don't cry; think of all the joys ahead of you."

CHAPTER 5

The lobby of the hotel had, the few times I'd seen it, been a sleepy place, with a drowsing clerk, a Coke machine, and the entrance to the night club-restaurant. Outside of the lights necessary for these, there were dark corners and overstuffed leather chairs, a few of them oozing their overstuffing.

New life had come into the old place. At least two dozen men and a couple of women were milling around, and the management had honored them with a lighted chandelier that looked about to fall from the weight of dust on its mass of tortured glass and metal.

Three of the men and one of the women were talking to a uniformed state police lieutenant over in one corner, near the Coke machine. I wouldn't say they had cornered him; he looked expansively happy, waving beefy hands and beaming.

Andy said: "I don't get my good-night kiss."

"I like the way you put that. I like it very much. Not so much as I would have liked kissing you." I thought: There's always my room.

"In front of God and the Associated Press? No thanks."

"There'll be another—" But the press had seen us they deserted the lieutenant, who went on waving his hands and talking for a good three seconds before he saw he'd lost his audience.

Then they were on me, and Andy fled, out of the front door and away. Maybe because the male reporters were gentlemen, or maybe because her shrill voice cut through them, the lady newspaper reporter got her question first: "You're Mr. Porter, I just know it, and I want to know, do you have a picture of your wife?"

"My ex-wife, and I don't carry ex-wives' pictures near to my heart."

A thin, bald gent, with his hat tilted back to show that grass didn't grow on his busy street, said, "How many times you been married, Porter?"

"Just the once."

He put the hand that held his notepaper on one hip, the one holding his pencil on the other, and shot his head out at me. He had a remarkably long neck. "You said ex-wives, not ex-wife."

A fat reporter came to his aid. "It's better not to hold out on the press, Mr. Porter. If you've been married before, we'll find it out."

The imaginary headlines swam before my eyes: POLICE BACK-TRACK BLUEBEARD. Or words to that effect. "No previous marriages," I said. "I guess I was making a little joke."

At once they all made notes on the folded coarse paper they carried.

ALLEGED SLAYER QUIPS. Maybe I should have been a headline writer.

The previously silent lady reporter edged up to me. She had a less piercing voice than her colleague, but was otherwise equally a reject. "You're very attractive, you know, Mr. Porter. I'll just bet you've got a new girlfriend."

"No such luck," I said, to be saying something.

Fat man said, "Wasn't that a girl that just came in with you?"

"The police chief's daughter," I said. At once I knew I shouldn't have, and tried to recover lost ground. "Maybe the cops are short-handed, and swore her in. Anyway, she drove me back from across the square." It wasn't a very good recovery. Bluebeard was quipping again.

They all turned, and pushed a young kid out of the crowd. It had been dark out on the courthouse lawn, but I thought he was the one who had tried to interview Henry Lighton and me, the one Henry had called Max. They were either too young or too old, the lawyer had said.

The rest of the mob started asking him if the girl who'd brought me to the hotel really was the police chief's daughter. They asked him so energetically that he didn't have a chance to answer for a while. When he did, he sounded miserable. "I didn't see her. But Chief McLane's daughter is tall and dark and she's not a girl. She's older, about twenty-seven or eight."

Although this didn't seem to go over so well with the two lady reporters, it did provide a diverting action to save me. The ladies just glared at poor young Max, and the thin reporter, who seemed to be a leader of some sort, chuckled, and then they were down my throat again.

One of the men in the back shouted, "You been released, Porter?"

"Yes."

"Going back to Chicago tonight?"

"I've been told not to leave town."

This made them all very happy. They made little notes again. All but young Max, who was trying to edge away. Henry Lighton had said it was Max's father's paper; I didn't think the son was going to follow in the paternal footsteps.

The thin man shot his head out again. "Have there been any other arrests?"

I said I didn't know.

"Then you're still the only suspect?"

"I don't know that, either. All know is, I was told I could get some sleep, and I'd very much like to."

Fat man took over. "What you so tired for? Just an ordinary day, wasn't it? Called on a few customers, took it easy, didn't you?"

"Ending up with being arrested, held, questioned. I'm not accustomed to that kind of night work."

A voice from the back said: "He's bluffing. I've seen a lot of murderers, and the cool ones are always bluffing. An innocent guy, now, he'd be in tears."

Even as my temper left me, I knew I was making a mistake. Alienating the press, it's called, I think. But I'd had all I could stand. I said: "That's probably slander. And if you want anything else, go see my attorney, Henry Lighton. In the meantime—" I raised my voice: "Lieutenant!"

He was out there beyond the crowd of reporters, looking lonely. He turned, and brightened; we all need to be needed. "Yes, sir?"

"I could use a little police protection. I want to get to my room, and I don't see how I can through this mob."

He waded over. He was a very different type from Lieutenant Gamble; fat where the plainclothes officer was muscular, dull-eyed where Lieutenant Gamble was sharp and alert looking. I guess it takes different types to do different kinds of police work; I don't know. I wish I'd never see another policeman again in this or any other life. "Break it up, folks," he said. "The poor guy is probably tired, and anyway, anything he's got to say, he oughta be saying it to the authorities."

But it did the work for me: they turned on him just long enough to let me slip by. They were asking him if he'd say I was being held incommunicado just as I made it to the stairs. The elevator was on the ground floor, but I thought I could do better on my own legs.

When I opened the door of my room, the phone was ringing. I snatched it up, and the operator said I hadn't stopped at the desk for my messages. When I confessed to this heinous crime, she said she had a call for me from Chicago; she'd ring me back if I would promise to stay in my room. I promised.

I used cold water on my face, and tried to think a cheerful thought, and finally the phone rang again.

The hotel operator said: "Your call from Chicago, Mr. Porter."

There was no hope she wouldn't listen in. How often does a town with a three-hundred-a-year police chief have a murder?

The call was from Harvey Planne. He said: "What are you doing in Lowndesburg, where the hell is Lowndesburg, and what the hell are you doing there? Police types have been all over me all evening."

Harvey was a lend-lease officer with the British in '42 and '43 and he never lost his British accent. If he had, he would have gone back and looked for it.

I told him it was rather complicated, and then I went into details. Despite my warning, I didn't feel he was, getting the story at all.

When I finished, he said, "Bit sticky, isn't it? I mean, time consuming, to say the least... Tell you what. I'll send you a month's pay, first thing in the Ack Emma, and you consider yourself on indefinite leave of absence. Don't worry; your job will be here, when, as and if."

When I cleared myself; as long as no shadow rested, on me and therefore on the firm; and if his father didn't object. Harvey was founder and president of Hydrol, but his father was chairman and sole investor.

But I might need the job back, so I thanked him as though he'd done me a big favor, and left him, I hope, thinking he had. But as for me, I was now on my own. I couldn't think of another friend that the divorce, had left me. Then I was alone in that damned hotel room, a picture of someplace in spring on the wall, and a hole in the door through which you could send clothes, and a bed and a closet and a chair. The drinks Henry Lighton had given me churned in my stomach and died an unhappy and protesting death and I felt like I'd like to die with them.

This morning—my God, just the same day, for it wasn't midnight yet—I had driven into Lowndesburg. Good job, good car, good weather. The chances of my driving out of Lowndesburg again, at the wheel, un-hand-cuffed, were not quite up to those of a Percheron winning the Kentucky Derby.

I was cooked, but good. I had a sadistic cynic for a lawyer, no friends, and a damned good case against me... The phone rang. I stared at it—it was probably the FBI joining the case, with a complete set of my fingerprints found on a long-handled stiletto—and it rang again and again. I picked it up. Henry Lighton said, "Paul, I want you to come back to the office."

I said, "No," and hung up. I didn't want to see anybody.

The phone rang again, and I sat on the edge of the bed and thought about Edith. She had been, and in my memory she still was, the most beautiful woman I had ever seen.

As soon as the ringing stopped, I snatched up the phone and told the operator I wasn't taking any calls. But she was a real hep girl; she said, "Not even the police? They're on the wire now."

"Put them on," I said. "If you don't they'll come over in person, and then you'll miss listening in."

She suppressed a giggle, and clicked some switches and said, "Go ahead, Lieutenant Gamble, here's Mr. Porter now."

The lieutenant's measured tones marched against my ear, which was aching no more than the rest of me. "Mr. Porter, I want you to know that we found the proper match up at Mt. Hilliard. And we've re-examined Banion and Crosley."

"The dendrologists?"

"I am glad to see you retain some of your sense of humor. So now, as the matter stands, it is certain that you only spent ten to fifteen minutes up at John Five's place, and that you lighted a match while there. Of course, we have only your word, your unsupported word, that you used that match to smoke a cigarette." He coughed. "With Henry Lighton as counsel, that might build up into something of a defense."

"You didn't call me to cheer me up, Lieutenant."

"Well, no. That is hardly my way. I wanted to tell you, we have obtained an order from a Chicago judge to search your apartment. Cook County officers should be entering around now. If there are any letters there—or other papers, such as newspaper clippings—proving that you knew where your ex-wife was, whom she had married, tell us now."

I watched the window curtains fluttering. If I jumped out of the window, I'd probably just break my arches, and have to go to the gallows with flat feet. Or death chamber. How did they kill you in this state? I said, "Lieutenant, there'll be nothing there. I didn't know. I don't suppose I could convince you of that."

"I am not much of a man for hypothetical cases," he said. "But let us construct one. You admit you didn't like your wife. Your ex-wife, I should say. So if someone else killed her, you'd be inclined to protect him within limits."

I said, "If that is a hypothetical case, so is the supposition that either a Democrat or a Republican will be the next President. Stop playing, Lieutenant. Maybe I would cover up for a guy like that. I don't know. I've never been privileged to be around any murders before, or any other police work, for that matter. I know that if I was silly enough to cover for a murderer, I'd drop the thing when it looked as if I might incriminate myself."

"At that time, you'd drop it, eh?" Lieutenant Gamble was probably nodding his head wisely. "Well, Mr. Porter, let me say that that time has incontrovertibly arrived. Yes. Have a night's rest, Mr. Porter, I'll be talking to you in the morning." And he hung up.

I started to ask my friend the operator for the name of a doctor who'd get me some sleeping pills. But Gamble maybe could build that into a sign of a guilty conscience. I'd see what a hot tub could do, first.

When I turned on the water in the bathtub, it ran just as slowly as you would expect water to run in a hotel in a town the size of Lowndesburg. The night club dining room seemed the only modem part of this dump.

I undressed slowly, hanging my clothes up with the neatness of a man who has been on the road quite a while. The water in the tub was warm, for a blessing. I slid into it, and stretched out. It was a very long tub. The outside was tiled, but I half suspect that under the tiles there were still lion's claw feet.

Aches and pains that I hadn't known were in me began going away. I rested the back of my neck against the warm edge of the tub, and stared at my knees, two craggy islands rising sheer from a soapy sea.

I suddenly started chuckling at my own idea. Like most men of my age—thirty in April—I have had my share of uniform wearing and weapon toting. While there are great differences in the armed forces—between, let's say, a Marine private landing on a hostile shore, and an Air Force cadet taking dual-control training in Texas—a few things are common to all.

A lack of bathtubs is one of them. Showers, yes—from holes punched in the bottom of an oil drum, to tiled luxuries in permanent BOQ's—but bathtubs aren't for the military.

Therefore, a man in a tub feels safe, civilian and serene. He may be worrying about love, money or getting fat, but he is not in immediate danger of being killed.

It was a good note to go to bed on.

And that was all for the night. I didn't think I could, but I slept, soundly, and without dreams until Lieutenant Gamble opened the door in the morning.

He stood at the foot of my bed, freshly shaved, neatly dressed, urbane as always. "Up," he said. "On your feet. Dressed."

A uniformed trooper, one I thought I hadn't seen before, was with him. Gamble jerked his chin, and the trooper slid his hand under my pillow, then jerked the bedclothes down. I said: "Hey," in a squawk of protest. But all that happened was that the trooper went over to where I had stacked my clothes.

One by one he threw my possessions at me—underwear, socks, shirt, then my trousers. He picked up one of my shoes at a time and ran his hand inside, then the shoes came flying at me, too.

I said: "I may not pay taxes in this state—"

Gamble said, "Your bill paid here?"

"No. I carry—"

Gamble looked at the phone, and the trooper went and picked it up. "Cashier, please."

I told Gamble that I carried a credit card, hotel bills were sent to the firm.

"You are somewhat severed from Hydrol Machines," the lieutenant told me. "I talked to Mr. Harvey Planne last night. You'd better pay your bill."

The trooper said, "Thank you" into the phone. "He owes nine dollars, even. His money's in his right-hand pants pocket."

Gamble snapped his finger. "Nine dollars, Mr. Porter."

"Thanks for the mister. I wonder if Hitler's storm-troopers were so polite."

Gamble snapped his fingers. "Nine dollars, please."

I was just putting on the pants. I snapped the top button shut, and fished out the roll of bills he'd made me take out of my wallet the night before. I gave him a ten dollar bill. He said: "Tester, you got a one?"

The trooper had to unbutton his hip pocket to get his wallet out. He took a bill from it, gave it to me. I rolled it with the others, and put them back in my pocket. Then I zipped my pants shut.

"Officer Tester will bring you a receipt later," Lieutenant Gamble said. "Now. Put your shoes on, your tie and coat if you want to. I don't believe in getting men off balance before I question them."

"Can I shave?" I asked.

"No," Lieutenant Gamble said. Flatly, infuriatingly.

"All right," I said. "I made a grammatical error. May I shave?"

"Still no."

"I had all night to cut my throat if I wanted to. Or my wrists. Or are you scared I'll assault you and your trooper with a deadly weapon, i.e., a safety razor?"

"I don't know," Lieutenant Gamble said. "There's a book. It says, don't let a suspect handle a razor. Thinking it over, the book may have been written when straight razors were still the only tool available for whisker removing. Shave, if it means so much to you."

But the trooper went into the bathroom with me, changed the blade in my razor for me, and took the razor back the minute I was through. He dried the blade before stowing the razor away in my toilet kit.

When we came back out, Lieutenant Gamble had neatly pulled the bedclothes up and was sitting in the room's one chair. He said, "That's all right, Tester. Go down, pay the bill, have a cup of coffee if you want to. I'll call the coffee shop if I need you."

Tester said, "Okay." He went away without slamming the door, and I was alone with Gamble.

He put that into words. "Now, we're going to talk, man to man. Just the two of us... I have seen a lot more trouble than you have, I'm sure. Let me tell you that the one, single thing that a man in your position can do is to co-operate with the authorities. In this case, I am the authority to work with, for the moment; pretty soon the district attorney will take over. We have an appointment with him in half an hour."

"Will my lawyer be there?"

Lieutenant Gamble shrugged. "That's pretty much up to the D.A."

"I thought—"

Lieutenant Gamble said: "I know, I know. Your rights. Your rights are to ask for your attorney, to stand mute until you are in the execution chamber. Then they usually talk. My rights—the rights of the authorities—are to take you over to the mortician's, presumably to identify the victim. I can then keep you there, in the presence of the corpse, as long as I want—up to forty-eight hours, I believe. That is cruel and unusual punishment, in my eyes, but not in the eyes of the law. I've never done it."

"You surprise me a little, Lieutenant. I should think you'd be a lawyer instead of a policeman."

He laughed, drily. "Very astute, Mr. Porter. I married in my third year of college, when I transferred to law school. Inadvertently, my wife had twins a year later."

"These things happen."

He nodded. "Do you mind if I smoke? I know it's before breakfast for you."

"Go ahead. I rather wish I had you to defend me instead of Henry Lighton."

Lieutenant Gamble was lighting his cigarette. He blew out the match with vigor, tossed the burnt bit of card board into an ashtray, blew out smoke. "Whatever you've read in whodunits, whatever you suspects the average police officer is anxious to get the truth. In that respect, I am as much your defense attorney as I am your prosecutor."

Talk, talk, talk. It went on, and I stopped listening. This was a hotel room, more like other hotel rooms than it was different; this was myself, more as I had always been than I was changed; but the man across the room, talking his rounded periods was a policeman trying to find out if I was a murderer.

All of last night seemed unreal, all of now was crazy. I'd gone through the looking-glass into a world that should never have been. I said, "I'd tell you anything, admit to anything, to get out of this."

"I suppose so," Lieutenant Gamble said. "But it's too late for that. You planned to kill Edith Hilliard. You went up there with that in your mind. You had first, very cleverly, used Mac as an alibi; she had written you that her husband owned these hilly woods, that if you came into the valley trying to sell a land-leveller—"

Like a fool, I interrupted: "A terracer."

He smiled. "Decided you do know something about it, after all?"

"I know I saw a terracer in McLane's window."

With his left hand, Lieutenant Gamble got a package of cigarettes out of his pocket. He tapped it on his knee till a butt rose, pulled the cigarette out with his lips, and used his lighter...with his left hand. His right hand remained immobile, on his lap. Presumably, if I were to jump him, a gun would be available to stop me.

"You know that any implement dealer around here would take you to see John Five if you offered him an exceptionally large commission on a...terracer? Yeah, a terracer. Who else around here would need one, but Mt. Hilliard? So you were smart. You picked on Mac, an ex-cop, a present hick police chief. You thought—how do I know what a murderer thinks? A man is crazy to murder at all—that since you would be in with the police chief, it would be easy to fool him. Maybe you thought Mac would close the case, confused, and that would be the end of it. Maybe you thought he'd be too anxious to get his commission on your rig to want to annoy you, but, of course, Mac is a policeman first and a moneymaker second."

Smoke rolled lazily out of his mouth. He smiled at me.

"Crime follows a pattern. I'm really not so brilliant as you might think; just experienced. I don't have to read your mind; I just have to have worked on enough similar cases. Actually, criminals are boring, they're so much alike; and the most boring of all are murderers."

I waved at the smoke with my hand. "I'm neither policeman nor lawyer, but don't you have to dig up a motive?"

He chuckled. "She wiped you clean, and she ran you under a vacuum cleaner. Then she wrote you and taunted you. The money that you missed so badly she was spending at the dime store; her new man had real dough, yours was to tip a bellboy with."

"Where do you cops get your talk?" I asked. "Is there a course in police school on how to talk tough?"

He smiled. "It is supposed to intimidate the suspect, Porter. I went to college; would you like me to say a long word for you? A man can stand most anything but laughter; ask any police officer. She taunted you a little too far, and you set her up for a strangling."

"I think you're the first man I ever heard say the word 'taunt.' I've read it, but I never heard it used out loud."

He stood up. "I told you I was a college man. All right. The district attorney is meeting us over at the court. He will have phoned Lighton... What's ahead of you isn't pleasant, but it's legal and it won't kill you. Suspicion of murder; bail refused; questioned at the state police barracks, driven to the city, held, questioned, driven to the scene of the crime, questioned; sooner or later they all talk. The sooner the pleasanter for all parties interested. Stand up."

I did. He pushed me towards the door. I moved.

Suddenly something whacked me hard, just below my ribs on the left side. My breath went out in a roar, and I put one hand on the bureau to steady myself. I turned.

Lieutenant Gamble was holding a short piece of cloth in his left hand. "Just a tube of nylon," he said. "Full of sand. Sifted sand; a pebble might bruise your skin. Never hit them on the right side, you might bust an appendix."

My breath was coming back. "Mine's out."

"You've got guts," Gamble said. "But the liver's on the right side, too. I had to show you I can get tough, too. Friendly, tough; it's all one to me. All I want is a confession."

I rubbed my side. "Last night you seemed to think me innocent."

Lieutenant Gamble looked gloomy. "That was last night," he said. "I spent the night trying to turn up any other possible suspect. I didn't. So now you're guilty... I have that much respect for my own ability. If there had been anyone else, I'd have heard of him by now. Let's go."

CHAPTER 6

The justice of the peace room across from the City Hall on the other side of the square from the hotel. It was a room that should have been, maybe had been, a candy store or a shoeshine parlor; narrow and long. A set of twelve legal-looking books occupied a glass-front case, an American flag drooped behind a yellow oak desk. The J.P. needed a haircut.

I was introduced to the district attorney as though we were going to be friends: Mr. Norton Prince. He had been to college, too, with a man named Henry Porter, from Chicago. I said it was a common name and a big city.

He nodded, respecting the wisdom of my observation, and turned to Henry Lighton. "We might as well get this over with."

Henry Lighton said we might as well, and we did. I was to be turned over to the sheriff and held for the grand jury. Henry Lighton applied for bail, on the grounds that I was being held on circumstantial evidence. Mr. Norton Prince cited a statute, and the J.P. denied bail.

Lieutenant Gamble took my arm, said, "Hold out your hands," and snapped cuffs on me.

"Are you the sheriff?" I inquired.

"All state police officers are authorized to act as deputy sheriffs. They passed a law ten years ago. Right, Mr. Lighton?"

Henry Lighton said, "Don't bother me. I'm thinking up angles about false arrest. About malfeasance based on malice."

Lieutenant Gamble said, "I do a neat, clean job. No angles, Mr. Lighton."

Mr. Norton Prince said he would buy Henry a cup of coffee. "We'll see you later, Lieutenant, Mr. Porter."

Gamble took my elbow, and said: "I'll lock you up at Mac's dog house. Prince wants to take you up to Mt. Hilliard later."

He pushed me ahead of him out on the street. Lowndesburg had turned out to see a real live murderer. Two state cops were holding the populace back. He shoved me at one of them, said, "Put him in the lockup, Marske, and get someone to sign for him. I'm going for coffee."

Marske's pal pulled a gun, Marske grabbed my elbow. "Out of the way, folks."

The folks broke, let us through, closed in behind us. I don't know if the drawn gun was for me or the crowd; the trooper holding it shot his sullen eyes in all directions. Marske was reasonably gentle pushing me ahead of him, and when we got to the steps leading down into Mac's police station, the pal with the gun stayed at the top of them. The office was empty, except for one man.

I was meeting all kinds of law officers. This one was neat in khaki pants and shirt, and his badge had come from a dime store; it just said, "Police," without any rank or the name of any city. He had lost half of one arm, his right one, and, his left hand held a ring of keys.

He unlocked one of the cells behind Mac's desk, and Marske took my handcuffs off with a key from his pocket. I'd learned something: all state police handcuffs worked off any state police key.

Marske said, "Lieutenant wants a receipt for him."

The one-armed turnkey grunted. "Sure. We're likely to lose him in here. Which lieutenant, Gamble?"

As he said it, he unlocked the iron-barred gate behind Mac's desk. He nodded for me to go through. "Sit in any cell, son, or stand around the aisle. We turned all our drunks out an hour ago."

He sat down at Mac's desk while I watched from the aisle of the four-cell lockup. He pulled paper towards him, held it down with the stump of his right arm, and wrote, clumsily, with his one hand. "I useta be on the state force," he said. "Sergeant Knowles. Heard of me?"

Marske said, politely: "I think so, Sergeant."

"Just mister, now. I'm sort of jail janitor here. I sleep back there, through that other door, and I fetch the meals when the prisoners need 'em—and we got prisoners—and I answer the phone."

"Tough," Marske said. He read the paper that was handed him, read it carefully.

"Not so tough," Knowles said. "I'm on half pay from the state, too.

Not bad."

Marske said something polite, and marched out. Knowles got up from McLane's desk, and came over near the bars. "Had breakfast, Mr. Porter?"

"No."

He thought. "I got a pot of coffee on the burner in my room, a couple of doughnuts. If those'll do you, you won't have to wait. Otherwise, I gotta send for the day cop, the traffic cop, to come watch you while I go out. Chief McLane decided to leave him on the traffic, thought I could hold you. How about the chow?"

"The coffee and doughnuts'll do fine, thanks. But why watch me? I'm not going anyplace."

Mr. Knowles said: "When I have a prisoner, someone stays with him. Supposing the building caught on fire, supposing you had a heart attack? You can't get out, can't even get to a phone."

I said I was sorry. "You're a pretty decent guy."

Knowles said, "I'm a washed-up one. I won't say that when I was a big muckamuck running around in a tailor-made sergeant's suit, I didn't have too much pride for my own good... I'll get that coffee."

He brought it back and handed it through the bars to me. Then he handed me one of those folding TV tables, tray first, then the legs. I fetched a stool out of one of the cells and sat in the corridor. He sat in the side chair, not at McLane's desk. He lighted a cigarette just the way Lieutenant Gamble had done, but in his case it was necessary since he had only one arm. That police trick must have come in handy when he lost the other one.

"I got a little radio if you need to pass the time."

"I think I'm only going to be here an hour. They're taking me up to Mt. Hilliard to see the place where—well, you know. I didn't kill her, before you ask."

"Wasn't going to," Knowles said. He blew out smoke.

"Incidentally, I lost my arm when a car turned over, before you ask."

"I wasn't going to."

We both laughed. Underground as we were, the noises of the town were soothing and distant. The one window in the cell block was above my head, and just at ground level, apparently. It was closed and barred, and the noise came down the stairwell from the City Hall lawn.

He said: "That damned Gamble asking for a receipt!" The stump of his arm jerked, once, as though a nerve hurt him. He put the cigarette in his mouth, and rubbed his short arm.

I said: "Yesterday morning I didn't have a care in the world."

"I was stashed up behind a bunch of trees, watching the highway, smoking a cigarette. These guys came along at ninety per. I took after them, and five minutes later I'd put the cruiser into a ditch."

"Life."

"And myself into a pension," he said. "The hell it's life... I was due to go off watch in twenty minutes... We got a visitor."

I thought it would be Lieutenant Gamble come to get me, and I think Knowles did, too, because he stayed in his chair. But it was Andy McLane. A black cotton dress showed under the same tweed coat she'd worn last night.

Knowles jumped out of his chair. "Hi, Andy. Sure nice to see you."

She said, "Hi, Knowlesy; hi, Paul. Okay to visit with your prisoner, Knowlesy?"

"You know better than that," Knowles said. "His attorney of record, Henry Lighton, has a right to see him; nobody else." He considered. "But that Gamble, and his receipt. I was a sergeant when he was still a rookie... How's a small-town clown like me gonna know that a prisoner's not supposed to have visitors? G'wan. Only I better sit between you."

He grabbed up his chair with his one arm, and swung right around the bars. "I'll sit down, and you can both talk over my head. Don't try and touch him, don't try and pass anything to him."

She got up close to where Knowles was sitting, and now she was only two or three feet from me. She said, "Gramps was worried about you. He sent me down here to see if there's anything you need."

"You're the damndest family," I said. "Yesterday I was admiring how well you got along with your father. Last night I had a big shouting match with him, and five minutes later you were walking across the square with me."

She said, "Well, Dad's all right, and I'm crazy about him, but Gramps is the real brain in our family. He thinks Dad shouldn't have called in the state police."

Between us, Knowles grunted. As though remembering him, Andy said, "Got a cigarette for me, Knowlesy?"

He grunted again, and got the pack out from under his badge. He did his act of making a single cigarette climb out of the package, and held it out to her, smiling.

Andy hesitated a moment, and then reached. But not for the cigarette. She grabbed Knowles's only wrist in her two hands, and twisted. Knowles came back against the bars. Andy was crying again. She said, "Paul! Hit him."

Knowles was making absolutely no effort to get away—which maybe he couldn't, if Andy had ever taken a Red Cross course in life saving. But he wasn't trying to yell, either, and that he certainly could have done.

I did nothing, and after a moment, Andy let go. Knowles bent over, giving her a free shot at the back of his neck, and picked up his cigarettes. "Here's your butt, Andy."

She took it, and he lighted it for her with a wooden match and his fingernail, turned, and held the package through the bars. I had cigarettes of my own, but I took one.

We all three blew smoke at each other for a while, without anyone meeting anyone else's eyes. Finally Knowles said: "You can't do things like that, Andy. Some people can, but you can't."

Andy said, "I suppose so," her voice completely dreary. "But Paul—"

"I know, I know," Knowles said. "You can't sock an unarmed friend, and Paul probably couldn't strangle his wife. I get a lot of time to think, back there in my janitor's room, listening to the drunks sing 'Sparrow in the Treetop'. It gives me lots of time to think."

"Knowlesy—"

"It's forgotten," he said. "You think I'd go out of my way to report this, or anything else, to Gamble?"

Andy said, "Or to my Dad."

"Mac gave me this job," Knowles said. "I'm obliged to him." His jaws moved as though he wanted to spit.

"Who rates higher," I said, "a sergeant of state police or a captain on the city force?"

Knowles said, "That's a damned fool question."

I suppose it was. At any rate, he didn't give me an answer. And I didn't bother to ask Mac when he came in a minute later, with a dirty look at Andy for hanging around a jailbird like me, a dirty look at Knowles for letting her, and no look at all for me.

The two tree men, Banion and Crosley were with him. Mac said, "Stand over there, raise your right hands." They did, and he said: "Do you swear to uphold the laws of this city and state and the Constitution of the United States?" and they both nodded.

Mac unlocked a desk drawer, took out two badges and handed them over. Knowles grunted, for no reason I could think of until I noticed that these were much more expensive shields than the one the turnkey wore.

I wondered what kept Knowles from greasing the steps down to the office some night when Mac was due to walk down them.

"All right," said Mac. "Take him up to the court room, boys." He turned. "Open the lockup, Knowles."

At least he didn't call the ex-sergeant Wingy. Maybe he hadn't thought of it.

Andy was peering into her compact mirror, straightening her lipstick, dabbing powder under her eyes. She said, "I'm going with you, Paul."

Mac said: "No."

Andy didn't hear him. The temporary cops each took an elbow, and we went out. I didn't say goodbye to Knowles; I didn't think it would help him with his boss to appear too friendly with me, and he needed the job.

For once there was no mob around the jail. With nothing to see they'd drifted away, maybe to watch the state officers eat their breakfasts.

I said, "I thought you lads were dendrologists, not cops."

Banion said, "I took a forestry degree. They give you a course in law enforcement in case you go into the Forest Service... Anyway, Mr. Hilliard is worried you'll get loose. What you did to Mrs. Hilliard he doesn't want done to him. So he lent us to Mac."

Andy was ambling alongside us. She said, "Danny, you look like a policeman, anyway."

Banion said, "Don't know how to take that, Andy. Say, they're changing the bill at the Metro today. Wanta go tonight?"

"No, thanks." She managed a smile.

The other temporary cop, Crosley, said, "Our prisoner's cut you out, Dan."

Dan Banion looked at me. "This dude?" he asked. "That on the level, Andy?"

Andy didn't answer. Banion shook his head and tightened his grip on my arm. "You ought to get someone with more staying power. This guy's got as much liberty left as a mouse with his tail in a trap."

"He's got Henry Lighton," Crosley said.

Banion said, "Yeah. Sure. That guy. Anyway, don't escape, Porter, or Crosley and I'll have to chase you. You really got the boss scared."

I didn't feel like chatting, but my ego demanded a show of nonchalance. "How come John Five had to send you boys down to be deputized? Doesn't he have private cops as well as private foresters?"

Crosley said, "Sure, do you think we're cheap? They're watchmen, though, not private cops, and John Five doesn't even call them that; they're fire guards. Which puts them under Danny Banion here and me, and so we're the ones he chose."

"I see. I'd kind of like to meet John Five."

We were circling the courthouse, going around to the front door. Banion looked across the municipal lawn and said: "Here come the ghouls," indicating citizens converging on us. We all started walking faster, and Danny Banion added, "You'll see John Five all right. He'll be at your trial."

Andy said, "Maybe there won't be a trial."

Still holding on to my arm, Crosley shook his head. "Oh, there'll be a trial all right. Henry Lighton always has a trial. He usually wins it, but going without it would be like asking a Barrymore to rehearse and then not give the show."

"Crosley's got the education," Banion said. "He's Yale School of Forestry. Me, I'm just Syracuse."

We went up the broad steps and into the courthouse. Up more steps and through a wide door that a bailiff in a neat blue uniform held open for us, and we were in a regular courtroom, complete with judge on the bench, a jury waiting to hear a trial, lawyers, spectators, defendant. Nearly as I could tell, the trial had been halted while Mr. Henry Lighton, and the Honorable Norton Prince, D.A., argued about me, because the judge seemed testy. He said, "All right, all right, Mr. Lighton, here's your man now. You applied for habeas corpus, and the court has granted it, the police have complied." He peered. "Who are you men? Where's police chief McLane?"

"Sulking in his tent, no doubt," Henry Lighton said. He chuckled.

"We're special deputies, Your Honor," Crosley said.

"All right, all right. You're Paul Porter, young man?"

"Yes, sir."

"You're admitted to ten thousand dollars' bail. Go over to the clerk there, and sign the papers he gives you. Your attorney has stipulated that you will not leave the county. Agreeable to you?"

"Yes, s— Your Honor." I didn't know much about bail, but I knew the lining of my own wallet: no ten grand. But maybe if I sold my car, it would bring enough to pay the premium on a bond. I'd held bonded jobs, and I knew about that kind of bond. Maybe this was similar.

Henry Lighton tapped me on the arm. His eyes were glowing with a deep fire I hadn't seen in them before, and he seemed ridiculously happy. "Over here," he said.

I followed him over to the low desk under the bench. "This is Mr. de-Vries," Henry Lighton said. "Clerk of this venerable court, and a jim dandy of a cribbage player."

I bowed, and tried to smile at the dandified old clerk.

Henry Lighton went on: "And you know Mr. Gray, of course," and I turned from the clerk to—of all people—Andy's grandfather. .

I hadn't seen him there. Even after looking at him, I could hardly see him; he was wrapped in overcoats, mufflers and shawls till it didn't seem likely he could move. Andy appeared from behind and gave him support. "Gramps, you shouldn't—"

"Do me good. Haven't seen the old courthouse in a spell. Always surprised me it stood up. Hank here—" he indicated deVries—"His uncle sold the county the rock, an' I always calculated he kinda cheated. Should have fallen down in the first hard freeze."

The court clerk chuckled, and said, "I'll be up to whip you at pinochle, cribbage, you name it, soon's this session of court's over. You sign here, Mr. Porter. Maybe you better read it first. Says you're remanded to custody Mr. Gray, your bondsman, an' he forfeits his worldly goods do you decamp. Better keep on lurin' him, Andrea, ten thousand dollars is a mite of money to lose."

A county full of bucolic characters. I signed the papers, and we went out in a little group, Henry Lighton, Mr. Gray, Andy, me. Henry and Andy were helping the old gentleman. I said I didn't know what had happened. Lighton laughed. "You don't have to. All that happened is that I'm a much better lawyer than Norton Prince. I got the judge to reduce the booking to suspicion of complicity."

"But Mr. Gray."

Mr. Gray cackled. "Just money, son. You aren't the running away type. And this'll fair put Otto in a tizzy, which is where I like to see him. Might make him so mad he'll move outa my house."

Andy said: "Gramps, you'd miss him."

"Didn't say I wouldn't. Henry, you drive me home. That damn car of Andy's is full of drafts."

The good people of Lowndesburg weren't used to seeing me without cops on my arms and wrists. There were people around the courthouse, but they paid no attention to me; but two men, obviously reporters, made a dive for Henry Lighton.

Softly as possible, Andy murmured, "Let's get away."

Her car was across the lawn, illegally parked on the wrong side of the street, but who gives a ticket to the police chief's daughter's car?

She said, "You don't want to drive, do you?" and didn't wait for an answer while she got behind the wheel.

She started before the motor was warm, and nearly stalled at the first traffic light. But she viciously pumped gas to the motor, and went on through the gray streets of Lowndesburg.

"I'd like to ask something?"

She said: "Sure."

"Who's watching the store? Your father's out police chiefing, you're chauffeuring fugitives; who sells feed and seed?"

Her eyes were on the road ahead of her "What's it to you? I understand you're unemployed, so even if some shoplifter steals that land-leveller, it isn't your business."

"In the first place, it's a terracer, not a land-leveller. In the second place, I'm not unemployed. I'm on indefinite leave of absence. Till I clear myself."

Andy said, "Oh. Your Mr. Planne took the trouble to call us, tell us he wasn't standing behind any checks you wanted to cash. A good friend."

"A boss," I said. I looked out at the streets. Yesterday had been spring, but now winter had come back; the light was cold and gray. One of those late snows was probably about to powder the Midwest. They don't do any harm to the crops. You have to know about such things when your business depends on farm prosperity.

It seemed a great many years since I had had any business to depend on anything.

"Andy," I said. "I seem to have asked this before... What's it all about? I don't mean my being accused of murder—I understand that—but all the rest? Your grandfather, Henry Lighton, you, for that matter? You never saw me before yesterday."

She turned her gaze away from the windshield a moment to look at me. Then she turned back, carefully twisted the car into the curb, and stopped. She left the motor running, for the heater.

"Gramps said I wasn't to answer any of your questions."

I said, "Oh. Just go along and be pushed in and out of jail whenever some member of your family feels like exercise."

"If you think I'm helping to frame you, get out."

She reached across me and twisted my door handle. Her weight was across my lap for the moment. "Go on, get out."

"Keep your chemise on."

She said, "Girls don't wear them anymore," and started up again. This was more like the Andy McLane I knew; I felt a little better.

"Where are you taking me?"

"Home."

"Maybe your grandfather will answer a few of my questions."

She said, "Maybe," and slowed down to let a car pass us. Nobody in it seemed to give me a second glance.

I rode along in a daze. I was a pawn in a game whose rules—if there were any rules—I didn't know. I was a puck in an ice hockey match. I didn't seem to have done anything but get kicked around, shoved, advised and then not asked if I was going to take the advice.

She stopped in front of Mr. Gray's big house and we got out. I said: "You must be the first police chief's daughter in history to help bail a man out of her father's hoosegow."

Now that she was on her own—her grandfather's—lawn, she was more at ease. She reached up, patted my cheek. "Haven't you heard about Dr. Freud? I'm in rivalry with my father."

"That's for boys, not girls."

"Maybe I'm queer."

"I don't think so," I said. I didn't have to bend far to reach her lips. They were firm and cold from the air.

But after a moment it was plain that she knew the trick most nice girls learn—learn young, if I remember my high school days correctly—of letting a man kiss them without committing themselves. I couldn't tell whether she was just being patient with me, or with herself, waiting for her heart to tell her whether she really wanted to kiss me. So I let her go.

She said, "Go see Grandpa. I'll make some coffee and bring it." Her voice said nothing had happened, but her eyes were bright, or maybe my ego made me think so.

In the daytime, the house was only slightly less gloomy than it had been the night before. The old man in the conservatory looked as if- he hadn't moved since we drank sherry with him.

He was listening to the radio. Somebody was banging away at the administration. Old Mr. Gray looked at me, smiled and slowly reached out and turned a knob. The sound died away. He said, "Half man and half horse."

I must have looked sufficiently blank, because he cackled, and said. "A cen-a-taur. Awful pun, and not original, anyway... How was jail?"

"I'm out on ten thousand bond. Your money."

His fuzzy eyebrows crawled up the drought-cracked river bed that was his forehead. "That's all right, boy. Don't go on thanking me. You embarrass me with all them kind words. Down, boy. Stop kissing me."

"You don't know me. And don't give me that line about Andy being interested in me. While we were going up for the hearing, she was flirting with one of John Five's private rangers. Anyway, anybody with a half a good eye could see you wouldn't have to buy her a husband."

"That's right, she could have any man in town, now."

The cracked old voice came down hard on the word "now." But maybe it was just age's inability to control any of its functions, even the voice...

He went on: "Think I caught cold, goin' down to that durned courthouse. Drafty old dump, ain't it? Did I tell you, the fella that's clerk of the court, his uncle..."

"You told me. What do you mean, Andy can get any man in town—now?"

"Jest what I said. Best lookin' gal in the county—now. When Mrs. John Five was alive, she could have her choice of Lowndes County's fellas, of course. A looker from way back."

The image of Edith came back on me. Desirable, alluring...but then, I would add, unattainable, and she would have been the perfect woman. It was when you got her that you got trouble.

Mr. Gray said, "You all right, son?"

Through the red haze that had bowed my head, I heard the front door close. I said, "Where did Henry Lighton go?"

"Back down to his office fer a spell. He'll be back to talk to you... Thinking about yer wife got you down?"

"It's hard to realize she's dead. Lieutenant Gamble was going to make me look at the body, but so far he hasn't."

The old man said, "Thank God for small favors."

Sitting there suddenly became impossible. I jumped to my feet. "I came in here to find out why I'm being pushed all over Lowndesburg—in jail, out of jail—but the talk got away from me."

"I'm an old man, son. I ramble. First sign of senility."

"You're about as senile as I am."

"I'm eighty, son. Never had a child till Andy's mother was born, Lissa we called her, and that was forty-five years ago. Was thirty-five then. Apple of my eye, boy, till she went up to the city to have a career, an' met Mac."

"We're rambling again. Why did you bail me out?"

"Don't shout at me. Got good hearing, fer all my age."

"Why—did you—bail me—out?"

A car started up outside. The door must have been Andy going away...

Old Mr. Gray said: "Don't believe in keeping nothing penned. Not dog, nor fox, nor man. John Five, now, he has his boys breed foxes up there on the Mount, and turn one loose fer him an' his bosses to chase. Onnacheral, I calls it."

"One minute your grammar's as good as a college professor's, the next minute you're playing the country clown."

He cackled his horrible laugh again. "You gettin' around to saying I killed Edith Hilliard, Paul? I couldn't strangle a new-hatched chicken."

He brought his claws up in front of him and flexed and un-flexed them a few times. Then his eyes brightened. "About time for my morning glass of sherry."

"I heard Andy go out."

"Mebee she had to go downtown to buy a fresh bottle... There's a car coming, now."

"Will you please tell me why you bailed me out?"

"Nope," he said. "That's not Andy's car. Don't know whose it is, an' my hearing's magnificent..."

Whoever it was knew the house well enough to enter without the use of the front door bell, knew it well enough to know where to find human companionship, or at least that of Mr. Gray. Masculine steps strode bravely towards us, and I felt apprehensive.

That old devil sensed it. "Scared, Paul? Want to take a powder?"

I saved what was left of my dignity by not telling him to go to hell. It was only Henry Lighton, my learned counsel.

He said: "I've been down talking to Otto and Lieutenant Gamble. They released your car, Paul; you'll have to drive me back downtown."

I nodded. "I've been trying to get Mr. Gray here to tell me why he bailed me out."

"The study of the mouths of donated horses is a notoriously unrewarding occupation," Lighton said.

"He never saw me before. For all he knows, I'm going away and forfeiting his ten thousand dollars."

Henry Lighton laughed. "You wouldn't get across the state line; you probably wouldn't even get to the county line. Our lieutenant, the good Gamble, is unhappy... It wasn't his fumble, it was Norton Prince's. With the growth of the big corporations it is harder and harder to find a good lawyer to stay home and run for district attorney."

Old Mr. Gray said: "Makes it hard on a real fine trained policeman like Gamble."

"You're right," said Lighton. "Would make an interesting article, if I were thinking of becoming literary, and you know I just might. The rise in training of the police officer, accompanied by the fall in training of the lawyer available for Political offices, and the cause of it all..."

"I'd like to read that. There's been changes in business, too," Mr. Gray said. "In the twenties, the salesman'd be a big fella, full of beefsteak an' bootleg, and if he brought an engineer along from the office, it'd be some measly little wretch that he'd stable down at the railroad hotel. Nowadays..."

My hand hit the table, hard. I shook it, feeling it sting even through the very real anger that was shaking me.

"It's no time to exchange rural philosophy. I'm facing a murder charge!"

Henry Lighton said: "Have no fear; Henry Lighton is here. I made a monkey out of Norton Prince this morning. I can do it again, on call."

Old Mr. Gray just sat blinking his eyes, a tree sloth awakened from a deep sleep.

I said, "Henry, I don't want to get off on a technicality. I want my name cleared, my job back."

He looked at me, and smiled. It wasn't a smile calculated to bring joy and happiness into my life. "You'll be cleared the way I think is best."

"If you don't mind, it's my life." It sounded school-boyish and weak as I said it. "I don't want to go to trial for something I didn't do."

Henry Lighton said, "Until you've been tried, dismissed, and the law of double jeopardy sets in, this will be hanging over you all your life."

"Or until the real murderer's caught."

Henry Lighton shrugged. "Then hire a detective, not a lawyer." He turned his tweedy shoulders away from me. "Mr. Gray, consider this. Can it be that the trend is away from the office man, the fellow who looks things up in books, and towards the field man, the fellow—learned enough—who uses books only occasionally and as a minor tool? The policeman and the engineer, for instance, though—"

The front door opened and closed. I left them there, and went to look for Andy.

CHAPTER 7

She was in the front room of the house, opening a bottle of sherry, just as her grandfather had predicted, but she was not alone. Danny Banion was with her, in his sturdy forester's clothes, still wearing his special policeman's badge. He was talking: "...could have knocked me over with a feather. Turning that guy loose!"

Andy's head was bent down over the bottle, as though she were struggling with the cork. But it was just a bottle of domestic sherry, the kind that is sealed with a simple metal cap. Her shiny hair had fallen forward, and I could not see her face.

She spoke with difficulty. "I don't believe Paul Porter's guilty."

"You're in love," Danny Banion said. "I don't know why, but you are! Come out of the clouds and use your head. Stands to reason, no guy but John Five would put up with the way that dame behaved. Believe me, I've had the night watch up at Mt. Hilliard, going around the house, checking the doors and windows. I've heard them at it; it sounded like she charged John Five ten grand for a kiss, and God knows what for anything more! So any real man, not John Five, but a real guy, would have—"

Andy's head came up; I don't think she saw me, but I stepped back into the wide hall. "Go to hell, Danny Banion. Go to—Mt. Hilliard. You ought to be there!"

He said: "John Five wants a watch around the clock; I got the night du— That stuff doesn't matter. Come to your senses, Andy. I'm quitting this job, going back into the Forest Service! C'mon with me, kid. It'll be a swell job!"

Andy started to cry, not politely like a movie actress, but loudly, as though she was at the end of her patience, of her very strength. I made as little noise as possible going out.

My car was at the curb. I had an extra set of keys my pocket, but I didn't need them. Henry Lighton had left keys in the ignition, the ones taken from me at the jail... Safe Lowndesburg, happy Lowndesburg where nothing so naughty as a car thief would dare to operate.

I didn't know where the county lines were, and if I went out in the country I was likely to cross one, thus forfeiting Mr. Gray's bail. So I headed downtown. Even in a small place like Lowndesburg, there ought to be one bar low enough for the customers to mind their own business...

I found it, finally, on the south end of town, near the highway. There was a shed for ice trucks nearby, and a filling station in front of the bar. Everything needed paint.

The inevitable juke box was playing, and two couples sat in the booths; there were three men at the bar. Everybody looked a little shabby and undersize. I got myself a rye highball, and carried it to one of the booths. After a minute the bartender followed me, and put a bowl of pretzels on the table; he didn't seem to have looked at me.

Now I was alone, out of the dreary weather, away from the curious people; now I ought to be able to think. There was some easy solution to my problem.

I was a big-city man, a successful man; surely I could out-think these hicks and rubes.

So I sipped my highball...and nothing came.

Maybe I ought to ask the bartender for a pencil and paper, I thought, and make a list of everybody I knew in Lowndesburg, and eliminate them one by one.

But the trouble was, I knew hardly anyone there, and in all probability, it was someone I didn't know who had killed Edith.

The only thing I was sure of was that old Mr. Gray knew all about it, or he wouldn't have been so damned helpful. But certainly he hadn't killed Edith; and also, just as certainly, I couldn't get him to tell me anything he didn't want to tell me. I wasn't as smart as he was, and any use of force would just kill him.

The juke box changed from one rock-and-roll number to another; a very slight change.

The front door opened, and a girl came in, as well as a burst of damp, chilly air. She started for the bar, then turned and walked over to my booth and sat down opposite me. I was surprised. Things were going on in Mac's town he didn't know about. B-girls, yet.

Not a bad-looking B-girl, either. Maybe not my type, but smart enough looking; clean white blouse under a red chamois jacket, hair permanented—or maybe naturally wavy—not too much makeup on.

I said: "I'm sorry, miss. I'm just sitting here thinking. I'm not in the mood for romps and frolics."

She said: "Wouldn't think you would be, Mr. Porter. Did that pug-faced police chief beat you up?"

It wasn't a vulgar voice; it had been to high school. But then, who hasn't? But it was a little high-pitched.

"You know who I am." After I said it, I gave myself a medal for elocution and extemporaneous speaking. That was a truly brilliant remark, and I am as proud of it now as I was then.

"Lou, the bartender, called me when you came in. He thought you might like to talk to me."

"I'm not in need of comfort."

"God," she said, "you're stuffy. No wonder your wife left you. Mister, I don't have to pick up dudes in a beer joint. But seeing that you and I don't like McLane any better than anybody else does, maybe I could talk to you. I'm Janey Dandler, by the way."

The name, of course, didn't mean a thing to me, but I seemed to have an ally. I began to brighten. She didn't look like a silver lining, but she didn't look like a dark cloud either. "Drink, Miss Dandler?"

"Sure." She turned her head and her voice went up an octave, cutting across the juke box racket. "Dry martini, Lou."

His lips shaped, "Sure, Janey," but the rock and roll kept me from hearing him.

I said, "I thought rock-and-roll was dead."

"It just smells that way," she said. "I figure you didn't kill Mrs. John Five."

"Nice of you, but how do you make that out?"

"If you had, Chief McLane would have pinched somebody else. That copper never made a right collar in his life."

She must have learned that talk from television. Maybe a new generation of underworld will grow up, talking the way the magazine writers of the '30's thought they ought to talk, as TV actors talk now: life following art.

Lou came and put a martini glass in front of her, poured her drink, and left her a generous dividend in the mixing glass.

I put a pile of coins on the table, but he shook his head. "On the house. You can buy the next one. You ain't sore because I called Janey, are you?"

"Of course not, Lou."

He said, "Swell," and went back behind the bar.

"You're popular here," I told Janey.

"Lou is Red's brother," she said obscurely, and drank half her cocktail. Her lips pursed in and out once in acknowledgement of its strength, while I tried to remember if I knew anyone named Red. "That don't mean a thing to you, does it? Red and I were engaged. Now he's in the VA hospital, with a ruptured kidney."

"A little light is penetrating my head."

"You talk stuffed up," she said. "You probably can't help it. My old man owns the taxi company. I'm one of the two dispatchers. My sister-in-law and I switch around, night and day; I'm night this week. Red was one of our drivers."

I kept my stuffed-up mouth from talking, since it seemed to annoy her. She drank the rest of her drink, without reaction this time, and started pouring her dividend.

"There's an old souse in this town," she said. "I guess more than one, but this particular guy, his name is Freddy Hughes, he gets a pension from some company he used to work for. He cashes it here, Lou keeps half of it, Freddy drinks up the other half. The rest of the month, Lou gives him so much a day for beer and groceries."

"It sounds like Mr. Hughes has it made."

She gulped the dividend. I raised a finger for Lou, pointed at Janey's glass, and mine. He nodded.

Janey said, "You think we're dirt, don't you? Night cab drivers like Red, bartenders like Lou, drunks like Freddy Hughes. 'Mr. Hughes!' 'A little light is penetrating my cranium!'"

"Head, not cranium," I said. "Don't make it any worse than it is."

"Sorry." Janey looked at me. "Like I said, maybe you can't help it. Anyway, while Freddy was still riding high, couple of months ago, good deal of money in his pocket, he passed out at the Red Rooster, a joint on the edge of town. They phoned for a cab, and I sent Red out there. He took Freddy home. I mean, I know he did, because he said so. Only, the next morning, McLane's traffic cop, Jess Fencher, found Freddy in a vacant lot, with his dough gone."

The juke box, for once, was silent. I nodded, and we were both still while Lou brought us fresh drinks. I tapped the coins and told Lou to take out for a drink for himself. "Don't use the stuff when I'm working," he said. "Nice story, ain't it?"

I had forgotten Red was his brother. I nodded, and he went back behind the bar, looking unhappy.

Janey said, "The rest of it won't last this drink out. McLane was still beating on Red, trying to get a confession, when a guy over in Millsville, just a passing no-good who peddles thread and stuff to little stores, gets drunk enough to start bragging about the neat trick he pulled here. Seems Freddy came to, and was trying to make it downtown when this salesman runs into him."

I sipped my drink. "I don't see where I stand."

She leaned across the table, her martini forgotten.

"You're not trash, mister, like Red and me. You got a fancy car and fancy friends. The word is, you're out on ten grand bail; you could melt

all my family and all Red's family including Lou's license here, and all
our friends, and we wouldn't make half that. I'll bet McLane didn't even
beat you, once."

One of the men at the bar got up and came over to put a nickel in the
damned juke box. We were both quiet while I thought it over. The music started again, but this time it was just a girl, singing in some quiet
rhythm.

"Make a beef, Mr. Porter," Janey said. "Make a stink. For the rich, the
law listens. False arrest, whatever—you got Henry Lighton, they'll listen to him. Break that McLane down for me, mister."

"And then?"

"Then we get a decent police chief here, we get to live a little. Listen,
I know you'll get off anyway; Henry Lighton never lost a case yet. But
do it the hard way, that's all I ask. Stand up and yell!"

She seemed on the level. I said, "That'll heal Red's kidney?"

"It'll make him feel like a man again. How do you think a guy feels,
taking a shellacking, and then scared to complain about it?"

Surprisingly, I answered that. J said: "I know. When I got out on bail
today, I felt just that way... I'll do what I can, Janey, but—there's nothing I can do. I wouldn't kid you. I don't know anyone in Lowndesburg,
and without knowing anyone how can I find out who killed Ed—who
killed Mrs. Hilliard? That's why I'd take the easy way out. The Henry
Lighton way. You're not asking me to take a chance on being convicted
of murder, are you?"

She made a sort of sideways sweep with her hand. "Hell, I don't know
what I'm asking." Growing up among the taxicabs hadn't refined her
overmuch. "You're not such a bad joe. Before you ask me, I don't know
who killed Mrs. John Five."

"Otto McLane?"

She made the gesture again, the throwing-away movement. "I'd like to
think so."

I said: "This is none of your business. But his father-in-law went my
bail, is paying Henry Lighton's fee. I'm not so rich as you thought me."

Her eyes lighted up. She turned towards the bar and whistled, undoubtedly a whistle she'd learned to summon sleeping cab drivers. Lou's
head snapped up, and he came towards us at once.

She said: "Old Mr. Gray greased Paul here out of the lockup. He's paying his lawyer. Whatya think?"

Lou got that same delighted look in his eye. Then it died. "Naw. Why
should Mac kill her? How would he even know her?"

"They're on a Civil Defense Committee together," Janey said.

Lou said: "Aw," in a disgusted way. "Naw," he said. "John Five had her bumped, of course." He turned and went back to the bar, a very businesslike man.

I stared at Janey. "Now, that's a dandy sort of suggestion right out of the clear blue sky."

"You're making noises like a stuffed shirt again," she said. "I suppose because John Five's got money, he wouldn't kill anybody? I suppose the rich don't spit when they got a mouthful? I suppose—"

I cut in before she told me the rest of the things she supposed the rich didn't do. I was beginning to wonder if any of her story was true. On the other hand, I hated to doubt it, since it made her my friend. I wasn't over burdened with pals.

I said: "Just because John Five's rich doesn't mean he murders his wives, does it?"

"Look at it with a little logic," Janey said. "She was a lousy wife to you, wasn't she? No reason to suppose she wouldn't be a lousy wife to him. You she can leave, and what would it mean to you? A few lousy grand. She leaves him, and—zowie—any jury gives her a few zillion bucks alimony. Especially looking like she did."

"Not a lady jury."

Janey looked gloomily at the table. "Especially a bunch of hens. Guys don't understand dames. They wouldn't be jealous of her. Especially the kind of bridge-playing clucks who like jury duty. Naw. They figure next week, maybe tomorrow, they're gonna buy a new bottle of face cream, or maybe a girdle, that makes them look just like Mrs. John Five. Yeah, she'd of got a big alimony, all right."

The cabman's delight lifted her head and sighed a deep, heartfelt sigh. "I wish I had a crack at that kind of money."

"John Five was up in the city when she was killed."

Janey almost spat at me. "Says he. Says Otto Goddam McLouse McLane. How d'we know? And anyways, John Five wouldn't do it himself. He's got a private army up there! It's half as big as the whole state police force, almost. He'd have one of them do it."

My head was shaking. "All right," I said. "I'll go along a little way with you, Janey. She wasn't the most joyous—she was a lousy wife." But even as I said it, I felt regret, loss. She'd been so beautiful... "She was cold, she didn't care for anything but money; what she got out of me—a marriage settlement instead of alimony, but it's the same—crippled me in the pocketbook, and she didn't need it. And now that you mention it, it was a woman judge signed the decree. But John Five—if he hired anyone to kill his wife, he could be blackmailed for life. And I don't suppose he likes to spend money and have nothing material to show for it."

"You can say that again," Janey said. "The few times he's used cabs, he asks how much before he puts in the order." She grinned suddenly. "Finalizes the order. And he don't tip. But blackmail? The guy that did the murder couldn't blackmail John Five without tipping his own mitt, and that would mean the electric chair. Naw, he'd shut up."

Lou had brought in a sack of ice cubes, was breaking them up behind the bar, using a softball bat. Some of the customers had left. There was now only one man at the bar, but another couple had been added to the ones in the booths. I got up and shoved a quarter in the juke box and punched two Dinah Shore records and a Belafonte that I remembered as being quiet. .

When I got back, Janey was frowning. "It's a matter of finding out which one of the Mt. Hilliard cossacks is suddenly changing his way of life," she said, a little quaintly. "Buying a new car, maybe getting married, something like that. Sooner or later, my drivers'll find out; they hear everything in town."

"Sooner or later doesn't do me much good," I said. "At any minute old Mr. Gray could cancel my bail. My boss tied the can to me for dragging the company name into this mess. Henry Lighton would pull out if Mr. Gray did."

She said: "Mr. Gray must think Mac's in this, or he wouldn't be siding with you. Hey, maybe Mac choked her, for John Five!"

I shook my head.

She said: "Naw," the light dying from her eyes. "He's a cop, that one... No, the old gent sprang you because he and Andy know how Mac is. They wanted to get you out of there before Mac beat you like he did Red."

It was as simple as that. Of course, Mac must have been in trouble up in the city. He wasn't so old that retirement would be for age; his resignation had been requested. He would never have quit police work till sixty-five forced him to, he was ten years short of that... Andy had suggested that Mr. Gray had bailed me because he wanted to annoy Mac. Henry Lighton had suggested that he'd done it because he thought Mac was slipping, had made an arrest on me because he was jealous of Andy's interest in me.

This girl thought it was because Mr. Gray was afraid Mac would beat me to death.

One way or another, it seemed fairly certain that Mr. Gray's interest in me had to do with Mac, and not with the murderer. Everyone in Lowndesburg thought so.

But the mystery of Mac and Mr. Gray was a little one, and it didn't seem to have anything to do with the big one, the only one that mattered— who killed Edith?

Janey said: "You met any of John Five's Green-and-Tans? He dresses them like forest rangers or tree surgeons, but they're there to guard him, believe you me." She giggled. "When I was still in school, a boy I used to go with and me, we thought Mt. Hilllard'd be a nice place for a picnic, like. We were just— It doesn't matter. You met any of the boys?"

"Danny Banion and his partner Crosley. Mac swore them in as special cops."

"You see what I mean?" she asked.

"If John Five knows who killed her, he wouldn't be so scared the murderer would get him."

Janey half turned her head to the juke box. "Who put that schmaltz on? John Five ain't completely dumb. He'd want to make noises like he was scared. Danny or Crosley didn't say anything about any of their men quitting?"

I shook my head. "They wouldn't be likely to chat about Mt. Hilliard affairs to me."

"Crosley's married," Janey said. "Married guys always need more dough. Danny is panting after Andy McLane, a good-looking dish, but a guy'd get Mac for a father-in-law."

"He's given up panting, as you put it. He's going back into the Forest Service, whether she'll go with him or not."

Janey snapped her head up. She looked at me, her eyes bright. "You got it!"

I looked behind me. I looked at my hands to see if symptoms of a disease had broken out. "I have what?"

"There's no money in the Forest Service," Janey said. "When I was in college I went with some boys in the forestry school. They said you almost had to have a private income to make out in the U.S. service..."

I was staring at her.

"Danny quit the Service to work for John Five. Now he's quitting John Five to go back. So, he's come into some dough."

Like an idiot, I said, "Where did you go to college?"

"State," she said. "I was a sorority girl, too, and I don't blow my nose in my fingers, they taught me better. Wake up, mush-head. We got your murderer, Danny Banion. John Five paid him enough to do it for Danny to live in the tall timber the rest of his life, making eyes at the trees."

"Banion seems too much of a boy scout for that sort of thing."

Janey began laughing. I guess I looked interested, because she said, "When I was thirteen my kid brother joined the scouts. When they met at our house, the patrol leader used to put the other kids to tying knots while he and I went out in the pantry. He was fifteen."

"You ought to write your memoirs, Janey You've got the experience, and you've got the imagination. That stuff about Banion is pure moonshine."

She looked at me, the dark eyes like buttons. "You don't want to get loose," she said. "Not if it means talking mean to somebody. You want to go to the chair, like a little gentleman, with your chin in the air, and a tight upper lip. You ought to be in the funny papers, mister." She got up and stamped high-heeled and hard-heeled, to the bar, and sat down on a stool, her legs very pretty and started talking to Lou. I scooped up my change and went after her.

Janey was saying: "The Dodgers ought to be hot as a homemade pistol this year..."

I went out. She'd given me plenty to think of; but Danny Banion? It seemed impossible, even if she and the patrol leader had played games in the pantry. Maybe Danny had been a Woodland Ranger instead of a boy scout...

CHAPTER 8

Spring was still in the process of avoiding Lowndesburg. I couldn't blame it; I wished I'd done the same. Everyone in this little town wanted me to do something for any reason in the world but one associated with my own best interests.

I got in my car, eyes down, frowning, and Lieutenant Gamble said: "If you drink, don't drive." He was sitting next to the driver's seat, relaxed.

"If you drive, don't drink," I said, completing the safety council slogan. "I won't ask how you found me; it couldn't have been hard."

"It wasn't," Gamble said. "My boys are watching all the roads, so you didn't leave town, and a Keystone cop could find a car parked in a town this size."

"I suppose if I start the motor, I get pinched for drunk driving."

"I'm only a lieutenant; we leave important cases like that to the captains and inspectors. I wanted to talk to you and this is as good a place as any other."

"Talk is turning my hair gray," I. said. "And all of it for my own good, till I take a second look."

Gamble said: "Oh?"

"A lady named Janey Dandler. A taxi driver, or something like that. She wants me to make a big false arrest case, because McLane punctured her boyfriend's kidney."

Lieutenant Gamble nodded his square-cut head. He said: "Give me the dope and I'll be glad to check it out for you."

"Why do you people say check out instead of just check? Anyway, it's probably true."

The lieutenant unbuttoned his coat, took a notebook out of his inner-suit pocket, a pencil from somewhere, and got ready to write. "Mr. Porter, never take anything for the truth that you have not checked out—checked, I'm sorry—yourself, to the best of your ability."

"It can't leave you much time for your regular meals," I said. "All right. Miss Jane Dandler told me she was engaged to a man named Red, who drove a hack for her father's company."

"Red?"

"She also told me, and he confirmed it, that said Red was the brother of a man named Lou who owns the bistro I just left. His name would be on the liquor license."

"Red told you this?"

"Red wasn't there. Lou…" I went on with the story. Gamble took it down in shorthand; of course he would know shorthand, as he would know fingerprinting, photography and any other simple arts likely to be of aid to the good state trooper.

I didn't discuss Janey's suspicions about John Five and Danny Banion. Not because I wanted to keep them to myself, but because I thought Lieutenant Gamble would laugh at me for even listening to that kind of story, not to mention paying for the drinks while I heard it.

When I finished, he stowed the notebook away, and said, "That should not be hard to verify or disprove, as the case may be."

"Part of it you'd know offhand. Does Mac have a reputation for brutality?"

His chiseled lips closed and he said nothing. It was as eloquent a nothing as you'd want to hear, if anybody ever wanted to hear an eloquent nothing.

"All cops are good, eh? All outsiders stay outside."

"Something like that," Lieutenant Gamble said. "Now, as I said, I wanted to talk to you. About Edith Hilliard. Edith Stayne Porter Hilliard."

"How about the notebook, copper? How about the speech that anything I say can be used against me."

Lieutenant Gamble sighed a patient sigh. He unbuttoned his coat again. "The notebook, certainly, if you don't mind. The other—that's England, not the United States. Or perhaps"—believe nothing you haven't checked out yourself—"it isn't even England, but just English detective novels."

We both sat. Finally the lieutenant sighed again. "What are you waiting for?"

"For you to ask questions."

He shook his head. "On second thought, maybe you ought to drive away from here. I am not unknown, and if Miss Dangler saw you with me, it might dam up any future information she was disposed to give you."

I started the motor. As the car pulled out of the parking lot, I said, "That is beneath you, Lieutenant Gamble. Attempting to disarm me by being less than a superman. Dandler, not Dangler."

He almost grinned. He stopped it when it was nothing more than a controlled smile, but he almost grinned. "All right, Dandler. Where did you meet your ex-wife, Mr. Porter?" So I told him. In '53 I was assistant personnel manager for a factory in Milwaukee, and she came to work as a stenographer. "She didn't stay in the pool long, of course. My boss snared her for a private secretary. So I saw a lot of her and—"

A car passed us, going very fast, almost going into the curb on the left to get by us. As it went ahead, it made a sirenish noise. There was lettering on the side, J. F. Gray's—Mac's car.

I said: "Follow that car, bud?"

Deadpan, Lieutenant Gamble said: "Follow the heap, chief." Then he laughed. "Only slower. I set some store on my life. And keep on talking."

"The assistant personnel manager sees a lot of the personnel manager's secretary. On the fourth date, I asked her to marry me."

Ahead, Mac's siren was now in full cry. Considering Mac, it should have bayed like a foxhound, but it sounded just like a police siren.

Lieutenant Gamble said: "I see. So you didn't know her too well... You were in personnel. So you had access to the files, of course. Where did she work before, where did her first husband work, who were her parents, her maiden name? I suppose you can give me all that."

I looked at him, startled.

He flipped a thumb forward. "The road, the road."

I looked at the road. "I don't ask a girl for references before I fall in love with her. I don't know anybody who does, or didn't, before I met you. Who was your wife's maternal grandfather?"

"Why, he was a storekeeper, postmaster and justice of the peace in Iowa," Lieutenant Gamble said, "though he was born in Canajoharie, New York. His family took him to Iowa when he was six. They had a farm there, but when he was thirteen he took to clerking in the local general store and—"

I yelled, "All right, all right. So you're perfect. I'm not. I don't know a damn thing about Edith except that she was beautiful, and I made the common male mistake of thinking that beauty connotes warmth, elegance of soul, intelligence and everything else that's nice, including sugar and spice."

"You don't even know who Stayne was?"

Ahead a knot of cars were stopped. One of them had a red blinker on the roof. I said, "I guess Mac's run the fox to earth," and began to slow down. "Why, Mr. Stayne was Edith's father, I presume."

"Nan for negative," Lieutenant Gamble said. "She gave a date and a place of birth on her driver's license. No such birth is recorded in Canton, Ohio. We've sent out to Nevada for her marriage license. If she gave the same date and birthplace there, it can be presumed that Stayne was a name from a previous marriage."

The knot of cars resolved itself into two private sedans, one with smashed headlights and radiator, the other with a smashed-in side; and Mac's car and a state trooper's cruiser. I stopped, looked at Lieutenant Gamble. A tall man in a trooper's uniform came over to us.

I said: "She could have changed her name."

"That would presume a criminal past," Lieutenant Gamble said, "and therefore that her fingerprints were on file with the FBI, which they are not." He touched his forehead in answer to the trooper's salute. "Yes, Roush?"

"We're a quarter of a mile inside Lowndesburg limits, sir," Roush said. "I'm letting the chief handle it."

"Right. You can resume patrol."

"Sir." Trooper Roush saluted, and started away.

I said: "Wait a minute," and Roush turned back, looked inquiringly at the lieutenant. "Lieutenant Gamble," I said, "you're slipping. How do you know this man is a state officer? He could have knocked off Trooper Roush, stolen his badge, car and uniform, and made up his face to resemble the victim. Hadn't you better take his fingerprints, compare his dental work?"

Lieutenant Gamble said: "Resume patrol, Roush. Mr. Porter's a humorist."

Roush said: "Yes, sir," in a tone that sounded as if he didn't agree about me. He went to his car, and started it before he'd taken the microphone out of his hand.

"Look, papa, no hands," I said. "Hey, I've got an idea. Edith changed her name from Stein to Stayne to avoid prejudice." Ahead of us, Mac was busy with his notebook.

"Was she Jewish?"

"No. But now that we've stopped kidding around, she could have lied about her age"

Lieutenant Gamble nodded, as though I'd said something wise. We both watched Otto McLane start to pace off skidmarks. The lieutenant said:

"Well, I thought of that. But the city directories for ten years back of the birthdate she gave show no one named Stayne. Or Stein. I thought of that, too."

"What don't you think of?"

Lieutenant Gamble snorted. "I don't think much of District Attorney Norton Prince for letting Henry Lighton get bail set on you. I'd like to see you in a cell. I would indeed."

"My pal."

He shrugged. "Call it my passion for neatness, Mr. Porter. I like all my clues neatly filed away, including suspects. Let's get out and listen to Chief McLane handle this case. It might be instructive."

Outside the car, it was not just a cool spring; it was a returned winter. I sneezed once, and Mac turned his head from his notebook, saw me, frowned and then saw Lieutenant Gamble and shrugged. He turned back to the drivers of the two cars, who were standing there as though they had been caught stealing sheep.

"All right," Mac said. "You can drive into Lowndesburg if your cars will go. Mr. Snider, I'm sure yours will. It's just a smashed door and some dents."

"About two hundred dollars," Snider said.

"Your own fault," Mac snapped.

Snider said: "I hit him with my side? You're crazy."

"You were going too fast," Mac said. "You saw Mr. Winfrey's car coming around that curve. You stepped on the brakes, and skidded right into his path."

Snider said, "Have a heart, Officer! My insurance—"

Mac said, slowly, "It's against the law to drive in this state without insurance. What were you going to say?"

Snider looked around at all of us. He shrugged, and got into his battered car, and started it, after a little trouble. The vehicle moved down the road towards Lowndesburg slowly and crankily, like a crab who has decided to go straight.

Mac said, "I gotta get this road clear. Try your car, Mr. Winfrey."

Mr. Winfrey smelled of money. So did his car, a Lincoln four-door. But you can't tell, these days of easy credit. "She oughtn't to be driven that way," he said. "The motor will overheat. Send me a tow car, Officer."

Mac said, "I like my streets clean. The weather bureau says there's a storm coming in; I want this heap off the road."

Mr. Winfrey said: "Listen, my good man—"

Mac's voice was a Boston bull's bark: "I'm not your good man. I'm police chief of this town. And let me tell you..."

Lieutenant Gamble had my elbow, was leading me away. The firm features of the lieutenant were drooping.

He got in beside me, and I started my car. I was headed back to town before I said anything, and then all I said was, "So?"

Lieutenant Gamble shrugged. "It didn't mean anything. Every cop has his off days, his off hours. It was cold out there, and that Winfrey was wearing an overcoat worth more than Mac makes in a month."

I stopped for a fixed sign, where the town really began. "You believe what you're saying, Lieutenant?"

His hand clenched and beat his knee. "I believe nothing till I've checked it—out. I'll make inquiries up in the city."

"What can you do? This is a democracy. The people of Lowndesburg can elect any police chief they want to."

He looked at me almost with affection. He said, "I wish I had had your nice, soft background. You really believe that, don't you?"

I asked, "Who's to stop them?" but I sensed it was a naïve question. .

"Why, I am," Lieutenant Gamble said. "It's a democracy, sure, but with only two parties. If the state police go to the bosses of those two parties and say they can't work with a local officer—or a district attorney—he doesn't get nominated." .

I pulled the car over to the curb, and parked carefully. Mac would be coming back in a minute, and I didn't want a ticket; and Mac would give me one, even though I was with a state police officer, if I parked an inch out of line.

"Your theory isn't working too well," I said. "How about Norton Prince?"

Lieutenant Gamble was in his frank mood. I was innocent—no, nice and soft were what he had called me—but I was dimly aware that he was most dangerous when he appeared most frank. He said: "Norton Prince does all right with the other Lowndes County lawyers against him. He's as good as we could ask. No one who would take the job is good enough for Henry Lighton, though."

"So you think I'll get off." I didn't make a question of it. Mac's car went by us, then, back into Lowndesburg. Mac had not looked at us when he went out, nor now returning; and he had given us only that one brief glance at the scene of the accident. Yet I was sure Mac didn't miss much.

Lieutenant Gamble said: "I'm only sure of one thing. And that is, when I get up on that stand in the court room, I'm not going to be asked why I didn't know this, that or the other thing about the case I was supposed to prepare. And so, my friend, I check everything."

"Out."

He didn't smile. "Sooner or later, I'm going to find out who Edith Stayne was. I think you know. If you do, tell me now." Any shade of friendliness was gone.

I said, "I really don't know."

"Got a copy of your marriage certificate, your notification of divorce?"

"I never had the first," I said. "The other's in a tin box in my bureau, in my apartment in Chicago."

"The Chicago cops will send it to me," Lieutenant Gamble said. "All right. Drive me downtown, the courthouse square."

I drove him there and let him out. He didn't say goodbye to me, or thanks, or anything else. He was, for the moment, through with me.

CHAPTER 9

Now I didn't have any place to go. Lou's bar was impossible, with Lou and Janey staring at me, urging me to go do something I didn't know how to do.

The hotel would be full of newspapermen, unless I stayed in my room, which was like locking myself in a cell. Cell, I could go to the courthouse and get one-armed Knowles to let me in, and we could chat. I could—

People were coming across the square towards my car. I'd been spotted. I had to go someplace. I started the car for that place, not knowing where it would be, not caring, just getting away.

It turned out, of course, to be Andy's house. Mac's house. Mr. Gray's house, really.

I had a nice, soft background, like Lieutenant Gamble had said. I needed a woman's shoulder to lean on. Andy's.

There was a driveway winding around a gnarled old tree to one side of the house. I followed it, and parked my car in the back yard, behind the house, where I hoped it couldn't be seen from the Street.

As I stepped out, I sneezed, twice. The change in the weather, the dragging fatigue of all the excitement, the grinding fear I carried were using me up. I was going to have a cold.

Not a serious thing, a cold in the head. Just fatal was all—to a man who had to use that head to stay alive. I didn't know whether I was that man or not.

Cars passed out in the street, and I waited till their noise faded before going back to the front door. But a noise at the back of the house attracted me.

Old Man Gray was rapping on one of the conservatory windows with his cane.

I went in to him. He looked at me, said, "Something the cat dragged in," and raised his cackling voice; "Andy!"

A door closed in the front of the house, and high heels clicked towards us. Then Andy came into the conservatory, closing the door behind her. She said: "Yes, Grandpa?" and then she saw me, and before I knew it, we were hanging onto each other, and I felt that I had come home.

Then she was crying on my shoulder, and I was patting her. "I didn't know where you were," she said, over and over again. "I was so worried—" She'd had time to think over my kiss, and she'd made up her mind the right way. Or, I worried, maybe she was just sorry for me...

She broke away, and sat down in the chair nearest the one her grandfather usually used. "Gramps," she said, "tell me to stop making an idiot of myself."

The old man sat down in his own chair, and shook his head. He'd dropped the role of cackling old gadfly.

"No," he said. "You're doin' right, Andy. You got a heart, an' you're doin' just right to show it. Not enough heart in this damned old world, as it is. You love the girl, Paul?"

I said, "I never knew what love was like till I met her."

"You want to marry her?"

Andy said, "Hey," but I just gave her a look and grinned and said, "Of course."

"Been waiting for this day," he said. He got his shawl and wrapped it around his shoulders. "I liked you from the time you sat here last night and wouldn't let me rile you. You're my kind of man, young fella, and I don't mind sayin' it. Not a bit."

I sneezed. He pulled back from me. "Don't do that," he said. "One good cold would kill me. You takin' anything for that sneeze?"

I shook my head.

"Vitamin C," he said. He was getting his cackle back again. "That's what the doc gives me if I sneeze. Fifteen hundred units of Vitamin C. Get him some, Andy."

"It's all out, I gave you the last of it Thursday."

"Well, g'wan downtown an' git him some. Don't just sit there!"

"I'll go get it myself," I said. "I'm not a baby, Mr. Gray."

"No, but you're a ring-tailed celebrity," he said. "The gal in the drugstore would plain faint away with ecstasy at the privilege of takin' your money, touching the famous hand that did or did not strangle Edith Hilliard. You stay here. On your horse, Andy."

If Mac had gone a little nuts, I could see why. Living with the old gent—especially living on his bounty—wouldn't be easy. I tried to make a pun of mutiny and bounty, failed, and accepted a glass of sherry from Andy. Mr. Gray already had his, was looking at it with the passion of a Tarquin for Lucretia.

Andy knew her grandfather; she was hurrying away. I heard the front door slam, the car start.

Mr. Gray took a sip of his wine, and said, "Where have you been, Paul? Had to get Andy out of the way; if things are goin' agin you, she'd whoop and holler. Report, youngster; how's it going?"

"I've been consorting with light ladies, or a reasonable facsimile of one," I said. "The queen of local hacky circles has been spilling the dope on Otto McLane."

He said, "Do tell," which he had probably picked upon a radio program thirty years before.

I told.

He nodded, when I finished. "Got to do something about Otto," he said. "He's gettin' queer an' queerer."

"Lieutenant Gamble's going to look into his record."

Mr. Gray shook his head. "Nope," he said. "Nothin' there. It's my fault, He was all right while he was up in the city. 'Twas me corrupted him, with my money, such as it is. Chance to draw his pension, *and* the income from the business, too."

I shook my head. "If a man's a louse, it's his own fault; not the fault of the innocent friend who unwittingly places him in ideal louse country."

The cackle was clear and unfeigned. "Got to remember that. Got to tell that to Andy... You been talking with Lieutenant Gamble, too."

I nodded, any joy dying in my heart. "That I have."

"And—" The old eyes bored into me from above the sherry glass.

I looked out at the darkening, lowering day. Little flakes of snow were coming down, mixed with the drizzle. "He still thinks I did it. He can't find any trace of anyone else, and he's conceited enough to believe if there was anyone else, he'd find him. So all he's doing now is tying up loose ends. He's trying to dig up a third husband for Edith, one before me, and find out where he was." I shook my head. "Two ex-husbands in this little town on one day. I don't expect it."

Mr. Gray said: "But they got no witness you killed her?" I shook my head.

"Then, boy, you'll probably be all right. That Henry Lighton eats circumstantial evidence like it was lady-fingers." He cackled. "Hope I'm well enough to go to the trial. It'll be a lolla—"

The phone rang before he finished the giant, long, old-fashioned word. He put his hands on the arms of his chair and started to rise. I reached forward to help him, and he waved me away with a thrust of his bony, wattled chin.

The phone had rung four times before he got to it. You would think they would have gotten a long cord, so he could have it near him, but maybe he didn't like phones...

He said: "Yes, who? Why, Hank, you old— He what...? By God, I'll— What do you think, Hank? Yeah, I know you're not a lawyer, but you hung around there long enough to— Ten days, huh? Well, by God, ten days from now you'll hear me down there, blastin' the calcimine off the walls."

He slammed the phone back in its cradle, turned and stared at me, began to shake a long finger in the air. "I was sayin' I had to do something about Otto! Well, he's done something about me! That was Hank de-Vries, down at the courthouse. Otto's gotten the judge to write out a paper I'm senile!"

Whatever was left in the old man—a pint of blood, a pound of muscles, a little marrow in his chalky bones—was shaking him unbearably. I stepped forward, grabbed him, tried to get him to sit down. But my touch made him shake worse, and I let go again.

I said: "That can't be done. There has to be a hearing, doctors have to examine you, you've got the right..."

His mouth was moving, as though he wanted to spit, but couldn't get up the moisture. "Injunction," he said, thickly. "Otto and I—partners. Enjoin me against spendin' my money—any money—own money—"

He staggered across the sunporch, tore at a picture on the house wall. It came down, he dropped it, shattering the glass, tearing the steel engraving of a paddlewheel Steamer.

"Bond," he said. "Cancel your bail-bond."

"Mr. Gray, sit down. Andy'll be back in a minute, we'll talk this over..."

"No time," he said. Two bricks came out of the wall, were dropped on top of the picture. There was the dial of a safe there. The bony claws spun the dial. "Henry Lighton will drop," he said. "Drop you." Color, not good red, but a murky purple was staining the old cheeks. There wasn't anything I could do; restraining him would only increase his rage.

The safe came open, and there was a sheaf of green in his hands. He thrust it out at me. "Take it to Lighton," his thick voice said. "Keep him on your side. Two thousand, been here for years."

And, by God, it had. The bills were the old, big ones that I hardly remembered ever seeing. I'd gotten them for birthdays when I was a very little boy...

But old Mr. Gray was shoving the money at me. Two thousand dollars; it would not keep me out on bail, but it would fee Henry Lighton to try and spring me some other way. I reached for it.

Mr. Gray's hands came open, and the money fell, as things fall in a nightmare just as you're going to touch them. Foolishly, I speared at the falling leaves like a puppy after a butterfly.

But then the money was forgotten. For the purple began to drain out of Mr. Gray's face, and he bent forward, clutched at his chest, his knees buckled, and he fell, though I tried to catch him.

He landed on the scattered money, but two thousand dollars, even in big notes, is no cushion. I dropped to my knees, felt for his pulse. It was there, all right; it fluttered for four or five beats and then was still.

And so was he. There'd been so little life in him that he started chilling at once.

I knelt there, staring at him. .

Outside a car came up; for a moment I thought it was Andy, and was thankful. But the steps that came back towards me were hard and firm and masculine.

Mac or Lieutenant Gamble or one of the special forester-cops, coming to pick me up; my bail was canceled.

I started to rake the money together, to take it or send it to Henry Lighton.

Which was a stupid waste of time. Now I realized how it looked: Mr. Gray dead, money on the floor, the safe open, the picture broken.

I had no right to the money; the injunction would cover it, too. And no one in his right mind could look at the scene and see anything but a guilty man—me—gathering this loot.

A desperate, guilty man who had undoubtedly killed Mr. Gray; maybe not purposely, but in the course of using violence to get him to open the safe.

Probably I didn't think all that just then; not in words, anyway. If I did, I was a mighty quick thinker, because in the time it took those hard footsteps to bang from the front door to the sunporch-conservatory, I was out the same glass door I'd come in through, out and in the back yard and behind the gnarled, leafless fruit tree there.

CHAPTER 10

Any fear I had felt up to now was kid sniff, nursery-grade fear. Now I was really alone, and on the run, and from something real. Maybe I hadn't believed they could get me for killing Edith, when I hadn't even been there; maybe, though I'd had some pretty bad moments in Mac's jail and in the hotel room with Gamble.

But I believed with all my quaking heart, with all my feeble brain, that

I could be arrested, tried and convicted for the murder of Mr. Gray. I'd been there, only too obviously; my fingerprints were all over the place. They could hang a motive on me; they could say I had flown into a rage when Mr. Gray told me my bail-bond was cancelled, had threatened him, and so he had gone to the safe, and since being threatened isn't good for sick men of eighty—he had dropped dead.

Maybe it wasn't murder. Maybe just manslaughter or homicide, or whatever they called the crime that put you in prison from twenty years to life. But with this against me, who'd help me with the charge of murder, the charge of murdering of Edith?

Not Henry Lighton, who loved money and hated the penniless. Not Andy, who had loved her grandfather. Not...

I forgot all that in the howling misery of knowing I had now lost Andy for good.

It was colder out than it had been yesterday. I had no overcoat. I shivered a little, and kept moving away from the house.

This was a back yard, a very big one. There was a ruined tennis court and a building that had been a stable, once, but was now locked up and dirty-windowed.

I could hide there. It was obvious I couldn't use my car; the man who had been on his way was now surely in the conservatory and would see me.

The man, I had to find out who that man was.

So I turned back for the house. First I looked around. Nobody could see into this yard; no other houses over looked it. If they had, it would have been dangerous to do what I did, which was crouch down like a kid playing cowboy and creep up on the conservatory bent over, making myself inconspicuous.

The panes of glass behind the plants were clean. I could see into the room clearly. Three people in there: Mac, Lieutenant Gamble and Henry Lighton. They were bending over Mr. Gray—over Mr. Gray's body.

I had to get going, on foot, of course, and quickly, before another sneezing fit told them I was there. I remembered the medicine Mr. Gray had sent Andy for, and wished I had it, but it was time to leave. Where did I go from here? I wasn't quite sure, but there were two things I had to do: find a place to hide, find Edith's murderer.

The latter seemed an impossible task. I didn't know a half dozen people in Lowndesburg and the valley, except policemen—I knew plenty of those. And since that seemed an unlikely field to plough, who else was there for me to suspect? The sensible thing to do was go back into the conservatory, talk to Henry Lighton. Even now he might—just might—be telling the lieutenant things in my favor. But I started moving towards the back of the yard. I went around the old stable; there was an alley there, unpaved. A woven wire fence had separated the yard from the alley, but it had broken down; some of it had, in fact, broken up, carried from the ground by growing shrubs and little trees.

The country was taking Lowndesburg back, as a jungle takes over an abandoned village. But this wasn't the jungle; it was the Middle West of the United States, the great Mississippi Valley.

Still, Lowndesburg was dying. With its part-time police chief and its one-armed jailer, with its battered hotel and its amateur farmers—one a semi-retired lawyer, one a distiller of apple brandy—Lowndesburg was dying. It might be reborn as a suburb—exurb was probably a better word—as superhighways, reaching out for it from the city, made commutation possible. But it was going dead for the time being.

And, dying, it had reached out and killed me, too.

Then, suddenly, I knew whom I had to see. John Five. John Hilliard V, the master of Mt. Hilliard, the man who married Edith after she had left me.

The master of Mt. Hilliard, the master of Lowndesburg, the master of all Lowndes County.

The state police could be firmly, impartially efficient; little Mac would bark and snap and growl; Henry Lighton could be learned and nationally known; but John Hilliard the Fifth, John Five, had the money, and money talked in a universal language.

Janey Dandler had claimed John Five had killed Edith, or had Danny Banion do it, this was too silly for words. And yet, it might be possible, but I'd need more than Janey's scraps of hearsay and bolts of hatred to sew it up. Still, I had better use Janey's idea. The time had come for me to use anything and everything I could lay my hands on. My hands and my feeble, sneezing brain.

To the sneezes, the wheezes and the running nose, a cough was now being added.

I looked around me. I surveyed the situation. Then I sneezed again.

Doctors will assure you that a head cold is seldom, *per se*, fatal. But I was about to be killed by one; this one was keeping me from thinking, just when thinking was the only thing that might keep me from the electric chair.

Full of self-pity, I kept walking.

Mt. Hilliard was about six miles out of town, a short jaunt in a car, a long walk for a man who was being hunted by all the police in the world.

Fortunately, the Gray house was on the edge of town. It was on the north edge, and Mt. Hilliard rose above the east road, but at least I was in a sparsely populated area. I headed uphill, going farther north than the Gray place. Here the houses were far apart, a house to an acre or an acre and a half; almost small farms.

A lot of the places were deserted, their windows broken, their porches falling down. On one big lot there was nothing left but a square hole in the ground and a chimney rising high; I could see where there had been a fireplace on each side of the chimney.

I kept on climbing.

The paving ran out, the houses got scarcer. Fields along here were sloping and they were going back into forest; second growth spruce and pine and hardwood were pushing in.

Rain began to fall again, and it got a lot colder, almost too cold for rain, before I saw what I wanted: a house with telephone wires leading in, no observant neighbors, and no signs of life.

The last took checking. The garage was open and empty and no smoke came from the chimneys; but I was cautious approaching. I peered in all the downstairs windows before I tried the front door.

Of course, it was locked.

Hope springs eternal in the heart of a fool. I fiddled around with my keyring, trying my car keys, the key to the office, to the apartment in Chicago, some keys I'd forgotten the use of, but none of them worked.

I tried a gas company credit card, like it says in the detective stories, but either I didn't know how to use it or this door had never read detective stories.

Then I tried windows, but whoever lived up here in the woods was a careful householder; the windows were locked. Finally I tried the back door, it was open. I walked in. But I was still cautious; I prowled the ground floor before I sat down at the phone. No signs anyone had been here for hours...

There were three taxi companies, none of them named Dandler: Checker, Yellow, and Lowndesburg. There was a private number for a Horace Dandler, and another for H. J. Dandler, Jr. I tried the first one; no answer. The second would probably be the husband of the sister-in-law who was the other dispatcher.

I didn't want to talk to anyone I didn't have to. I tried Yellow, and when a man answered, I hung up; then I tried Lowndesburg, and Janey said: "Taxi," and I said: "Have to talk to you, Janey."

She was a smart one; or maybe she'd been thinking of me. She said: "Where?"

"About four miles past Mr. Gray's house, on the road that goes uphill and then turns toward Mt. Hilliard."

"Brown house with green trim? Two-story?"

"Yes."

"McAllister's," she said. "They'll be home in an hour or so. Wait in the first bunch of pine trees away from town."

"Okay, Janey."

"I'll be a little while."

I hung up. I'd made two phone calls; I shoved a quarter into the lining of an overstuffed chair, looked around to be sure I hadn't left anything—though I hadn't much to leave—and went out the back door, eyeing the ice box as I went by. Eating was a half-remembered habit.

The road was clay, slippery, and inclined to ball on the feet. I stumbled on, and then pines were dark on either side of me. Leafy trees were still in bud, and liable to lose these if this frost got any worse. The pines were rough barked, but their needles made dry standing and they kept the drizzle dripping in predictable places. I found a dry place to lean and lighted a cigarette.

That cigarette was out and another one was started before a car pulled into the pine grove, stopped, and Janey got out. There was a man at the wheel of the car, and I nearly turned and ran when I saw him; I had been sure she'd come alone.

She said, "What are you doing up here?"

"Waiting for you. I've got to see John Five; maybe you can figure a way to help me." But I was looking over her shoulder at the car. .

"That's my brother," she said. "And he's got a gun pointed at you."

"I didn't kill Mr. Gray. MeLane got an injunction out, claiming the old gentleman was senile; it killed him."

She said, "It sounds like Mac," and then was silent a minute. Then she said, "Got a cigarette? I forgot to bring any. Had to get my sister-in-law to watch the switchboard, she'll probably smoke them all up."

My hands were shaking so she had to take the package from me, light her own smoke.

"Mac," I said, "he's as bad as you said." Mac was the key to this girl.

"The old man was good to him. How the hell can I get you to see John Five?"

That was a question beyond my abilities. I stood there, shivering in the cold and wet, and said, "You know everything that goes on. How do I get through the Green-and-Tan?" '

She shook her head, frowning. "Danny Banion's on night duty, or it would be a cinch. He's a sucker for girls. But Crosley... Lemme talk to my brother."

She went back down to the cab. Brother, whatever his name was, climbed out, a service .45 big in his hand, and they stood talking. The automatic pointed at the ground, but Janey stood with her back to me, so the brother could keep an eye on my dangerous face.

Then she turned, and waved a hand at me, and I went down, too.

"Get in the cab."

Dear brother added: "Keep your hands in your pockets. I don't want your fingerprints all over the heap."

"My fingerprints have frozen and fallen off."

"Very funny."

He got in the driver's seat, and Janey and I got in the back. She was eyeing me with less of a frown, but she looked worried. "You're freezing to death."

I said that death would be a pleasant relief from the way I felt.

"It's colder up here than it is in town. Wetter, too. This weather will break, we get it every spring."

She had a woolen muffler around her neck. She unwound it and handed it to me. It did some good. But my teeth kept on chattering, and she reached over, pulled me down on her shoulder, put her arm around me. That did a lot more good, but she was as impersonal as a veterinarian. Brother pulled over to the side of the road, stopped the car, said: "Here."

We got out. He U-turned the car, and was gone.

"He'll wait around the next bend for me," Janey said. "He never liked Red, to begin with."

There wasn't, anything I could say to that. I changed the subject. "Isn't he worried about his tire tracks?"

"We get our tires from Monkey Ward or Sears and Roebuck. So do half the other people in town. No sweat on that one."

Ahead of us a dirt road crossed the one we were on, which had been paved once and then gone back to dirt. A sign said that trespassers would be prosecuted by the Hilliard Land & Improvement Company.

I couldn't see any improvements, but the crossing road looked queer. I went and put my hand on it. It was springy; John Five had hauled tanbark up here for his bridle path.

"Twenty miles long," Janey said. "All landscaped, all paved so his horsey-worsies won't hurt their feet."

"Their footums," I said.

"Shut up," she said. "My brother said the guard was due to ride by here any minute, and horses don't make any noise on that stuff."

"That how you got caught when you were in high school?"

"Yeah." She giggled a little, though we were both talking in whispers.

"What were you doing?"

"Shut up," she said again. "Start downhill. I'll keep the Green-and-Tan here for about twenty minutes, one way or another."

"Or another," I said.

"Depends on which one it is. Good luck. You'll see Mt. Hilliard in about twenty minutes, if you keep walking downhill. It's up to you."

The tanbark was soft and comforting under my feet. I stopped once and dug down; it was a foot deep, at least. Twenty miles of it must have cost John Five a small fortune. ,

I began coughing again; I couldn't sneak up on anyone that way.

There was a very nice tulip tree overhanging the bridle path. I rested under it, lighted a cigarette and tried to figure how many ten-ton truckloads of tanbark had been hauled up here. The cigarette, perversely, stopped the cough.

I was facing the valley, but not much of it could be seen. John Five's dendrologists, helping nature, had planted trees that kept an equestrian from being bothered by a view of the machine age that had developed below. An occasional roof could be seen, a patch of cement highway catching the patchy sun; nothing more.

I put out the cigarette and started walking.

The wrong time was on my wristwatch when I got to Mt. Hilliard. Understandably. I had not wound it the night before. But the hunger in my belly, the ache in my legs, the watery light in my eyes all told me I had used up the morning and part of the afternoon.

The bridle path ended in the woods, with stables and white-fenced corrals, or paddocks, or whatever they were called at Mt. Hilliard. This plant was set down in the woods, on a lower level than the house and the garage; broad, gentle steps led from one to the other.

There were men working around the stables, several of them, leading horses in fancy overcoats around, and polishing leather. Two men were busy putting new shoes on a long-legged red animal who didn't seem to be appreciating the honor.

As I watched from the woods, he kicked out—though one man was holding his hoof up on a knee, another was holding his head—and the man at the hoof end swore. He let go of the hoof and stood up, shaking his hand, which had turned bright red.

Everybody around came to inspect the wound, and I used the opportunity to work halfway around the ledge and get to the stairs going up to the house.

But I didn't use the stairs. I went up the steep slope of the woods alongside, using the trees and shrubs for cover, moving cautiously.

Hungry and dog-tired, I lost my breath quickly. I sat down under a little moose maple and looked back down.

I'd come higher and farther than I thought. The stables were dwarfed, now; the big red horse was only a toy. Sunlight played on the scene, and the man with the ripped hand now had a bright white bandage around his palm. It looked like a Currier and Ives print, and gave the impression of an age, an innocence that I doubted had ever really existed.

A man could feel like a god, coming down this hill and seeing that layout below him and knowing he had made it and owned it.

I hurried up the hill to meet that man.

My journey ended near the back door and the big garage. Yesterday had been Thursday, and the servants were all off; today was Friday and they were hard at work, proving to their master that a day's pleasure had not ruined them for his devoted service.

Two chauffeurs were out polishing cars; a gardener was covering shrubs with gunnysacks and tying them down against the winter, A maid came to the back door and put a load of trash into a can.

I hadn't a prayer in the world of getting across that service yard to the house. I'd seen six or eight men down at the stables, three up here. No doubt there were enough women servants in the house to overpower me by sheer numbers. And the Green-and-Tans would be on call, with riot guns.

I picked another tree—a black walnut—and rested under it. I couldn't smoke here, or John Five's fire department would start blowing off sirens.

Edith had certainly fallen into it. As I thought back our arguments over whether we could afford to eat dinner at a restaurant three times in one week were a little silly. If she and John Five had had arguments like that, it would have been as to whether it was entirely sensible to buy more than three restaurants in any one week, the bookkeeping being what it is.

When I had been married to her, she had made me almost angry enough to kill her, if I'd been built that way. And all my vaporous reflections boiled down to the thought that John Five had felt the same way, and maybe had been built that way. A big maybe.

But would she have bedeviled a man with all this money?

Not if he was generous. And John Five looked mighty generous to what was his: his horses, his cars, his trees, his shrubs and his house.

Surely his wife would have had all the conspicuous expenditure her cold heart could desire.

"She wouldn't irk him," I told the black walnut. "She wouldn't irk him."

And on that quaint line, I fell asleep.

CHAPTER 11

I know it sounds unbelievable: that a man in my position, hunted, harassed, in imminent danger of losing life, limb and liberty would choose that particular time, that particular piece of hostile territory, to take a nap in. Since then I've asked a couple of doctors about it; one of them had the answer. He said it hadn't been physical exhaustion that made me cork off, but mental retreat: the human brain can face just so much frustration, just so much despair, and then it quits; it needs a rest.

At any rate, I didn't feel rested when I woke up. I was stiff and miserable with cold. My neck felt as though any sudden movement would snap it like an icicle. Both my wrists were numb and sore, as though I'd kept my fists clenched all the time I slept; and my back ached.

It was not quite dark yet, but there were lights on in the house. The chauffeurs had put the cars away; now one of them came out and went down the line of drive-out doors, testing the locks. Then he went back into the house. People kept passing in front of the kitchen windows, which presently began to fog over.

I got my feet under me and stood up, rubbing the back of my neck, twisting my shoulders and hips to get my circulation going.

Not knowing the inside of Mt. Hilliard, how could I plan? The master would be in the front part of the house, having a cocktail or sherry while his faithful army prepared his dinner.

Or the master would be upstairs, having a bath, a nap, or a massage.

Or the master would be in the attic, chasing bats.

How could I tell?

It was getting dark enough to do a little scouting. With luck I might see John Five through a window. I'd know him: he would be eight feet tall and made of solid gold.

I moved downhill over the crisp grass. From the feel of the air, there might be a killing frost tonight.

The gravel on the parking lot crunched louder than the grass had.

The minute I put foot on it, it made a noise that sounded—to me, at least—like an entire regiment charging down a gravel bed.

I jumped back, and stood on the grass, waiting. Waiting for what? For workmen to come and replace the gravel with tanbark? I took two steps out on the gravel, brave Porter, bold Porter.

A voice behind me said: "Hold it. Hands in the air, and feet right where they are... No, don't turn around."

Crunch on the gravel, pat, pat as hands went over me, presumably looking for a gun. "All right. You can take your hands down."

I did, and turned, sneezing into the face of Danny Banion. True to his green-and-tan uniform, he didn't flinch or step back, but stood his ground boldly, holding a pistol on me. "Golly," he said. "You."

"What's left of me."

"You don't look good, and that's a fact But what are you doing up here?"

I felt like saying I didn't know. But it didn't seem like a good idea. So I tried: "I've got to see John Five."

"That's the screwiest thing I ever heard of," the dendrologist said. "He doesn't want to see you. He's got a twenty-four-hour watch out to make sure he doesn't see you."

"You searched me. I'm not armed."

Danny Banion shook his head. "Whoever killed Mrs. Hilliard strangled her; he didn't need a gun."

"Do I look like I could strangle anybody, just now?"

He laughed. "You sure don't, Porter. But Hilliard'd fire me if I let you in to see him."

"What do you care? You're going back in the Forest Service anyway."

He pushed his hard-brimmed Stetson back on his forehead, holstered his gun. "I always feel like a kid playing cowboy wearing one of these damned things," he said. "Listen, man, you sure you aren't out of your head, running a fever? You could have pneumonia, the way you look."

Now was the time to prove I had sales ability, the power to dominate a vis-à-vis, as some professor had called it in college. "Banion, I'm out of my head, but not with a temperature. The minute I show my nose in town, I'm pinched for a murder I didn't commit. John Five, Mr. Hilliard—"

"Call him anything you want to," Danny said. "Like you said, I'm quitting this tin-soldier job, heading for the tall timber. But I can't figure out how you know it."

I went back to my theme: "John Five couldn't have liked Edith any better than I did. No man could who'd been married to her awhile. He's the man with the power, the money; maybe he'll give me a hand. If he doesn't, I'm no worse off than I am now. I couldn't be."

The Stetson dipped back and forward as he nodded. The sky was purplish-black now. Danny Banion said: "Maybe if he sees you, he'll call the cops, and I won't have to run a night patrol. It's going to be a stinker out. Still…"

"Down in town, they're saying maybe you killed Edith…for John Five…and enough of his money to make up for the size of a Forest Service pay check."

The big forester took a step forward, and I thought he was going to sock me. Then his laugh rolled out, hearty and frank. "Forest Service pay's not so bad. And I got it figured out where you heard that screwy story: Janey Dandler." The noise I made was approximately, "Oh."

"Sure," Danny Banion said. "Crosley got a two-way report from one of our jeeps, working down the bridle path you probably got in here on.

Picked up a dame with a sprained ankle, walking back from a tough date. When I heard it was Janey Dandler, I kind of wondered. The only date she ever found too tough would be maybe an honest wrestler."

I made my noise again: "Oh." Or maybe, "Ugh."

"For a guy that Andy McLane thinks is a hot shot, you chase some funny dames."

My vocal chords got more talented. "She has a grudge against Otto McLane, for beating up and framing her boyfriend. She wants me to get Mac for false arrest, to give him some trouble, like the kind he dishes out."

Danny Banion tilted his hat forward again, and nodded against the growing gloom. "Sure. She has a grudge against me, too, for knocking Red clear across the street once when he was drunk and picking on me. He's strictly a no-good, Porter. And Mac didn't frame him; he just couldn't get enough evidence to bring Red to trial."

"How about some kind of salesman over in the next county who confessed to robbing whoever it was that was robbed?"

Danny Banion looked at the sky. "It's a hell of a night to stand out in the cold hashing up the affairs of Janey Dandler and her Red... That was just hacky talk, the salesman and his confession. Janey wanted Mac to run over there and pinch every salesman in sight, but it was just hacky talk; cab drivers are a bunch of old women for gossiping. No, Red rolled Freddy Hughes as sure as Freddy's next drink... Come on down to the estate office, and I'll call the police to come get you."

He reached out for my elbow. I let him take it; he had the gun, and I didn't have anything but a cold and a faint hope that he'd help me. "Banion, give me a break. Five minutes with John Five wouldn't hurt anybody; especially with you there to grab me if I got rambunctious."

The dendrological brain chewed on that. Finally he said, "Andy thinks you're the king of the woods, and I never knew her to be far wrong." Faith died hard in that big man. "Okay. If you slap him with a feather or throw a powder puff at him, it's both our necks. His money swings big weight around here."

"Maybe you can teach me dendrology in our prison cell."

His hand on my elbow propelled me towards the house. "I don't know why everybody thinks being a dendrologists' so funny. It's what I am; a guy who majored in dendrology at forestry school. It's one of a half dozen branches of forestry, and it doesn't sound any sillier than silviculture, does it?"

I had to admit it didn't.

The front door of Mt. Hilliard was locked. Danny Banion fished a big ring of keys out of his windbreaker and opened it, and we went in. A

wave of heat met us; it was the finest thing I have ever felt; I loosened
Janey's muffler so as to enjoy it on the swollen glands of my neck. Then
I sneezed twice, while Danny Banion knocked on the walnut door of a
room off the big entrance hail.

The door opened, and at last I got to see John Five.

He wasn't eight feet tall, he wasn't coated with platinum, or even gold.
He was just a man of medium height, a little plump, a little effeminate;
not queer, but soft in his way of talking and moving, uncertain.

He said, "Yes, yes, Banion, who is this?"

I remember what a salesman had told me, and looked at his lapels. Sure,
the stitches were twice as close together as on any suit I'd ever worn; and
that was the privilege of great wealth.

I said, "Mr. Hilliard, I'm Paul Porter."

He said, "Oh, my God." He jumped back a foot. "Get out of here. Banion, get him out! Don't let him hurt me... Don't hurt me, Porter. I have
not done anything to you!"

Danny Banion's voice was that of a male nurse, and since Danny was-
n't the male nurse type, it was easy to see why he was quitting this soft
and well-paid post. "Mr. Hilliard, I searched him. And I'll grab him if
he needs it."

John Five was blinking at me as I would blink at a caterpillar six feet
long.

"You're Porter. The—" He broke off.

"The murderer, Mr. Hilliard? But I'm not. Mr. Hilliard—" the respectful
use of his name seemed to calm him—"Mr. Hilliard, I'm an innocent
man, being framed. The only thing I ever did wrong was marry Edith.
You did as bad yourself."

His eyes popped a little, in the soft light that came from the fanned glass
over the front door. He said, "Come, now, you can't talk about Mrs.
Hilliard that way."

This was so silly I almost breathed naturally. "She used to be Mrs.
Porter."

The hand that came up to brush at his face was remarkably firm-look-
ing. Perhaps that came from holding the reins on all his horses. But his
gesture was ridiculous; as though cobwebs entangled his face.

"Mr. Hilliard, I have to find out who killed her. Or they'll kill me."

He said, "Well, do come in, Mr.—"

"Porter. Paul Porter. I told you."

"Of course."

He stepped back and walked into his study, not looking to see if
Danny Banion and I followed him. Danny shut the door, and John Five
turned to the right, went into a small room, leather furniture, leather

lampshades, Navaho rugs on the floor. There were silver cups on the bookshelves—but no books—and photos of horses on the walls. This was a den. I never knew anyone who had a den behind a study, but apparently John Five liked to retreat. Danny Banion said, "He was walking in here, not sneaking or anything. When I jumped him, he neither put up a fight, nor ran away. He said he wanted to talk to you. I didn't see the harm."

"No, no." John Five dropped into a leather chair, very shiny-looking, very soft. There were several other chairs, and they looked very inviting, but if I sat on one he might be afraid my poverty would rub off on the leather.

I said, "Just five minutes of your time, Mr. Hilliard. You might help me. I don't think anybody can, but you're my last chance."

He seemed pleased. I don't suppose anyone had ever wanted to lean on him before in his whole life, except financially. "I don't see—" he said. He stopped as though wondering where that sentence should have gone. He tried another. "You shouldn't hold a grudge against me. Edith was already divorced when I met her, out in Nevada. I was buying quarter horses."

Danny Banion's patient voice said, "He isn't armed, and he's just about pooped out—exhausted, Mr. Hilliard. Doesn't seem to be any danger."

"No, no, Banion. Hadn't you better be seeing to the night watch?"

Danny Banion shrugged, and managed not to smile. Since the watch was being kept to see that I stayed out, and I was now in, there was a certain amount of pointlessness involved. But John Five was paying the bills.

I winked at Danny Banion as he exited in a semi-military manner. His lip quirked a little. I'd gotten to like him awfully well in our few minutes together; if Andy McLane really preferred me, it seemed she was being kind of silly.

John Five squinted at me, waved at a chair, and I sat down with a sigh.

CHAPTER 12

John Five went around, turning lights on and off until he stopped squinting. "Sherry, Mr. Porter?"

"If I can have a cracker or something with it. I'm about beat."

He looked at me directly and said, "You do have a bad cold. This is no time of year to be out without your hat and coat," as though he were my old aunt. He opened a knotty pine door, and there was a little icebox. He put a plate of cheese next to me, brought crackers and the glass of sherry; stood, indecisive a moment, opened a door, went into a tiny lavatory, brought back a box of tissues and put them next to me, too.

It was the damnedest performance any suspected murderer ever saw.

He said: "A cold's the worst thing in the world," and sat down opposite me. Then he took out his handkerchief and held it in front of his nose and mouth. "I certainly don't want to catch your cold."

I ate cheese, I gulped the warming sherry, I blew my nose; the last was the greatest pleasure. "Mr. Hilliard, I'm being killed by coincidence."

Again, that wavery gesture of the strong left hand. "I don't understand talk like that. I'm a very plain-spoken man myself. A businessman."

I had heard different. But I looked at his clear eyes, his clear skin, his white teeth and made myself look pleasant. "By sheer chance, I was in Lowndesburg when Edith was killed. By sheerer bad luck, I was up here, at Mt. Hilliard."

He nodded. "I don't know that I like that," he said. "We don't encourage tourists up here, you know. Why, last year, some people wanted to picnic in my finest grove of dogwoods."

"I came here on business, to see you. To sell you a terracer."

"Oh, now, really, Mr. Porter. I don't even know what a terracer is. Why in the world should I want one?"

"You own land and horses. With a Hydrol Terracer and a small tractor—say a D-30—you could raise all the hay and grain your horses need."

He seemed quite interested. "My land's quite hilly."

"That's what a terracer is for. It lets you use steep land without subjecting it to erosion... For instance, you could run a long, narrow contour all through your woods; raise spring barley or any other small grain on it, then turn it under and it would be a fireguard the rest of the year, protecting your woods."

He chewed his lip. "Not bad. Could you arrange a free demonstration?"

I hit the leather arm of my chair with my palm. "Damn it, Hilliard, I'm not here to sell terracers. I just told you all that to prove that I had a legitimate reason to come up here yesterday."

"Yes, yes." He had that vague look about him again; I must remember not to frighten him with loud noises. "Spent an awful lot of money on forage last year. Timothy hay, in particular. Just bulk, you know, not much nourishment in it, but the horses..."

He grinned suddenly. "I'm not as scatterbrained as all that. I'm trying to remember, someone tried to sell me a dingbat like that, once before. If he'd explained it the way you did, I'd have bought it..."

"All right, Mr. Hilliard. But I—"

"Don't you see?" He was very patient. "I suppose you don't, what with the cold, and gulping down sherry the way you are. If someone knew that you'd be sent here to close a terracer sale, it would be a way of setting up a suspect to take the blame for Edith's murder." He yawned. "I certainly regretted marrying her, didn't I? I guess that's why the police were so fussy about making me establish an alibi for yesterday. Anyway, McLane and that state captain made me go with them while I interviewed the men I was with yesterday. I got myself clear. I guess you weren't so lucky."

He went on: "Yes, setting up a date for you and me to talk terracing—and killing her at the same time, right here—one of us would be sure to hang for it."

I had been sitting here, thinking he was a dope—and he had put the killer right in my lap. And done it in a dopey way.

A girl who looked like Edith could have any man in the world. She'd had me, she'd had rich Hilliard. She'd had another guy, and laughed him off—and he'd killed her.

"Mr. Hilliard, who was Stayne?"

He said, "Stayne, Stayne? I don't know any Stayne. I was at a horse show last month, lost out in the green hunter class to a man named Stone—no, it was a woman, Mrs. Hilary Stone—but I don't know any—Stayne, did you say?"

"Edith's name before she married me. Edith Stayne, when she came to work where I was working."

He nodded, but he was being vague again. "Yes, yes, I remember that. I was introduced to her—I mean, when we were introduced—a lady is never introduced to a man, is she?—she was Mrs. Stayne Porter."

I sneezed twice into John Five's Kleenex, coughed once. He moved away from me, nervously. "Very distinguished," I said, when I could say anything. "Mrs. Stayne Porter. Very upper-class. Only, who was Stayne? The state police are pretty sure that wasn't her maiden name. She must have, been married before."

John Five chewed his upper lip and considered this. "Poor Stayne," was his conclusion. So now we knew who Stayne was: the third member of our club.

Then the vagueness rolled back for a moment. He said, "All you have to do, Mr. Porter, is find out who sent you up here, and you'll find he's the murderer." He yawned. "I presume you'll find he's this Stayne fellow, too. Yes, yes. Under another name, of course. You don't suppose Edith had been carrying on with him all the time, do you? While she was married to me, and to you, too, of course. I'd not like to think that, but women, you know. I mean, if he was poor, and—are you rich, Mr. Porter?"

I said that I managed to eat every day.

He stared at me. I don't think he'd ever heard that some people don't eat. Then he laughed. I'd made a funny. "Do you have any horses?"

"Too bad. I find them the most diverting of occupations. I do my best thinking in the saddle. You really ought to take it up."

I promised that I would. "But this Stayne thing, Mr. Hilliard."

"I can't help you there. Really, it's up to you. As I say, just think back to who told you to see me. Who sent you to this part of the country at all."

It should have been simple to figure out. But in the condition I was in, nothing was easy; I felt like leaning back in John Five's fine chair, going to sleep and letting the police come and get me. I made a superhuman effort to keep my eyes open. "Why, of course, everything in our company starts with the president, Harvey Planne. He told me to take a turn through the northern Midwest, or I wouldn't be here."

"Any chance he could be this chap Stayne?" John Five asked. He chuckled. "I'm quite, like those district attorneys on television, don't you think?"

Through the fog I made an answer. "Harvey Planne's father is well known in Chicago, has been for years. Unless Harvey used a false name—no. He was still in the Air Force overseas when I met Edith, had been since she was too young to marry."

"They're not always the age they say they are," John Five said, his brain yawing like a sailboat again. "Chap I know, goes in for palominos, can't say I admire his taste, got into serious trouble. Girl looked nineteen and was only fourteen; lied to him of course, cost him a pot of money."

I took another sip of his sherry. My throat tickled, and I lighted a cigarette, which should have made me cough more, but didn't. "No," I said. "It's not Harvey Planne. And he wasn't here, because I talked to him on the phone last night. Nobody knew I was coming to Lowndesburg. Nobody. I saw the sign at the crossroads and remembered we had that terracer here, and—like that—made up my own mind."

John Five sighed. "It was such a good idea." He sounded as though he didn't have many ideas, and hated to see one wasted. "Ah, well."

"No," I said. "I just came into town and called McLane, and then I phoned the distributor in the city and—"

John Five had made a sort of noise. I broke off and looked at him curiously. "Otto McLane? But he's the fellow tried to sell me the terracer once before."

"Sure, he's the only agricultural dealer in town."

"Don't like the fellow," John Five said, with an unusual show of firmness. "Please, be sure and turn your head when you sneeze. I hate colds! No, I don't like Otto McLane. Impudent little upstart. Gave me a ticket for parking in front of the firehouse, and I'd left my keys in the car. If they wanted it moved, they could have moved it."

"Nobody seems to love Mac in Lowndesburg" I said. "He only knows one way of being a cop, and that's the big-city way. I can see it wouldn't sit so pretty in a tiny town... One of your dear citizens down in Lowndesburg even suggested that he killed Edith. Then she changed her mind and suggested that you had her killed. By Danny Banion."

John Five said: "Oh, no, I wouldn't do that. Why, Banion could blackmail me for a fortune."

"Not without indicting himself," I said. I helped myself to another cracker, another swallow of sherry.

John Five's simple face lighted up. "You know, you're right," he said. "If he exposed me, think what he would do to himself! I never thought of that."

"You didn't have Danny do it, did you?"

Polite laugh. "No. I wouldn't have used Banion, anyway. My personal groom, the one who takes the horses to the shows, used to be a gunman in prohibition days. Say, shall we have him in, he tells marvelous stories?"

I sighed, starting another series of sneezes. John Five jumped up and moved hastily out of range, though I twisted my head away and covered my nose with Kleenex.

Then his brain skidded back into the road. He said, "Porter, are you stupid or frightened?"

I said, "Both, I suppose," which seemed frank enough.

"I don't care much whether Edith's murderer is caught or not," John Five said. "Except that I suppose it is bad for the whole community for a murderer to go at large. Don't you think so? But I have told you who did it, and you don't seem disposed to take any action at all."

I half expected him to add that he didn't know what the lower classes were coming to.

"Very sorry, maybe this cold's frozen my brain."

"McLane," he said. "Otto McLane." He looked around cautiously, but there were no police spies in the trophy shelves. .

"Because he gave you a parking ticket?"

"My dear fellow. Who else knew you were coming up here, and at what time? Who told you what time to come here?"

"A girl down in town suggested Mac, for about the same reasons you have; she doesn't like him. But she dismissed the idea as crazy. Murderers usually have a motive, or so I've heard."

John Five nodded. "Of course, he knew her. Everyone in Lowndesburg knows the Hilliards, of course. She was on a Civil Defense Committee with him, too. I made her join. Our position here, you know, demands that we participate in village activities. And then, there should be someone on every committee like that to see that not too much money is spent."

"Otto McLane, Mr. Hilliard."

But the boat had yawed again. "Taxes are frightful," John Five said. "In a way, it's a good thing I don't have a son; there wouldn't be a thing to leave him. If I told you the tax I pay on Mt. Hilliard, you wouldn't believe it. School tax and road tax, gasoline tax, inheritance tax, income tax, it's Communism, that's what it is."

"Edith's murder. Otto McLane.'

He shifted sails and came back into the channel. "Well, the minute she was killed, your state policeman found out she hadn't been born Edith Stayne, didn't he?"

I had to admit that. I was beginning to get disgusted with the whole conference; there was something gruesome about Edith's two ex-husbands quietly talking over her death. One of us should have missed her, at least. Him. He was being Mr. D.A. again. "You admit McLane is a policeman."

Sneezing, I nodded. When I could speak, I said, "A good one."

"So he found out Edith had been married to a man named Stayne. And he got in touch with Stayne, and Stayne paid him to kill her."

He had figured all this out because Mac had given him a parking ticket once. He wouldn't let it go.

"You admit that no one but Mac knew you were coming here just when you did," he said.

"Mac and his daughter."

"Ridiculous. Miss McLane a murderer? I'd never believe it."

"I wouldn't either," I said. I was very tired. "I didn't mean to imply it."

John Five started trotting around the little room. "Too bad about her," he said. "Nice girl; be hard on her to find her father's a criminal. But I suppose policemen's families are more hardened than other people. Do you suppose so?"

There wasn't any sense in answering him. Two people had tried to help me—besides Andy. Janey Dandler and John Five. Both of them had mentioned McLane.

Probably if John Five knew about the Queen of the Hackers, he'd change his mind sooner than be associated with such low company.

So why not, I asked my rheumy brain. Why not Otto McLane? True, my first impression of him had been one of great liking. But when a man has a daughter who is a pretty girl, and a young man happens to need a pretty girl, said young man is going to stretch like a toy balloon to like the father.

True, also, that there seemed the remotest connection between Mac and Edith.

But—I was stopped in all other directions. Well, at least I could make some effort to find out if there was any connection. It would be doing something, and I felt intensely that I had to do something or go, framed, to the chair.

So I gave in to John Five, which was a little like losing a wrestling match with a three-weeks-old kitten.

I said: "Mr. Hilliard, I think you're right. If you'll lend me a car, I'll go downtown and try and hang it on Mac."

"A car? Really, a car? I don't know."

Patience, understanding and conviction oozed into my voice. "Your cars are known all over the county. In one, I'm not likely to be stopped. And if I am stopped, it might be by a policeman who doesn't know me, or you, and maybe I could bluff through."

"I'm pretty well known. My picture is in all the horse-show magazines frequently."

"Admittedly, I'm taking a chance. But without a car, I'm throwing the game."

He pondered this awhile. "Do you have a driver's license?" he asked, finally. "You see, my insurance is invalid if I lend the car to anyone without a driver's license."

Someone defined experience as what you get when you're looking for something else. Patience is what you learn under the same circumstances. So I hauled out my license and my insurance cards, and finally satisfied him. He went with me out of the inner den and through the study to the hall, a long distance for John Five to go with a common man.

In the hall he pressed a button, and a grayish man in a blackish suit popped out from the inner reaches of the castle. "Call Banion and tell him to meet Mr. Porter at the garages. He's to let Mr. Porter have the station wagon."

The butler said, "Yes, Mr. Hilliard." Unlike his appearance, his accent was pure Middle-Western. John Five turned back into his double-barreled retreat without wishing me good luck or goodbye or good anything at all. The butler opened the front door, asked me if I knew where the garages were, and shut the door behind me. I heard the jingle of the bolt being shoved home.

It was fully dark now, and cold as a Pigmy in Alaska. I went around the house as I had done yesterday, in my carefree youth. Floodlights played on the garages, and Danny Banion, gun strapped over a forest-green short-coat, was unlocking a stall.

"My God, you look awful," was his way of making me feel better. "Want me to loan you an overcoat?"

"There's a heater in the car, I'm sure. You're not a bad guy, Danny." He swung the big door up. Inside, a station wagon gleamed. He said, "I was all right once, and I will be again, when I get to where a tree isn't a post for scratching John Five's back. I can't give you a gun, but anything else?"

"Tissues."

"In the glove compartment," he said. He sighed. "The chauffeurs put fresh boxes there every time they polish the cars, which is once a day. Where to, Porter?"

"Down into Lowndesburg," I said. "I've gotten so I feel naked without my head in a lion's mouth."

Danny Banion nodded. "I didn't know whether you knocked off Mrs. John Five or not," he said. "But no guy that Andy liked would have killed her grandfather. So I'm for you."

I wanted to get into the station wagon and start the heater. But here, in the garage, we were sheltered from the wind. "Nobody killed Mr. Gray," I said. "I was with him. Mac played a dirty trick on him, and the old man shook himself to death."

Danny Banion shrugged. "Mr. Gray and Mac squabbled a lot, but I always thought they liked each other. Well, on your way. In ten minutes I got to go saddle a horse and ride around the home place. Security." He spat on the garage floor and walked out into the night. When I pulled out, I saw him swinging the garage door shut.

CHAPTER 13

Nobody stopped me on the way into Lowndesburg, but twice I passed roadblocks on the exits. My spirits lifted as the heater took hold; I was headed for the police station, and it seemed a safe thing to do; the roadblocks indicated that nobody was fool enough to think I'd head into Lowndesburg, or into the jail if I was still there.

Lieutenant Gamble must be going nuts, I thought; such a good cop, and unable to find a full-sized man in a child-sized town.

But I was hardly in the business of preserving the amour-propre of state policemen. I was hardly in business at all.

A stop light and a street lamp came together, and I was halted under the latter. My hands on the wheel caught my eye; they were stained black. Fingerprint powder. I was sick to my stomach. I should have thought of it; this was the four-hole station wagon in which Edith was strangled.

Some minion would catch John Fivish hell for not doing a better cleaning job.

But me, I wanted to step out of the car, and run. The death, and the person who had died, came unbearably close for a moment.

A recurrence of coughing and sneezing combined with my nausea to double me over in the seat, down against the wheel. I was dimly aware of a car pulling alongside, more than dimly aware that if there was a car, I'd have to control myself.

There was a car, the driver had his window down, was peering at me. I un-cranked my right-hand window.

"You all right, mister?"

I nodded, my eyes streaming. "Sudden cold. Takes me bad."

"Better get home and to bed." The light changed and he pulled ahead of me. He hadn't recognized me. I probably didn't look human.

I wiped my eyes with John Five's tissue and drove on, too. I tried to think of anything but Edith.

During my months on the road, I had read a lot of detective stories. I don't go for anything much heavier; and reading passed the time more cheaply than sitting on a chrome bar stool, spending money.

So I had become a sort of expert on crime stories. The people in them suffered, they knew fear and apprehension, they were shot at sometimes; but they never had my trouble.

I was trapped by my own stupidity, my own inaction. Where a private eye—at least a fictional one, and I didn't know any others—would have thought of a dozen things to do, and done them to exhaustion and success, I couldn't think of anything, really. Where an amateur sleuth—paper—would have had a handful of suspects to track down and confront, I had only one: Otto McLane.

So I wheeled Edith's station wagon down into town and started looking for McLane. I didn't expect to have much trouble; he was certainly looking for me, too. He and every other cop in the world. Even a dope such as I was knows where to look for a police chief.

I drove to City Hall.

It was past dark now. But City Hall Square was the only part of Lowndesburg that was lighted; there, I had no trouble seeing. The hotel and shop lights added to the glow provided by the municipality's high globes. It wasn't bright as day, but it was brighter than my mood.

Sneezes and chills still racked me. I parked where I could watch the entrance to the basement police station, and left the motor running while I tried to size up the situation, using the brains I'd been given. They didn't seem adequate.

There were no state police cars in sight. Maybe there'd been an earth-quake or a tornado at the other end of the state; maybe my future mess-mates at the state penitentiary were rioting.

I glanced at the ammeter on the car. The idling motor wasn't charging the battery; I had the fan on, the heater going full blast.

If I turned the heater off, I'd freeze, and I had an idea that if I turned the fan off, I'd suffocate; so I put my foot on the gas pedal to keep the battery from running down, which meant that pretty soon I'd be out of gas.

Obviously the police had had this car. John Five's lads hadn't had a chance to refill it with gas, if they hadn't wiped off the fingerprint pow-der.

Something was going to have to be done soon, and there wasn't any-body but me to do it. Stupid, law-abiding me. I watched City Hall. No police cars around. Nor Mac's car. There were some sedans and coupés on the other side of the square, near the movie house, but they didn't look in any way official. There was a lighted window in the police basement, and there was a glow from the firehouse around the corner...

It looked safe enough, but I couldn't be sure. Maybe I ought to just take John Five's car and try and get through the roadblock. Maybe in a few years someone would confess to killing Edith, and I could come out of hiding again.

Suddenly I laughed at myself. Of course. There was a radio in John Five's car. There would be. The dashboard clock said four minutes to the hour, and news broadcasts come on the hour...

I shot an extra minute of electricity to be sure the clock was right—though being John Five's clock, it wouldn't dare be wrong. The tubes warmed, the set hummed, a disc jockey promised to rejoin me in five min-utes, and I got a break; the newscast was local, rather than national.

The announcer was a girl, with a lilting, flute-type voice designed to be distinctive, to make you remember her. She said that three people had been killed in traffic accidents in the state, making the year's toll nine hun-dred and forty-two dead as against nine hundred and thirty-six on this day last year. She said that a warehouse had burned down in Libertyville, at an estimated loss of two hundred and six thousand dollars.

She said that at the quarter, one basketball team was twenty-two points ahead of another.

She said that a man described as Paul Porter, alleged by the police to be "the most cold-blooded killer ever to operate in this state," has gone to earth in a motel in Mublenville, a hundred miles north of his scene of operations in Lowndesburg. State police, National Guard and special auxiliaries have surrounded the area, and a mobile public address system is being brought in to demand Porter's surrender. Sheriff—"

I switched it off. The majesty of the law was, for the moment, aiming its guns at another innocent bystander.

It would be nice if I could say that I worried about him, that I hoped he wouldn't get himself killed by some fumbling fool with a gun, but the truth is I was thinking about myself.

I switched the motor off, too, and climbed out of the station wagon, strolled across the last year's grass of the courthouse lawn to the blue light.

Knowles was alone in the police office; he was reading a magazine under the unshaded light over Otto McLane's desk. The magazine lay flat on the desk, and he held it in place with the stump of his right arm, turned the pages with his one set of fingers. He looked up when I came in.

"Evening, Sergeant."

He flipped the magazine shut. It was a book for gun fanciers. Without any apparent surprise, he said: "Come on in. It's a quiet night; they haven't rounded up a single D and D yet."

"D and D?"

"Drunk and disorderly. My regular customers."

"Before you ask, I didn't kill Mr. Gray. In fact, I haven't killed anybody."

Knowles stood up, wriggling his shoulders as though they ached. "Nothing to me. Cops round 'em up, I hold them. With more or less success."

"I gather I'm no longer out on bail."

"Naw. Mac's got the estate tied up. Andy tried to bail you, but there was some kind of technicality. Anyway, the judge denied her, for all Henry Lighton's spouting off."

I sat down on the straight chair he usually used. I sneezed. I had forgotten to bring the tissues in from the car. He opened a desk drawer, and shoved a box at me.

"So?" I asked, intelligently.

"So you're a fugitive, pal. But like I say, it's nothing to me. I'm not a sworn police officer, just a civilian employee of the department." He touched his ten-cent-store badge, awkwardly. "This doesn't mean a thing. He moved from behind the desk. "Coffee?"

"I need your help, Sergeant Knowles."

He shook his head. "I wondered why all the sergeants. I'm just a janitor, Porter."

"Then I need a janitor's help."

For a moment the glaring light brought something into his face: strength, maybe even cruelty, a reminder of what he must have been before his accident. But it faded, or maybe had only been a trick of lighting or of my watery eyes. "Like I said, nothing to me. I just hold them. I don't pick them up, and I don't help them, either. You want that coffee? You look frozen."

"I hear they have me surrounded up north. Yeah, I'd like the coffee." He went over to his hot plate, got down two thick mugs from the shelf above it. He poured. "That motel thing? That always happens. Some hawk-eyed citizen spots your man; some bright-badge sheriff sees a chance to get his picture in the papers."

"Still, if it wasn't for that, this place could be covered with cops." I shook my head for no cream or sugar.

Knowles said: "That's what you think. Wet roads—there's cops working traffic. A fire here or there, and the nearest state trooper goes in to see the sightseers don't run over the hoses. Night like this, there'll be a couple of attempted holdups, and three fights in unincorporated territory. All state police business."

"Still—"

"Ah, the state probably loaned a sergeant, a corporal, and four troopers to that sheriff up in Muhlenville. For various reasons. Yeah, it cuts down. Gamble and McLane are each holding down a roadblock they'd rather have a trooper handle."

He made pretty good coffee. I drank it hot enough to burn my tongue, and said that I still needed his help.

Knowles looked at the ceiling. "Tell your story," he said. "Where's the harm?"

"Two people—who I'm sure aren't working together—would like to see Otto McLane hang for killing my wife. My ex-wife."

He set down his cup, wiped his lips with the back of his hand. "Screwy."

"I thought so, too. Maybe I still think so. But I've got to be sure. And the only way I can be sure is to find out how much connection there was between Mac and Edith."

Knowles nodded. "Yeah," he said. "Mac's no guy to do anything on impulse. I mean, he's getting screwy—losing his youth hurts him worse than me losing my arm hurts me—but even if she maybe laughed at him, called him an old man, he wouldn't strangle her. He's right inside the letter of the law, that cop."

I said, wearily: "One more country heard from. It's what everybody says about Mac. But if he knew her well, if he had time to plan—"

Knowles drained the cup. "I got to go in the cells to wash the cups," he said. "No running water out here. Why, mister, it's not for the likes of a janitor to criticize a police chief. Chief McLane is a fine man. Very careful. Writes everything down. Files everything, right in that file by his desk. Yes, sir, you'll never catch our chief doing anything slipshod. You through with that coffee?"

I nodded, handed him my cup. He peered into it.

"Needs a good scrubbing."

His hand was big; it held both cups and the coffee pot handle without effort. He trudged to the cells, and through the unlocked iron door, then to the last lockup, clear in the back. The pot clattered, and then water was turned on.

There was the filing case; here was I. I got there fast, but for a moment my thoughts were back in the cells; how does a one-armed man hold a cup still while he scrubs it?

Then I had the file open. Headlights, Cracked, Citations for. Highway Jurisdiction. Hilliard, Edith Stayne. I took out the folder.

Letter to Las Vegas attorneys. Letter to the Chief of Police, Moberly, Missouri. I glanced at that one. It was asking for whereabouts of and any information concerning Carl Stayne.

Letter to Carl Stayne, on 119th Street, New York City. Are you divorced? Would like to know whereabouts of your former wife. Letter from Carl Stayne...

Clump of Knowles's feet coming back. I slid the folder back into its place, and closed the filing case. I had enough. There was a connection between Mac and Edith. A great big, fat connection. Mac had been looking into her past. Otto McLane was a blackmailer. There was no other explanation possible; there wouldn't have been any other explanation if my brain had been rested, and virus-free.

Knowles put the pot and coffee cups into a cupboard and turned to me. I guess my face was pretty transparent; he swore with fervor.

"I'm going, Sergeant."

He said, heavily. "I couldn't stop you."

"No. And thanks."

"For the coffee? Nothing." His hand came up and rubbed at his face. It hit him hard, I guess; I suppose he'd been a policeman all his adult life, and knowing that there were honest, almost perfect cops like Mac—for all his faults as a human being—had comforted him.

I remember Gamble when he saw Mac using his office to push motorists around; but police brutality was one thing, and police crookedness another, completely. I wasn't a cop, but I felt bad, too.

I felt worse when I got outside. Andy!

This was the end of anything between us. She didn't like her father today, but she had liked him yesterday. In time, she'd probably like him again; after all, what he had done to Mr. Gray he had apparently done for reasons convincing to himself.

Apparently, but not really. As a murderer, as the guilty man in the case he was supposed to be working on, he couldn't take any chances on my getting away; I was his scapegoat.

So he had shocked Mr. Gray to death in order to frame me.

But it seemed doubtful that Andy would believe that. If I got Mac arrested, indicted, convicted and electrocuted, she probably wouldn't believe it. She'd think I'd framed her father, and that was the end.

So maybe I ought to quit. Give up my life for love, as the poets say.

It is a safe bet that no such poets ever had to choose between life and love.

But there's no money in writing: I could not love you half so much loved I not myself more.

Philosophical thoughts of a dope about to tackle a tough and experienced cop.

And a cop who had me where he wanted me. I was a killer on the loose; I was, according to Flute-Voice on the radio, the worst thing that had ever hit this state, barring a cyclone or two.

Mac could shoot me on sight, and get commended for it. I didn't have a gun, and had no way of getting one. I didn't have a friend. Janey Dandler had made it clear that in getting me into Mt. Hilliard she'd run out of favors; John Five had run out almost before he started; Danny Banion, Lieutenant Gamble, the bartender, Lou—whom else did I know in Lowndesburg? .

Mr. Gray, who'd really helped me, was dead. Mac was my enemy, on the hunt for me. Andy was her father's daughter, Henry Lighton, money's lover.

Whither, Porter? There was no answer.

Jail suddenly looked good, but not Mac's jail. Knowles was on my side, but it would be too easy for Mac to send him on an errand, and fire him if he didn't go.

And then I'd be dead in a cell, instead of on the first pavement Mac saw me treading.

If I could make it to Lieutenant Gamble, I'd at least live to go to prison or the chair; at least I'd survive long enough to have a trial, maybe an appeal, maybe a commutation from the governor—or was that just melodrama?

Until you have thought of a life sentence as attractive, you have not fully lived. My advice is: don't live. It hurts too much.

So I got ready to give myself up; it became my version of going on fighting.

First, I had to get away from City Hall, from the square. Sooner or later Mac was sure to come back to his office, and Mac was what I didn't want *to meet.*

I climbed back into John Five's car, and started it up again. The gas gauge needle barely moved as the juice was switched on. And gas was how I measured time now; on foot I was a walking quail; which is the same as a sitting duck.

CHAPTER 14

Away from the square, Lowndesburg was poorly lighted. I drove along, the tires humming on the damp pavement, I turned corners, I went straight awhile; the aimless wanderings of an indecisive fugitive.

Then I saw a light ahead: a market, closed, but with night lights left on, no doubt to alert Otto McLane's night man if burglars were working inside. Outside there was a phone booth.

I would phone, I would order my forces. I would go down fighting.

At which point the station wagon, which seemed as fond of me as the rest of Lowndesburg, spluttered and died. I had used up the last of John Five's gas.

Like everybody when that happens, I stepped on the clutch as quickly as possible, and I undoubtedly twisted and jerked at the wheel, trying to get more roll with body English. And like everybody, I found that what had looked like a level street was really slightly uphill; the car stopped, started to go backward, and I set the hand-brake.

About two blocks to the market and the phone booth. Nothing to do but walk.

Only two minutes, maybe three, but I felt as conspicuous as an overcoat on a bathing beauty. A man as lightly clad as I was, out on a night like this, would attract a second and a third glance from any passing motorist, and my face had been in all the local papers; the mad-dog-killer.

I walked as fast as I could, I hunched my shoulders vainly trying to look smaller, and it didn't work; the second car that passed me stopped, and the driver yelled: "Out of gas?"

I nodded, and walked on.

"Want a ride to a filling station?"

I shook my head.

The driver said: "Hey, you're Porter."

Janey Dandler's brother, the hacky. He pulled over to the curb, got out. He was not a very big man, but he was taller than Janey, and broader than I; what he gave away in vertical inches he made up in chest girth. He stood square in front of me. "Thought you was up at John Five's."

"I was. I'm not anymore."

"Yeah. Wise guy." He shifted his squatty bulk as I tried to step around him. "Listen, wise guy. Stay away from Janey."

"I don't plan on ever seeing your little sister again."

"She's older than I am; she ain't my little sister. But I don't want you seeing her, all the same. You get me?"

"I get you. Now you get out of my way."

Dandler shifted again. I'm not an aficionado of the prize ring, but to me he moved as though he'd worn gloves and fancy trunks in his time.

He said, "Janey, she's got a nose for picking no-good bums. Red, and Freddy Hughes for a while, and now you. Leave her alone."

For no reason at all, I said: "You drove her up to see me today."

"Sure. She's my sister. When she asks for my help, I come through. But she ain't here now, so I'm saying: leave her alone."

"Get out of my way, Dandler."

This was spreading joy and good cheer. He grinned a happy, jubilant grin, and rocked back on his heels a little, giving the effect that he had sunk into the pavement a quarter inch. "Try and make me."

The habit of being a sucker was now so ingrained in me that I threw a punch. He brought up one palm, caught my fist, and squeezed it a little before he threw it away. A little—no more than the closing of a bank vault door on it would have done.

When he threw my fist away, I went, with it.

Since the sidewalk was paved, I fell on the pavement. He pulled his heels out of the concrete, walked over to stand over me and asked me if I wanted any more.

"No," I said. "Less. I want a good deal less."

But I got up. With my cold it wasn't good for me to lie on the pavement. I said: "I was just going to phone. Do you mind?"

"Janey?"

"Good Lord, no. Can't you get an idea through head of yours? Janey's nothing to mc.'

Now, I supposed, he'd really give me the works for spurning his sister. "She ain't?"

"No. She wanted me to mess Mac up because it would make the case against her Red look better. That's all."

Dandler chewed on this. He finally said, "Nothing would make that Red look better. A bum and a no-good from way back. When she was going with Freddy Hughes, the lush, Pop and me thought she couldn't sink no lower, but she did."

"That's all there was between Janey and me. When she found out I couldn't do any better against Mac than anybody else could, she threw me away, like you did."

Dandler chewed some more. Then he said a good word for Mac, the first I'd heard in Lowndesburg. "Mac's not so bad. If you gotta have cops, he's not worse than the next one. I'm sorry I knocked you down."

"That's a very flattering way of putting it. Thanks."

"Get in the cab, and I'll drive you around to Lou's and buy you a drink. Lou ain't so bad, neither, for all he's Red's brother."

"I'm a fugitive from justice," I said.

"Huh?" Then he got it. "Oh, yeah. A lamister. Well, lie down on the floor of the heap, and I'll bring you a snort. You can use it."

I wasn't at all sure that I could. It might thaw me, and it might melt me down to a weak puddle of indecision. But I finally nodded, on the principle that any change could be a change for the better, and got into the back seat of his cab.

He made the springs creak a little as he got behind the wheel; he was certainly solidly built.

We drove a little while, then stopped where lights streamed down on me, curled on the floor. Dandler got out, went away, came back after a while, and started the motor.

He tossed something over his shoulder and I picked it up. It was a half pint of cheap rye.

I sucked on it, and felt warmer, or at least, less cold. The car stopped again.

We were in front of the closed market. "You was going to phone," he said. "Want me to get gas for that station wagon?"

"Sure. But why?"

"I knocked you down," he said, persisting in his flattering distortion of the facts. "I swung when I shoulda been listening. Pop says I'm too fast with my fists. I'll get a can of gas from our garage."

"Thanks. There's probably a reward for me by now."

His short figure was as erect as de Gaulle's. "Nobody in our family ever yelled copper, and nobody never will. Not even on a punk like Red."

If I had known Latin, I would have translated his statement and had it carved on a Dandler family shield.

It was as noble a sentiment as has ever been voiced.

So now I could make my phone calls. There had been a time in my life when using a phone was a simple matter, but since my arrival in Lowndesburg, nothing was simple.

Not even blowing my nose. I had again forgotten to bring tissues from the stalled car.

My first time got me Henry Lighton. By luck, he was at his office; the phone book listed it, his farm, and an apartment in town.

I told him who I was, and then proved it by a series of magnificent sneezes and coughs.

His response was gratifying. "Where are you? I've worried myself bald-headed about you. Don't you know you're in a position to be shot on sight? The streets are full of sharp-eyed young troopers with virgin guns."

"I'm in a booth. Do you think the police have your phone tapped?"

His voice was a snort coming at me from the night. "They'd better not. Where are you? Can I come and pick you up?"

"I want to talk to you. I want to talk to Andy. After we talk, I want to give myself up to Lieutenant Gamble."

His polished voice was dubious. "I don't know about Andy. Her grandfather—"

"Try her," I said, and started to hang up.

He said: "All right. Don't come here; too close to City Hall. My apartment."

I checked his street address against the map in the back of the book. It looked easy to get to.

I wanted to get out of the booth, but I had to shoot another dime.

I called the state police number on the cover of the phone book. Gamble was out. I got a man at his desk, a corporal something or other. "This is Paul Porter. I want to talk to Lieutenant Gamble right away."

"Now, hold on, Mr. Porter. It may take me some time to get the lieutenant."

"I'm not holding on. Phones can be traced."

"Call him at 3-7717." That was one alert corporal.

My third dime got me Lieutenant Gamble. It sounded like a railroad station, but he answered the phone himself. I could hear lots of other voices in the background, all men. -

"I think I can trust you, Lieutenant," I said. "If I tell you where I'll be in twenty minutes, will you keep it to yourself and give me the twenty minutes?"

"Now, Mr. Porter—"

"Yes, or no?"

"Yes."

"Henry Lighton's home in town, not the farm. Bring some of your men if you want to, but nobody else."

"Oh?"

"I won't discuss it. I'm hanging up, and you can go back to looking for me."

"You're not easy to find, and that's a fact. Reporters from the wire services are on their way in to rib us. All right, it's a deal. Henry Lighton's in twenty minutes."

That call had been hard to make; I was not exactly a police-loving type of citizen any longer.

The next call was almost impossible. My fingers froze and wouldn't hold the receiver; the coin wanted to go anyplace but in the slot. But it was only Knowles's calm, slightly bitter voice that answered: "City police."

"Is Chief McLane there?"

"Out on a call. Any message?"

"Porter, Knowles. I'm going to be at Henry Lighton's in twenty minutes. I'd rather he didn't get there before then."

Knowles's drawl was still calm. "Then you shouldn'ta called till you were there. If he calls in, I gotta tell him right away."

It was too late now. I hadn't managed this any better than I'd managed anything else in Lowndesburg.

I hung on the phone, trying to think of some way of swinging Knowles back to my side. I had called up, of course, to try and get Knowles to delay Mac for my needed twenty minutes. But Knowles had gone back to being a cop; or maybe he was resting on dead center again, a janitor as he called himself, helping no one, hindering no one.

Feebly, I said, "It's very important to me."

"I just take messages for the chief."

"I know, I know, you're just a janitor."

Down the block, the chunky figure bending over my car could only be Dandler. I started walking. The wind had shifted, the air was almost balmy. Spring was coming back to Lowndesburg; I could enjoy it from my cell.

He flipped the cover over my gas tank cap, and said, "All set. I'll give you a push to get the gas circulating."

"And then goodbye?"

"You was right," he said. "Janey'd never have nothing to do with a punk like you. Put your car in second gear."

But because he had thrown me down, or maybe because I was anti-cop, he pushed his hack against the rear bumper of the station wagon, and shoved me down the street.

Before we got to the market, I remembered to turn the ignition on, and the station wagon shot ahead. In the rearview mirror I saw the cab U-turn and get away from there without waiting for any thanks.

One wise Dandler.

Using the box of tissues provided by John Five, I hacked and coughed and blew my way to Henry Lighton's street, as indicated on the phone-book map.

Of course, not a house number was visible, but his house was 942, and this was the nine hundred block; it oughtn't to be hard to find. .

Strictly speaking, Henry didn't have an apartment, he had a tiny house. He was just parking his car in the driveway as I came down the block. I wondered how he'd shaken off reporters and cops, maybe he'd told them he was out of the case. Maybe he was. But he'd been cordial on the phone.

I parked behind a little coupé and crammed my pockets with tissues. Then I got out.

When I walked alongside the coupé, it was lettered: J. F. Gray's Feed and Seed Co. I went back to the Station wagon.

Under the seat there was a crescent wrench, small enough to go in my pocket, heavy enough to knock a man out, if it connected with his chin. Maybe.

Passing the coupé, I was scared all over again. But there was no place to go but ahead. I rang the doorbell.

CHAPTER 15

Henry Lighton had had time to get his hat and coat off.

He opened the door at once. "Man, something for sore eyes."

"I'm sore all over, not just my eyes."

He laughed as though I'd really been witty, and bowed me into the living room. "Welcome to my pied-à-terre. Two rooms and bath... Paul, if you ever think of buying a farm, come to me. I've slept out there three nights in the last four months."

"McLane's car is out in front."

"Wrong again. That's Andy's coupé. She's here." He laughed his pleasant laugh again. "Can't you smell her perfume? I was kidding her about it."

"Not with this cold."

Andy's voice said: "Here's a hot rum and butter for you." She came through a door, a little kitchenette was behind her, she had copper mug in her hand, steam rising from it. Her face looked grim and drawn, as though she'd been crying.

I said, "Thanks."

She shook her head. "Don't bother with thanks. You're cold and you're sick."

I held the mug, the heat rising to tantalize me. Then I set it down. I had Dandler's liquor in me, I didn't dare take any more. "You don't think I killed your grandfather, do you?"

She bit her upper lip. "I don't know what to think, any more. About anything."

"You know what Mac did. What your father did. Tried to have Mr. Gray declared incompetent. The old gentleman got so mad he had some kind of attack. Just fell over on that pile of money."

I reached out for her. She stepped back.

"The police say you—that you were trying to get the money. That you maybe tortured him to find out where it was. And then knocked him down when you found out it was old-fashioned bills, no good to you."

She'd retreated as far as the wall of the little entrance hail. So I could get my hands on her shoulders.

"What police told you that? Your father?"

"What difference does it make? Dad wouldn't lie about police business."

I closed in a little and almost had my arms around her, but she slipped past me, into the tiny living room. I followed her. She had begun to cry, and I had to comfort her. Henry Lighton's dry voice stopped me. "As I understand it, the police will be here pretty soon. Lieutenant Gamble called me. He's giving you—" Henry Lighton glanced at a flat, gold wristwatch—"twelve minutes from now. You'd better let your love life go and talk to your attorney."

He was leaning on a little bar at the back of the room. Behind him there was a tiny combination icebox and stove, a liquor cabinet, some ranked and highly polished glasses.

I said: "Mr. Lighton, I didn't kill anybody—neither Edith nor Mr. Gray. I haven't any money—my car, some clothes, a couple of hundred dollars I could borrow on my life insurance, a half month's pay coming to me. But I've always made good money, and I should again. Take my case, and I'll pay you back, some way, some time."

He nodded his neat and shining head. "I cost like hell. Ten thousand dollars for a murder case. Are you willing to sign a promissory note, at six per cent?"

I said: "Yes, but—"

He said: "Ah, hah," with triumph. "You don't plan to dicker, do you?"

"I was just going to say, but don't you want some proof I'm innocent?"

"Once you've retained me, you're innocent."

Andy said, suddenly, "Your hot rum," and went out into the hall. She came back—there were no distances in that tiny house—and said, "Oh, Henry, it's left a ring on your lovely little table."

Henry Lighton waved this aside. "Don't you want your drink, Paul?"

"I had one before."

"You'll go a long time till the next one. I won't put up bail for anybody; and it might take some time to sell your car and pay a bail bondsman .

. . Is the car paid for?"

"Yes, but I'm trying to tell you I know who killed Edith."

He waved his hand; the wristwatch caught the light and shot it around the room. "Don't tell me anything till you have retained me, my friend." He reached under the bar, brought out a folder, opened it, laid a paper out. "I just happen to have brought a note from the office. Sign right here."

I stood staring at him.

"Come on," he said. "Time's wasting. What is it Clifford Odets always has his characters say...? 'I can hear the whistle blowing'."

Fascinated, I moved towards the bar. He held out a fountain pen. I took it from him.

His eyes were bright, his lips a little wet. There wasn't a hair out of place on his head, not a speck of lint on his flannel suit, but he didn't look urbane any more.

"Sign it, Paul," he said. "I'm your only hope."

Andy cried, "No," and broke the spell.

I turned towards her. She was crying now, openly. "Paul, there's something wrong. He looks like—like Mephisto in Faust."

Henry Lighton's laugh was light and clear, and thoroughly amused. "Now we're setting our little melodrama to music," he said. "I always look like that when I think about ten thousand dollars. Like you, Andy, I believe in the young man; I think he's going to make big money." He drooped a little, and added, sadly, "Maybe I should have made it twenty thousand."

A lot of talk, but of all the things he said, the one that moved me most was his saying that Andy believed in me. She must have said something to him while I was prowling around outside.

Then I remembered that I was about to alienate her forever and a month.

But I signed the paper.

Henry Lighton picked it up, waved it in the air, and kissed it. "God, how I love money... All right, start talking. The good lieutenant will be here in a minute or so; perhaps you ought to talk fast, but clearly. If we need more time, he'll certainly give it to us; a fugitive surrendering through his lawyer is always in a strong position."

Andy said, "Paul, you said you know who killed Edith Hilliard."

Henry Lighton said, "The state's got a damned weak case on that one, anyway. Happenstance and coincidence never hung a man with a good lawyer. Or is it hanged? But the matter of Mr. Gray, that's serious. You were there, he had just told you that you had to go back to jail, he took out of his secret cache money—under duress or not; who can prove?—

which had not seen the light of day in thirty-odd years—a very serious set of facts."

"But no one killed Mr. Gray. He dropped dead."

Henry Lighton leaned his elbows on the bar, rested his chin on his hands.

"Would a jury accept that? Possibly, in view of his age... But you were alone with him. And I don't see how I can prevent that fact, and the other facts submit ted above, from getting to a jury. The other case, that of Edith Stayne Hilliard, consists of allegations not facts, and these I can quite probably get barred from the record. Meaning, no jury will have to consider them."

He straightened up, came from behind the little bar.

His walk was a saunter. I am sure his mind had created a judge behind the little bar, a jury in Andrea, a press table in me.

"I'm a lawyer's lawyer, and no ham," he said. "The law, as decided by a judge, is clean and beautiful; the facts, as decided by a jury, exist in a shadowy territory, a Cloud Cuckoo Land, if you please, where anything can happen, and the most brilliant man cannot say it nay. Case against Paul Porter, in the matter of Edith Stayne Hilliard, thrown out for lack of evidence. Yes. You understand, we'll not be so lucky as to have only the local worthy who is district attorney of this county to contend with; there'll be the attorney general of the state, perchance, and quite possibly a special prosecutor, all planning to nourish their measly careers on this fat table of publicity spread before them.

"Ergo. In the matter of Edith Stayne Hilliard, no case. Then, what happens to the matter of the death of J. F. Gray? Why was the defendant there, what possible motive could he have for acting against a lovable old man? 'Well, this, that bail—' 'But I object, your honor. The prosecution is seeking to inject matter from a dismissed case.' Double jeopardy? Perhaps, but certainly matter that could not be proved in one case cannot be testimony in another. Aha!"

Andy said, "Henry, listen to Paul."

But he was off again. "Certainly there will have to be two trials. At an interval, too. By the time of the second trial, the attention of the whole country will be fastened on Paul Porter, a poor wretch in the toils of ambitious politicians. It's going to be a lovely mess."

Andy said again: "Paul knows who killed that poor woman, Henry."

Henry Lighton dismissed the whole matter with one graceful hand. "It doesn't apply any longer. I'm not going to fight facts with facts; I'm going to fight allegations with law, good solid law. No, I don't care."

I had my eyes on Andy's lovely face. It could be mine, to kiss at will, to gaze upon in my home for the rest of my life. Men have stolen, killed, for much less beautiful objects—diamonds, oil paintings; all I had to do was keep my weak mouth shut.

And then, I couldn't. My lips opened and the words came. "I care. She was my wife, she was a human being. Maybe she made my life miserable, wiped out my life savings—you'd call that corny, Henry—but I'm not John Five to say: 'she annoyed me, off with her head.' I care. And I don't care for her murderer to go marching around the world, free."

Henry Lighton went behind his little bar again, selected a glass and a bottle and poured himself a short, straight drink. "You should have been a lawyer, Paul. You'd have done beautifully in the magistrates' courts, or collecting small debts."

I looked at Andy, at her glowing eyes, and I said, "Otto McLane killed Edith."

The glow went, and shock spread, from her jaw line slowly up her cheekbones to her forehead. "Oh, Paul."

I said, "Hear me out. Then maybe you'll never listen to me again, because I know you, Andy; not long, but well. You're loyal. You're mad at your father now, but once he's in trouble, you'll forget that, you'll stick by him."

Henry Lighton drank his little drink, and clacked the empty glass on the bar. "A lawyer with a fool for a client is in a better position than vice-versa. Paul, you're out of your mind. Mac? Never."

"Hear me out, counselor. One, Mac's been slipping; that was why he had to resign from the city force; that was why he resented old man Gray—I'm sorry... Mr. Gray. He's been using his badge and uniform to be unnecessarily harsh and brutal; Lieutenant Gamble and I saw him, yesterday, or was it today, pushing motorists around and enjoying it."

I stopped, and looked at the two pairs of eyes that watched me. Neither of them was friendly.

But I'd bitten it off, I had to chew it. "Two. He wanted to get out of here, out of the business that had been given to him, but not completely out of a house that wasn't his. He needed money for that."

Henry Lighton said, "I happen to know that Mac's pension was more than sufficient for a widower."

"Peanuts," I said. "Popcorn money. He wanted the big money, the kind that makes people look up to you. Where to get it? The Hilliards, John Five and his wife, have the only big money around here. Edith looked easier than John Five. She was. He found something on her, he attempted to blackmail her, and Edith—Edith never gave a damn for anything but money, but that she loved with a love that passeth understanding—"

Andy said, "A bush-league edition of you, Henry. I'm not going to listen to this." Anger only accentuated her beauty.

But I went on. Henry had offered me a way out, a lawyer's door to walk through; I could have stood mute, as he would have said, and had my freedom and Andy, too; but I talked. "Three. No one but Andy and Mac knew I would be at Mt. Hilliard at just the hour I was."

"Then I murdered her, and framed you?" She was trying not to cry.

"No, Mac did."

Henry Lighton was smiling at me. "Someone ought to collect the weird things a desperate man comes up with. Forget it, Paul. Have no fear, Henry Lighton is here. I'll get you off with ease, without this fantastic hodge-podge."

And Andy said, "I don't think I can ever forgive you for even thinking of it. But just tell me one thing, Paul: how in the world could you ever connect Dad with Edith Hilliard, except as the most casual of acquaintances?"

I said: "Go down to the little hole that Lowndesburg calls its police headquarters. Look in his file. He's got a thick folder on the background and life of Edith Stayne Porter Hilliard. He's been writing to cops all over the country getting the dope."

My cough came back on me. I doubled over with it. Henry Lighton reached down under the bar, got a glass of water, put it on the bar; he didn't hand it to me.

I got up and took it, and drank it down, blew my nose, and went on. "He was ready. He tried to blackmail her. You didn't know Edith as I did. She never put out money; it was strictly one-way with her. She was going to expose him."

Henry Lighton raised a hand. "I would be ashamed to lay trash like this before a jury," he said. "Conjecture, pure conjecture, and not even very, logically devised. How could she expose him without exposing herself, losing her mink-lined nest at John Five's?"

"You didn't know her," I said again. "All she would see was that Mac was forcing her to pay out money. She would never do that. You just didn't know her well enough."

"But Henry knew her very well," Andy said. "Better than anybody in Lowndesburg, except John Five, of course."

"I am one of the leading experts on the late Edith," I said. "On the other hand, I certainly don't know Mac as well as you do, Andy. But I should say that all he would see was his honor about to be smirched, his reputation as a police officer destroyed. I don't know whether he loves that honor more or less than he loves you, or his own life—but I'd guess the three ranked about even with him."

So I'd said it. I was left breathing hard; my lungs or bronchials or both were filling with the cold.

"Henry, I'll take that drink now. I've made my speech."

He nodded, absentmindedly. "Quite a speech, too. Straight whiskey do you?" He turned to his neat bottles, his sparkling glasses. "I almost believe you." He raised a hand. "Almost, but not quite, Andrea."

Then he was pouring me a shot. I stood up again to get it. Something had crossed my rheumy mind. I should have taken that folder out of Mac's files. By now he had probably destroyed it, my luck being what it was.

"I still say," Henry Lighton said, "I'm not taking any of this into a public court. Your defense, Paul, will be strictly on legal grounds."

The liquor started me off coughing again. My eyes watered, and I mopped them. "But Mac—"

"Mac can take care of himself. Damn good care of himself," Otto McLane said.

CHAPTER 16

He stood in the door from the hall, a gun held big in his hand. He still wore his police uniform with the brass eagles on it. I now noticed that the LPD on his lapels did not quite cover the marks of the city's insignia; this was his old uniform, thriftily converted.

He said: "Damn, Porter, you had me fooled. I took you for a cream puff."

The bore of the gun was big enough to cover the whole area of Henry Lighton's little living room. I wondered idly if it was a .38 or .45 or maybe even bigger; the only hand-held elephant gun in the world.

Otto McLane was, for the moment, a pit bull, the white kind with the squinting, flat, pink eyes. He said: "An old copper like me, taken in by a set of narrow lapels and an Italian necktie. You got a good brain, boy. I could have made a policeman out of you."

Andy cried, "Oh, God, Dad," and buried her face in her hands, sobbing.

"Where's your fancy state trooper, Porter?" Mac said. "I bet you phoned him to pick you up here."

My voice was distinctly hollow. "I don't know."

Henry Lighton said, quickly, "Mac, if you overheard all this—and it seems you did—remember I never took any stock in it."

I was very pleased to hear that Henry's voice was hollow, too. He seemed as frightened as I was.

Mac said: "Have no fear, in your own words, Henry. Otto McLane's here, and he's a good cop; he takes 'em alive when he can, and he usually can."

Andy said, "Dad, Dad…"

McLane's chuckle was a growl. "Andy, your Paul Porter made a lot of sense. How come you didn't believe him?"

Andy said, simply: "You're a lousy hay-and-grain dealer, but you're a good cop."

"Carve it on my tombstone," Mac said. "And keep the hands on the bar, Henry."

I sputtered something that was meant to be: "What?" or maybe just: "Whoosh."

"Henry didn't believe you either, Porter," Mac said. "Why should he? He croaked your ex-wife."

Henry Lighton said, "This is double-feature night at the Fantasy Theater."

McLane said: "Lieutenant Gamble should get here sooner or later; there must be one guy on the state force who had a street map of Lowndesburg. I'm waiting till he goes to make my pinch. There's less accidents when there are two cops to cover each other. I was searching your flat here, Henry, when you and Andy came barging in. I took cover in your clothes closet—damned if you don't use perfume. I always thought it was just good soap."

Henry Lighton said, "I wish I had a recording of this. It seems highly saleable to the smaller television stations."

Mac said: "Sure, so long as I can see both hands on the bar."

Lighton said, "Do you mind if I pour myself a drink?"

"To throw in my eye? No, thanks. I've known all along, Henry, you were in on this. Where I made my mistake… I thought you sent for Porter to do the actual knockoff. He had a good motive for it, and I wrote you down as a guy who'd play it cool, have an alibi for the killing time."

"Gaudy talk, Mac," Henry Lighton said. "And, in front of two witnesses, it constitutes slander."

I presume that my jaw was on my Italian necktie by now. Actually, I don't remember where it was.

"Sue me," Mac said. "Edith Hilliard liked money, but she didn't mind spending a little, Porter, to protect a lot more. So you didn't know her as well as you thought you did. An old cop usually finds out that most husbands don't know their own wives, but that ain't what we're talking about. You're a good lawyer, Henry, and you're John Five's lawyer. When he got married, you started making sure his new wife didn't have attachments that could mess up the Hilliard estate."

"Of course," Henry Lighton said. "But, Mac, you are making too much of what was my plain duty."

Mac laughed again, his pit-bull laugh. "When you found out she was never divorced from Stayne—because she didn't want to spend money getting rid of someone who'd run out on her—it became your duty to try and shake her down, didn't it?"

Henry Lighton took the advice he would have given a client; he said nothing.

Mac kept on talking: "She came to me. There's no private detective in Lowndesburg, and if there was, those guys are punks. She offered me a reasonable fee to get you off her neck. Incidentally, I found Stayne; did you? He's running a tire recap shop in San Diego, California. He went and divorced her in Nevada two weeks ago, at her expense—not that that makes her marriage to either Porter or John Five any better."

Andy said, "Dad, I never dreamed—"

"Ah, it's legal, baby; a part-time police officer can do private chores, beyond the call of his duty, and get paid for it."

"I wasn't thinking of that," said Andy.

Mac said, "I told her not to tell you, Henry, who was doing her work. That seemed to protect her; you wouldn't bump her off while you knew someone else was aware of the blackmail attempt."

My nose started to run again. I fumbled in my pocket for tissues, and my fingers closed around the wrench. I'd put it there ages ago to protect me from Mac, when I thought Andy's car was his, in front of Henry Lighton's.

Mac said: "When she got it in the neck—" I could see out of the side of my eye Andy wince—"I just didn't know. It didn't seem like you to do anything like that. Then John Five mentions a husband named Paul Porter, and I had a Paul Porter right in town. I'd even seen him get sick when he caught a glimpse of Mrs. John Five. Whammo, I got it. She'd left him broke, she'd left him mad; you got hold of him, Henry, and offered him a little dough and your protection as a great lawyer to do something he wanted to do anyway; and he done it."

I said, "No, Mac, I had nothing—"

"Aw, punk, I know that. I been in there listening. It woulda worked, too, but you wouldn't powder-puff out; you kept on slugging, climbing around in the rain, and goddam—you come up with, it's me that done it."

He'd had some culture before; but he was dropping back to the linguistic level of the beat-slogging patrol man. He said: "You told it so good, you almost had me believing it," and laughed his growl again. "If you'd been in with Henry, you never woulda bothered. Of course, I had alibis all over the place; I was at a town council meeting from after you left my office till the mayor dropped me at Mr. Gray's house."

"Oh." That was me, the brilliant conversationalist. "I never thought of that."

"You done good," Mac said. "For an amateur. And there's your lieutenant, just pulling up in front of here. Later than a cow in a horse race."

Henry Lighton said, "Now that there'll be a competent officer here, I have every intention of moving my hands, Mac. You can't shoot me and claim some nonsense—"

Mac said: "Hold it, Henry."

Henry Lighton said, "Hands in the air, as they say?" and started to raise them.

His suit cuffs slid back, disclosing lovely white cuffs with massive gold links. It is peculiar what you see at a time like this.

Then a tiny, tiny pistol appeared in one hand, and the manicured fingers worked for it—and I threw the wrench.

It missed Henry Lighton completely and broke a bottle of rare old Scotch on the back bar.

But Mac didn't miss; the little guy became a Doberman for jumping. The sights of the pistol came down on Henry Lighton's head, and the legal coiffure was no longer immaculate.

And Lieutenant Gamble came in with a trooper behind him, like the Seventh Cavalry in an old-time movie—only this time, the soldiers arrived just as Geronimo scalped the last settler.

Lieutenant Gamble said, "I'm sorry, we had a flat tire, and the jack kept slipping."

Mac straightened up from behind the bar.

This time his laugh was real. He said, "Didn't you never think of radioing for another car to pick you up, Lieutenant? They got radios in all the cop cars now, and from what I hear, they work real dandy."

Lieutenant Gamble blushed.

Mac hauled Henry Lighton to his feet. The lawyer's eyes were opening again, but a thin trickle of blood was running towards the left one.

Lieutenant Gamble gave that a big old reaction: the Seventh Cavalry sort of inviting the Apaches to the USO for an ice cream soda. He jumped forward, and pushed Mac away from Henry Lighton and towards his trooper. "Hold Chief McLane, there."

The trooper dropped a hand on Mac's shoulder; he was a good eight inches taller than Mac. He said, "You won't give me any trouble, will you, Chief?"

Mac winked at me, and suddenly, I felt wonderful, runny nose, scratchy throat and all. Otto McLane liked me. It was as big a laurel wreath as being asked to be Secretary of State by a President you'd vote for.

Lieutenant Gamble was sort of brushing Henry Lighton off, and using his own handkerchief to mop at Henry's ruined hairdo. He said, "There's a first-aid kit in my car, Mr. Lighton. I'll get it and patch you up, but maybe you ought to telephone a doctor to come over here. His testimony will be valuable to us later."

Mac said: "While you're cleaning up, Lieutenant, there's a little bitty old gun behind the bar that I'd pick up, if I was you. Your patient there was gonna plug me with it, but hell, I've rubbed up against so many rough characters in my life, the skin on my belly's probably too calloused to get hurt from a derringer."

Lieutenant Gamble gave up his ministrations to turn on Mac, who was still calmly wearing the trooper's hand on his shoulder. "In case you think I'm outside my jurisdiction, Chief, being inside yours, I'll remind you that there is a state statute covering incompetence, dishonesty or brutality of local officers, both county and municipal."

"Sure," Mac said. "Statute 2911, and Paragraph Four covers brutality. That what you think I've been doing?"

Andy began to laugh. It started as sort of a mild giggle, and then rose and got a honking quality I didn't like; it was too close to hysteria. I went over and put my arm around her, and she leaned against me and seemed to take some comfort. She calmed down.

Despite the fact that I was still, in his eyes, prime suspect in a murder case—and Andy could be my moll, about to slip me a rod—Lieutenant Gamble hardly glanced at us. He was busy with Mac. "What do you call it, if not brutality, when legal counsel feels it necessary to carry a gun before conferring with a police officer sworn to keep law and order?"

"Wow," Mac said. "If I could fling that kind of language around, they might let me work the telephone switchboard at headquarters." He turned his head, looked up at the trooper. "Don't bear down so heavy, son. I'm old and frail."

From inside my arm, Andy said, "Stop it, Dad. You're making an enemy out of Lieutenant Gamble, and it isn't necessary."

"It don't matter to me," Mac said. "I'm leaving the state. I got an offer to run the plant police for a factory with more people working in it than live in this whole county."

By now, something seemed to be getting through to Lieutenant Gamble. Mac wasn't talking like a man about to be broken for police brutality, and Andy wasn't talking like a girl being hugged by a murderer, and Henry Lighton wasn't talking at all, which was perhaps the most unusual thing of all.

The trooper took his hand off Mac's shoulder, which called my attention to him. From his carefully immobile face, and the brightness of his eyes, he looked exactly like a private about to see a lieutenant made a damned fool, which was exactly what he was.

Mac said: "Henry Lighton killed Edith Stayne Porter Hilliard Five. I got him dead to rights. When I flung it at him, he tried to plug me with the derringer that's lying behind the bar, which I wish you'd pick up. So I slugged him on the head."

Lieutenant Gamble looked at Henry Lighton.

Henry said, "I am not saying anything at all. I stand mute." But his face gave him away.

Lieutenant Gamble took a pencil out of his inside pocket and went behind the bar. He bent over and straightened up with the pencil inside the belly-gun's barrel. He laid the little gun on the bar, took an envelope out of his side pocket, and teased the gun inside the envelope with the pencil.

"I like to see a real cop work," Mac said. "Beautiful."

Lieutenant Gamble looked at his trooper, and said: "You don't take shorthand, do you? Well, go out to the car, and radio for a trooper who does. I'll want to take Chief McLane's statement down."

"Later," Mac said. "Later. I'll meet one of your boys down at my office and give him the whole thing. It's a water-tight case."

"I'm sure it is," Lieutenant Gamble said.

"If you hadn't gotten a flat tire, you'da been in on the pinch," Mac said. "But that's police work. Rain today, snow tomorrow. Take him away, Lieutenant. Get his head patched up, and heave him in my lockup, or take him to headquarters with you." He looked, for all the world, like a performing poodle.

"It occurs to me," Lieutenant Gamble said, "that the attorney general isn't going to be happy. Whoever has to prosecute Henry Lighton is going to have a bad time in court."

"Not with a case that Otto McLane worked up," Mac said. "When I pinch them, they stay pinched... Now, get him out of here. I got work to do. Andy can't run that feed-and-seed store, and I can't take my good factory job till I find her somebody who can. How's about it, Porter? If you was a dealer, you could give that yellow-bellied boss of yours some bad times. He's got it coming to him, running out on you when you was in trouble. Guys oughtn't to run out on a friend of Otto McLane's."

All that occurred to me was that if my plans went the way I hoped they would, I was in for some bad times myself, if my children took after their grandfather.

THE END

Richard Wormser Bibliography
(1908-1977)

Mystery/Crime Fiction:

The Man With the Wax Face (1934)

The Communist's Corpse (1935)

All's Fair (1937)

Pass Through Manhattan (1940)

The Hanging Heiress (1949; reprinted as The Woman Wore Red, 1958)

The Body Looks Familiar (1958; abridged version pub in *Cosmopolitan* [Sept 1957] as "The Frame")

The Late Mrs Five (1960)

Drive East On 66 (1961)

Perfect Pigeon (1962)

A Nice Girl Like You (1963)

Pan Satyrus (1963; science fiction satire)

The Takeover (1971)

The Invader (1972; Edgar Award winner)

Westerns:

The Lonesome Quarter (1951)

The Longhorn Trail (1955)

Slattery's Range (1957)

Battalion of Saints (1961)

Three-Cornered War (1962)

The Ranch by the Sea (1970; originally published in *Blue Book* [Dec 1951] as "The Kingdom by the Sea," and reprinted as Double Decker, 1974)

On the Prod (1970; reprinted as The Trouble Seeker, 2017)

Horse Money (2012; four stories)

As by Nick Carter (from *Nick Carter Magazine*):

Bid for a Railroad (Jan 1934; reprinted as Murder Unlimited, 1945)

Bloody Heritage (July 1933)

Crook's Empire (April 1933; reprinted as Empire of Crime, 1945)

Crime Flies High (Aug 1933)

Death Dollars (Nov 1933)

Death Has Green Eyes (May 1934; reprinted 1945)

Death on Park Avenue (July 1934; reprinted as Park Avenue Murder, 1946)

Gate of Death (March 1934)

The Gilford Mystery (April 1934)

Gold and Guns (Oct 1933)

Letters of Death (Sept 1933)

Maniacs of Science (June 1933)

Marked for Death (March 1933)

Newspaper Racket (Feb 1934)

Six Rings of Death (May 1933)

Thefts of Yellow (Dec 1933; reprinted as The Yellow Disc Murder Case, 1948)

The Twenty Year Crimes (June 1934)

Screenplays (all written in collaboration):

Start Cheering (1937)

Let Them Live! (1937)

Fugitives for a Night (1938)

The Plainsman and the Lady (aka Drumbeats Over Wyoming) (1946)

The Phantom Thief (1946)
Perilous Waters (1947)
Tulsa (1949)
Powder River Rustlers (1950)
Vigilante Hideout (1950)
Rustlers on Horseback (1950)
Fort Dodge Stampede (1951)
Captive of Billy the Kid (1951)
The Half-Breed (1952)
A Perilous Journey (1953)
Crime Wave (1954)
The Outcast (1954)

Novelizations/Adaptations:
Thief of Baghdad (1961)
The Last Days of Sodom and
   Gomorrah (1962)
McLintock! (1963)
Bedtime Story (1964)
Operation Crossbow (1965)
Major Dundee (1965)
Torn Curtain (1966)
The Wild Wild West (1966)

As by Ed Friend:
Alvarez Kelly (1966; movie tie-
   in)
The Green Hornet: The Infernal
   Light (1967, TV tie-in)
The Scalphunters (1968; movie
   tie-in)
The High Chaparral: Coyote
   Gold (1969, TV tie-in)
The Most Deadly Game: The
   Corpse in the Castle (1970, TV
   tie-in)

Children's Fiction:
Trem McRea and the Golden
   Cinders (1940)
Ride a Northbound Horse
   (1964; Spur Award winner)
The Kidnapped Circus (1968)
Gone to Texas (1970)
The Black Mustanger (1971;
   Spur Award winner)

Non-Fiction:
The Yellowlegs: The Story of the
   United States Cavalry (1966)
Southwest Cookery, or, At Home
   on the Range (1969)
Tubac (1975)
How to Become a Complete
   Nonentity: A Memoir (2006)